The Irregular

H.B. LYLE

The Irregular

Quercus

New York • London

Quercus

New York • London

ISBN 978-1-68144-027-9

Library of Congress Cataloging-in-Publication Data

Names: Lyle, H. B., author.
Title: The irregular : a different class of spy / H. B. Lyle.
Description: First edtion. | New York : Quercus, 2017.
Identifiers: LCCN 2017031175 (print) | LCCN 2017039923 (ebook) |
    ISBN 9781681440255 (eBook) | ISBN 9781681440248 (library eBook) |
    ISBN 9781681440279 (hardback) | ISBN 9781681440262 (paperback)
Subjects: LCSH: Intelligence officers–Great Britain–Fiction. | Secret service–Great
    Britain–Fiction. | Leaks (Disclosure of information–Great Britain–Fiction. |
    Undercover operations–Great Britain–Fiction. | Conspiracies–Fiction. |
    Espionage, British–Fiction. | GSAFD: Spy stories.
Classification: LCC PR6112.Y44 (ebook) | LCC PR6112.Y44 I77 2017 (print) |
    DDC 823/.92–dc23
LC record available at https://lccn.loc.gov/2017031175

Distributed in the United States and Canada by
Hachette Book Group
1290 Avenue of the Americas
New York, NY 10104

www.quercus.com

For Annalise

1

Leyton knew something was wrong.

He had a clerk's eye for detail, for a set of numbers that didn't quite match. The Underground train lurched and screeched over the points at Portland Road Station. Leyton ducked down and pushed through the crowded carriage, hurrying. "Watch it, mate," a coarse voice called after him. Someone laughed. Tobacco smoke hung above the nodding heads.

Leyton had seen the two men at Moorgate, their eyes flickering as the train steamed into the platform. He'd turned away but caught sight of a tall, angular thug with an outsized Adam's apple and shovel hands. Beside the giant stood an ape-like accomplice, dressed in a sailor's peacoat and a tweed cap. Leyton guessed they had boarded the train but didn't wait to find out. The latch between carriages pinched his hand as he forced it open.

"Careful, dear," an old woman called. "Wait until the next station."

He stopped, momentarily thrown by her kindness. The train clanked and clinked and he vaulted into the next carriage, acrid dust and smoke prickling his nose. Glancing back, he could see no sign of his pursuers.

The train rattled into the next station and Leyton took off his hat and mopped his brow, slick despite the December cold, his eyes smoke-stung. His thoughts jumbled and clattered—he suspected he'd seen the ape-man, or rather his tweed cap, at the docks and again on Farringdon Road, but he couldn't be sure. He should never have tried to go to the telegraph office. Stupid mistake. Kell would be livid, if he ever got to Kell. He should have posted the information, as insurance, but they were watching every step. At least, he thought they were. The crowd swelled past him to the doors. "I say, mind out there." Leyton turned his head. A tweed cap blurred to his right. He felt a sharp pain in his back and a cold hand on his neck. The ape-man in the tweed cap pressed toward him from behind, breathing stale gin and death. He gripped Leyton around the neck.

Leyton swiveled, panicked, afraid, invisible to the passengers streaming off the train. A mauling, sweating rugby scrum flashed into his mind, the hated schoolboy torture. In that same instant, Leyton, acting on instinct, drove his fist full-bore into the man's bollocks. The man's cap came off and he released his grip. Leyton fled onto the platform.

The concourse teemed with New Year's Eve revelers.

"Help me," Leyton gasped to a station guard. "I'm an agent." He scanned the platform gates behind him.

"It's barely seven thirty, sir." The guard glanced up at the clock. "Bit early to be the worse for wear?"

"No, you don't understand."

"'Ere, look at that," a woman cackled to her friend. "'E's got no hat."

Leyton startled at her, confused. Over the heads of the throng, he saw the tall thug pushing his way through. Leyton ran. "That bloke looks like he's pissed himself," the woman screeched.

The laughter of the two women pursued him out into the watery street, the two heavies hard behind.

He should never have gone to the telegraph office, not even tried to telephone. He should have gone to Kell instantly. What he had in his pocket would blow the whole thing wide open. He might even get a medal—he'd be back in the Admiralty and Kell would get his pound of flesh. But by God, Kell was right. It would blow Whitehall sky-high.

Leyton hurried out onto Baker Street, the pavement dark and slick beneath his feet, the rain loud and heavy. Faint pools of gaslight dotted the road, up toward the sinister mass of Regent's Park to his right. He hesitated, took a few steps toward the park—thinking of the thick bushes and trees, the lack of streetlighting. But that scared him even more and he broke into a run south toward Oxford Street and Whitehall, toward Kell. The rain thrummed hard on the pavement and he couldn't hear the steps behind him, but he knew they must be there. His hand pressed against the bulge in his breast pocket, his head swiveled as he ran, looking for anywhere to hide.

"Watch out!" a cabbie hollered as his taxi swung past, the two lanterns on the front flickering in the backwash of a passing omnibus. The motorized taxi splashed away from him, back toward Baker Street Station. As it reached the corner, Leyton saw the two men now following him, illuminated for an instant by the cab's headlights. The tall man stooped. Beside him was his accomplice, tweed cap back on, his squat frame radiating violence even from a distance. They upped their pace.

Leyton sprinted. He vaulted over the wall to a churchyard, scampering between the gravestones. If only he could get to Kell, get to the War Office, this would all be over—once he'd delivered the package there would be no need to kill him, no need to—*Bang!* The bullet chipped the wall just as Leyton rolled over it and away into a deserted street. He dodged left down a side road, right, then left again into a dark street. Gasping for breath, he stopped for a moment. A light at the far end fizzed. Wheezing, Leyton knew he'd never outrun them. He ducked under a builder's wire and felt his way into a half-built terrace. The walls felt dank and unplastered, the floor squelched underfoot, and it was coffin-dark. He slumped onto the floor, propped himself up, and waited. Above him, the rain rattled harder on what sounded like corrugated iron. Two sets of feet pounded past.

A heavily accented voice shouted, "Wigmore Street?" Then the footsteps petered out.

Leyton exhaled. He patted again at the documents in his pocket just above his heart and silently cursed the day he agreed to work for Vernon Kell.

"I need a smoke," he said aloud, to reassure himself that he still existed as much as anything else. He shuffled his hips and pulled out a crumpled pack. His head twitched—was that a sound? No, the squeaking of his sodden clothes as he moved was all. An odd smell of burned cloves pervaded the air. Leyton sniffed again, trying to place it. He must be in a warehouse, he reasoned, as he fumbled for matches.

"At last," Leyton mumbled through his cigarette. The smell, it suddenly came to him, was that of the Batavian tobacco the Dutch sailors smoked in the docks. Strange smell for a building site in Marylebone. He dismissed the thought, struck the match in a bright bloom, and illuminated both his own face and then that of his killer.

* * *

So far, Wiggins hadn't enjoyed 1909. Three weeks in, the rain hadn't stopped, the wind sheeted down in icy blasts, and the mercury seemed stuck at thirty-two degrees. And he still hadn't paid his rent for the last month. He'd taken to leaving his window open despite the wretched weather and climbing up the drainpipe, so as to avoid Mrs. Balducci and her baleful eyes asking for money in silent reproach.

He adjusted his elbows on the handrail of the iron fire escape, which scaled the side of a tall brick warehouse. Below him, Wiggins could see the entire street—a shabby affair that ran into another even shabbier terrace. Pelham Road looked like a damp and miserable place to live. Wiggins's two colleagues approached the door of number fifteen, their collars turned high, beetles inching down the road. The taller one turned toward Wiggins and raised his head. Wiggins lifted a tired arm in reply.

Go!

The two men paused for a moment, nodded, then pounded at the door with sledgehammer fists. "Open up!" No reply. After a second attempt, they gave up and looked back toward the fire escape in mute inquiry. From his viewpoint, Wiggins took in the crooked terrace—the snub chimneys coughing out pathetic wisps of smoke, the mean and muddy roadway, unpaved, the stench. He saw too the back entrances that led to a small, crowded alley. The scene looked

no different from the East End slums of his youth, twenty years earlier. London may be on the up and up, Wiggins thought, with its
underground railway and traffic lights, with telephone exchanges
and motorcars and brickwork sewers—but as far as he could tell the
poor still had nothing. He nodded his head at his colleagues down
below. They lifted their feet in unison and battered at the door with
sharp, heel-led kicks. There was a vicious grace to their movements
that made Wiggins wince.

He kept his eye on the back of number fifteen and, just as the
front door flew off its hingeing with a great crack, a small figure
leapt from a window and flitted through the yard and into the alley.
"He's out the back!" Wiggins shouted as he slid down the fire escape
and hit the ground at a sprint.

Heart pounding, he ran left, then took the first right. Out in
front, the prey popped out of the side alley, starting at the sight of
Wiggins. "Stop!" Wiggins shouted. The small figure, ragged shirt
open at the collar, hatless, cut across the road and down toward
Shoreditch. Wiggins ran on, his sinewy frame able to keep pace
with the young man ahead, who slipped, catching his foot on the
curb, one foot now shoeless.

Wiggins glanced down at the discarded boot: foreign-made,
repaired many times, sole ripped from the upper like a broken
accordion. He saw this in the instant it took him to run past. Value:
nil. The man's debt: one pound, five shillings, and sixpence, interest
included. Leach and Son, Wiggins's employer, wouldn't take kindly
to a single, tatty boot in lieu of such a sum. Wiggins lost sight of
the man, but then he reappeared as he ran into a cigarette seller, the
wares fluttering skyward. The man, now severely handicapped by
his unclad foot, slowed and held a hand to his ribs.

They ran past Liverpool Street Station through the ever-growing
traffic, toward the river. Wiggins gained on him, dodging the trams,
but suddenly the small, stumbling figure dropped out of sight in the
sea of bowler hats and unfurled umbrellas. Wiggins came to a halt,
head swiveling. City workers spilled out of Bank Station. To his left,
King William Street tapered north.

A newspaper boy shouted out the titles of the first editions: *"Globe, Star, Standard, News. Globe, Star, Standard, News."*

Wiggins glanced up at the bank, squat, imposing. Rainwater tattooed the umbrellas above the rich felt hats, the long-striding pinstriped legs that rushed past the beggar tucked into a nearby arch, nothing more than a pile of clothes, a hopeful hand, too poor even for a bowl.

Wiggins cursed. He'd never lost a runner, at least not unless he'd *wanted* to lose one. He rubbed his hands on his sodden thighs, trousers slick with rainwater, the buildings closing in like an early night, gray as the sky. His eyes played over the faces rushing past him.

He looked again at the beggar, twenty feet away now, and shook his head in disgust. All this money, all these rich men—and not one able to spare even a penny for the poor. Rain pelted his face. He would go back to Leach and Son later that day and draw his measly retainer. No commission today. No money, just like the wretched beggar under the blanket. *Empty-handed.* He opened his eyes. Beggars never leave a bowl empty—you need a coin to start the flow, otherwise the punters walk straight past. And what kind of beggar ever goes empty-handed at Bank, surely the most lucrative pitch in the City? Didn't Neville St. Simon make tens of pounds a week?

Wiggins jerked his head round just as the beggar leapt from his place, tossed the blanket aside, and ran. "Cheeky sod," Wiggins whistled under his breath. He heaved another lungful of London's vile stink and resumed the chase.

As they approached London Bridge, the man ducked down to the right of the bridge toward the riverbank. Wiggins veered left and dodged between the ribbons of traffic and people crossing the great span. He jumped onto the balustrade, in front of hurrying women (machinists, judging by their fingertips). "Excuse me, ladies," he said and swung down to the walkway below, just as the beggar rushed toward him.

Wiggins grasped his prey between two hands. "That way's been closed all week." He nodded at the work gang constructing the riverside path running west. The man felt slight and loose in his hands, like a child of twelve, a bag of bones. "I'm not the police," Wiggins said. "Mr. Leach just wants his money."

The boy—Wiggins could no longer think of him as a man—struggled in his grip. One of his eyes was almost closed and seemed sightless. The boy fought on for a moment but then relaxed, resigned. He looked up at Wiggins and, with an exhausted sigh, murmured, "*Pazhalsta. Pazhalsta.*"

"Again!" Tobias Leach boomed. "If you weren't the best man I know at finding the blighters, you'd be fired by now the number you let get away." He wagged a fat, black-nailed finger at Wiggins, his arm barely squeezing through the glass hatch of the office.

"He was too quick," Wiggins replied.

"Too quick my foot." Leach puffed out his cheeks and ducked beneath the hardwood boards that served as his desk.

A piercing screech emanated from deep within the office. "Is that him lost another?"

"Shut up, Ma, I'm running things."

"Drop him, I say. He's too soft. Like that fat gut of yours."

Leach snapped his head round and bellowed into the darkness. "I said quiet, Mother. I'm running things now. How's a respected man of business to put up with this caterwauling?"

The unseen mother cackled. "Respected man of business? A fat piggy like you. Drop him, I say."

Wiggins stood on the street and scratched at his chin. They'd all heard Ma Leach's judgments before, though no one was known to have seen her outside since the death of Queen Victoria, all of eight years ago.

Leach and Son occupied a small yard off Commercial Road, just to the east of the City, from where the breathless Tobias dispatched bailiffs to the worst areas of the metropolis, collecting money owed to one sharker or another, for a cut.

Tobias slapped a single coin on the counter. "Is that all?" Wiggins said.

"And think yourself lucky," Tobias belched through the hatch. "No collar, no commission."

"I've got rent to pay."

Leach grimaced, his version of a smile. "You could always take out a loan. My rates are very reasonable."

Wiggins turned away and looked down at the fat round coin in the palm of his hand. If it weren't for Bill, he might soon end up like the poor one-eyed bastard he'd let go by the river. "Oi, Wiggins!" Tobias called after him. "Some toff was asking after you. Said he'd be back at three."

"I couldn't care less about no toff," Wiggins muttered over his shoulder. He folded up the collar of his greatcoat and thrust his hands deep into its pockets.

"Be here at eight tomorrow," Leach shouted.

Wiggins hadn't gone ten yards when a crisp, cultivated voice sang out from a doorway. "Excuse me, may I have a moment of your time?"

The man stepped into the light, his eyes darting to and fro. He wore a gray wool suit, pressed collar, and a polished watch chain. Wiggins stopped and eyed the man carefully, noted the hand-stitched shoes, the Jermyn Street umbrella. About his own height, five nine or so, he had a delicate manner and sharp eyes, partially hidden by small glasses: an elegant, glossy owl. "You don't appear to be getting on too well with your employer," he said.

"What's it to you?" Wiggins replied.

The owl smiled.

"My name's Kell. Vernon Kell." He held out his hand.

Wiggins regarded the offer of a hand but didn't take it.

"Is there somewhere we can talk?" Kell returned the outstretched arm to his side.

Wiggins looked along the street, the horns sounding, the clopping of the dray horses, the smell of beer, the chugging of the motorcars, the street. The dirt. A lamplighter edged his way along the curb—a memory of running under the wheels of a hansom cab, hanging off an omnibus, the first time he bunked a tram, stealing apples from Mr. Jones's cart on Kingly Street, the shit, the dirt, holding the horses for the gentlemen of Mayfair for a shilling if you were lucky, for the back of their hand if you weren't, the dirt, the light, hiding in the rafters of the music hall on Swallow Street or the old Blockmaker's before that—*Get out of it, you dirty bastards, don't come back*—the sweating impresarios and painted whores tossing him a florin on Sundays. The street.

"Here will do," said Wiggins.

The two men stood six feet apart and waited. "You don't strike me as a spit-and-sawdust man," Wiggins added, nodding at the beer hall across the road.

"What I have to talk about is *sensitive*," Kell said.

Wiggins glanced back along the street but did not speak.

Kell clucked his tongue. "Can we at least walk?" he said after a moment, pointing along the pavement. The tip of his umbrella twitched.

The two men fell into step westward, toward Aldgate and the City. Kell placed his feet carefully, high knees, stork-like, his umbrella keeping time on the flagstones. Wiggins ambled beside him, hands thrust deep into the pockets of his greatcoat. He gripped an inkpot in his pocket, filched from Leach's desk moments earlier. A horse-drawn bus clip-clopped by, passengers huddled on its open top deck. The wind bit. "You come highly recommended," Kell said as they approached the bustle of Aldgate East.

"Mr. Holmes was always good to me."

Kell blinked back surprise. "How . . . ?"

Wiggins shrugged.

"The debt business doing well?" Kell resumed.

They stopped to watch a man heave beer barrels off a cart in front of them, his bare arms glistening despite the cold. "You asking what I get paid?" Wiggins said.

"Yes. I suppose I am," Kell replied as they set off once more.

"Is that something you always ask down your gentlemen's club? *Polite* conversation, is it?"

Kell inclined his head in apology. "Nothing more than a professional inquiry," he said.

They'd reached Aldgate East Station and Wiggins drew to a halt, pointing north. "This is me. And not you."

"Back to Mrs. Balducci?"

"Now look here, Mr. Kell, what exactly do you want?" Wiggins snapped. "You may be pally with Mr. Holmes and God knows, you know things you shouldn't, but I don't need a job. 'Specially not with the army; I'm done with the military."

"What makes you say military?"

Wiggins cast his eyes over Kell as he spoke, pointing gently with a half-raised finger. "When I see a man hold his umbrella like a swagger stick, then I *think* he's military. When he holds his feet together at the heel, carries his chin yea high above the horizontal, *and* wears an Albany collar that's more starch than cotton, then I *know* so. Infantry?"

Kell's eyes widened for an instant. As he recovered himself, Wiggins grinned. He liked this owl better than most officers he'd come across. He at least looked as if he knew one end of a gun from the other.

"It's not army," Kell said at last.

"What is it then?"

"I can't tell you that, not now. Not yet."

Wiggins snorted. "That ain't much of a show." He smoothed his hair. "You've got an offer, you just can't say what it is?"

Kell clenched and unclenched his fist. "Shall we just say His Majesty needs you?"

"You mean government?"

Kell nodded.

"Sorry," Wiggins said. "Ain't my style. I don't do official. Now, if you don't mind, Mr.—Kell, was it?"

"We need good men, Wiggins. Do you love your country?"

"Don't give me that bollocks, Mr. Kell. I'm not some kid. I've fought the Boer, as you probably know, and I ain't going to take that horseshit from you or anyone else." Wiggins cleared his throat, spat, and set off up the hill.

Kell reached for his arm. "Wait! I apologize. As you say, I know of your war record. I don't doubt your patriotism for a moment. I am just in a very difficult . . ." Kell stopped and took a deep breath. "Please, take my card. Telephone the number, or leave word at my club. I urge you to consider my offer."

Wiggins looked down at the address:

Kell, Whitehall 412. White's.

"Good day." Kell tipped his hat and stepped away, stooping only to release his umbrella.

"Here," Wiggins said as an afterthought. "How about my mate Bill? Constable William Tyler. He's police, Tottenham station."

Kell paused, dipping his head sideways.

Wiggins held up the card. "I'll tell him you're looking."

Kell stopped in his tracks, then pivoted and marched back toward Wiggins. His face loomed close. For the first time, Wiggins could see Kell's strength, his resolve, perhaps even ruthlessness. Kell's voice remained as soft as before but each word sang cold. "Tell no one. Mr. Sherlock Holmes assured me you were a man of utmost discretion. It would be unfortunate, for you, if you were not." Kell enunciated each word carefully. "I repeat: tell no one."

Kell didn't like it underground. He steered between the people spilling out of the station and marched instead toward Fleet Street. The traffic thickened and he could barely make out the advertisements painted above the shops opposite. *Pears Soap Cleans.*

Wiggins impressed him, the quick deductions, but also how he stood up for himself. Kell needed good men. The boys sent to him were all very well with their impeccable French and German (not to mention Latin and Greek), their long sleek bodies and first-rate swordplay, but they were useless agents. Martindale had sheared off his own thumb while undercover at a factory in Liverpool; Russell had been run out of Tilbury Docks on the first day—a gentleman con man, or so everyone there thought, with his manners and his haughty lisp; and his best man Leyton was missing.

Kell caught sight of his own reflection in a shop window and pulled his collar straight. Wiggins looked a mess. He wore his hair too long, a whore's length, and he couldn't have shaved within the week. An athletic build, however, Kell reflected, with strong hands—strangler's hands—and the kind of loose-limbed gait that wouldn't look out of place in even the poorest neighborhoods. A former street kid, no doubt, but something otherworldly about him too: his skin was ivory and his eyes shone an electrifying blue—as if plucked from some Nordic prince. Perhaps he had Irish blood in him, Kell mused. Whatever else, though, the man dressed an absolute fright.

The steeple of St. Clement Danes reared up as Fleet Street turned into the Strand. Kell strode on. Something was definitely up at Woolwich. Otherwise why would Leyton disappear? One of the few men he had at his disposal who could go undercover at the country's most important munitions factory had vanished. Kell had always enjoyed hide-and-seek as a child, but then he had known the rules, known his opponents. Here, now, in a city of six million souls he had no idea who was friend or foe, or how to go about telling one from the other. He was a blind man. Great Britain stood in grave but ill-defined danger from the other imperial powers across the Channel, the Empire's wealth too ripe to ignore, and its leaders, his leaders, too full and fat to notice.

His boss at the Ministry, Major General Spencer Ewart, director of military operations for the British Army, was gravely concerned with the threat from Germany. He had a degree of authority within the army but no one beyond that listened, certainly not in Whitehall. The high-ups in the Liberal Party were willfully blind to the potential dangers of espionage, apart from the insufferable prig Churchill, but he didn't have the clout to raise the budget of Kell's meager counterintelligence unit.

He had to make do with fools, and too few of them at that. What he needed was a good agent, someone who could actually find things out—then at least he might get the money to expand. But right now, all he wanted to do was find out what was happening at Woolwich Arsenal. And find Leyton.

His secretary's light was one of the few still on when he arrived back at the War Office. "Any word?"

"Yes, sir," replied the secretary, a pink-faced, chinless young man with a girl's lips.

"Thank God." Kell pounced on the list of messages. "But what's this? Nothing from Leyton?"

"Oh, no, sir. Sorry. It's Lieutenant Russell, actually. He's written, telephoned, and even wired. He's eager to be employed, I think. Tired of kicking his heels."

Ewart wanted Kell to appoint Russell as a nominal deputy. Kell sighed. He'd probably have to find some harmless task for the well-connected fool. "Take this down, and wire it immediately to Mr. Holmes." Kell paused while the secretary grasped a pencil. "He said no stop. Other ideas question mark. Kell stop."

Later, as Kell prepared to dine alone—his wife now a regular attendee at meetings of the National Union of Women's Suffrage Societies—the great, retired detective's reply clattered along the corridor in the form of the commissionaire. "A telegram, sir."

It comprised three words: WIGGINS THE BEST.

2

"It's bitter out, ain't it?"

"The usual," Wiggins grunted at the barmaid. "And rum, with a slice."

"Charmer." She turned to the bottled wall behind her. "And we're out of lemons."

"Not my fault your little 'un's ill." He placed a shilling on the bar, the same shilling he'd palmed from Vernon Kell's expertly tailored pocket earlier that day.

"Oh, a cough is all." She planted a tankard on the bar and thrust out her left hip. "I'm not gonna ask how you know. And trust me, Wiggins, you'll never get a woman with those tricks. It's unsettling, so it is. A woman'll think you know what she's thinking, and she don't want that, whatever she says."

"I'm flirting," he said.

"Ha! You don't need to flirt, darling, you just need to smile. And don't be so curious—we don't like it. No wonder they's always running off."

Wiggins grunted. He rarely revealed how he deduced things. It was a question of looking: the bottle of Labo-Cooper medicine by the till, the small rattle set beside it. Throw in the heavy bags under the barmaid's eyes and the little patterned handkerchief poking from her bustle (quite separate from the beery bar cloth slung over her shoulder) and it was quite clear to him the child was ill.

A hand smacked the bar. "Missus, service here. Service."

"Jesus, gi' us a moment," she said. "Wiggins, you're the peachiest bloke I ever did see. Why, if I weren't married I'd . . ." She grinned. "But why is you always alone?"

Wiggins held up his drink. "Don't die thirsty," he said and wedged himself into a corner.

A hand slapped the bar again. "Service! Heavy," he shouted. "I want heavy." Draymen stamped their feet as they pushed through the swing doors, the tram drivers laughed loud. A trio of signalmen played dominoes, slapping down the tiles staccato. The piano struck up and a deep baritone bawled out: "The night was mighty dark so you could hardly see . . ."

"Shut up, you!"

The piano twanged.

"Where's that blasted key? Lock it, I say," the landlord roared. "If I hear another line about that fucking shining harvest moon I'll brain you. This is Tottenham, we don't have harvests here."

As one, the whole pub broke into the song, spiting the landlord in good humor. And then a shout once more above the hubbub. "I said HEAVY." Wiggins stood up. The barmaid glanced back along the bar. "It's all right," she mouthed.

The man, cheeks blood-cracked, glared along the bar at Wiggins. "Want some, do you, squirt?"

Before Wiggins could answer, a familiar figure materialized behind the loudmouth. "No, he doesn't," the policeman said.

"Hello, Bill." The barmaid smiled.

"Best get off, eh?" Bill addressed the loudmouth.

"It was him," the man spluttered. "He was threatening me. All I wanted was a pint of heavy."

"That squirt? He threatened *you*? Do me a favor." Bill stood broad and true, his pinched mustache an afterthought on his wide face. The angry man looked about him. His mouth opened and closed and opened again. "Oh, fack off," he said and stomped to the doors.

Bill and Wiggins shook hands. "I had it."

"I know that." Bill smiled. "I just didn't fancy arresting you for disorder. Ta, Elsie," he called as two pints of black and tan with rum chasers appeared.

"Good day?"

Wiggins gulped down the rum. "Let another lad go. Bag of bones, he was. Worse than Knightly."

"Thinner than a streak of piss, him. How he got into the gunners I'll never know." Ale foamed on Bill's lips and a tiny splatter dribbled down his chin. "You should get another job, mate. You're wasted at that."

Wiggins drew his hand across his mouth. Vernon Kell had said something similar.

"Join the force. Better than the army, so it is. You can go home for one thing. Seriously, you've got more brains than half of Scotland Yard combined."

"You think they'd make me a detective?" Wiggins swirled the rum in his glass.

"If you put the time in." Bill paused. "Twenty years?"

"Orders don't sit well."

"Probably best," Bill said after taking another gulp of beer. "You'd do half of us out of a job. And I'd have to put up with all that clever-clever crap."

An oil lamp burned in the window. "Quiet, now, quiet," Bill said as he crashed the door open on its hinge. He turned back to Wiggins. "Em'll be asleep, so take your boots off here." His whisper echoed down the hallway like the rush of an Underground train as it entered a station. He motioned to Wiggins and began pulling off his own boots, bumping against first one wall then the next before settling for the floor with a heavy thud.

"Bill!" Emily Tyler appeared from the parlor door, fully clothed and holding a lamp in her hand. "Look at the state of you. You're on the morning shift, you great lummox."

He righted himself with Wiggins's help and turned to his pocket-sized wife. "I shall be on the front line, at seven sharp. London's finest." He hiccuped and she laughed. "We aim to uphold the law, to . . ." he slurred. "What's the rest?"

"Bullshitter," she said, her round nose wrinkled in amusement. "You stink of beer." She looked at Wiggins. "I'll take him up. There's a cot made up in the kitchen for you."

"No need," Wiggins said.

Emily tutted. She pushed her head under Bill's arm and moved to the stairs. "Don't be daft. Get to bed."

Wiggins pulled the coarse blanket around him and closed his eyes. The cot creaked with every move. Smoke tickled his nose from the smoldering kitchen fire. His dreams ran back to the streets, the barkers, the gangs, the horseshit. *Wiggins,* a voice in the darkness. *Fuck off, you little shits. Vermin, you are. Where's me leather? Want your boots polished, guv'nor? A penny a time. Nobody wants you, she's gone, even your own mother, you miserable scrote. It's for your own good.*

"Your mother is no longer with us, Wiggins. This gentleman will look after you now."

"Where's she gone?" Wiggins, seven years of age, looks up at the Doc, the presiding benefactor of the Strand Union workhouse. "Can't I stay here?"

"You cannot. You are an orphan now."

Orphan.

"We will take good care of him, Doctor, do not worry." The Master of St. Cyprian's grins.

Tommy, Willis, and Sal—the rest of the Irregulars—encircle him then disappear once more. And the tall, thin man with the piercing gaze. *Can you do a job for me? I'll pay.*

A small boy running. *Wiggins, get back here! Where are you, Ma?*

In the early-morning gloom, a little boy runs across the heavy mud of the riverbank, the lights on Tower Bridge picked out against the waning night. He runs up the tidal steps, his feet sure and soft despite the darkness. Batters through a back door left swinging on its hinges. A body, Ma, a body, the boy cries. She flashes a look that says *Do not lie to me,* and then rouses her old man with the news. He coughs a cough that tells of brick dust, smoke-filled rooms, and a life not long to go. But he pulls on heavy boots and thrusts his hand toward the boy. His hand is calloused and heavy. It is the first time his father has held the boy so and the child will remember it long after the cough has sent the man the same way as . . .

"It's a body all right," the man says. "My old man used to pull 'em from the water. From his own boat."

The man takes a different direction from the house; the boy told to hurry home. He interrupts a constable's morning tea. The constable wakes the coroner, who in turn demands a detective on the case. The waterman trudges back to his son and wife. A young sergeant rifles the pockets of the body and tries not to look at the second mouth agape across the neck, washed gray by river water.

"Anything?" the inspector asks.

The young sergeant hands him a single embossed card. The inspector trudges through the station to the one, prized telephone and shouts into the horn. After clicks and whirrs and two false starts (the inspector is still suspicious of the device and even pens a telegram while he waits) an irritated voice comes on the line.

An hour later, Vernon Kell appeared to view the body. "His name is Leyton," he said to the inspector. "He worked for me. There was nothing on his person other than my card?"

"No, sir."

"I'll have it back if you please."

The policeman hesitated, then picked up the soggy card and handed it to Kell. "Do you know if he, er, had any enemies, sir? Or next of kin?" Kell stared at the inspector. "Not that I'm suggesting they're the same, of course, just for the formalities . . ." he tailed off. "Perhaps I should call in the Yard."

"I'll deal with matters from now on, Inspector." Kell pulled a letter of authorization from beneath his overcoat. "Have your men take the body to Barts. And if I see any of the details of this affair in the newspapers, I shall know what to do and who to do it to. Understood?"

Kell followed Leyton's body to the basement of Barts Hospital, where he had already sent the Home Office pathologist. It didn't take a genius to work out what had done for Leyton. A deep slash across his throat that sliced the windpipe in two, the poor man's head attached to the body as if by the starch of the collar alone.

"Didn't drown," the pathologist said.

Kell clicked his tongue. "How long ago did he die?"

"Impossible to say."

Kell's temper cracked. "You've given me about as much as the wretched flatfoot in Rotherhithe." He thought of Leyton's pretty wife in Croydon, a picket fence around the small front garden, a life Leyton might have had; a War Office functionary instead of the dead man he, Kell, had turned him into. Kell didn't actually know if he lived in Croydon, if he had a pretty wife or a wife of any kind. Next of kin, the inspector had said. Next of kin. "Is there nothing you can tell me?" he pressed. "Other than that a rather obvious flesh wound nearly took the man's head off?"

The flustered doctor rinsed his hands in a sluice.

"I'll have to report it as murder," the doctor said eventually. "At the very least Sir Edward Henry must be informed."

Kell picked lint from his coat. "Very well. If you think of anything, please inform me." He pulled a card out of his wallet and laid it on the side.

"Well, there is one thing," the doctor said suddenly. "There was a considerable amount of time between the death and entering the water."

"The body was thrown into the river already dead?"

"Yes, but some time after the death. Days, possibly a week or two. Hard to tell but he was almost bloodless when he went into the water."

Kell glanced at the pile of clothes beyond the corpse. "And yet no bloodstains?"

"Not one."

No papers, either, Kell cursed inwardly. Whoever killed Leyton knew who Kell was—the visiting card attested to that, a message, a warning, or a courtesy. No courtesy shown to Leyton: bled, then dumped, probably as part of a torture routine. Which meant whoever killed Leyton knew about Kell, while Kell in turn knew nothing—not who killed Leyton, nor why, nor what was happening at Woolwich. He doubted anyone else on his staff had a clue either, despite their brilliant manners and first-class educations, especially the enthusiastic idiot Russell. They knew nothing. He looked again at the card. Sighing, he set his lights to Scotland Yard and the tire-some task of talking to Sir Edward Henry, commissioner of the Metropolitan Police.

Four miles due north of Barts, Wiggins woke up. He swung his legs out of the narrow cot and pulled a hand through his hair. A dull ache pinched above one eye, the familiar sign of a hangover. Some-one had left a large jug of water and a glass for him on the table. The house appeared empty. Bill, he knew, had gone on early shift. Wiggins planned to go to the station on his way to work, as Bill had promised to stand him a loan but didn't have the cash on him. When do loans become charity? Wiggins thought as he shrugged on his jacket.

He drank half the jug and listened for any sound of Emily but she must have gone out too. On the sideboard was a piece of pie wrapped in a linen handkerchief. Wiggins breathed in the smell of pastry, lavender, and the same indefinable something that he'd caught the night before when he spoke to Emily. He held the hand-kerchief to his face a moment longer and then thrust it deep into his pocket.

Tottenham Police Station was the largest building on Chestnut Road. It stood three windows high by three wide by three deep, a brick cube—no digressions, no frills. Wiggins pulled his collar close, turned off the High Road, and approached the steps up into the station. He looked up and down the street quickly, as he was used to doing whenever he arrived anywhere. A childhood habit that stuck.

On the opposite side of the road, the gates to the rubber fac-tory swung open. A few loafers idled nearby. Two men in particular stood out, huddled together under tight hats, hunched and rocking from one foot to the other. Farther down on the left, near the factory office, a tangle of foreign workers—cheap labor after a spare day's work. One of them was shouting and gesticulating. A car came out of the factory gates and turned right toward Tottenham High Road.

Wiggins had to get to work, so he hurried up the steps and put his hand to the heavy police station door.

A pistol barked.

First one shot, then two, then a third punched the air. The two men he'd noticed ran out in front of the factory motorcar; each held up a pistol.

The windshield shattered. One of the men rushed forward and tried to wrestle something from the passenger. Wiggins started toward them but the other man, a red scarf at his throat, turned and shot without hesitation. Wiggins heard the bullet chip the wall behind him as he ducked.

"*Davay!*" the man with the scarf cried as the other pulled clear from the motor, a cotton bag in his hand. The two men took off at a fast pace down the street, letting off shots as they went.

Wiggins rushed into the police station and down the hall, into the sergeants' room. "Bill, Bill! There's an armed robbery out there, you deaf bastards."

"Get the guns!" Bill cried as he grabbed his hat. "In the cabinet upstairs."

Wiggins ran back to the street, Bill at his side.

By now the two gunmen were a few hundred yards down the road but Wiggins could see a straggle of people following them. He and Bill caught up with the pursuers and joined them, ducking every minute or so as the gunmen—seemingly in no real rush—turned and took potshots at the growing crowd.

"Who are they?" Wiggins glanced around at the pursuers.

"This is Tottenham," Bill said with grim pride.

Up ahead, the road ended and the horizon opened up. Wiggins pointed. "They're breaking for the marshes. If we're quick, we can catch 'em by the bridge."

Together they ran at right angles and then swung through rows of squat, new-built terraces.

"There," Wiggins shouted. "They'll come down Park View."

"They've got guns," Bill said.

"And we got surprise."

Ahead of them on their left ran a single row of terraced housing, with a break in the middle that led out to the railway lines. Beyond stood the Tottenham dust destructor, ribboning smoke into the air, its great chimney dwarfing the surrounds. "They've got to come through," said Wiggins. "You wait here and I'll go round the back of the destructor. I'll pile in from the side and then you can pick up the pieces." Bill looked doubtful. "We only need to stop 'em for a minute—they've got half of Tottenham on their tail."

Wiggins skidded across the wasteland and into position. In the distance another barrage of shots rang out. He craned his neck away from the road, so as to hear more accurately. Judging sound had been a problem ever since a dud shell went off at Ladysmith and burst his right eardrum. As he strained to hear, he saw a young boy race out in front of him. The boy stopped and stared along the road, his leg jiggling in excitement.

Wiggins shouted at him. "Hop it!"

The boy, who couldn't have been more than six, glanced at Wiggins but didn't move away. Instead he pointed in the direction of the firing: "Bang bang."

Wiggins shouted again but the child, twenty yards out into the road, directly in the line of the fleeing gunmen, simply laughed and paced toward the noises. Wiggins looked back to his right, to Bill's hiding place, then back to the kid, and at the empty space on the far corner where soon (how soon?) two armed men would appear.

"Christ." Wiggins dashed out to the boy. He grabbed him around his waist and hustled to the other side of the road. As he reached the lee of a coal shed, the gunmen rushed past, leaving Wiggins, still clutching the boy, too late to ambush them. He clung to the child as he watched, the boy's breath hot and fast.

As the gunmen reached the break in the road, heading out to the railway footbridge and the marshes beyond, Bill stepped out in front of them. "Bill. No!" Wiggins shouted, rearing up.

The gunmen didn't hear him. Instead, they drew to an abrupt halt at the sight of Bill and his uniformed frame.

"Come on. Give in, the game's up," Bill said in his distinctive, loud, clear tone. He held up his hands, and walked slowly forward. Wiggins threw down the boy and shouted again.

The man in the red scarf lifted up his left arm and loosed off two shots. Bill clutched his face and toppled to the ground, like a tall tree felled.

Wiggins rushed to Bill's side as the gunmen sped on. Blood pumped out of his left cheek but his eyes were open. "It's all right, mate, I'm here," Wiggins cried, scrambling in his pockets. He pressed a handkerchief to Bill's face. "Stay awake, Bill, it'll be all right, you'll see. Ambulance!" he shouted.

The handkerchief pressed to Bill's face turned crimson. Blood kept coming, soaking Bill's mustache, Wiggins's hands, sleeves, even his hair. A towel appeared from somewhere, and then more people, as Wiggins tried to stanch the flow. They carried Bill into a nearby house. All the while, his eyes open, staring at Wiggins, transfixed, frightened.

"Stay awake, Bill, stay awake," Wiggins pleaded.

Then he saw it in his eyes, the fading light. He and Bill had seen it in South Africa, Knightly dying of a bullet in the gut; he'd seen it in Whitechapel, in the poorhouse, always ever only a moment.

"You coming?" the medic called to him as they pushed Bill's stretcher into the ambulance, but Wiggins shook his head.

"His name's Tyler," Wiggins shouted at them. "Constable William Tyler." He watched as the ambulance drove away.

The street had filled with people. Men, women, and children milled around. Wiggins looked at the blood-sodden handkerchief in his fist. A cotton memento that earlier had smelled of pastry and lavender and a happy home.

People streamed across the railway bridge and out over the open marshes. Rumors echoed through the throng as they marched on, tracing the escape of the gunmen. *There was a gang I tell you, fifteen of them at least. Shut your noise, it was two—I saw it all. You was hiding under the kitchen table. A copper's been shot, I hear. Two,*

three. Four. Some old bird threw a potato at them, so she did. Is it a
child dead? Where's the police, where are they? Is it Rooskies?

Through it all, Wiggins stumbled on. It was a carnival: wild with
rumor, gobs agape, steam rising into the air from their yapping,
mingling with the falling mist. Hostages up on the marshes. A large
gang. Theft, anarchists, charlatans, louts, the jabberers echoed in his
ear. Rooskies.

He knew most of it couldn't be true. Yet he knew Bill was dead. It
hadn't occurred to anyone to go home, to hide, to let the coppers do
their job. The jamboree traipsing across the marshes was nothing if
not democratic. A shooting party, out on the marshes looking for
game, joined the melee. They'd opened fire on the fleeing gunmen
and claimed to have at least winged their men.

Eventually, the pursuers thinned out. Wiggins reached Billet
Lane over the other side of the River Lea. Bystanders on the high
street chattered. The gunmen had commandeered a tram, so one
shopkeeper said. "There was two of them, shooting and shouting
and all whatnot." He waved his hands about wildly. "They jumped
the number seven, I saw it all. Now, who's for half a pound of bacon?"

Wiggins glanced around. A constable he recognized from the
Tottenham station jogged past.

"Hey, Jim," Wiggins called. "What's the latest?"

"We've got a call to go to Hale End. I think it's all up."

Wiggins ran with him, down a shortcut, until he met a wall of
police—like at a football or cricket match—surrounding a small
cottage next to the pub. Another rumor rippled through the crowd:
attempted double suicide. One by the train tracks less than a mile
away, the other in the besieged cottage. Jim put his hand on Wiggins's shoulder, then joined his colleagues in the scrum trying to
hold back the onlookers.

Wiggins found Emily at her neighbors', the Jellys. He pushed
through the door to the parlor. Emily rocked forward, keening.
Mrs. Jelly, a stern woman of forty, looked up sharply as he entered.
Her long-boned hand held Emily's like a mother with a child.

"Please, I think you should—"

"Em?"

She looked up through red-raw eyes and searched his face. "He's dead, H, he's gone," she said in a moment of clarity. But then, distraught, she collapsed back in the chair.

Her hair hung loosely around her hunched shoulders. Wiggins felt his attention drawn to a mole on the point of her left clavicle, usually so carefully covered. It flashed in and out of view behind her collarless shift as her racked body bobbed. He hadn't seen that mole for years.

"I'll find out who did this, and why," he said. "I promise."

He went to the Tylers' empty house and lit the oil lamp in the narrow hall. Bill's blue-and-yellow "going out" scarf hung loosely on the banister; the fire in the parlor remained unmade. Wiggins strode over to the Welsh dresser and helped himself to a bottle of sloe gin he knew Bill liked to have on hand. Bill had no need for it now.

3

"It was here, at Tottenham's very own O.K. Corral, that the desperate anarchist Lepidus chose to make his last stand. Hundreds of brave citizens on his tail, the full might of the Metropolitan Police massing at the gates. His partner, the coward Hefeld, had already turned a gun on himself and now only Lepidus remained, the death of a child, of a policeman too, gnawing at his evil heart. Trapped, alone, crazed by Rooski madness, he places the gun on his own temple and pulls the fateful trigger . . ."

Wiggins looked up at Oak Cottage, a small, gray-brick affair with two windows, one above the other, and a door in its left corner. Bullet holes pockmarked the walls. He'd walked the four miles to Hale End from the police station that morning, amidst crowds of sightseers. The story was all over the newspapers less than twenty-four hours after Bill's death. They were already calling it the Tottenham Outrage.

"Oi, you, have you paid?" The speaker waved his derby at Wiggins. "This is a guided tour." The man gestured. "Pay your penny, or sling your hook."

"A penny?"

"An honest price. Now, where were we, gentlemen and the lady . . ." He tipped his hat.

Wiggins spoke to the policeman stationed at the door. "I won't be long," he said. The copper, a friend of Bill's who knew Wiggins, nodded.

"Be quick," he said. "The inspector's due."

"It was in this very cottage," the guide's voice boomed, "that Lepidus left a bloodied dagger, the handle embossed in the German language with the legend Give us this day our daily bread. On the blade, ladies and gentlemen, etched no doubt by the hand of the dead man, one simple word: heaven . . ."

Up the cottage stairs, Wiggins cast an eye about the room. Lepidus was dead, and Hefeld lay dying in hospital, but there was more to the case, he knew. Bill hadn't died as part of a robbery gone wrong. A single bed had been pushed up against the wall, underneath the front window where Lepidus must have witnessed the gathering police. A bloody stain marked the wallpaper, a chair remained upturned. From the pattern of the stains, Wiggins reasoned that Lepidus—pacing in agitation—was injured before receiving the shot that killed him. Size eleven police boots had stomped around the room. Wiggins picked out an impression of a square-toed shoe or boot—quite distinct from police-issue, and which also differed from Lepidus's boot marks. They were the shoes of a small man. Dust on the back window of the unoccupied cottage had recently been disturbed, consistent perhaps with Lepidus looking for an escape route. Or signs that someone else had escaped, dropping down into the garden below.

He put his face to the floor, ran his hands along the skirting, traced every crease and crevice in the boards, as he had watched Sherlock Holmes do.

"Get that arsehole out of here, Constable." A voice rose from the hall below. "I will not have wretched barkers profiteering from the death of one of my officers."

Boots crunched on the stairs just as Wiggins's eyes snagged on a glint in the hearth.

"Another bloody trophy hunter?"

Wiggins leapt to his feet to find a man the size of the doorway, with ginger whiskers and liver spots.

"Beat it." The inspector half raised a hand but then stopped and glanced back to the stairway.

"A pal of Tyler's, guv'nor. An army friend," Wiggins said. "Just curious, is all."

The inspector's voice softened. "You can't be in here. This is a crime scene."

"Understood." Wiggins hesitated then squatted down. "What's that?" He pointed to the far corner, a faint print on the floor.

The inspector bent down to look, distracted, allowing Wiggins to scoop up the glinting object in the hearth.

"I don't see anything." The inspector righted himself. "In any case, we had the cottage surrounded. No one else was here. Lepidus and Hefeld acted alone. And we got 'em."

"Didn't they shoot themselves?"

The inspector growled. "Didn't I ask you to leave?"

Wiggins stepped to the door. "What happened to the money?" he said.

"What do you mean?" The inspector's whiskers twitched.

"I heard it was a payroll robbery."

The inspector looked away for a moment then regained himself. "I'm not here to answer questions; now get off before I have you arrested. Leave it to the professionals."

Wiggins had worked for Sherlock Holmes long enough to know the cops didn't like unexplained dead ends, not when they already had a man in stir. Once out of sight of Oak Cottage and the inspector, Wiggins opened his hand. He dusted off the ash and held up to the light a small brass eight-pointed star, inlaid with red enamel. Lepidus, or whoever it was in the cottage, had left something behind.

Ducking his head into a biting January wind, Kell picked his way across Whitehall to the Cabinet Office and reflected on Ewart's singular failure to persuade anyone of the threat of German spies. His boss insisted Kell attend the monthly meeting of the Committee for Imperial Defense. As head of counterintelligence, he was wheeled out to offer speculation on the threat of foreign agents in lieu of evidence. Perhaps Leyton's death would sting the ministers into action, though somehow he doubted it. To make matters worse, the Commissioner of Police, Sir Edward Henry, had refused to turn over the investigation to Kell's office, refused even to believe that Leyton's killing was an espionage matter.

"Look alive, Kell," Ewart called from the Cabinet Office doorway. He'd driven the two hundred yards from the War Office. "This is it. Our man—what was his name again?"

"Leyton, sir."

"Yes, yes. His murder. This will make their whiskers stand on end."

"There is only one item on our agenda today, gentlemen, I am afraid, which Sir Edward will report on when he arrives." The Permanent Undersecretary sniffed. He fashioned a watch into his hand, like a magician's trick, and stared at it. "Which should be any moment now."

"But I must insist," Ewart began. "We have a man, one of our agents—"

The heavy oak doors of Cabinet Briefing Room A swung open and Sir Edward Henry appeared at the head of the table. He handed his hat to a minion.

The Undersecretary rolled out a lazy, elegant arm. "A seat, Sir Edward?"

Sir Edward Henry glowered over his beak of a nose. "As you all must know, there was a gunfight in Tottenham yesterday. At least one of my constables is dead. William Tyler. A child slain. Panic and mayhem. The press are already calling it an outrage. On the streets of London," he barked.

"Is the situation under control?" Ewart asked. "Will my troops be needed? We have the footguards at Chelsea."

"Of course they won't be needed." Sir Edward looked daggers across the table. "*My* men have already solved the case. One of the killers is dead, from his own hand. The other's in hospital. Under *police* guard." Sir Edward outlined the details of events. When he'd finished, a brooding silence settled over the room.

Finally, the Undersecretary coughed. "Who are these people? What do they want?"

"Russians, we think. Common criminals. After a payroll."

The Undersecretary hummed. "Odd, though, isn't it, these Russian gangs? Nothing more to it than money? There seem to be rather a lot of these incidents." He said this last word with mild distaste, as if his favorite horse kept running lame.

Sir Edward nodded grimly, his sideburns bristling. No one challenged him, the members of the committee having no more knowledge of Russian gangs than they did of the lives of their children, or the mating practices of Canadian wild geese. The Undersecretary sighed.

Kell, who sat against the wall behind Ewart, fought to hold his tongue. "Captain Kell," the Undersecretary began. "You look as though you have something to venture on the matter? Please."

"I think, er, that is I'm led to believe, that many of these immigrants claim to be anarchists or, indeed, Bolsheviks."

"Bolsheviks, eh?"

"Yes, sir. Further to this, I fear some of these groups may be funded by external forces, foreign powers."

"The Germans!" Ewart boomed, triumphant.

Sir Edward slammed the table. "Stuff and nonsense. Major General, you're obsessed with Germany."

Kell winced. It was true, his boss Ewart was obsessed. On his very first day in the job, Kell had been told to concentrate on little else. The unit's stated aim was counterespionage, but Ewart had informed him that he was to find evidence of German espionage—that only this evidence, and nothing else, would do if the department were to survive and thrive.

Ewart was a difficult man, but Kell thought he did have a point. Europe was an armed camp, with Britain on one side and Germany on the other. Less than two years before, the British had signed a treaty with Russia to go with their agreement with France a few years earlier, which had secured an enviable defensive block—the so-called Triple Entente. But the Germans themselves were allied with Austro-Hungary and Italy. Most in the government, certainly most of the gray faces around the committee table that day, assumed that the strength of these treaties ensured a permanent peaceful stalemate. Kell wasn't so sure.

"You know nothing of Germany, or of policing," Sir Edward rumbled on.

"I know more than—"

"Gentlemen, enough," the Undersecretary cried. He held up a clerk's note. "We must adjourn. The Prime Minister wishes to meet with the full Cabinet at once."

Everyone rose and filtered to the doors, but Ewart couldn't let it go. "Sir Edward, I demand an apology."

"Or else what? Will you call me out?"

Kell stood behind his boss and hoped to disappear. The committee men muttered as they passed. He looked up to see a familiar face pushing toward them through the departing throng. "What have I missed?"

"Good day, Churchill," the Undersecretary drawled. "I had no idea you were a member of this committee."

"These are grave times, grave indeed," Winston Churchill said. "As president of the Board of Trade, I insist on being informed." He nodded at Kell. The same age, they knew each other from Sandhurst, though they rarely spoke.

"It's German imperialist troublemaking," Ewart cried, glaring at Sir Edward.

"Prove it," the chief policeman retorted, red-faced.

Ewart looked at Kell expectantly. He shrugged.

"You see?" Sir Edward turned to Churchill and the Undersecretary. "Not a shred of evidence. And until you find any, I warn you to keep your noses out of police business. Now, if you'll excuse me, I have a job to do." He swept his coattails aside and strode off.

"This is a disgrace, Captain Kell, a disgrace," Ewart blustered. "We must rectify this parlous situation immediately. I told you, get me evidence." The older man then also pulled at his coattails in theatrical style and followed Sir Edward down the corridor.

Churchill raised an eyebrow. "Could do better, eh, Kell?"

Oh, sod off, Winston, Kell thought but did not say. Instead, he nodded mutely and waited while Churchill followed the others to Number Ten. The Undersecretary whispered to Kell as he left: "The club. Seven fifteen. I'll be in the Bengal Lounge."

"Do you know, until Clive took Calcutta, Bengal had a larger economy than the whole of Western Europe?"

"Oh, leave off, Soapy," Kell said. "I'm too tired for another one of your history lessons. And thanks for landing me in it today, most generous of you."

The Undersecretary, Soapy to his friends, curled himself into the red velvet chair opposite and smiled. "You've ordered yourself a drink, I see. Cigarette? They're Turkish, I've just had them made up." He sparked up with a polished silver table lighter. They bathed themselves in smoke.

"Bad business in Tottenham," he went on after a moment. "The PM's most put out. Press will have a field day, of course. Not to mention Sir Edward."

"He's going to the funeral?"

"Wouldn't miss it for the world, preening old fool—still, he's not a bad policeman for all that."

"He's not too keen on me." Kell sipped a straight Scotch.

Soapy paused, then picked a shard of loose tobacco from his lazy bottom lip. "You suspect agents provocateurs?"

"I suspect everyone."

"Ha! It's deuced inconvenient that they appear to be Russian, though. Did you know the Tsar might be coming to London this summer? He and the King want to toast the success of the Triple Entente, if it still holds by then." He dragged on his cigarette and released the smoke through flaring nostrils. "But you really think Germany is sponsoring this sort of thing? Whipping up mayhem and murder?"

"Honestly, Soapy, I don't know. It could all have been trumped up by Special Branch. Melville and his gang are always putting temptation in the way of fellows. Or it could be foreign-power sponsored. Aside from Tottenham, what I know is that a man of mine was murdered, probably while working for me. I know that our factories leak information, our naval yards are as open as Covent Garden, and our diplomats fritter away sensitive details like cheap champagne. We are not secure, and our greatest rivals must surely realize this, if not now then soon."

"Are you sure your man was killed by Germany?"

"No, but I suspect."

"That word again."

Kell sighed. "You're right. I have nothing concrete, but . . ." He left it hanging there, his mind still taken up with how little he could do—almost nothing—to find Leyton's killer. Without an agent who could successfully infiltrate the lower classes, he was at a loss. "And I don't have the resources to investigate properly."

"If it were up to Ewart, we'd declare war on the Kaiser today and be done with it," Soapy chuckled. "A word of warning though, old man, keep out of Sir Edward's business. All these Russians, these gangs—he's right, you know, it's police work. Not War Office bag at all."

"Has something been said?"

"Let's say the PM has never been too keen on what you chaps are trying to do. Spying just ain't cricket, is it? Rocks the boat all round. So if you do find some German spies—big if, I'll wager—that's all well and good, but don't bother with anything else. Leave the criminals to the police."

"I understand."

"Jolly good. You look all in. Let's have another drink and talk about something else. How is the lovely Mrs. Kell?"

"As well as usual."

"My Alice said she saw her the other day, in Hyde Park. Some sort of demonstration? I told her it couldn't have been Constance. Mistaken identity." He fiddled with his cigarette case. "I was right, of course?"

"Of course," Kell lied.

"It's these motorized taxis Alice insists on taking. They go so bally fast you can't see a thing. You've seen the *Mail*? They've offered a cool thou to anyone who can fly the Channel in one of those heavier-than-air machines. Never happen, of course, but still, hideous idea. Now, shall we risk the dining room?"

4

No detail, however small or trivial, should ever be ignored.

Wiggins examined the back of Bill's coffin. The funeral cortege plowed through crowds three deep. He walked two rows behind Emily and the rest of the Tyler family. The Union Jack swaddling the back of the horse-drawn hearse darkened with rain. In the days since Bill's murder—'the Tottenham Outrage,' the press called it—Wiggins had tried to find out more about the killers, who was behind them, about the possibility of a third man in the cottage: anything to make sense of his friend's death. The newspapers talked of a London that was full of disgruntled Russians (Lepidus and Hefeld were two) frequenting political clubs and drinking dens and calling for the death of the Tsar—but it was all a far cry from a Tottenham beat bobby.

Emily's sobs rose above the clip-clop of the horses as they approached the church. "Oh Lord, take me too," she wailed. Wiggins pulled at his hip flask. The police and the newspapers had closed the case between them. Two lone killers, a robbery gone wrong, and the missing payroll? The work of an opportunistic trophy hunter apparently. And the death sentences had already been passed. Lepidus had bled to death at Oak Cottage, and Hefeld was about to die in hospital—both from self-inflicted wounds.

Wiggins fingered the eight-pointed red enamel star in his pocket. He thought of the bloodied footprint in Oak Cottage. And where was the money?

Crowds filled the doorway of the church and lined both sides. Wiggins settled into a pew midway down the aisle, and looked up at Bill's coffin center stage. There must have been another man. He pulled again at his flask, the cheap gin stinging his nose. A woman to his right frowned. The vicar's words left him cold. Now was not a time for platitudes and acceptance, for pondering a great scheme. It was a time for anger.

As the mourning party broke free of the church, Wiggins put his hand on Emily's shoulder. "I'll find out who's behind it, I promise."

She looked blankly at him.

The liquor rose to his head. "We'll find these bastards."

A policeman, one of Bill's ex-colleagues, ushered him away. "Shut it, mate. You're not wanted here."

Wiggins looked around. Mourners glared, shook their heads, the start of a scene. "Sod it," he cried and stalked off. What he needed was a drink, and not the kind where you sat around with dark-suited men, coppers all, and cursed blind fate. A drink and answers.

Kell shifted uncomfortably in his seat. Next to him, Sir Edward regarded the congregation with ill-concealed disgust. In front of them, William Tyler's coffin lay draped in a damp Union flag. The priest spewed forth the same comfortless crumbs he'd heard umpteen times before. Kell caught sight of Wiggins, sitting a few rows behind the widow, lank hair tucked behind the ears, unshaved, hand clamped around a liquor flask. He looked drunk. Holmes's telegram came back to him: WIGGINS THE BEST. He didn't look like it now.

Kell wondered how his wife might behave at his funeral.

Relations between them were currently strained. Over breakfast, he'd brought up Soapy's remark concerning her presence at the Hyde Park demonstration.

"Well, of course Alice saw me. *Because I was there.*"

"I know that, dear. I was merely trying to explain how it looks."

"She looked like a startled turbot," Mrs. Kell said. "She quite goggled."

Kell exhaled loudly and paused. A kettle whistled in the kitchen below. "It's a question of appearances." He tried again. "A suffragette."

"I am a *suffragist*, how many times have I told you? I believe in universal suffrage, the vote for all men and women, not in smashing windows." She crunched into a corner of buttered toast.

"The distinction, I think, is moot—at least where appearances are concerned. A man in my position—"

"A man in your position," she cried. "Jumping at shadows, chasing whispers, conjuring up the Kaiser. A man in your position surely has nothing to do with the vote."

Kell sat silent. His wife put down her teacup and placed her hand on his, mindful perhaps of going too far. He gazed at her for a moment. She was a slight woman with asymmetric features, a feline nose, and an air of unhurried beauty. Only after they had married did Kell realize quite what a granite will she had, every bit as exceptional as her forensic eye and scalpel-sharp tongue. They held a hiatus of affection, then she reached for the teapot. "I am sorry to put it so bluntly, but it's true. The War Office has nothing to do with voting rights for women, now does it? I don't know what Soapy was thinking when he brought it up. He and his silly, soppy Alice. Soapy and Soppy, what a pair."

"But we dined there on New Year's Eve. You said you enjoyed it?"

"Oh, it was fine. Wilkins, more hot water," she bellowed down the hallway. "Now, before I'm terribly rude about your position again, how is the German-hunting going? Rooting out the duplicitous Teuton?"

"Leyton is still dead, if that's what you mean."

"Oh, don't be such a sourpuss. That wasn't your fault."

Wilkins, the cook, entered and plunked down a jug of steaming water. Kell waited until she had departed. "That's as may be, but he was working for me, and I have no idea who killed him. Ewart is convinced the Germans are behind it and threatening us at every turn. I tend to agree, but there's no real evidence. The few agents I have left in the field provide me with little."

"What do the police say, about Leyton?"

"Less than nothing. There's an inspector who is willing, but stupid. All he can tell me is the body probably entered the river somewhere between Richmond and Battersea. And Ewart doesn't really care who killed poor Leyton—all he wants is to prove a link to Germany. I think he gets most of his intelligence from the *Daily Mail*."

"Never believe what you read in the *Daily Mail*. One of the first things they told us at the meetings. Famous liars, particularly about suffragists. Are you sure there's a threat? From Germany, I mean? It all seems like so much hot air and bluster. We should ask Gerta."

"No, I don't think—"

But Mrs. Kell was already screaming up the stairs to the nursery. "Gerta, Gerta!"

The nanny came into the dining room and stood facing Mrs. Kell. Gerta was in her early twenties, and her cheeks shone pink and fresh. His wife spoke. "Gerta, now tell me. Do you think your fellow countrymen and -women are planning to invade England?"

"No, Mrs. Kell."

"Would you want them to?"

"No, Mrs. Kell. I love England."

"You see." Mrs. Kell turned to her husband with a smile. "Nothing to worry about. Thank you, Gerta. Tell the children I'll be up to see them at three. You may go."

"One more thing," Kell said, startling the young girl. "Er, Gerta. Do you think women should have the right to vote?"

"Vote?"

"Yes, in elections. Politics. Should women be allowed to vote?"

Gerta looked from one to the other of them, alarmed. "I know nothing about this. In Germany, I do not vote." She hesitated. "I do not know about . . . ?"

"Don't bully her, Vernon," Mrs. Kell said. "Off you go upstairs, Gerta. You know that means nothing."

He shrugged and snapped open *The Times*.

"Do you honestly believe that you are intellectually superior to me?" she went on.

"It's not as simple as all that, dear."

"Well, if not me then Marie Curie? Is she not your equal, or at least that bellowing buffoon Ewart's? Are you and he planning on winning the Nobel Prize any time soon? And don't say 'it's different' because it's all brain work. I've never met a woman in my time not worthy of the vote, even Alice. The Chancellor of the Exchequer agrees with me, does he not?"

"Lloyd George is a Liberal."

"Well, maybe we should be too."

"And Welsh," Kell added under his breath.

"Give me one good reason why women shouldn't be allowed to vote? *Prove* your case, or else."

"Or else?"

Mrs. Kell stood up, irked. "You'll see." She said no more. Kell closed his eyes and listened as she clattered the china, scraped her chair, and exited the room.

Somber music filled the church. "Captain Kell," Sir Edward hissed. "Pull yourself together. We must follow the widow out."

Kell snapped open his eyes. A choir of small boys sang into the rafters. Kell fell into step behind Sir Edward and followed the congregation from the church. Wiggins had disappeared.

* * *

Stumbling down an ill-lit alley south of Whitechapel, Wiggins groped at his fly, finally alighting on a dark alcove. He pissed long and hard, trying to forget—the coffin, Emily's tears, the ranks of public mourners. He slapped his face with his free hand and breathed in the steam and acrid stench.

He had tried some Russian clubs, but all his efforts to find the associates of Hefeld and Lepidus had failed. Most hadn't even let him in. As he swayed drunkenly against the wall, he heard a song in a language he didn't recognize, soft and angel-high. Suddenly, out of the darkness, a woman walked up the alley toward him. Wiggins tried to doff his cap, remembered his knob in his hand, twisted back into the shadows. "Sorry, miss, shit, ah . . ." He splashed his trousers. A faint tinkle of laughter reached him through the night as the woman carried on her way. Wiggins burped.

Farther along the alley, the woman stepped into a pool of waxy light outside a pub. Three toughs tumbled through the doors. Wiggins looked up at the noise as he buttoned his fly.

"All right, Jam?" the tallest of the three called out to the woman. "Any bargains tonight?" He plucked at her arm and thrust his pelvis toward her. "I might shell out for a quick 'un."

His companions laughed. The woman turned, shook her head, and muttered something before hurrying on.

"Don't turn your back on me, you Rooski Jew-bitch." The tall man jumped forward and grabbed her shoulder.

Wiggins drove his fist into the man's throat. The tall man reeled back, pawing at his neck. Wiggins swiveled and kicked the next man in the balls full force. He lifted off the ground, a look of shock and surprise on his face twisting into sudden agony. The third man, a butterball, roared in rage and leapt onto Wiggins's back. In an instant Wiggins dipped, twisted, and threw his wobbling assailant over his shoulder—a perfectly executed Bartitsu move.

In seconds, the three toughs were utterly defeated. The first man slumped in a corner struggling for breath as he held his neck; the next wheezed, bent double, hands clutching his bollocks; and the third lay on the flagstones, his huge stomach rising and falling in fast jerks.

"Scram," Wiggins panted. "Unless you want more?"

The men gathered themselves, silenced by the unexpectedness of Wiggins's attack. They barely mustered a curse between them as they pulled each other out of reach. Wiggins watched carefully until they disappeared onto Whitechapel itself. Boxing technique, basic martial arts, and a good old dose of street fighting: enough to sober anyone up. The "bollock" move was a favorite from his days as a young runner—Mr. Holmes would not have approved. But then Mr. Holmes hadn't had to look after himself on the streets of London from the age of seven.

The woman stared evenly at him, her face half-lit by the flickering torch and framed by a tight headscarf. Wiggins picked up his cap. "I apologize for my fellow countrymen, miss . . ."

Her faint smile turned into a look of puzzlement. As her expression shifted, Wiggins realized the shadow was a large birthmark that spread from the inside tip of her left eye down past the point of her chin.

"I thank you," she said at last. She spoke slowly, as if the words were recently acquired but sincerely meant.

"Russian?" Wiggins said.

Her mouth turned up again in vague amusement. "Latvia," she said.

"What's your name?"

"Bela," she said after a moment.

"Wiggins." He hesitated. "Do you know where I can get a drink?" (He couldn't quite bring himself to say "we," though he dearly wanted to.)

She pointed past him to the very obvious pub.

He laughed. "No, I mean a Russian drink, or Latvian. You know, spirits? Nearby."

Her eyes flicked down the alley involuntarily, surprised. "No, not for you. It's dangerous." The smile disappeared.

He stepped toward her, emboldened by her kind voice. "Do you know what this is?" He pulled the eight-pointed star from his pocket.

"Sorry, I must go. You drink in there." She tried to press a coin into his hand but he waved it away.

"Go," she said again, pointing to the pub.

Then she stepped forward, reached up, and kissed him on the cheek. It was so quick, so unexpected, that Wiggins stood still. "Thank you, Anglish," she called before vanishing into the night.

The adrenaline was wearing off. The Drowned Sailor was a rancid boozer, but it was close. He ordered a pint of black and tan and blinked his eyes against the stale haze. Wiggins had given up smoking at the age of twelve and never regretted it. He pushed his foot hard on the rail to stop it shaking and drafted half the beer in one gulp. "Again," he said, though he barely had the money for more.

Heaviness returned to his limbs, his focus softened, and he ordered a gin, trying to dispel the iron-filing itch in his mouth. What he couldn't shake was the thought that he'd let go of a lead. Her eyes, dark, quick, and strangely memorable, flashed for an instant in his mind.

"Barman, is there anywhere round here that sells real liquor?" He held up the empty gin glass.

The landlord swiped a wet cloth down the bar. "They'll have brandy at the Ten Bells," he said. "And rum at the Blind Beggar, no doubt. But you don't look like you've got the gilt for either."

Wiggins ignored him. "Something Eastern. European, like. Ain't there some Rooski dives round here?"

The landlord stopped wiping. "What do you want with that? Them places is dangerous for the likes of you."

"I know some," a ferret of a man called down the bar and sidled over. "For the price of a drink, of course." He swilled around his near-empty glass and raised it slowly.

Wiggins hiccupped. "I'll give you the rest of mine and nothing more. And if you're wrong, you'll regret it."

The man sniffled and soon enough took Wiggins outside. He pointed down the alley—the direction in which Bela had gone. Wiggins pictured her face, her laughing eyes. "It's two doors before the end, red door on the right. Knock three times, I reckon."

Wiggins swayed onto his heels, then handed the man the remainder of his beer. "If you're wrong . . ."

"Oh, I'm not wrong." The weasel gulped his drink. "But you're mad to go down there—don't you read the papers? They're murderers. It's an outrage."

Wiggins teetered down the alley. He found the red door, continued past, then stopped at the corner. There was no light, no sign to suggest anything other than a private home. He turned up his collar, pulled his hat low, and untucked his shirt. It was not a good time to be Eastern European; he'd seen enough of them to know that look of fear, that desire to melt into the background. He hunched his shoulders and put his fist to the door. Part of him wondered whether he shouldn't come back in daylight, or at least sober. But he needed to find out somehow, and if not today, then tomorrow, or soon he would have to knock on this door or other doors like it. He rapped three times.

Nothing happened. He stamped his feet. Still nothing. He knocked again, louder, less fearful now but more annoyed, indignant. What kind of bar was this? He was used to frosted glass and pianos and shouting and fighting and bursts of coarse laughter and beer and spit on the floor, and a front door banging and crashing near off its hinges. Not the cold silence of a blank wooden door. At that moment, as he half turned away in frustration, a small man bumped into him.

"*Izvineetye,*" he said as he and another man pushed past. Instead of knocking, the man simply shoved the door open and the two men went in. As they did so, one of them held the door open for a moment and Wiggins followed with a gruff nod.

The two men, deep in conversation, hustled down a thin corridor. Lit only by a dim gas lamp, the walls were streaked with grease and dirt. Wiggins kept behind the men as they went through a second door at the end of the hallway. He stepped into the bar after them.

Smoke stung his eyes and he ducked his head instinctively, squinting. The room was surprisingly large, despite a low ceiling, and stretched out into shadows at the back. As his eyes grew accustomed to the meager light and the tobacco haze, he felt the rich swell of chatter die down and eventually stop.

Five or six men sat around a miserable fire. Wiggins strained to make out their features. Eyes glowed from beneath beards and hats and scarves. Down the left-hand side of the room a few planks laid on thigh-high barrels doubled as a bar. Rough fabrics hung on the walls. Wiggins picked out other men sitting farther back in the darkness. He felt their stares. Over and above the tobacco, the bar stank of mold, cinnamon, and a sweet-rotten tang Wiggins couldn't place. The two men he had come in with now turned, standing at the bar, and shrugged slightly, regarding him anew.

Wiggins tried to smile. No dice. He glanced about him. Finally, a heavily accented voice sounded from behind the makeshift bar. "Police?" The barman, similarly bearded, held a bottle in his hand—by the neck. The wall hangings behind him rustled.

He held the barman's eye and slapped his hand on the bar. "Drink," he said. The barman stared.

"I've just buried my best friend," Wiggins said in a loud voice.

A door wheezed open somewhere off past the bar, then slammed. The barman shifted his grip on the bottle and looked past Wiggins to the men knotted around the fire. Wiggins didn't turn back, kept both hands foursquare on the bar. He may have been drunk, but he wasn't senseless. The barman furrowed his brow and Wiggins concentrated on counting each crease. *One, two, three.* Someone called out a single word. *Four, five, six.* The barman drew up the bottle in a sudden flourish, then in one swift movement slapped down a metal beaker, upturned the bottle, and splashed in a full measure of booze.

Wiggins gulped down the drink with a great show of bravado that he didn't feel. The spirit, for that's what it was, hit the back of his throat like a white-hot hammer. He gasped and held his hand on the bar. His eyes watered, his chest burned, but bit by bit the fire subsided. He stared hard at the barman, whose face came slowly back into focus. Was that a smile?

"Again," Wiggins croaked and placed his final coin.

A murmur of conversation resumed. Wiggins took in the rest of the room, this time ready for the burn. The group around the fire caught his attention. They looked at him with an unhealthy degree of fascination. Wiggins felt his legs loosen and his jaw slacken. He finished the drink but it didn't do any good. The room tipped ten degrees to the left, and the conspiracy of men stared at him—expectant. Wiggins looked at his beaker—was this one spiked?

"What is this?" he said to no one and stumbled toward the fireplace.

"*Voy!*" someone shouted at him, and he felt a hand on his shoulder. One of the men rose from his fireside seat. Wiggins caught sight of a jagged gash across the man's chin and wondered if this was the reason he wasn't bearded. And then, as the man approached, Wiggins saw the large symbol, hanging on the wall above the fire. An embroidered red eight-pointed star.

Hands throttled him from behind. A welter of shouts broke out as he struggled against the barman's tree-trunk arm. He kicked someone hard but the man with the scar slapped him around the face then plunged a fist into his stomach.

Wiggins strained and bucked but the barman was too strong. He dragged him toward the rear of the room. Out of the corner of his eye Wiggins saw one of the men walk behind the bar and pull out a knife. Its blade flashed in the light of the bar-top candle.

They pulled him outside into the blackness of the yard. Someone rammed a dirty cloth into his mouth. Three or four men tugged him to his feet and hustled him through the starless night, first around one corner, then another, and a third. Wiggins tried to pick out familiar words, all the while thinking of that long, flashing blade.

The men came to a halt and Wiggins's stomach lurched. He had a sense of being near the river. A Londoner, born and bred, perhaps it was right to end his days in the Thames. It washed away all the city's shit.

The Russians argued. Despite not knowing the language, Wiggins could tell by the stifled urgency and the half-seen pointing that they were discussing where to dump his body. The man with the scarred chin had obviously decided how to kill him. Wiggins heard the knife slicing the air. Practice.

Wiggins writhed against the barman once more but the grip was firm and true. He breathed heavy garlic into Wiggins's ear and laughed. Finally, after another round of whispered discussion, the four other men standing above him—little more than bearded silhouettes—came to some agreement. The armed man whistled the blade through the mist-wet air.

"Goodbye, Anglish," he said.

"*POLISKI!*" A woman's cry pierced the night.

Footsteps neared.

The men stepped away and exchanged hurried words. The female voice moved closer, quiet but urgent, calling out in Russian. In seconds, the barman released Wiggins with a violent wrench and the men hustled off into the darkness.

He recognized her smell first, as she bent over him, and then the voice—sounding so different in English. "You stupid man," Bela said as she knelt over him. "Stupid, stupid man."

"I . . ." He tried to cough life back into his throat.

"Run," she said. "Don't come back here. I am sorry for your friend. But go now. There is no police. If you don't go, they will come back for you. Nikolai will kill you." She pulled him up and then pushed him away all in the same movement. "Run," she said again.

Wiggins held on to her arm for a second. "Thank you," he said, but she was already gone, after her compatriots. His survival instinct kicked in and he stumbled off in the other direction, the lights of Cable Street blinking into view.

He held his hand to his throat, bruised by the barman's arm. The street lamps hissed along the otherwise deserted street, the shop fronts shuttered. Over the sound of his own heaving breath, he heard the slow lope of leather shoes.

"I've been . . ." Wiggins spluttered.

"On the piss, son?" said the policeman.

"No, yes."

The policeman shook his head and made to continue on his beat, unwilling to concern himself with a time-waster. Wiggins grasped his arm. "I've been—"

"Get your hands off me."

"I've found an eight-pointed star. At Tottenham and now here, in the 'Chapel. It's a link, you stupid bastard. The Outrage . . ."

"If you don't calm down—"

"Listen." Wiggins pulled at the policeman's cape, half to steady himself, half in desperation.

The policeman, as his notebook later reported, and as he testified to the local police court, immediately took all necessary measures to subdue the defendant—both on his own and later in conjunction with a colleague who had come to his aid on hearing the whistle. The magistrate noted Wiggins's black eye and broken lip with regret, ascribed it to the evils of strong drink, and sentenced him to sixty days in prison for assaulting a policeman and resisting arrest.

5

Sixsmith didn't like the sea. The wind sheeted in from the Channel, and stray salty flecks tattooed his face. Out there past the navy yard in the black was the raging, monstrous ocean. He whipped his head round. Was he being watched? Or was it the tapping of a buoy out in the harbor? He turned away from the front, collar tight against the rain, and hurried past the glowing doorway of the Eight Bells up the hill toward the Grand Hotel.

"I wish to make a telephone call," he said.

"Booth one." The bellboy pointed to the only telephone.

Sixsmith glanced around the hotel lobby but saw no one.

"Operator," he spoke into the horn, "get me Whitehall 412, fast."

Kell closed his eyes. The violin hit high, sweet, heavenly notes, then came the rest of the strings, and finally the brass. His fingers tapped time on the empty seat next to him. Constance was at a meeting and so he attended the concert alone. He had recognized a few faces when he arrived, and nodded curtly to a man from the Admiralty. On those evenings when he went out without his wife, he felt it easier to keep his distance from conversation, her absence so often a dominant, if silent, subject of any interaction. The wives were worse than their husbands, their lips tighter, their brows sharper.

The audience erupted for the half and Kell jerked awake. Musicians hurried from the stage and the concertgoers bubbled around him, alive with conversation. As people hubbubbed out of the exits, a gangling man pushed his way against the tide toward him.

"Excuse me, madam, sir. Apologies. Was that your foot?"

"Russell," Kell said. "What are you doing here?"

Lieutenant Russell stood before him, a six-foot-three man-child, whiskerless, with impeccable manners and, as far as Kell was concerned, a mind as feeble as his voice was loud. Kell had finally acquiesced to Ewart's promptings and made him nominal deputy of the unit.

"Good evening, sir," he foghorned amiably. "How is the music?"

"Mozart has his moments."

"Lady Agnes." Russell bowed to a grand old woman swathed in purple velvet. "I'll pass on your good wishes to my mother of course. How is Fifi?"

Russell turned back to Kell, having finished another round of pleasantries with the stately dame. "Who the devil is Fifi?" Kell hissed. He hated himself for asking but couldn't help it.

"A Pomeranian. At least, she was last time I looked. Lady Agnes calls all her dogs Fifi."

"What do you want?"

"I almost forgot. A telephone call. Sixsmith, sir. He said he would try again at nine."

"He shouldn't call." Kell scrambled to look at his watch. "Not on the office line anyway." Something was wrong, he knew, as he hastened to the cloakroom.

Russell lumbered after his boss. "Sounded a bit, you know, rattled. I came as fast as I could. He's stationed in Portsmouth, isn't he, sir? Perhaps he has news about Leyton."

Kell glanced up quickly as he collected his coat and gloves. "Did he say that?"

"Oh, no. He just said he'd call again. I only thought . . ."

Kell passed his ticket to the gangling lieutenant. "The second session is Mendelssohn—perhaps you'd like to take my seat, Russell?"

"But shouldn't I come with you? This is it, isn't it, sir?"

"What?"

"The great game for Europe."

Kell almost shouted at the idiot. But he didn't have time. Instead, he pulled on his overcoat and regarded Russell for a moment. "The great game for Europe? Is that what you'd like?"

"Isn't that why we're here, sir, for king, country, and empire?"

"Not tonight, Russell. Tonight, you are here for Mendelssohn."

Kell's shoes beat a sharp report on the new flagstones of Knightsbridge. The concert didn't finish for another hour and he couldn't see a cab, so he kept walking. As he did so, he became aware of steps behind him. He went to cross the road and glanced back, ostensibly looking for a cab. An angular figure, his face obscured by a spotted scarf pulled tight, flitted out of view. Kell reached the opposite pavement and increased his pace. He ducked down a back street as he approached Grosvenor Place and waited in the shadows. Then he stepped out quickly, back into the light cast from a street lamp, and caught hold of the man.

"'Ere, wot you doing?" The man pulled away, but Kell had him by the lapels.

He hesitated. "Who are you?" Kell searched the man's face.

"Get off, or I'll call a copper."

Kell relaxed his grip, suddenly unsure. At that moment a cab pulled up in the background. Kell caught a brief flash of someone leaping into the carriage and then it clattered past him in a whoosh of dust and tack. He stepped back.

"I beg your pardon," he said. "I mistook you for someone else."

"Too fucking right, mate."

He reached the War Office with twenty minutes to spare. As he settled into his chair, telephone in front of him, it occurred to Kell again that someone knew a lot more about him than he did about them. It could be a German spymaster, a criminal gang—he had no clue. He couldn't even be sure he was being followed. The truth was that he, Captain Vernon Kell, responsible for military counterintelligence in the British Isles, had almost no idea who he was fighting against. The closest he'd come to real intelligence had died along with poor, headless Lawrence Leyton. Hopefully Sixsmith knew more.

At nine o'clock, the telephone failed to ring.

Kell clicked his tongue.

In the days after Leyton's death, Kell had tried to reconnoiter Woolwich himself. A futile exercise, he'd discovered soon after exiting the train station. A foreman doffed his cap, a flower seller put on her best toffee accent as he passed, a policeman wished him good morning. He couldn't hide who he was. He didn't belong at Woolwich Arsenal, didn't fit in amongst the vast whirring machinery, the dirt, the grime; sheer hard, physical work simply looked alien to him—and everyone he passed knew it.

By nine thirty, the telephone still had not rung.

Sixsmith worked in the Portsmouth naval yard as a clerk. Kell had placed him there last November. Though he'd come up with little of interest, he'd managed to maintain his cover, which was a damn sight better than the rest of the depleted department. Perhaps at last Sixsmith had something for him. Or perhaps he too was dead.

Eleven o'clock. No call.

Kell stared at the silent instrument in front of him. A night chill crept down his back. He'd never liked the blasted things, couldn't trust them. Like ghosts speaking from the grave, or hallucinations.

He shot to his feet and grasped the telephone, as if to throttle it. "Get me the exchange. Hello, yes, this is Captain Kell at the War Office. Whitehall 412. I received a call on this number about half past seven this evening, can you tell me where it came from?"

Eventually, after much complaint and heavy sighing, the girl from the exchange gave him the name. Kell called the hotel, only to speak to an irritated receptionist. Sixsmith was not a guest, he said. The lobby was empty at that time of night, sir. Don't you know it's late? It took Kell another two hours to whistle up an army driver and car.

"It's gone one, sir," the duty QM whined, but by two o'clock Kell was on the way.

London's tentacles reached long and wide. Vernon Kell sat in the back of an army-issue Austin as it rattled south down Clapham Road on the way to Portsmouth. Less than a mile away, in Brixton, Wiggins stared into the blackness of his piss-dank prison cell. He kept in his heart a picture of the girl with the angel-high voice and a birthmark splashed across her face, an image that had been his companion for the first thirty nights of his stretch and would continue to be for the next thirty. The cell prompted darker thoughts, too, the worst of life mixing with the best. As he slept, he dreamt of his childhood on the streets of the uncaring city.

A city whose tentacles spread wider, past the pleasant Hampstead villa where Kell's wife slept, beyond the limits of the new Underground and suburban trains, even farther than the main lines steaming forth to Glasgow, Bristol, Aberdeen. The tentacles spewed farther still, from the docks to Pondicherry, Melbourne, Singapore, Wellington, the West Indies, and beyond, webbing the planet; stretching to the poppy fields, the gold mines, plantations sugar-rich, the cotton fields. The wealth of the world pouring back along the filaments, back to London—the beating heart and head and guts of an empire of 370 million souls, a quarter of the globe.

Kell knew: an enemy that struck here would strike everywhere.

Thwack!
"This is a merciful mission."
Thwack.
"I strike only to help."
Thwack.
"You may only be seven, but I must release the evil within."
Thwack.
"St. Cyprian's will save you. I will save you."

Wiggins didn't feel like he'd be saved. His arse stung something rotten. He didn't cry. Wouldn't cry. The Master had held his hand when he walked him out of the Strand Union, Doc Rogers smiling sadly after them. As soon as they were out of sight, though, the Master threw his hand away, disgusted. He pushed him through the roads north of Oxford Street toward St. Cyprian's in Marylebone. The Master beat him that night, as a welcome, he said, to keep him straight. He pushed him into a dark, airless room and whispered, "Sleep." The room sounded to Wiggins like a huge slumbering animal or monster: children squashed together any old how, on beds, on the floor, curled in corners. Wiggins, small for his age, crawled beneath one of the few beds and made himself smaller still.

"Where you come from?" a high-pitched voice squeaked in his ear.

His eyes stung with held-back tears. He didn't want to think of where he'd come from. He said nothing and shifted his head away.

"Did the Master smack you, did he? With the paddle? He does that to keep you straight. So *he* says. I think he likes it. What's your name? 'Ere, go on. I'm Sal."

"Wot kind of name's that?" Wiggins said, surprised. "You a girl?"

"Might be," she said.

"Why you here?" Wiggins said quietly. "Ain't there a girls' place?"

"No chance," Sal hissed. "They send the girls out to Blackheath, or God knows where. I'm London, me."

Wiggins wiped his face with the ripped collar of his shirt. He tried to stifle a sniff.

"'Ere, give over. The others will hear ya," Sal whispered again. "Don't worry, he's had his fun now, he'll leave you be."

The Master did not leave him be. Every second or third day: "I must release the evil from within," he said. "We need to keep you straight." Wiggins was confused. He knew his mother had scared people and that he should never tell anyone how she died. But hadn't she released the evil in her already, weren't that the point? Why else would you kill yourself, if not to kill the devil inside?

"He don't like you, Wiggins. I mean, he don't like anyone, but he sure as teeth don't like you. Or maybe he likes you too much." Sal shrugged. "You're too pretty."

Wiggins frowned. Sal was always saying things he didn't understand. Of course the Master didn't like him.

In the daylight, Sal had proved to be a freckled redhead with boy-short hair and oversized trousers. She was seven too, she told Wiggins, although the way she spoke made her seem older.

Only Wiggins knew she was a girl.

The orphanage was spread over a warren of rooms off St. Cyprian's Church in Marylebone. Its corridors echoed with the sound of crying children, and the malevolent jeers of the black-toothed deputy Bane. The Master never raised his voice. Wiggins and Sal hid as much as they could, primarily from the Master, but also from Bane and even some of the older boys. Violence cascades down.

"The Master ain't no churchman," Wiggins chirruped to Sal. "He's scruff."

"He's a phil-an-throp-ist, so he says," Sal replied.

"I've heard of them," Wiggins said. "They's trouble."

"Wiggins!" The Master's hand clasped his ankle and dragged him from under the bed. "The evil is strong, we must release it." Sal held his hand for a second and then he was gone.

The Master, black-suited, bounced on the balls of his feet. He rubbed the wooden paddle against the seat of his trousers as he pointed Wiggins to his desk. "Evil must be defeated. I fear we have not made as much progress as I'd hoped." His left eyelid drooped.

"I ain't done nothing, sir, honest."

"Silence."

Wiggins turned his head to the desk. He could hear as the paddle scratched against hard worsted trousers. The office reeked of stale sweat and spilled ink. Urine stains streaked the floorboards beneath his feet, the marks of boys past. The Master breathed deeply. Wiggins scanned the desk, anything to distract him. "Don't hit me, sir, I ain't evil. Promise I ain't." He turned away from the desk and faced the man.

"You dare disobey me?" the Master demanded.

Sal's words flashed into Wiggins's mind. Maybe he likes it.

The Master raised the paddle in his right hand. "Turn," he said.

"Do you like it, sir? Do you?" Wiggins said. "I could do something else if you want."

The Master tensed. His eyes widened. His jaw worked. And then he roared.

* * *

"A gentleman made a telephone call at seven thirty last night." Kell pulled off his gloves and stared hard at the concierge of the Grand Hotel, Portsmouth. "Where did he go?"

"Sorry, sir. I'm the morning man. You'll have to ask Albert. He knocked off at seven."

Kell sniffed. A vaguely exotic smell hung in the air, something he couldn't quite place, familiar and novel all at the same time. "And where might I find Albert?"

"He comes on at six." The concierge had decided Kell was neither a potential guest nor a tipper. He fussed and fumbled at the desk in pointless busyness. "Is there anything else I can do for you? Sir," he added after a pause.

"One thing," Kell said carefully. "You could inform me of your next of kin. I wouldn't want them to worry, you see. It can be so distressing for family when their loved ones are taken to prison, don't you think? It's better if they know."

"I'll check the book," the concierge offered. "Here it is, yes, that's right—a telephone call was made around that time. You see? But we don't keep records of walk-ins. The caller wasn't a guest is all I can say, sir."

"Were any other calls made that night? Afterward?"

"No, sir."

"Would he have made the call from here?" Kell pointed to the booth.

He examined the small telephone kiosk but nothing seemed amiss. There was no note. Just the mouthpiece and horn, hanging limp.

Kell didn't like dealing with the local police, but he had no choice. He'd drawn a blank at Sixsmith's digs, other than to confirm that he hadn't returned the previous evening. There was nothing for it but to raise an official alarm. He flashed his credentials and, after a number of confused conversations with ranks ever ascending, he spoke to an Inspector Grimes.

"Sixsmith's a small, slight fellow. Blondish hair, thinning at the temples. Worked as a clerk at the naval yard. He tried to speak to me last night from the Grand Hotel, couldn't get through. And then he didn't return to his lodgings on Alexandra Road."

The inspector blinked, heavy-lidded. "Is that so unusual, sir? We don't normally classify a person as missing until—"

"Look," Kell interrupted. "I have reason to believe, well, that his life is in danger."

"Why's that, if you don't mind me asking?"

Because he is one of my only agents left in service. Because the last one was murdered, bled to death; because Sixsmith tried to call me and is now missing. "Because, Inspector," Kell said at last, "I say so."

The inspector nodded and went to the door of his own office, leaving the desk free for Kell. "I must use your telephone," Kell said. "Report back to me in two hours."

Kell looked out onto the drab Portsmouth cityscape as Grimes padded off. Mist hung in the air, but the inspector's office offered no comfort. Not even Scotch.

The telephone rang. "I have your call, sir."

"Thank you, put it through. Lieutenant Russell, is that you?"

"Yes, sir. I've been manning the line, sir."

"Has Sixsmith reported in?"

"No, sir, not a dicky bird. Will you be coming back soon, sir? Should we inform Jones—where is he, come to think of it?"

"Jones is . . ." Kell paused. "Jones is none of your concern. I will be returning shortly, if we can't find Sixsmith. I have a car."

"Take the Petersfield road, sir. They've recently laid a new surface, far better than the Guildford route. Absolute bone-wobbler, that one."

"Thank you, Russell."

"It's only Jones, isn't it, sir? He's the only one left."

Before Kell could answer, the office door swung open. "Captain Kell?" A constable stood before him, eyes hooded by his helmet. "Inspector Grimes says you must come at once."

* * *

Wiggins may have been short, he may have been seven, but he was old enough to see murder in a man's eyes. As the Master roared, eyes bulging, Wiggins dived between his legs and out into the hall.

"Bane!" the Master bellowed. Boys scattered through St. Cyprian's, terrified.

Wiggins barreled down the corridor, eyes wild. "The gate's open," Sal cried from the dorm doorway. "The coalman's here."

He swerved toward the front door.

An arm shot out of nowhere. "I've got him, sir," Bane called. The assistant, no more than eighteen, grinned, black-toothed and rank.

Wiggins swung for a second as Bane gripped his collar. But then the ragged shirt fell apart and Wiggins was away. He burst into the sunlight, Bane cursing in his wake.

He dodged left, right, and then the coalman towered before him. Wiggins looked up at him and froze. The coalman winked white in his tar-black face and Wiggins bolted out into the traffic.

"Oof, sorry, lad," he heard the coalman say.

From the other side of the road, Wiggins caught sight of Bane, sprawled in a pile of coal on the orphanage steps, the Master trapped behind. He was free.

Free to do what? He ran wildly down unfamiliar streets. Finally, after losing himself in a crowd, he came across a park. He hid in some bushes and tried to think what to do or where to go. Mary-the-bones wasn't his manor. Wiggins was a Soho boy, and since he and his mother had been in the Strand Union he also knew the neighborhood north of there. He'd never once been west of Mary-the-bones Lane, not in all his days. But he was hungry now, and though it was warm, he didn't fancy staying the night under that bush. Park-keepers were to be avoided. They often carried sticks specifically for the task of beating small boys.

He snuck out into the nearest street, looking for something to eat, a click, anything. The roads were wider here than his own

Soho patch. Cleaner too. He couldn't see a costermonger or a rubbish dump. Adults rushed around, towering over him, unheeding. He slumped down on the steps of a terraced house and eyed the passersby.

"Got a tanner, sir?" he called out. "Tanner for a poor choirboy?"

No one even slowed. Not to look at another long-haired scrote knocking around the streets, begging. Two men approached. One tall, thin, with a sharp face and a clean shave. The other square-shouldered with a bushy mustache and kind eyes. Wiggins glanced quickly at their boots as they neared, searching for an angle.

"'Ere, mister. Gi' us a tanner. You've been down south, ain't you, mister? Don't wanna leave London."

The two men stopped and the tall man regarded him with the clearest eyes Wiggins had ever seen. His insides shriveled. "What was that you said?" the tall man asked.

"A tanner, sir." Wiggins put out his hand.

"After that?"

"You've been down south."

"How did you know?"

Wiggins pointed. "Chalky boots, guv, chalky boots. That's south, ain't it?"

The man twinkled. "Or west, don't forget it could be west. My dear fellow," the man called to his friend. "Do you have tuppence for the boy?"

"A tanner, mister. Go on."

The tall man turned back to him. "Tell me, how many people have gone past since we started talking?"

"Five, sir. Three gents, a lady, and a sweeper."

"And on the road?"

"A four-wheeler, two cabs, and a hurdy-gurdy. Where's me tanner?"

The man offered the sixpence piece. Wiggins went to take it but the man withdrew it. "And what street are we on?"

"Dunno. I'm new round here. I'm Soho."

The man pursed his lips then handed the coin to him carefully. "You *must* know London, if you are to survive. Do you know your letters and numbers?"

"Course." Wiggins had only just mastered them before his mother died, but master them he had.

"Well, learn the street names. There is no excuse. Now be off with you, scram. Out of my doorway."

Wiggins jumped into the street and turned back to the man, triumphant—a whole sixpence.

"Gotcha!" Bane gripped him by the upper arm and pinched hard.

Wiggins struggled and kicked but Bane dragged him away. "Ever so sorry to disturb, gentlemen. This evil boy has run away."

"Where from?" the tall man asked.

"St. Cyprian's, sir. He's too stupid to know it's just around the corner. Now, Wiggins, the Master is par-tic-u-lar keen to see you. 'E was ever so de-stressed at your absconding."

Wiggins fought uselessly as Bane hauled him across and down the street. He looked up once and saw the tall thin man gazing after him. Over his head, in the glass above the door, Wiggins could just make out the number: 221B.

"He must have fallen, sir. There are no marks."

Sixsmith's body lay crumpled at the bottom of a dry dock.

"Let me see," Kell said. From the vantage point at the top of the dock, Sixsmith was little more than a punctuation mark on a blank page.

"It's a good sixty feet, at least," the inspector said.

More, Kell thought, as they climbed into the great gouge mark in the docks. Many a huge ship had started here, slipped into the sea. And now here was Sixsmith's body, like a wind-blown piece of confetti left after the grand departe.

"The coroner's been called, of course. But it looks like a broken neck—it's a death trap, this place. They's always losing men down here when there's a job on."

"But there is no job on now."

"No. He hasn't been robbed, though, sir. Wallet, money, latchkey—it's all there."

"Anything else in his pockets? Documents, letters?"

"Nothing."

"Inspector!" The word echoed around them. They craned their necks to see a constable hailing them from above. "There's a witness."

It was dark by the time they made the Eight Bells.

"As I told the constable," the excited publican said, "I saw a man matching that description drinking here last night."

"Fair hair, slight?" Kell asked. He had to raise his voice over the hubbub of the bar.

"He was hitting the bottle something fearful. Now, can I get you anything yourselves, gents? Inspector?" The publican grinned.

"Not while I'm on duty, Jack." The inspector glanced at Kell. "Would you say he was the worse for wear?"

"Up the pole, he was. A little fellow like him, wouldn't take much. Rum, sir? Keep out this drizzle."

Kell clicked his tongue. "Did he drink alone?"

"Yes. No, hold up. There was a bloke he came in with, maybe. It were full, rammed here. Big fella, stank of Christmas."

"Christmas?"

"Like an orange. If that was him. Had an Adam's apple as big my fist. But I can't say they drank together, as such, sir. I couldn't swear to that. But he left alone, I know that. Lilting so he was. A half-pint pot, sir?"

"I think it's pretty clear, sir," the inspector said as he and Kell walked back to the Grand Hotel. "Your man, Sixsmith. Got blind drunk, stumbled out onto the quay—perhaps he wanted to go back to the office, collect something he'd forgotten—and fell into the dock. It's not as uncommon as you might think, not around here. I've seen it before and I'll see it again."

Kell said nothing. It didn't fit. Sixsmith wasn't a drinker, for one thing. And it *was* uncommon. How many other counterintelligence officers fell to their deaths in such circumstances?

"Thank you for your help, Inspector," Kell cut him off. "It seems your theory fits all the facts. I will ask you to keep investigating, however. Let me know if there is any further mention of the tall man with the Adam's apple. I will show your final report to the Minister."

"The Minister?"

"Yes. I trust you'll do a good and thorough job? And now I must find my driver and get back to London."

Kell had nothing to gain by staying longer. As with Leyton's body, there wouldn't be any more evidence. Unless someone came forward who saw the deed, Sixsmith's demise would be recorded as an accidental death.

The driver sat slouched in the hotel lobby, an air of mutual mistrust hanging between him and the concierge. Kell flicked his head at the door.

"To Whitehall. Oh, and take the Petersfield road—it should be quicker."

The driver nodded.

Kell wrapped a muffler around his neck and cursed the day he sent Sixsmith to Portsmouth. He cursed the cold wind whistling through the motor's cab. And he cursed the Austin's stinking engine, filling his nostrils with the smell of petrol and burning grease. The car rattled and coughed out of town and hurtled northward into the night. Kell massaged his temples. Leyton murdered, Sixsmith too, most likely, and he had nothing to go on, no clues. Why had Sixsmith called? There was nothing of note in his digs, nothing at the naval yard. And what was it Leyton had discovered at Woolwich? What could he do?

These questions crowded in on Kell as the car engine roared. The faint lights of a small town prickled the darkness up ahead. "That's Petersfield," Kell shouted. "Open her out, can you? I can't stomach much more of the countryside."

They flew down a wide high street, asleep and poorly lit, and then back into blackness. Kell pulled the driving blanket up to his throat, closed his eyes, and let his thoughts wander once more.

Someone kicked him in the back. Twice, three times. He jolted awake. "What the hell was that?"

The car swerved wildly and the driver shouted, "Sir! Sir!"

Kell swiveled as the car lurched. Behind them, a black van was pressed up against the back of the car, forcing Kell to his knees, a dark shape bearing down. "Hurry, man," he called to the driver.

His hand felt his hip on instinct, but of course he was unarmed. It was bloody Hampshire, for Christ's sake. The van crunched against them once more and the car leapt forward, spurred by the bump. "We can distance them," Kell cried. He opened his door and hung out the side, pretending to draw a gun, anything to put the van off the chase.

"A hill," the driver gasped. The car kicked against a slope. The van's lights fell away.

"We can make it." Kell glanced forward. The car's headlights flashed and flailed into the night, the engine at its limit. But then it whined horribly and began to splutter.

The driver cursed. Foul smoke bubbled from the engine. Kell glanced back, then the car kicked into life again. They swerved left and right, the car rattling. The van gained on them, as if suddenly lighter. Kell, hanging from the door, watched in horror as it came alongside and swerved into the back of their car. As it did so, the road twisted violently to the right, around the cusp of a hill.

For an instant, Kell saw two grinning specters in the cab of the van.

And then the car flew off the road into blackness.

"You only got to Baker Street?" Sal said for the umpteenth time.

"I didn't know," Wiggins groaned. He lay beneath the bed on his stomach, Sally by his side. The other boys left them alone; they'd heard the beating Wiggins took. It had been the third one that week; his back, arse, and legs throbbed. And yet the Master still didn't seem satisfied. It didn't seem like he'd ever be satisfied.

Since his recapture, Wiggins had drawn a mental picture of the surrounding area. One of the other boys had a penny map and let Wiggins pore over it obsessively. He memorized everything he could. The tall man had told him to *know* London and know it he would. Wiggins clung on to an image of the man's face, not kindly exactly, but not cruel either. Trustworthy. The man had liked the trick with the chalky boots, just like Doc Rogers at the bone shop—always chalky boots when he came back from visiting his sister. Wiggins remembered things like that, details.

He remembered anyone who gave him a tanner too. Wiggins had stuffed it in his mouth the minute Bane nabbed him. Now it was nestled in his pocket. Something to hold on to.

"I'm gonna run again, Sal," he said quietly. "I can't stay."

Sal nodded, a filthy red curl falling across her face. "Wait for coal day," she said. "I'll run a dodge."

"What will you do?"

"Just be ready—coal day, remember."

This time Wiggins knew where he was going. A boy had told him about the empty railway sidings up past Paddington Station. The map was in his head now; he'd remembered its every cut and cross, all the street names. He'd hated his mother for teaching him to read, but now he realized what power it gave him; he could *see* a way clear, on the pages of a map. He wouldn't be nabbed again.

Coal day arrived and still Sal hadn't told him the dodge.

"Be ready, is all, by the doorway there."

The Master had most of them arraigned in the classroom, as usual, although no learning took place. He would walk up and down in silence, examining each of the boys in turn. You weren't allowed to move. Every now and then he smiled, and that was worst of all. You knew you were in for a beating then. In the dorm, Bane was supervising the "cleaning." This involved kicking and cuffing the boys as they scrubbed the grime-encrusted floorboards and walls and windows. Sal was in the dorm while Wiggins tried to avoid the Master's eye in the classroom.

Wiggins sat perfectly still. Only the muscles in his calves twitched. Bane's voice trailed off in the background. In the silence,

Wiggins heard the great creak of the coal-hole cover opening. The Master heard the coalman too and went out to speak to him. At that moment, Bane let out a great scream that echoed throughout the building.

"Master!" he shouted. "Master!"

The boys scuttled to the classroom door in time to see the Master rush past. "What is it now, Bane?" he called as he loped along the corridor.

This was his chance. Wiggins shot through the door. From behind him, he heard the Master cry out in horror.

"A *girl*?"

Wiggins scuttled past the kindly coalman.

"Go on, my son," the black-faced titan cried.

He made the street and tore right up Marylebone Road, then left and right again. He took tiny backstreets and alleyways, dived under wheeling cabs, risked a horseshoeing, all to make good his escape, to find the sanctuary of the train station. Finally, he gathered the courage to look behind him. No one had followed, not the Master, not Bane. Sally had revealed her secret. She had saved him.

"Is he all right?"

"Broken bones, but alive."

"Thank God for that, Russell. We're in trouble. Have you left word for Jones?"

"We still can't reach him, sir. Should I go to Harwich myself?"

Kell sat back in his chair and ran his hands across the desk. "No," he said. "Give me a moment, please."

The driver had survived the crash. Kell, hanging from the door, had been thrown clear and had come to in a mulberry bush. Their attackers hadn't lingered, but it took Kell an hour to find help. He'd left the driver with a local quack, commandeered a police car, and taken a train from Petersfield back to Waterloo. Now, mid-morning, he was facing an entirely new fate.

He was a target. The service was a target. Someone was trying to clear up the whole lot, even him. He'd have to speak to Sir Edward, organize a police guard. Humiliating enough, but not as bad as being attacked, being *at war*, and not even knowing the enemy.

"Sir." Russell poked his head around the door. "An urgent telephone call."

"What about?"

"It's the Hampstead police, sir. It's about your wife."

6

"I never want to see you again."

"Won't you miss me?"

The warden grunted. He turned away from the counter and went off in search of the few possessions Wiggins had on him when he was arrested. Wiggins felt like a seven-year-old once more. Prison did that to you.

After he'd escaped St. Cyprian's thanks to Sally, he had taken his tanner and his newfound knowledge of the area and raced up to the railway lines at Paddington. He'd lit on a deserted archway and made a camp for himself. That first night, as he picked at a rotting orange he'd scavenged from the gutter, young Wiggins listened out for the trains rattling to and from the station. At some point, when the night was at its blackest, they stopped.

The next morning, alone, he ventured out and bought a penny bun for breakfast. The station concourse teemed with people. Wiggins scooped up a mislaid shawl, a half-eaten chicken pie, and five par-smoked cigarettes. He realized that no one saw him, that if he were careful he could ghost through the day without attracting any attention, feeding on the flotsam and jetsam of London's traffic. But he wanted one man to notice.

Wiggins still had nothing to his name, he reflected, as he regarded his scant belongings in the warden's box. No job, no home, and now an ex-con to boot.

The warden placed the lonely objects on the counter with an unhurried grace quite at odds with his lumbering gait and red-faced panting.

"You've got card-sharp hands and no mistake, Mr. Potts." Wiggins nodded. "Were you once in Monte Carlo? Or perhaps the penny game at Margate?"

"I can still have you up before the governor," Mr. Potts nodded gravely. He passed Wiggins a pencil and a sheet of paper. "Sign here."

Wiggins mentally checked off each item. A shilling. Check. A British Library ticket. Check. Notebook. Check. A red enameled eight-pointed star with gold trim, origin unknown. Previous owner presumed to be one Jacob Lepidus, deceased. Check. A battered gold, oft-pawned pocket watch that loses two minutes a day. From the Doctor. Check. And one business card, crumpled and water-damaged but the number still legible: *Kell, Whitehall 412. White's.*

"Ta-ra, Mr. Potts." Wiggins grinned. "Stay away from those tables."

"I never play for money," the warden called after him.

Wiggins pulled his cap close over his eyes and strode down Brixton Hill. Pale sun bounced off puddles, the London planes rustled green despite the grime. Wiggins took a left and worked his way through the urban cottages and ugly new terraces of south Stockwell. Every now and then he pulled Kell's card from his pocket. He'd known good officers and bad in the army, been demoted by some of the good ones and promoted by the bad—the rank made no difference to him, only the pay. Kell had an air of competence, but then this was the easy part; all those Sandhurst-trained haw-haws had the confidence, the expectation, of command. What they didn't have was the brains to go with it, nor even the common sense or animal cunning to realize their own limitations, or the wisdom of their subordinates.

At the approach of the river near Battersea he cut down a small cul-de-sac of railway cottages, cloaked by the billowing smoke of a matchstick factory. A wall ran directly across the end of the road. Sulfur caught in his nose, an acrid tang wafting over the smoke, but he didn't hesitate. Keeping his pace even and quick but not hurried, he stepped into the front garden of the final house, took two long strides, and pushed up off the windowsill. He leapt onto the wall and easily hauled himself over and onto the grass verge beyond.

A scrub embankment rose up to meet the train tracks. He hustled along, ducking slightly as a train neared on its way into town. Glancing up, he could see the passengers crammed against the windows, swaying. Wiggins made his way to the huge splayed tangle of tracks at the junction south of Nine Elms. He checked his watch. Unless the timetables had changed in the last six months, he'd be fine. He sat beside a large bush, a major signal fifty yards up the line, and waited.

After a number of expresses screamed over the points en route to London, a slithering train of six carriages rolled slowly from the other direction and came to a halt at the signal. Wiggins stepped out, glanced toward the guard's van, then pulled himself up onto the footplate. He opened a door to one of the compartments and climbed in.

"Morning, madam." He tipped his hat to the only occupant of the compartment, an old woman dressed in a pile of coats. Wiggins sat down opposite. Their compartment had a door on each side, but no connecting corridor, along with the rest of first class.

The woman frowned. "This is the eight-thirteen to Shoreham-by-Sea, isn't it? The express?" she said eventually, eyeing the window.

"I hope so, madam."

The train lurched into life and within minutes they found themselves steaming southward. Wiggins checked his watch again, nodded, and closed his eyes for a snooze.

An hour or so later, the train slowed to a stop in the middle of nowhere. Trees and foliage filled the view on either side. Wiggins snapped open his watch, checked in both directions, then quickly pushed open the door.

He tipped his cap once more. "Cheerio, madam."

"Wait, young man. I'll need your help with my luggage." The woman gestured to a large case on the overhead rack.

Wiggins hesitated. "But this isn't Shoreham."

The woman looked at him as if he were the greatest fool in Sussex. "This is the nonstop?"

"Believe me, madam, you don't want to get off here."

Wiggins dropped to the ground and waited for the signals to
change. The old lady peered down at him, puzzled and also, he
thought, secretly excited. She had a glint in her eye and at least an
hour's worth of scandalized anecdote to share over lunch.

The train left him as he pushed through the tangle of undergrowth
and out into the open fields. He'd made the walk before—westward
from the points—and each time something about the emptiness of
the countryside unnerved him. Nevertheless, after forty minutes
of hard hiking he approached a small, well-appointed cottage. He
slowed as he reached the wild blackberry bushes that protected the
cottage's rectangular garden. Picking a hidden spot proved easy, and
he settled down to observe for a few minutes.

Wiggins had first waited for him twenty-six years ago, though
he didn't know his name then, only his address. In the days after
his escape from St. Cyprian's, Wiggins—keeping an eye out for
Bane—had stood watch on 221B Baker Street and hoped for another
tanner from the tall man.

"Got another test for me, mister? Anything you want for a tanner?" Wiggins jumped out at him one morning.

The tall man stared down at him. "I wondered when you'd come
back," he said. "You've been watching my rooms. Why? Come on.
Be quick."

"Want a job, don't I."

"Do you know what I do?"

"Nah."

"Well, what have you observed about me?"

Wiggins screwed up his face. This was important. "You're not the
average gent. Up at all times. You get lots of visitors." The small boy
paused. "Visitors in trouble, I reckon. No one looks happy knocking
on your door."

The man chuckled. "True enough, but what does that mean?"

Wiggins thought hard. "You ain't a doctor but I reckon you help people."

"That's as good a definition as any. Anything else?"

"Who you live with, your mate. He's a good 'un."

"Really, why do you say that?"

"He puts up with that awful bloody music."

The man fell silent for a second, and then burst out laughing. "Ha! I shall tell the Doctor. What's your name, boy?"

"Wiggins."

"Can I trust that you won't be detained again?"

"No chance."

"And are you learning your way around London? That is critical."

Wiggins held up a penny map he'd found. "I can read and all."

The man raised an eyebrow. "Then I think, young Wiggins, that I will have need of your services. Look up at my windows each day—that one second on the left. If you see a violin in the window—the cause of the awful music by the way—then you are to ring the bell and ask for me. In the meantime, here's a guinea as a retainer."

A guinea. Wiggins gasped.

"Can I trust you?"

"Course, guv."

"You may need friends to help in your tasks. I will need you on an irregular basis, but need you I will. And make some friends."

Wiggins's eyes shone. "Who are you?"

The tall man pulled himself taller. "I am the world's first and only consulting detective. Now, be off with you before your gruesome jailer returns."

Wiggins, guinea clamped hard in his fist, stepped away but then looked back at the man, who had his foot on the doorstep. "One thing, guv'nor, who do I ask for, when I ring?"

The man turned and raised his chin a touch. "My name is Sherlock Holmes."

* * *

Wiggins now watched as the retired detective, clad head to foot in white, emerged from the cottage and edged down the garden toward his bees. Holmes reached one of the boxes at the far end and slowly pulled out a shelf. Dark smudges bounced and drummed around him, and Wiggins could hear soft buzzing. The old detective was unfazed. When he'd finished, he strode back to the cottage with the same even tread. He showed no sign of noticing Wiggins.

Wiggins hesitated. Now that he'd made the journey, he wasn't quite sure how to approach his mentor. The bees scared him. Wiggins pictured himself caught amid a frenzied storm; he wouldn't know how to behave if the bees kicked off, if they rioted. Would he be killed? That wasn't the only source of his reticence. It was one thing to turn up at Baker Street, on a case, but quite another to appear out of the blue in deepest Sussex. He was an ex-con now too, which didn't help. Maybe Holmes wouldn't want to see him? But with Bill gone, who else was there? Before he could make any firm decision, the back door of the cottage opened once more.

Holmes, this time dressed in a light jacket and tweed trousers, stepped out onto the paving stones round the back of the house. He placed something on a table, then folded his long body into a garden chair and turned his face, eyes closed, to the sun.

"It is uncommonly warm for April, wouldn't you say, Wiggins?" he called out. "Won't you join me for a drink?"

Wiggins extracted himself from the hedge. "You always did have a keen eye, Mr. Holmes."

Holmes wafted a hand toward the vacant chair. "I thought it a little early for beer, even for you," he said as Wiggins sheepishly took his seat. "So I assume you'll be happy with a glass of this cordial, to which I'm partial."

Wiggins nodded, then remembered to take off his cap. Holmes poured two glasses of the oily liquid. He fixed his guest with the cool, hard, penetrating stare that had been dissecting London's criminal class for the past thirty years.

"Unmarried, still. Perhaps not a subject on which I can pass judgment. Drinking too much—though not lately—and, oh dear, yes, oh dear." He muttered to himself. "Underused, certainly. Bored and recently bereft. No." Holmes put up his hand before Wiggins could speak. "There's no need to explain, my dear fellow. Tragedy comes to us all."

Holmes took a delicate measure of his cordial. "I've been expecting you," he said after a moment. "Though I must say you took a lot longer than I anticipated."

"I was detained."

"At His Majesty's pleasure, yes. What have I told you about the East End, Wiggins?"

"It's not like it used to be, Mr. Holmes."

"And yet still you manage to find yourself arrested for assaulting a policeman. Don't look so surprised—I deduced it from the court reports, not your appearance. Now, I can understand, better than you may think, the upset a friend's death might cause. But Tyler died at the hands of common thieves. They are dead, God has seen justice done, what else do you need to know? It is over."

"I owe it to Bill, sir. You always told me about the importance of friends, and he was one of the best. And I reckon there was others involved—"

"I know, the missing payroll," Holmes interrupted.

"And I don't think they's just thieves either, there's politics."

"For all the outré cases I've been involved in—documented and somewhat embellished by the good Doctor—there are tenfold more that are mundane, tawdry, and commonplace. And yet the ordinary and the bizarre, the weirdest crime and the simplest murder, at bottom most always have one of two motives behind them. Love or money, Wiggins—there's not much else that drives a man to crime." Holmes paused to examine his guest. "They were armed thieves. They play at politics, but they are criminals. And your friend was a brave man. That's the end of it."

"But it's personal."

Holmes threw up his hands in irritation. He leaned forward and took a sip of the cordial, then looked out across the garden. "The day of the amateur is over, Wiggins. We live in a different age. You can't hope to work alone." He held up his long, bony hand to still any protest. "Detection is a state-run business now. You need to have the apparatus, the backup. Need I remind you that your last effort at investigation left you in prison?"

Wiggins unfolded and folded his cap. "You think I should work for Mr. Kell, then?"

"I told him you were the best. He's a good man, but they don't know what they're doing or how to do it. Kell has been trying to recruit me for years, but I am, as you know, retired. He is clever, but he has no idea how the streets of London work, how its underbelly lives and breathes. Yet this is where the game is played, under our very noses. Don't worry, Wiggins, he may be what you would no doubt call a toff, but you can trust him."

Wiggins looked at the ground between his feet. Snail trails criss-crossed the flagstones. "So I should forget about Bill and take the shilling?" he said at last.

"There's a conflagration coming, Wiggins, and we must do all we can to stop it, or at the very least prepare. There are large and growing forces ranged against us, on the streets of London even now—hostile foreign powers. Kell is doing what he can and I urge you to help him, not only for your sake, but for the sake of this great country of ours. Forget about the political playacting of immigrants, you must fight the countries that are against us. You must work for Kell, work for the Empire."

Wiggins squinted up at the older man, surprised at this sudden fervor. He remembered, years ago, the big fuss Mrs. Hudson had made when Holmes shot the old Queen's initials into the wall. "VR" pockmarked above the mantle. But he hadn't been there, hadn't seen such patriotism writ large on the great detective's face, as it was now, burning in his eyes. It was easier to be a patriot if you hadn't been a soldier. Perhaps Holmes might think differently if he'd seen the camps of Bloemfontein, all in Britain's name.

"Besides," Holmes went on, "a man in your position, if he were to conduct his own private investigations—say in the East End—would be much better placed to succeed if he were working under government auspices."

"I ain't no bloody snitch," Wiggins said, then remembered himself and coughed.

Holmes tutted. "You wouldn't be. But working for such an organization—however badly run it is at present—is one of the few ways outside the official police to pursue your other . . . interest, shall we say? Although you must never mix the two. If Kell found out you were working on your own investigation, he'd dismiss you at the very least."

Wiggins nodded slowly as Holmes went on. "Mark my words, the Tyler fellow died an heroic death, but a pointless one. He was unlucky. Nothing can bring him back."

They relaxed into their chairs. Wiggins knew Holmes was a kind man, despite his cold, rational exterior. If he could help, he would. The old detective drew a deep breath.

"If I were to advise you to pursue this investigation—and I'm not, by the way, but if I were—then I would suggest getting to know the world. Join in. Go to one of these anarchist meetings. These criminals appear to justify their insanity with politics. So find out about their politics—establish personal contact. The vilest murderer, the most ruthless criminal, the terrorist even—at heart, they are all human, all individuals. Make friends. And be patient." He fixed his eyes on Wiggins. "I told you that when we first met, did I not? Make friends."

"Yes."

"What an age away that was, a different world. You were so young, Wiggins, a child."

"No younger than half the others on the street."

"True. You were an apt pupil, though, the very best." Then he nodded and changed the subject abruptly, and talked for a few minutes about the countryside and the pleasures of keeping bees.

Finally, Holmes rose from his chair and ushered Wiggins through the house. "One more thing. Take this." He handed Wiggins a sovereign.

"Mr. Holmes, I don't need charity."

"It's not you I'm thinking of," Holmes replied. "I fear my already rather dubious reputation in the village will tumble further if it becomes known that my visitor intends to evade paying his train fare in *both* directions."

Wiggins laughed. "If you think anyone else will notice, Mr. Holmes."

"Oh, believe me, Wiggins, more is noticed and commented upon in the sleepy English countryside than ever causes remark in the busiest street in London. Behind these pleasant hedgerows and quaint cottages lie some of the sharpest-eyed sentinels that ever drew breath."

Holmes saw Wiggins to the gate. "Goodbye, Wiggins, and good luck with Kell. Whatever you do, don't tell him about your personal crusade. He won't like it." Holmes waited for Wiggins to nod. "Good. And who knows, in the future we may be working together again, but this time against a far greater danger than ever the criminal classes could contrive."

"Thank you, sir," Wiggins said and then quickly added before the older man could turn: "One thing, what's that cordial we drank?"

Holmes smiled. "It has a certain kick, doesn't it? Not quite what it was, but still pleasing. Watson prescribed it one gloomy day and I have taken it ever since. Unfortunately, you can't buy it here. I have it shipped over from an agent in New York. It's called *Coca-Cola*."

Kell stared at the documents strewn across his desk. For weeks, he and the department had searched for the killer of Leyton and Sixsmith. Ewart still wanted evidence of German espionage activity. Information multiplied in the form of letters, telegrams, memoranda, reports, files, the occasional photograph, and even, in one case, a hurried note scribbled on the back of *Ally Sloper's* one-penny paper. This last proved to be an observation that many of the beggars congregating around London's major train stations seemed to be of German extraction and, as such, might prove a threat to national security. Yet on the other hand, there had been no more information on the man seen with Sixsmith in Portsmouth. The coroner had reached a verdict of accidental death, with no evidence to offer. Kell had no idea why he was killed. There were no leads. He'd even pulled Jones from Harwich, fearful of another death.

The police had drawn a blank on finding out who had run him off the road in Petersfield. Are you sure it wasn't an accident, sir? Could your driver have fallen asleep at the wheel? Kell felt besieged at every turn. But not like the heavy gunners at Ladysmith, not a real siege against a visible and knowable enemy. Kell was besieged by the unseen, by a force only limited in power by his imagination. Sir Edward at Scotland Yard had agreed to provide a police guard at the house, but he too seemed unwilling to really believe in any danger. The police had proved utterly useless, except in one respect.

When it came to apprehending suffragettes, the constabulary apparently excelled. On the morning of his return from Portsmouth, the Hampstead station had called: "It's your wife, sir." He'd rushed headlong across London, anxiety-filled, only to find his wife alive and indignant, sitting on a cell bunk at the police station.

"It's totally ludicrous," Constance said when he arrived. "These lumbering flatfoots seem to think I broke the windows at Radlett's on the high street. Now, really."

"Perhaps we should go home. I've had a rather trying night and the sergeant has agreed to discharge you, under my recognizance."

"Quite right, too," Constance said loudly as they swept past the charge desk. "I have done nothing wrong, other than fight grave injustice."

The sergeant eyed them carefully but said nothing. Once outside, Constance turned to her husband. "Where have you been? You look dreadful."

When he explained what he saw as the danger, his worries for her and the family, his desire for her to head to the country, she flatly refused. "Never," she said. "I shall stay. I will not be hounded out of my own house by anyone, be they German spies or otherwise." When the police guard arrived she further observed, "Is this

some elaborate ruse you've hatched to keep me away from suffragette meetings, Vernon? Am I really such a threat?"

No, she was not a threat—at least not to him anyway. Kell smiled
to himself, polished his glasses, and glanced out on Whitehall.
The traffic clattered and sang. For all her faults, his wife was not
one to be intimidated. And now, at last, amid the piles of useless
paper collecting on his desk, he had a piece of relevant, concrete
information.

The leak at Woolwich Arsenal had been confirmed. Bethell at the
Admiralty had a friend who sold heavy tools and traveled exten-
sively throughout Europe. This salesman, a Glaswegian named
MacDiarmid, occasionally visited German factories as a guest.
It was at one of these factories—the Krupp munitions works in
Hamburg—that MacDiarmid had noted the superheating of shell
casings. He found this an unusual innovation and reported it to
Bethell when he returned to London. MacDiarmid wasn't to know,
but such a technique had been invented at Woolwich near the end
of the previous year—a great leap forward, so the boffins said, and
as such, a closely guarded secret. And yet, four months later, Krupp
knew.

Leyton must have discovered the source of the leak, and that
supply line of information must still be open, otherwise why kill
him? There would be no need, if the mole didn't need protecting.

Kell replaced his glasses and turned back to the desk. A newly
installed electric lamp cast a golden pool around him and his work.
He picked up MacDiarmid's Hamburg report once more. There it
was in black and white: British technology in the hands of a foreign
power, an imperial rival no less, direct from the Arsenal in less than
six months. Woolwich held the key. "If only we could get in there,"
he murmured.

"Is that what you want me for?" Wiggins said.

Kell jumped in his seat. "Who's there?" He stood up and pushed
back from his desk.

Wiggins stepped into the light. "It's me, Wiggins."

"How the hell did you get in? This is a secure building."

"Is it?" Wiggins lifted his eyebrows.

"How long have you been here—in this office, I mean?" Kell took off his glasses again. He tried to sound haughty, schoolmasterish, to cover his shock.

"Just arrived," Wiggins replied. "Should I sit?"

Kell gestured to the chair opposite. "I didn't hear you."

"You was busy talking to yourself." Wiggins slumped into the high-backed chair and looked carefully about him. "And I'm used to getting around unnoticed, like."

"Yes, well." Kell draped a newspaper over the documents on his desk and sat down. He took a deep breath, placed his fingers together, and counted to ten in his head. Wiggins slouched in the chair, his hair longer than at the funeral, his chin stubbled. Kell was struck once more by his startling blue eyes, so at odds with the black hair. "I do not approve of trespass," Kell said at last. "But I will admit that I'm impressed. Is this the kind of, er, unusual skill you learned while working for Mr. Holmes?"

Wiggins brushed an idle hand across his leg. "Where I come from, you wasn't worth nothing if you couldn't get into a place like this."

"It's a good job you're not criminally inclined."

"As far as Mr. Holmes knows anyway."

Kell frowned sharply. "I take it you've had a change of heart? Are you looking for a job now?" Kell shuffled paper absently. Wiggins could be the break he needed—a rough, working-class man rather than the long-boned twits he was presently forced to rely on. But he hadn't forgotten Wiggins's drunken appearance at the funeral. "Are you sober?" he said.

Wiggins hesitated. "I haven't had a drink in months."

Kell looked over his glasses at him for a long time, but Wiggins seemed sincere.

"What's the job?"

"I can't tell you much, until you agree," Kell said. Wiggins nodded, a diffident flinch. "Excellent," Kell went on, his bounce returning.

"We'll talk about pay in a moment. I take it you have somewhere to stay this evening?"

"No."

"Money?"

Wiggins looked between his feet. "Some," he said. Then he looked up. "I'm ready to sign up. Mr. Holmes said you might have use of my talents."

Kell nodded. "Indeed I do. Or rather, the country does." He stood up. "But this isn't the time or place. Tomorrow, we should meet—I'll have to check a couple of things, make sure everything's in order."

"But what about the work? What is it?"

"That can wait. Suffice to say it is of the utmost importance to the security of the Empire."

Wiggins rose slowly and followed Kell to the door. "You'll be working for me, directly, of course. My agent, as it were."

They faced each other by the open office door. Wiggins paused, pulled his fingers through his hair, and nodded again. It felt to Kell like a handshake.

"Here." Kell dug into his pocket and pulled out a few coins. "For this evening. Find somewhere to stay, temporary, where you're not known. It is important that you keep all this to yourself. We'll work everything out tomorrow. I'll expect you here at three." Kell felt his equilibrium restored.

Wiggins looked at the money in his palm. "I don't think that's a good idea," he said.

"What do you mean? Why?"

"I take it when you say 'agent' you mean the secret kind, judging from what Mr. Holmes says. And there ain't that much secret about you or your office."

Kell felt himself flush as Wiggins went on.

"I found you, and I'm just a nobody off the street. There's a bloke outside in a tweed cap with one eye larger than the other and a sailor's tattoo who, I'd wager a pound to the penny, is watching you. He didn't see me come in, because he's waiting for you to come out. So if you want to keep me secret, we should meet secret."

Wiggins was right, Kell now knew. True counterintelligence work required secrecy, not just from the enemy but from everyone. Especially if you didn't know who the enemy was. He resolved in that instant to keep Wiggins's existence a secret from all but his immediate superiors, and even then never to identify him by name. Kell had lost too many men to be careless again. He nodded. "Where?" he said.

"Outside Fortnum and Mason's, main entrance."

Wiggins stepped into the corridor. "But how will you get out?" Kell said. "Won't he see you?"

"He won't see me."

Kell sat at his desk, confused, unnerved, yet elated. He wasn't used to being ordered about by a man as socially inferior as Wiggins; a man with barely a guinea to his name, a torn cap and ragged clothes. It was unnerving, too, to be so thoroughly out-thought. For Kell had no doubt Wiggins was right: any meeting between them should be conducted in secret and certainly away from his office. Wiggins would be a difficult agent to control.

But what an agent he could be, Kell smiled to himself. He lit a cigarette. No one on his staff could have stolen into the building so effectively, past the policemen and the most officious doorman in Whitehall, let alone found his office—not even with their best Sandhurst accents and fine manners. And what of the reverse? Could any of them melt into a working-class milieu like Wiggins? A pub, a music hall, a munitions factory? Wiggins was like a stray cat; a lifetime spent keeping to the shadows, working for Holmes, the army, London. In that moment Kell believed the great detective was indeed right: Wiggins could be the best.

7

Wiggins scrambled on the road for stones. It had taken him days to track down little Sal. The Blackheath Orphanage for Girls rose grim against the sky. A huge building with sharp turrets and black windows, it was designed to eat motherless children. Wiggins kept to the shadows as he paced around its walls.

Sherlock Holmes had told him to find friends, and after his escape from St. Cyprian's, Wiggins realized he had only one. Sal. He watched (or *observed*) as a row of girls came out into the yard. They walked in desultory circles, heads bowed, while a black-clad specter oversaw them from a high doorway. Wiggins spotted Sally, her red curls uncovered. A proper girl.

He crept across the road and scouted down the side of the building, stones at the ready. Then he took aim and hurled the pebbles at the large, high windows, cracking one and smashing a second outright.

The girls cried out and their jailer shouted. As she hurried from her post and rounded the corner, Wiggins called in a soft, high voice: "Sal, Sal, over here."

Her head whipped round. As the rest of them rushed to the scene of the damage, she hurried over to the gate.

"Wiggins, what are you doing here?" she whispered through the railings.

"Let's go," he said. "Come on."

Sal glanced back, excitedly. "Where?"

"Paddington. I've found a spot."

"But what will we do for poppy?"

"I've got a job, ain't I," Wiggins said proudly. "It's irregular, but it's a job."

Wiggins had followed Sherlock Holmes's advice as a seven-year-old, and he followed it now, more than twenty years later, as he stepped across the traffic-choked Strand. He had until the afternoon before he had to meet Kell at Fortnum's. The morning was his.

While Wiggins was in prison, both the police and the press had lost interest in Bill's death. Fresh murders decorated the front pages; society scandals; rumors of a state visit by the Tsar; the Imperial Exhibition at the White City; the touring Australian cricket team; Blériot's flying machine; Harvey the Notting Hill strangler and his sensational trial; the people's budget—the world kept on turning, the presses rolling, Tottenham and Bill Tyler soon forgotten.

But not by Wiggins. He knew someone else had been in Oak Cottage that day. He'd seen the boot marks, the bloodstain—and what about the stolen money? There must have been a third man, a mastermind behind the whole bloody scene. The eight-pointed star held the key. The police had closed the case and wouldn't want to know. Holmes had told him not to let Kell in on his "interests," and so Wiggins was going it alone. He was determined to find out who was behind Bill's murder, who gained by it—and who would pay for it, at his hands. Street justice, just like the old days. Bill deserved it.

He hustled down Villiers Street to the river, noting the new stall-holders and the old, the vintners, Faulkner's hotel and washroom—for toffs in need of a bath and a piss—and the aged beggar. "Morning, Otto," he called out to the hunched mendicant.

"Shsss," the beggar hissed and beckoned him over. "Arthur now, Viggins. Un gut English name."

Over the years, Wiggins had come to know many of central London's regular panhandlers, and Otto had been working around Charing Cross since Wiggins was a boy. "You're as much a Londoner as me," he said.

"Vor is coming," Otto said. "Arthur is better than Otto, no?"

"I always liked Otto," Wiggins said, almost to himself. He looked down on the top of Otto's head, noticing the few strands of thin white hair, the dry, peeling skin. "There's always talk. If you believed half you heard on the streets, we'd be fighting the Americans next, then the Russians, then the French, the Austrians, the Spanish, and not forgetting the Turks. Germany can wait."

Otto wagged his finger. "Beware the Turk," he said. "You can call me Otto, if you vont, but quiet, quiet. Where have you been anyway? I don't see your old friends, no."

"The Irregulars? Way too old for that."

"Young vons, I don't see so much now. It makes me sad."

"You can still pick up a runner at the Cheese, down Fleet Street, but they's older now."

"Ach, I miss the young vons. Spare any change?" Otto gestured at a passerby.

Wiggins plunged a hand into his pocket and flipped one of Kell's last shillings into the hat. "Don't die thirsty," he said in farewell.

He stepped among the boatmen on Embankment Pier, a faint smell of tar and coal and damp wood and the memory of brine hanging off them. He quickly found out who was going east and cadged a lift from a cargo launch heading back to the docks.

After a jaunty trip down the Thames, flitting between the thick traffic, the launch pulled in at Wapping. The wharf was alive with steamboats and sailing skiffs dwarfed by the towering sea ships moored in dock. Wiggins made his way up Red Lion Street, the London Docks to his left. A city all its own, the ships like great buildings straining for the sky, the quays awash with citizens of all the world: thin, straggly-bearded Lascars, Negroes from the West Indies, Portuguesers, dash blond Swedes, all crying out in their different tongues amid the tar-barrel reek and the smell of cinnamon from the East, tea from Assam, and tobacco from all over. The dock echoed with the yells of traders, warehouse hands, and two-a-penny street sellers.

Wiggins pushed north up onto Cable Street and toward the Russian drinking den where he'd so nearly met his end. He'd been so boozed that night he couldn't have sworn to the identity of any of his attackers, bar the man with the scarred chin.

He took up a position on the corner with a clear view of the drinking-den door. Two hours later a man bustled along the alley-way jangling a floret of keys. This was no bearded Russian, though, no hardened immigrant drinker with a chin scar and a three-foot razor-sharp blade. The man stood barely an inch over five feet, wore a loud chequered suit and had bright ginger whiskers that crept from beneath his hat like a fox's ears. A property agent on his daily rounds.

"Is this the laundry?" Wiggins asked, just as the man thrust a key into the door.

Ginger Whiskers contrived to look down his nose at Wiggins, even though he was nearly a foot shorter. "May I help you?" he said.

Wiggins put on his haughtiest voice. "I am prospecting for rental properties on behalf of my employer, with especial regard to the proximity of laundries. He is of a very particular bent when it comes to matters of hygiene. Has this property been long empty, may I ask? And is there a laundry hereabouts? The agent on Whitechapel, Nelson, he says there's nothing around here and that I should look elsewhere."

"Ha!" the man crowed. "Nelson is a damn fool. This is a new rental." The agent smiled. "Very desirable location, close to all ame-nities, reasonably priced. I'm sure your employer wouldn't be disap-pointed. Although I should say I've already had interest. If you don't snap these up, they go quickly." He lowered his voice. "We are even prepared to let to the Sons of Judea, if you take my meaning—for a premium, of course." The man winked.

Wiggins cast his eye at the line of derelict houses opposite, the half-mooned glass in the windowpanes and the peeling paint. "How long has it been empty? And who was the last tenant?"

"Oh, well, you can't expect me to reveal such details. Commer-cially sensitive, I'm sure you understand."

Wiggins sighed. "Is there a laundry nearby?" he said again.

"Of course, of course—all conveniences here. There are two down Whitechapel—Chinese." He whispered this in a deep undertone. "Or back along the passage, past the pub. Mostly Eastern European, but some locals."

"Aren't they all locals?" Wiggins said and turned up the alleyway toward the pub.

"Discounts are available, bite now or be sorry," the agent called after him. He had confirmed what Wiggins suspected: the Russians were long gone.

The laundry belched steam. Wiggins felt it on his face before he saw it, the hot moisture prickling his cheeks. A faded sign marked the laundry's huge doorway in an alley off an alley with cobbled stones running into a bubbling drain. Wiggins walked past to a courtyard farther along. A gang of children played in one corner, their squawks and jibes rattling off the high walls. They threw and kicked a rag ball among themselves, made from the laundry scraps, no doubt. He knelt down and retied his bootlaces, scanning the children as he did so. None of them had shoes.

One of the children stood out, or rather stood apart. Moving toward the ball in half-apology whenever it came near, but too slight to make his presence felt. Wiggins noticed him. The last pick, the weakest; spent their lives on the sidelines, watching. He beckoned him with a long finger.

The small boy padded over. His clothes hung off him. "Speak true, and I'll sort you." Wiggins held up a penny. "Lie, and you're mince."

"You ain't no nonce?"

Wiggins smiled. "Does one of the laundry girls have a birthmark, right across one side of her face from here to here?"

"Yeah, I seen her." The boy thrust out his hand.

Wiggins held the coin. "But you ain't seen me, right?"

"You *are* a nonce. Give me my money."

He handed over the penny and shook his head. "When does she work?"

The boy chewed for a second and grabbed his chin. "If only I could remember . . ." He posed deep thought.

Wiggins pulled another coin from his pocket and the child smiled, fat and broad, as he took the second penny. "I seen her in the mornings. Once anyways. Want to know anything else?"

"I doubt I could afford it."

The boy skipped away, past the others and out along the alley, suddenly aware of his newfound riches. Wiggins fished out the old Doctor's battered Hunter: still two minutes slow. He turned westward. On the way, he made sure to pass the Anarchist Club on Jubilee Street. One of the cons in Brixton, a peterman working out of Lewisham, had spoken of it. That's where it all happens, he'd said, all those Eastern European nutters, Jews, Bolsheviks, spouting their claptrap. The peterman had even been to a lecture there, he said, but found it absurd. He worked hard for a living, he told Wiggins, and didn't expect to have to give it away to the poor. He'd dedicated hwis life—and his father before him—to blowing safes and why couldn't the likes of these wasters also learn a trade?

Wiggins examined the crude posters stuck up outside the club. They listed guest speakers, times, places, extolling revolution. He jotted something on his shirt cuff, checked the corners for a tail, then set off once more.

Kell stood by the entrance to Fortnum's, jostled and harried at every turn as the masses strolled down Piccadilly. Idle shoppers, the new "tourists," loafers, pests all. Wiggins was already seven minutes late. Kell despised tardiness. He began to regret his high spirits of the night before. He'd gushed to Ewart that morning about recruiting a new kind of agent, gushed like a fool.

A mama went past, a governess and two children in tow. *She* didn't look like a suffragist, Kell thought as his eyes dwelled on the disappearing governess's behind. His case against votes for women, he decided, rested on war. He'd yet to outline this theory to Constance in full, but surely, he would argue, one couldn't expect a woman to command armies, to fight at all, which was the chief purpose of government. Ergo, they couldn't be expected to vote. He sighed inwardly: if ever there were a woman fitted and prepared to be a minister of war, it would be his wife.

Eleven minutes late. On hearing about Kell's new agent, Ewart had muttered about recruiting from the proper class, the right sort of people. Kell was loath to admit his boss might be right, that Wiggins was and always would be too much of the street. He'd wait the time it took him to smoke, he decided, and dug into his pocket with weary despair. As he pulled out his cigarette case one of his battered visiting cards came with it, fluttering to the ground. He stooped to pick it up, and noticed unfamiliar writing on the back of the card, etched in pencil—a note:

You are being followed. Take underground from Pic.
Cir. 2 stops, then cab to Regent St. Theater.
Take aisle seat stalls. W.

Kell whipped his head round. There was no one there. Ever since the attack in Hampshire, he'd checked every street he entered, watched for exits. Even at the height of a bustling afternoon in town, he was on guard. He examined the card again. Placed there when the deliverymen buffeted past, he assumed. Christ, the man could have taken his wallet and watch without a by-your-leave. Of course, he could simply wait, flush Wiggins out, or return to the office even. He disliked being told what to do. Except that Wiggins infuriatingly had a point. Certainly, he had the upper hand. Kell rammed the card back into his pocket, tossed the cigarette aside unsmoked, and headed to the station.

He glanced about nervously as he walked, hesitated at the window of Hatchards to see if he could spot anyone suspicious in the reflection of the bookshop's convex windows. Nothing, apart from the omnibuses, motorized taxis, horse-drawn four-wheelers, hansom cabs, costermongers' carts, and the hundreds of hurrying pedestrians that made up the traffic of a normal spring day on Piccadilly.

Kell descended the station stairs and headed across the ticket hall toward the lifts, a first-class ticket in hand. A great hubbub broke out behind him.

"He's fell," someone called out. "Mind out there, watch it, give him space."

A crowd bunched at the bottom of the stairs. Kell caught sight of a hand splayed onto the tiles, heavy knuckles briefly visible through a thicket of legs. "Careful, it might be broken," a voice said.

Kell knew enough to keep moving. He took a train two stops to Down Street and then hailed a cab.

The theater had been newly converted into a cinematograph. Kell found his way down the aisle and took a seat. As he slumped back he lit a cigarette, sending a twisting stream of smoke out into the light spilling from the screen. A man leapt in and out of a bed-room, at great speed, but Kell was too distracted to work out what the images meant. They never stopped, never settled. It was impossible. He closed his eyes.

"You took your time," Wiggins whispered in his ear.

Kell started and turned in his seat. "Stay looking at the pictures," Wiggins said from the row behind.

"Is this all really necessary?"

"You saw him at the station?"

"I saw *someone*," Kell said. "Did you injure him badly?"

"I tripped him, is all."

A black card popped up on the screen, casting a gloom. Two of the audience got up and left. A third snored heavily. The organist abruptly segued from jaunty action to funereal dirge.

"There's a couple of questions I need answers to, if you don't mind," Kell muttered, irked. "How did you find my office? And get in?"

"Easy. Your card. I telephoned the exchange."

"The exchange has strict instructions not to give out my details."

Wiggins sighed. "Which means you must be War Office, Admiralty, or Special Branch. No one else would bother. Simple from then on."

"But how did you get in?"

"Past the most fearsome commissionaire in Whitehall?" Wiggins said. "Give me some credit. A brown coat, a bit of the old chitchat, and Bob's your uncle."

"And how did you know I was being followed today?"

Wiggins shook his head. He waited as a couple walked past them to the front of the stalls. "Because *I* was following you."

"But I saw no one."

"Well, that's the point, ain't it? Now, Mr. Kell. Your turn. What's the plan?"

The screen burst into light.

"Yes?" she said abruptly. Her face—oval in a headscarf—showed no surprise. She angled her birthmark away from him.

Wiggins blinked, struck mute. He'd tried to find her every day for two weeks and now she was finally in front of him "Don't you remember me?" he said at last.

"I remember you. You piss in street. And you like fighting."

Wiggins felt the heat in his face but took heart from the arch in her eyebrow. "It's Bela, right?"

She nodded. "Why you follow me?"

"I wasn't, I didn't . . ." Wiggins tailed off. "Only from the . . ."

Wiggins *had* followed her. He'd waited at the laundry then trailed her bobbing head down the passageways and alleys of Whitechapel until the junction with the main road. He'd been debating with himself whether or not to stop her when she'd swiveled to face him of her own accord. Wiggins squinted in the morning sun, his cheeks pinched by the cold. He knew he'd gone red but he couldn't think of anything to say, which made him redder still.

Bela frowned and smiled at the same time. An apple cart clattered past and Wiggins had to step toward her to get out of the way. She looked up at his face, now close. "How did you know I work at laundry?" she said at last.

He coughed. "Can we walk?"

She glanced about her. "I must go."

"Two minutes."

They broke out onto Whitechapel. Bela held a small canvas bag in front of her. Wiggins thrust his hands deep into his pockets. "You saved my life."

"You made mistake. You speak Russian, maybe Nikolai and the others like you more."

Wiggins scratched the back of his head. "Would that have made a difference?"

"I go this way." Bela stopped at a crossroads. "You go that way." She pointed.

"Sorry. I should . . . I don't know. My friend died . . . killed. I wanted to find out why."

"Why would I know this?"

"I'm not asking for help. I just wanted to . . . Can I see you again?"

"See me?"

"For a drink?"

"Drink? I think maybe you are not a good man to do this with, no? Last time, it not end so well."

"Tea?"

"What would your wife say?"

Wiggins shook his head. "I ain't married."

"I must go."

Wiggins pointed up the street. "There's the bus. I'll treat you."

"Treat?"

"Pay." Wiggins took her arm and she didn't resist. They stepped up onto the open top and sat at the front, faces turned to the milky sun. "I've got money now."

"What is your job?" Bela asked, folding her hands on her bag.

"I'm a watchman down a big factory, in Woolwich. Good money."

She tucked a stray strand of hair back in her headscarf. "What do they make?"

Wiggins tapped his nose.

"You don't like the pub, you don't like tea. How about a stroll? I could take you to the park."

"Which park?"

"Victoria, Regent's—we could even push the boat out and walk down Rotten Row."

Bela looked puzzled. "Why?" she said.

"You don't make it easy, do you?"

The bus jerked beneath them, the conductor singing out the stops each time. Wiggins searched his hands for something to say. He cracked his knuckles.

"What does a watchman do?" Bela said.

"Watch. I used to be in the army. I'm on a late shift today, so I come down to the laundry. In passing, like . . ."

Bela gave him a sideways look, amused.

"What do you do for larks?" Wiggins plowed on. "How about the pictures? The cinematograph."

Bela half smiled. His powers of deduction often failed when faced with a woman.

"The female mind is irrational," Holmes once told him when he was tasked with following a posh bint up St. John's Wood way. "They are ruled by emotion. Your job is simply to record her movements, gather the data. Her mind will forever be a mystery to you."

As an eight-year-old, Wiggins had taken this perverse advice to heart, and he'd been no better at dealing with women since—other than Sal, but she was a mate. Bill had had a bluff way with women. Not just with Emily, but the pretty Spanish girls who used to promenade the quay in Gibraltar, swaying their hips and toying with parasols. Talk to 'em, Bill would say, show 'em your medals. Girls don't bite.

"I'm going to this meeting, in Jubilee Street." Wiggins finally found Bela's eye as the bus juddered forward. "Politics, like, you want to come to that? On Friday." His insides shrank with shame. Politics?

Bela frowned. "Is this the Anglish way, what people like to do? In my country when a man talks to a woman he asks her about music. Or maybe he has a flower. Or maybe he says, do you walk here every day? Will I see you here again? But the Anglish, are they so serious? I don't understand."

"Sorry, all I meant . . . actually, I'm not sure," Wiggins floundered.

Bela burst out laughing. "No, I am sorry. I make fun. I know this place." She stood up, eyeing the next stop. "I will go," she said, smiling still. "But only if you tell how you know I work at laundry?"

"You'll come?" Wiggins squinted up at her, surprised.

"How you know?" Bela said again.

Wiggins examined her half-brown, half-white face—the birthmark's permanent shade all the more pronounced in the sun. "Your shoes." He pointed. "I noticed the night we met. The suds marks on the uppers—too extensive to be only home washing. And your fingertips. You've had your hands in water all day."

Bela opened and closed her hands quickly as the bus slowed. "You are odd man. I think I understand why you are not married."

"What?"

Bela was already halfway down the aisle toward the stairs. She didn't turn back to reply but her clothbound head inclined to the left in acknowledgment. Wiggins released his fists as the bus pulled away, the engine grinding. He breathed in deeply and ran a hand through his hair—which all of a sudden felt far too long.

*　*　*

Wiggins may have felt unsure in the presence of a woman, but Bela knew men. A lesson learned long ago.

"You Grybas girls will kill me," her father shouted. "One, all of town wants to fuck, the other with a face like a cow shit on it. Sarah, you will have to marry Vincas—he's the only one who'll take you before Bela, and nobody wants Bela."

"Vincas is a lunatic," Bela said. "Sarah can't marry him."

"Shut up." He slapped her with the back of his hand. "None of this would have happened but for you. I've lived with this for eighteen years. Everyone thinks we're cursed. I should never have married a Jew."

Bela held her face and avoided his eye. Her younger sister Sarah gripped her arm tightly, but said nothing. Vincas, the eldest son of old Marinsky the flour merchant, was known throughout the neighborhood and even the whole of Dvinsk. When he was a child he tortured small birds, then cats and dogs. And now he wanted to move on to her sister.

"I can't support the two of you forever." Her father pulled at his knuckles, checked that the skin hadn't broken on his hand. "You think I have rubles coming out of my ears?"

Bela felt Sarah tremble. Their father paced the small room, chuntering. Bela knew he couldn't be swayed by reason, he could barely be swayed at all, except by the prospect of booze or money. She played her only card, all she had left to save her sister. "I'll marry him," she said in a cold whisper. "Promise to let Sarah have her pick, and I'll marry Vincas."

"You dare make bargains with me?" Her father loomed over her, spittle flecking his chin. "Smart-ass bitch. I should string you up and be done with it." He pulled his hand back, sneering. "Ach, what do I care—if Vincas will take you, then Sarah can fuck who she likes." He kicked open the door to their two-room shack and stumbled out into the night, once more blaming his own inadequacies on the facial blemish of his oldest daughter.

"Vincas? Bela, are you sure?"

"He can't be worse than *him*," Bela replied. She looked at her beautiful, flawless little sister and gently stroked her hair. She'd been looking after her for more than fifteen years and now this was the last thing she could do for her.

Sarah held on to her sister. "Mother—would she have protected us?"

"I was three, little one, I don't know. But I will protect you. Make sure you choose a husband well, but quickly. Father won't wait forever."

"Stasys will do fine," Sarah smiled hopefully. "When he is of age."

"He is poor."

"So are we. But he's kind."

Two days later, Bela returned from work to find Sarah at the door. "He wants you at the Marinskys' now," she said. "He's waiting."

Bela charred for a rich family in town, the Plovs. That afternoon, she ditched her apron, sloshed her face from the bucket inside the door, and squeezed Sarah in a tight hug. "Don't worry," she said and set out for the Marinskys'. A grit-rich wind stung her face. Winter was coming. Life in Dvinsk was bound by the seasons. The stinking heat of July, the desperate paralysis of an ice-bound January, hoping for that sliver of comfort in spring and autumn. She longed for a world of the middle ground, the mild, where it didn't feel like you were on the very edge of life all the time.

She read of such places in the books of the Plovs' library. One of her tasks at the house included cleaning out the fire from the night before and setting a new one. The room looked out over Nevsky Park and contained books from floor to ceiling, a leathered treasure trove of browns and greens and age-beaten red spines. Her aunt had taught her to read many years previously, hidden from her father. Every Sunday morning when Bela was little, they would go through the letters. Her aunt never spoke of Bela's father, just the letters, the words, a rare power.

Access to the library enthralled Bela. She never dared take a book, or even suggest to the master that she might borrow one. Instead, she would pull one from the shelf and keep her place with a tiny strand of hair, hoping that one of the family wouldn't be reading that volume. In addition, she'd take scraps of the newspaper left out to set the fire, mostly the classified adverts. Only once did she take anything home.

The previous January, when the streets were ice-slick and Nevsky Park a virgin white, she picked up a volume of Blok's verses. The library fire crackled. Inside the book she found a pamphlet, *Common Cause*. It was full of revolutionary ferment and froth, a dangerous article to possess, seditious. Bela thought it must have been left there by Dimitry Plov, recently home for the holidays from university in St. Petersburg. Certainly left there by accident, he would not complain at its removal, could not. Bela held the flimsy paper, fingered the bold lettering of the heading. She turned the phrases in her head: "the workers must unite," "fair pay for a fair day" . . . The library doors creaked.

"What's taking you so long?" Dunya, the housekeeper, snapped. "The mistress will be back soon."

"Sorry." Bela ducked her head. "I am finished." She scuttled out of the room, her right hand pinning the pamphlet in the folds of her skirt. She had her prize.

She read that pamphlet often, in the mornings before her father rose. Sarah's reading improved under her guidance. Using the scraps of newspaper, and then the pamphlet, Sarah learned to read well. It was Bela's greatest gift to her sister. Their father didn't know they could read since he couldn't himself. He didn't even know Bela spoke Yiddish *and* Russian. He could barely master one language. And yet, he was her master.

Bela finally reached the Marinskys' place. Her father stood outside the large double doors of the flour warehouse. He grunted as he saw her approach. "We've been waiting for you. In the back."

She followed him through the deserted shop. Flour dust hung in the air. She licked a stray speck from her lips. In the back room, a gas lamp burned in the middle of the table, despite the daylight outside, a show of meager wealth. A fireplace gaped cold, the exposed brickwork dirty and unkempt. She glanced up quickly. Around the table sat old man Marinsky, his eldest, Vincas, and the younger son, Arvo, who couldn't have been more than sixteen. If anything, he was more distasteful than his older brother: as cruel and sadistic, but with a cold intelligence about him, difficult to read.

No one asked her to sit down.

Her father, standing also, coughed. "Good news," he said at last. "Vincas has agreed to the match."

She nodded and kept her eyes on the floor.

"And you know young Arvo here. He plans to go to America next month. And Mr. Marinsky has kindly agreed to let him marry Sarah before he goes."

Bela looked up, startled. "But," she cried, "you said—"

Her father slapped her. "Shut up. Sorry, sir." He nodded at Marinsky.

Bela held her head down and fought back tears. Her father had never hit her in public before and her face burned with shame. She was used to the pain, but not the humiliation.

"I trust this disobedience is a display of sisterly love," old man Marinsky said after a pause. "Rather than a sign of things to come? We are risking much, marrying someone of her background."

"Don't worry, Papa," Vincas replied in a quiet, half-amused, half-drunk slur. "She is nothing I cannot handle. I like spirit."

8

"Watson, you're late."

"Sorry, sir. The trains at Woolwich."

"Trains! In my day we walked to work." Old man Rayner coughed into Wiggins's face. "Fack trains. They ain't good for nothing but excuses. This is the last time. There's plenty scum out there who'd jump at this job. It's a cushy billet."

"Yes, sir," Wiggins replied.

Rayner had been waiting for him at the main gates, theatrically looking up at the large clock above the entranceway to the munitions factory. Now, as they paced toward Workshop 4, he glanced back at Wiggins. "Wipe that facking smile off your face," he rasped.

Wiggins grinned wider. He'd come directly from his meeting with Bela and couldn't help it. Her dark-light, harlequin face flashed in his mind. He liked a girl with spirit.

Rayner dredged up a plump gobbet of phlegm and arced it toward the wall. "And you say you was army? If you'd been in my outfit you'd have been flayed for lateness. Twice!" He thrust out two gnarled fingers to emphasize the hideousness of this crime.

The old man, Wiggins's boss for his first two weeks at Woolwich, talked often of his "unit" in the army. Wiggins watched the back of his boots as they whipped up angry whirls of white dust. He didn't have the heart to point out the telltale signs: the peculiar scars on Rayner's hands (multiple nicks and scratches and various minor burns), the way he tucked in his shirt, even the hunch of his shoulders. Rayner, nominal head of security for the shell shed, a self-important, trumped-up sentinel, far from being the one-time sergeant major of some crack infantry regiment as he liked to hint, had obviously been a cook in the Army Service Corps.

"Get on your rounds, sharpish. Take a look-see as per, and meet me back here before I go." Rayner pulled open the door to a small wooden guardhouse. It smelled of burned creosote and damp socks. "And sign in. How many times do I need to tell you, anyone staying overnight has to sign in and sign out. Any bags?"

"Does it look like it?"

"Don't sauce me. And don't touch anything in there neither. It's treason to monkey around in the shed."

"And treason's a death penalty," Wiggins said simultaneously with the old man, annoying him further. "Don't worry, chief, I'll keep me hands pocketed, so I will."

Wiggins began his stroll round the perimeter of Workshop 4. He looked askance at the massive brick building. It was low-ceilinged and loud and he thanked Christ he didn't have to work in there all day. A tall chimney at the far end belched black smoke at an alarming rate, and the earth around him was flecked with unworldly white dust quite unlike chalk. Wiggins pulled open the door to the shed.

The noise was terrific. Metal on metal, replicated hundreds of times a minute, in close proximity, pounding at his ears more than any big gun he'd had to handle in the army, not even that Congreve nightmare. The Empire was at peace, apparently, but the workshop felt like war itself. He walked along the far edge of the huge, hellish brick hangar, full of men stripped to the waist, like moving organic parts of a bigger machine; they looked as one, glistening with sweat and dust and dirt, sinews straining. Iron filings clung to his hair and the white dust clouded his eyes. The place reeked of scorched iron and sulfur combined with a rank odor of men hard at work. A foreman caught his eye and spat. Wiggins couldn't blame him. For all the talk of outsiders looking in, everyone knew the real job of the watchmen was to watch the staff. Like a redcap.

Wiggins had never felt more disliked in his life than he did in his first two weeks at Woolwich. The workers regarded him with outright disdain or else they simply avoided his eye. Only one person went out of his way to be friendly. On his second day, as Wiggins strode across the workshop floor, someone ran into the back of him. "Oof."

He turned to see a boy of around seventeen sprawled at his feet. "Watch it," Wiggins grunted.

"Watch me, why don't ya?" the boy said. "Watchman."

"Clever dick."

The boy clambered up. "Milton."

"Is that a question?"

"Nah, it's me name, ain't it." He thrust out his hand. His head jiggled from side to side, all abuzz. A lank flap of blond hair fell over his eyes.

Wiggins regarded the boy. He was one of the factory runners. They took messages from the floor to the office, to accounts, to security, outside. They went everywhere, saw everything.

"We do the shit," Milton said by way of explanation. "Not as bad as working for Rayner, mind. See ya."

"Wait up. I'll shout you a pint. You're the only body who's said a word to me since I got here."

"You're the snitch, ain't ya?" Milton grinned. "But I talk to anyone, me. I'm not so popular myself."

"Why?"

"I'm bad luck." Milton smiled, open and artless. "Cos of this." He pointed to his foot and then ran off.

As he loped away, he swung his right leg around in a swift arc. His head rose and fell in time with the strange, almost mechanical movement of his legs. The boy had a club foot.

Two weeks in, Wiggins had failed to speak to anyone else on the factory floor. Maybe he was bad luck too, he thought, as he wandered on through the factory, past the great whirring machines. Milton might be bad luck, but what of Bela, did her face mean ill fortune? He smiled at the memory of his successful meeting with her earlier in the day. Her birthmarked cheek must have been a cross to bear—the cruel jibes of children, the stunted interest of men. Perhaps it was good luck in Latvia? He didn't know.

"Have a good one, Jonny," Milton called out, startling Wiggins. "You look like a mouse couldn't get past you." He laughed.

"Cheeky," Wiggins said as he made it back to the guardhouse while the rest of the workers made for the gates.

"You still owes me a beer," Milton said over his shoulder as he joined the stream heading home for the evening.

"No fraternizing," Rayner rasped. "And no kipping. I'll be back at six tomorra."

At eight o'clock the next morning, Wiggins kept his latest appointment with Kell. "It's cracked," he said.

"At last!" Kell exclaimed. He sat behind Wiggins on a sparsely populated tram. They rattled around the corner at Westminster Bridge Road and headed up toward town. Kell hunched forward to hear. Wiggins looked out of the window. "Go on," Kell said.

"Money, ain't it? Who doesn't have it, then gets it. You said your man, the dead man—"

"Leyton."

"Right. He was numbers, in the clerks' office? And they wanted him dead."

Kell nodded quickly.

"You've been through anyone who's left since and they're clear. Anyone stupid enough to spill the beans, *then* leave with the dough is asking for it. Besides, no point in binning Leyton if you're gonna scarper. So, the rat's still there and has access to shell design. Whoever they are—"

"Germany, surely?" Kell interrupted.

"We know the information got to Krupp's is all," Wiggins said. "Not who stole it." He closed his eyes and intoned: " 'Do not theorize without data.' Do that, you get all out of whack. A wise man told me that, sort of," he went on in his normal voice. "Whoever it is, the Woolwich connection is too juicy to let go."

The brakes kicked and screamed. Kell waited while a trio of new passengers swung down the aisle and the conductor cried out, "Off!"

"And? Get to it, man."

Wiggins paused. "The rat's not from the factory floor; can't be. Got to have access to the office, right? So—links in the chain, the old man says—it has to be either a clerk, management, or a third man I ain't sure of yet."

"Management!" Kell gasped.

"Or relations thereof." Wiggins took off his cap. Should he shave the sides of his head, he wondered suddenly—the Latvian look. Would she like that? "The rat's close to things," he went on to Kell. "Has to be. There are two men we need to look into before we make a move."

"At last." Kell pulled a notebook from his breast pocket. "I'll have the police bring them in immediately."

Wiggins exhaled. The tram swung away from the river into Northumberland Avenue. He steadied himself on the seat in front. "Is that smart?" he asked. "We don't want 'em to know we know, do we, sir? Better if I worked out which one it was *and* who they report to?" Wiggins swiveled in his seat to look at Kell directly for the first time since their meeting began. His chief's eyes stared wide and puffy, long unclosed, and he clutched the pencil in his hand too hard. The tips of his boots twitched and his right knee rose and fell repeatedly. It didn't take Sherlock Holmes to deduce that here was a man under pressure. Wiggins relented. "One of the underclerks is up to no good. Name of Basil. I'll look into him, sir, he's my bag."

Royston Basil, a round-faced and furtive man, occasioned much comment among the workers at Woolwich. He wore tinted glasses and had a haughty air that made him disliked. Wiggins didn't care about his manners so much as his dress sense. He wore calfskin gentlemen's shoes and a bespoke overcoat. A cursory examination of his cigar ash further confirmed Basil's expensive tastes: he smoked Marquis No. 6, a rare and pricey brand. Suspect number one. Wiggins coughed into his hand, a new habit, and continued his rundown. "The second man's one of your lot. A gent. Charles Tinsley?"

Kell gaped in astonishment. "Good God, you don't think . . . He went to Eton."

"So did Colonel Sebastian Moran."

"But . . ."

"And Jonathan Clay," Wiggins added under his breath.

"Moran was an assassin."

"It takes all sorts."

"I mean, Tinsley's the Deputy Assistant Director. He's an Honorable." Kell shook his head. "No, I really think this is an outrageous suggestion. I can't go to my chiefs with this."

"I thought your job was to find spies?"

"Yes, but . . . it won't go down well at all."

"Look, just cos I'm suspicious don't mean he's bent. Best if you look into him yourself, sir; he's a man of your circles."

"How am I meant to do that?" Kell asked.

"Ain't that your job?" Wiggins dropped his voice. "Go gentle like, don't ring his bells. What's the word at his club—is he a gambler, is there a debt? Does he have German relations, say?"

"Half the aristocracy are German."

Wiggins shrugged.

"Why don't we bring in Basil, and the other man?"

"Scotland Yard would trample over everything. And they'd take the credit."

This last point struck home. Kell leaned back. "You are sure this is progress?" he said as he closed his notebook.

"All we need to do is watch 'em. A tail is always progress, one way or the other."

Kell looked up sharply as Trafalgar Square disappeared off to their left.

He got up but Wiggins thrust his hand out and grabbed him by the wrist. "You dandy, sir?"

"I'm fine," Kell muttered. "Damned impertinence." He shook his arm clear and hurried to the doors.

The conductor bowed slightly as Kell fluttered off the tram and pigeon-toed back down the Strand. Wiggins gazed after him for a moment as Kell's figure weaved along the busy street. The tram jolted forward. He wondered about his new boss. An improvement on Leach surely, but still, it worried him.

"What can you deduce about me?" Kell had asked at the Regent Street Theater, after they'd first agreed to work together. Wiggins threw him some chaff but evaded the main deduction: Kell's marriage was unhappy. At least, that's what the signs suggested. Wiggins had already noted the absence of the wedding ring on at least two occasions and it was clear to him that Kell's real mistress was his job. It made him untrustworthy in Wiggins's eyes. Not because he couldn't trust him with money or a woman (he was sure he could with both, if he had either), it was because Wiggins couldn't know what he wanted. You can always trust a selfish villain to follow his self-interest, but when a man starts thinking of his duty, anything is possible. He'd seen it in the officer class in South Africa: a duty, so it was said, to dump the Boers into typhoid-invested camps and let them die of dysentery and measles. Wiggins sniffed. A man wedded to his job could disappear within it; you couldn't fully trust him to do anything. The rules of the game were all that mattered. But Wiggins thought of himself too: what did the job make him? Was he a redcap now, after all—a policeman without a uniform, leading folk to the gallows all the same?

"All change, all change," the conductor cried. "This is Aldwych."

Kell raced back to the War Office through the crowds of the lower Strand. He came out onto Trafalgar Square. A burst of pigeons made him jump. "Tuppence a bag!" a seed seller cried.

"Blasted menace," Kell muttered. Though whether he meant the birds or the seed sellers, or the gaggle of day trippers tossing out the scraps, wasn't clear. The pigeons fluttered down again, obscuring his view.

He'd seen no one suspicious since Petersfield, though a policeman still stood guard at his Hampstead home. The commissioner of police, Sir Edward Henry, didn't believe any "cock and bull" story about spies running Kell off the road, but he gave him the guard all the same. Sir Edward wasn't the only one to remain unconvinced of the German espionage threat. The swells on the Committee for

Imperial Defense still openly derided the idea. In the last meeting a wag had even asked whether he should be worried about the number of German waiters in London. Only one man in the Cabinet took the idea seriously. Churchill, still president of the Board of Trade, had co-opted himself onto the committee and spoke up in support of Kell. "This Krupp's business is worrying, is it not?"

"What was that, Winston?" Soapy said from the chair.

"Is it not to be deplored that German industry has been found to be stealing our most valuable technology, right from under our very noses? Is it not doubly deplorable when these technologies are a means of war? Should we stand by and do nothing, or should we act?"

"Steady on, Winston, this isn't a public meeting, you know," Soapy said. "And that's far from proven anyway."

Churchill glared around the room. He looked like a starved baby, wispy-haired with a petulant, spoiled mouth. Kell remembered him from military college. A man who even then suffered from a surfeit of self-regard. His meteoric political rise had, in Kell's eyes, only inflamed the affliction. "I knew Captain Kell at Sandhurst," Churchill continued, lisping. "We argued often. I would not call him a friend. But Captain Kell is not a man who starts at shadows, he is not a man who conjures up ghosts out of thin air, or who sensationalizes for his own aggrandizement. In short—"

"Yes, short would be good, Winston."

"In short, we should heed his words. We should empower him, give him every means at our disposal to find out and eliminate these threats to our great nation."

As Kell walked up Whitehall, he sighed to himself. Nothing had yet come of Churchill's fine words. Kell needed more substantial proof. His grand dreams of a Secret Service, fully funded, home and abroad, remained unrealized—ironically, for want of accurate intelligence. Even the Krupp's link had failed to sway the committee. It could have been a coincidence, they muttered. Britannia ruled the waves. Why all this worry about Germany? And should we really be involved in spying? Isn't it a bit like playing sneak? This was the sort of thing he had in his way. It didn't help that Ewart was such a buffoon. Kell could hardly blame them for not taking the man seriously. He needed incontrovertible proof that German spies were working on mainland Britain, and that was that—otherwise the service would remain a dream, and he'd be out of a job.

Yet for all his thwarted ambitions, his fears of attack, the worries over Constance up in Hampstead; for all this, hope lightened his step as he headed toward the Savile Club. For the first time since Leyton's death, he was following a lead, albeit one he doubted would go anywhere. The notion that Charles Tinsley was in any way involved in spying seemed absurd.

The Honorable Charles Tinsley's nominal title at Woolwich was Deputy Assistant Director. It was a position handed out by the government to the son or nephew of someone important as a political sop and a way of keeping an appearance of nobility at the Arsenal. Tinsley came from an aristocratic family. Kell had seen him at society events, a lean, spry fellow of thirty-five with coiffured hair and a face like a hungry horse—too big and too toothy for his body. Not his sort at all. Wiggins had been even more disparaging when Kell pressed as to the reasons for his suspicions.

Kell called in at the Savile. He never felt truly at home there. Too many actors, writers, and other unreliable sorts. He preferred the more formal atmosphere of White's and the Bengal Lounge. Tinsley was a Savile man, though, and Kell was determined to prove capable of at least basic fieldwork—as much to himself as to Wiggins. The commissionaire at the club directed Kell north toward the Marshall Street Baths.

He strolled through St. James's and cut into Soho proper, trying to keep his bearing erect and formal—not easy when every second person was a whore. "Out for a morning stroll, sir?" a middle-aged lady of the night winked at him. "Discounts for the 'andsome."

"No, thank you. I am quite well," Kell muttered as he passed through Kingly Street. Shit streaked the roads. Dogs barked unrestrained.

Ten minutes later, he stood swaddled in towels, steam prickling his beard, peering into the mist of the main Turkish bath. Many of the men chose not to cover themselves at all, which made identifying them all the harder. Nevertheless, he picked out Tinsley away to his left and tried to saunter past unawares. The effect was ruined when he lost his footing on the steam-slicked tiles and Tinsley himself offered a hand.

"Watch out, old fellow," he said. "Floor's deuced slippery."

"Thank you." Kell found himself locking eyes with Tinsley. "Yes, er, sorry."

"New here?" said Tinsley.

"Yes."

"No need to be shy."

Kell nodded and took a seat across the room. He mopped his brow. Sweat trickled between his shoulder blades. He kept an eye on Tinsley, who lounged with a couple of other men. They talked in low tones. Occasionally Tinsley would glance at him and offer a lazy smile. Kell was loath to look too closely. The steam had misted his glasses and his sight was poor without them.

He thought again of his own position—vision clouded, opaque, enemy unseen, threats mounting. So far, he'd been a very poor spy. He peered again at Tinsley and his companions, huddled close together, conspiratorial. Perhaps Wiggins was right about him.

"*Bonsoir, monsieur*," a voice whispered.

"I beg your pardon?" Kell stammered.

"Your first time?" the man went on in a French accent.

"I can't see you," Kell said in despair.

The voice chuckled. "*Pardon*, I am behind you. *Voilà*, I am here. *Je m'appelle René. René LeQuin.* You are new here?"

Kell squinted at the man, seeing little beyond a large black mustache.

The mustache grinned. "*Bienvenue*. Fresh blood is always welcome."

"Blood?"

LeQuin purred. "There is no need to feel intimidated."

"If you'll excuse me." Kell rose unsteadily and stepped away. Great plumes of steam rolled into the room and he lost sight of Tinsley. He gasped against the heat. Sweat poured into his eyes.

"Are you quite top-hole, old chap?" Tinsley asked.

Kell recoiled. "Sorry, I . . ."

"The name's Tinsley." He offered his hand, formally this time. "We met when you first came in, but I'm afraid I didn't introduce myself."

Kell hesitated, then shook the proffered hand. He wiped his glasses on the towel and stared at the fine red hairs of the naked Tinsley's legs. They quivered slightly. "I'm terribly sorry, but I really must go. I quite lost track of the time," Kell stammered.

"Oh, it's easy to lose yourself here," Tinsley said.

"Goodbye," Kell called over his shoulder as he left.

Kell dressed hurriedly. He couldn't wait to be clear of the place. As he pushed through the swinging doors of the dressing room, he suddenly turned—was someone watching him? He couldn't shake the feeling. It gave him the creeps, all those men, all that tackle swinging free. He shivered despite the heat. What was it the Frenchman had called him? Fresh blood.

9

The Anarchist Club wasn't an obvious choice for courting. Wiggins had been there three times already and not seen a smile cracked once. That night, he arrived well before time. The club occupied a terraced house on a street off Commercial Road, in an area that straddled the Jewish quarters around Brick Lane. Inside, oil lamps cast yellow fans down each wall of the lecture room. At the far end, a small wooden stage had been erected. On it stood a locked upright piano, a stool, and an improvised lectern. Wiggins entered, nodded to a man setting out chairs, and took a position at the edge of the seating—from where he could see both exits, as well as being in reach of a large sash window. As ever, his biggest fear was coming across one of his attackers from the drinking den. A fear, as yet, unrealized.

Slowly the place filled up. The low murmur of voices grew. Wiggins picked lint from his new shirt and straightened his cuffs. The uppers of his leather boots shone dully in the light. He'd even gone so far as to oil his hair. A faint smell of almonds clung to him, not unpleasant.

He'd expected the club to be exclusive to bearded men, but women and children had come to hear the lectures. It was the women that surprised him most, for they spoke too—not much from the stage, but in the question sessions and the debates. Where Wiggins came from, women didn't really do politics; or at least, none of the men listened to them. Where he came from, not many of the men did politics either—they kept their heads above water, did as they were told, and got on with it.

A speaker ascended the stage. The babble of English, Russian, and Yiddish quieted. Wiggins couldn't see Bela in the crush. He loosened his collar. It occurred to him she might expect a level of political understanding and call upon him to have an opinion—it was he, after all, who had asked her to the lecture.

"Comrades," the speaker bellowed. "I have here a few words from our good friend Lenin." He held up a thick wad of pages. The audience remained quiet, rapt, as his loud, urgent tones washed over them.

"My name is Kent, Richard Kent. I have lately been traveling on behalf of the Trade Union Congress throughout the Continent, communing with fellow workers, unionists, members of our movement—miners, dockers, railwaymen, factory workers, mill workers even. In Germany I was lucky enough to meet and talk with Comrade Lenin." The crowd whooped and cheered. "He is a very impressive man, and while I don't agree with all he's got to say . . ." Kent looked down for a moment. "Anyway, Mr. Lenin spoke very highly of this country and even, yes, even of this very club. He pressed upon me a number of his newly translated pamphlets and asked if I would read one to you on my way back to Manchester. Of course, you already know this—I doubt there'd be quite such a crowd for a humble Oldham-born trade unionist such as myself, although I have been known to address more than five thousand people at a time. Right, anyway. The talk I'm going to deliver to you tonight is one that is close to the heart of myself, the union movement, and, of course, since he wrote it, Mr. Lenin. Forgive me—or him, yes, ha ha—if this is a bit of a mouthful, but detail is important. Here we go: 'Note on the Draft of the Main Grounds for the Bill on the Eight-Hour Working Day.'"

A rather dry and technical discussion followed about a bill that had been presented to the Russian parliament, with general remarks pertaining to the hours of all working peoples. Wiggins's mind turned to Woolwich and that dark, satanic Workshop 4; he thought of Milton—the runners did a fourteen-hour day— and those titans of the forge, their sweat-bathed brows wrinkled with exertion. They entered those gates before Monday's sun rose and hardly saw natural light again until Sunday.

The audience clapped and stamped their feet. "Thank you, thank you so much." A younger man popped up onto the stage. "Please, for our friend Comrade Kent and, of course, for Lenin!" The young man then launched into a speech. It was passionate, naïve, but oddly moving too, this dream of a better world, of a socialist utopia. The talker tailed off, however, and many in the audience either got up or broke into discussions of their own. Wiggins stood and looked around for Bela.

She hovered by the entrance, beside two huge men in matching kaftans. Wiggins raised his hand and she inclined her head, neither happy nor sad as far as he could tell. He held his cap before him and shuffled down the ranks of chairs.

"Wait." A hand clamped his arm.

Wiggins turned. The hand belonged to a man in his late twenties, with a close beard and revolutionary's hair split by a stunning gray streak. His nose had been broken at least twice, Wiggins thought, and the skin above his left eyebrow bore a pale scar. But above all this, and the fact that he stood two inches taller than Wiggins, the man exuded power. His eyes were a bottomless brown so deep as to be almost black. They swallowed the light. Wiggins glanced down at the hand on his arm but the man did not let go.

"We speak, yes?" the man insisted in a heavily accented voice.

Wiggins glanced at the exit.

The man went on: "I have many friends here. You have none, I think. Only a big bear hunts alone. Sit, please." He let go at last. "My name is Petr, or Peter you can call me."

Wiggins took a seat and waited. Peter sat down next to him and eyed the room as he spoke. "Do you like it here? No, no, please don't try to deceive. You have been here before, I think. More than two times."

"You keep score?" Wiggins said. "I'm new to politics."

"Is this your country?"

"London, yes."

Peter revealed a set of wolfish teeth. "We have other clubs, other meetings. Here it is a little bit, how you say, for the old ones, for the women? Sometimes the wolves like to run, no? Some of us are more used to action. Maybe you should join us at these clubs and see if this too is interesting?"

"Action?" Wiggins moved forward in his chair.

He'd started tentative conversations with a few of the regulars but no one seemed like gang material. None of them could hold up a banner, let alone a payroll. This man in front of him was different. Peter looked like he could collect on an armed robbery, could even plan the Tottenham job. For all his easy manner and fine-toothed smile, Wiggins had noticed the bulky, lopsided hang of his left jacket pocket. A Mauser, he guessed.

Peter traced fingers across his scarred forehead. "We believe actions create more noise than words alone. Thinking is nothing without action."

"Are you criminals?"

Peter laughed. "This is a word used by capitalists to talk about people without capital, to disguise their own historical crimes. No, we are anarchists—this is an anarchist club, no? I think maybe you can help us—you look strong, clever. You look like a soldier."

"Ex-soldier."

"You see, strong," Peter confirmed. "So many here are too weak." He made an odd sucking sound with his mouth and licked his lips.

"I might be a policeman."

Peter shook his head. "Ha. You are not police." He pointed to a man in the front row, whose face was hidden by the peak of an enormous cap. "*He* is police. Special Branch. Klaus. His Russian is terrible. We took him drinking, for fun, because he spoke so bad. He is from Germany, but he pretends Poland. No, you are not police. But you can help, I think." He sucked again, then suddenly thrust a hand into his right pocket.

Wiggins flinched.

"Mint Imperial?" Peter said, offering a rumpled paper bag. "English sweets, they are best."

Wiggins took a mint. He sucked it for a moment and said nothing.

"Sweets in Russia is like licking *turd*." Peter reveled in the word. He grinned. Then he pulled out a piece of rough card. He wrote down an address and handed it to Wiggins. "Come, Tuesday or Thursday nights. I am there. We can talk again. If you don't want to help, you don't have to. There are no masters here."

"No masters?"

"No gods, no masters: that is who we are."

Wiggins stared after him as he left, shocked to hear such a thought put so bold. No gods, no masters. Peter gave a low whistle and two young men by the stage hastened to follow him. As he reached the door he leaned down and handed sweets to a brace of small children. Wiggins pocketed the address. There had been no indication that Peter recognized him from the drinking den, or that he had any connection to the men who'd killed Bill—but he was connected to something.

It was not every day you met an armed man in London; for all Sherlock Holmes advised carrying a firearm east of Aldgate, Wiggins knew few that did.

"You didn't like it?"

Wiggins twitched out of his reverie. Bela stood in front of him, arms folded across her chest. "It was new, at least."

"Mr. Kent has never spoken before. Maybe this is why so many people came?"

Wiggins blinked and then smiled. "Right, I get it. If they'd seen him before, no one would have come."

Bela looked at him like he was an idiot. She wore a loose scarf around her head. He could see her hair. Thick strands of brown-black, like a delicate veneer of worn and polished rosewood. She inclined her head to the door and he followed her.

A knot of men stood outside smoking. One of them called out in Russian to Bela and sniggered. Bela didn't break stride, but said something over her shoulder. The men burst into laughter, all except the first speaker, who looked shamefaced.

"What was that?" Wiggins asked.

"Men. Always the same. They think big words make them look big. This man, he ask me once to go walking with him. I say no. Now I tell his friends why."

"He looked like he could handle himself."

"I can handle myself too."

"Will you get stick, walking out with an Englishman?"

"Oh, I do not care what they say. I walk where I want to." She glanced at him. "And with who I want to."

Wiggins smiled. He noticed she wore gloves, despite the mild night. "Where are we going?" he said.

"Walking safer than drinking."

They rounded a corner and continued on into the near darkness of the ill-lit East End. "This Lenin geezer, seems like a popular sort," Wiggins said after a moment.

She shrugged. "Many people like him. My country has many problems, he has many answers."

"You said before you was from Latvia. That's part of Russia, right?"

"The Tsar thinks it is part of Russia, but we do not."

"One of the many problems, eh? Is that why you're in London?"

She nodded in a strange, half-hearted way—as if she couldn't quite decide what to think. "Why did you save me? You are Anglish. I am Latvian. You could have been killed."

"I was drunk." He grinned. "Why did you save *me*?"

She motioned her head from side to side but didn't answer. They turned onto Whitechapel. Despite the late hour, the street was alive with hawkers, loafers, hookers, and restaurant-goers. "You couldn't walk around here twenty years ago, not at this time of night," Wiggins gabbled. "It was cut-throat dangerous. But since the Jews moved in, it's safer."

"You were almost killed."

He smiled. "But I weren't, thanks to you. Asking for it any road. Drunk. Round here has always been for new folk. Before the Rooskies it was the Huguenots and God knows who else. Always here, out east. The whole world comes to London—I've met Chinese, Yanks, Frenchies, blackamoors from the Caribbean, Indians, Dutchmen, Spaniards, Siamese. There ain't no color or size or shape on the planet that ain't been here one time or another. I've even seen an Andaman Island Pygmy when I was young. This, right here," he slammed his foot on the ground, "this is the center of the universe, so it is."

Bela laughed.

"Sorry," Wiggins blushed. "I gets carried away."

They looped back south, skirting a large goods depot. Wiggins ushered Bela away from the horseshit stench. Carts waited all day and all night to pick up cargo and the horses stood for hours at a time. "It smells that way, I know," Bela said. "It is not a secret."

Wiggins glanced behind him. He strained to hear. Was there a step echoing theirs? Did the shadows move?

"And your work, you told me but I forgot," she said.

"Out Woolwich way, it's nothing. But it keeps the wolf on a leash."

"An important factory you said before?"

"Very important." He pushed his chest out and they both laughed. The road ahead, tapering east, darkened further. They skated past unlit goods entrances. Wiggins checked behind him once more, unsettled and uncertain. Bela slipped on one of the cobbles and Wiggins caught her. She placed her hands on his chest but didn't push back, as he expected. Instead, she brought her lips up to his and pressed against him. They kissed. Wiggins leaned back against the wall, surprised, delighted.

It was not the kiss of a beginner. She kissed like she meant it. Finally, Bela broke away. "Funny man," she said, her hand lingering on his chest. "I go now, don't follow me."

"Can I see you again?"

She looked at him, dark eyes barely visible in the quarter-light of the far-off street lamp. "Find somewhere for us to go. The street is no good."

* * *

"The streets ain't no good." Sal plucked at her curls listlessly. "I need grub."

"It's better than Blackheath," Wiggins said.

They sheltered in a doorway on Praed Street, along from Paddington Station. Wiggins hopped from foot to foot, hoping to catch the eye of a benefactor. Sal slumped beside him, disconsolate. "I thought you said you had work."

"It's on-off, I told you."

"I'll say. No work, no pay, nothing."

Wiggins hesitated. "But I told Mr. Holmes I'd get a gang. Look out for stuff, eyes all over."

"Well?"

"I only know you."

Sal stood up. "Then let's get over there."

"But . . ." Wiggins faltered.

"Alls you do is *tell* him you've got a gang. Then *we* can do the job."

"Ain't that a porky?"

Sal scoffed. "We'll get a gang, stupid. You can be the leader."

Thirty minutes later, Wiggins presented himself at 221B Baker Street, ready for work.

"Found yourself a team, have you, young Wiggins? Please, don't steal that paperknife—it came from the Emperor of Japan. The silver lighter, too, should remain, I think. It is the Doctor's favorite." Sherlock Holmes chuckled as the small boy routinely tried to filch his possessions. "Look at me. A shilling-a-day retainer when you're on a job, plus a bonus. Fair?"

"Some of them are mighty hungry," Wiggins said. (Sal, who waited outside, had coached him in what to say.) "There's a pair of twins and all."

Mr. Holmes peered at him and raised an eyebrow. "A shilling a day it is. Now, there is a small matter down at the docks that needs the attention of your . . . gang?"

"Like a nail gang?"

"No, you will *not* be thieves."

The door swung open and the kindly man with the mustache arrived, exclaiming loudly, "Who's this young fellow?" The man bent down and examined Wiggins, his breath reeking of strong baccy, his hands of soap. He straightened. "Well, Holmes, this is all very irregular."

"That's it," Holmes cried. "Watson, meet Wiggins. The head of the Irregular Division of the Baker Street Detectives."

10

Wiggins checked his watch against the huge clock high above the gates of Woolwich Arsenal. Two minutes late, again. He waited for the end of the working day. The factory horn was due any moment, and Wiggins settled himself to observe the workers as they left.

A hand clamped his shoulder. "Oi!"

Wiggins twisted round in surprise.

"The old bastard ain't worth it."

Wiggins released a breath. "Milton. Shouldn't you be inside?"

"Errands, boss has me running errands," the runner replied. He let go of Wiggins and started to massage his right leg. Milton never commented on the pain his club foot must cause him. "Knocking off now, all done," he said cheerfully.

Wiggins eyed the runner, listened to Milton's calloused hand rubbing against his trousers. The great horn sounded over Wiggins's left shoulder. He started, unsure. Milton smiled, wide and innocent. "Don't do it," he said at last.

Did Milton know?

"You and Rayner. He got you put on two days a week. You're here to give him a beating, right?"

Wiggins shrugged. He fingered the cosh in his pocket. Best to let Milton think that. The great factory gates swung open. Wiggins turned away from Milton and scanned the throng hurrying away from their daytime prison. He caught sight of Royston Basil. The underclerk twisted a large umbrella, his dark glasses tinted purple. His clothes were too rich, his gait too furtive, his shoes a—

"Jonny," Milton cracked his knuckles. "Fancy the Hulk?"

Wiggins looked back at the young runner and grinned. "Now you're talking." Basil would have to wait.

They drank at the Old Sheer Hulk, standing outside on the pavement. It was a warm night and it seemed as if half of the Arsenal stood around them quaffing pints. "You all right for brass, Jonny?" Milton passed him a pint of black and tan.

"I've got another billet—up Rotherhithe way—night watchman."

Wiggins didn't tell him about the room he'd rented off Essex Road. Kell was paying him more than he had ever earned in his life, plus the Woolwich wages. Enough to let something half decent above a pawnshop, with its own door down a side alley. Bela had wanted him to find a place off the street, and so he had—though whether she'd really want to visit or not, he didn't know. He hoped. The black and tan slipped down easy, and he wondered about a rum chaser.

Milton drew on a Woodbine and coughed. "Rayner's a pillock but he ain't worth a fist. Army sends 'em funny sometimes, don't it?"

"Funny, am I?"

"Nah." Milton grinned. "But the army. Sends them doolally. My old man gave everything to the British Army, so he did. Never the same again. Broken, he was, broken. Left us wiv nothing."

They got very drunk. Or at least, Milton did. His lazy right eye grew lazier and his slack jaw slacker as the night wore on. In the end, Wiggins slung the feather-light runner over his shoulder and carried him home.

"Number five," Milton slurred as his chin bounced on Wiggins's back. "It's number five, down on the right."

"Is that your right, or my right?" Wiggins chuckled.

They were in one of the dingy streets in Charlton that ran between the railway line and the river. A lone gaslight cast a faint glow from the end of the road and the street stank of blocked drains, or no drains at all, more like. Wiggins eased open the door of number five with his boot.

"I've got a knife, mister," a high-pitched voice echoed out of the darkness. "I'll stick ya."

Wiggins froze, unable to bolt or see an attacker. Milton burped. "Mavis, it's me," he said.

An oil lamp flickered and the room came into view. "Mavis, my little sister," Milton said as Wiggins shrugged him to his feet.

Mavis, thirteen or so, had the same open face as her older brother but her eyes were sharp and lively. She placed the knife on a side table.

The room looked surprisingly comfortable, with a plush bed in one corner and heavy curtains over the small window. Then the bed moved. Pinned beneath the covers lay a girl of six, tousled blonde hair awry. She looked at Wiggins with curiosity.

"Meet the family," Milton said. "That's our Annie in the scratcher. You should stay."

Wiggins shook his head. The sight of the two small girls—with seventeen-year-old Milton as their sole breadwinner—upset him. They looked like they were doing well, but as an orphan you were only ever a hair's breadth from oblivion. And always that tugging at the heart, the why should this be me? He never knew his own father, who could be alive still for all Wiggins knew, and his mother long dead in a pauper's grave.

"I best get home. Mavis." Wiggins tipped his cap at the older girl, offered the little one an enormous wink, and opened the door.

He began the long walk back. The wind picked up, the air cooled, and then a rain burst slicked the streets. Wiggins turned his collar close and strode on, picking his way through the dark, on the look-out for a night bus. He crossed the river at Tower Bridge just as the rain stopped. The air tasted bitter still; the river stank. He paused on the northern edge, just as the darkness turned from pitch- to blue-black, breathing in the foulness. His belly felt heavy with stale beer. That evening's truth was hard to stomach.

No amount of summer rain could wash the taste away.

* * *

There was nowhere to go.

She lived with Vincas now. The northern ports had long since frozen solid for the winter. Sarah had been gone four months and still no word. Bela woke every morning, dreaming of her sister's tears. Two days after their double, hateful wedding, Arvo and a weeping Sarah had made off to the sea, and America.

"Write to me," Bela whispered. The secret only she and her sister shared, the power of the written word.

"Where?"

"Write to the Plovs' cook," Bela said.

"What will I do without you?"

"I will come for you, I don't know how, but I will come for you."

"To New York? How?"

"Enough of these tears."

Bela feared dreadfully for Sarah. The ship might have been wrecked, Arvo might have already killed her, anything could have happened. She simply didn't know. To make matters worse, Russia itself was in turmoil. News reached Dvinsk of trouble in St. Petersburg, of mutinies and nascent revolution against the Tsar, but nothing was certain. Each report came followed by its opposite until no one in town knew what to believe, only to be fearful and nervous—of the revolutionaries, the mutineers, or, worst of all, the Tsar's own secret police, the Okhrana.

Vincas didn't care for politics. He didn't care for much other than vodka and the slaking of his more private tastes. When Bela first moved into the Marinsky house, she'd expected the same brand of sporadic violence her father employed—a means of control and of venting his own anger and drunkenness. Vincas was different. He delighted in hurting her. On those occasions where she'd committed some minor slight or misdemeanor, he would grin and pull from his waist a long leather belt. It slithered from the loops.

Bela tried to make friends with old man Marinsky, hoped he might come to her aid or at least temper his son's malice. He did not. The rooms they all shared above the shop resounded with her cries, until she realized crying out only made things worse. Belt marks slashed her back, the air vodka thick.

"You are learning, bitch." Vincas spat, laughed, and left.

She learned too the one thing that would often forestall a beating, though it sickened her. Vincas fucked her whenever he wanted, drunk, sober, morning and night. He didn't need her permission. And he didn't care when it hurt her. The first time, their wedding night, he laughed when he saw the blood. But though he did it whenever he liked, Bela realized he preferred it when she seemed enthusiastic or aroused. She never was. That it made a difference to Vincas amazed her. Didn't he know she hated him, that her very soul shriveled at his every touch? Yet if she showed she enjoyed his vulgar thrustings—or, even better, initiated them—then she avoided a belt lashing. It gave her wounds time to heal.

It didn't take Bela long to realize too why the Marinsky family had agreed so readily to the double match. They needed a woman in the house, and all of its work had fallen on her. Vincas forbade her from working for the Plovs. Denied the secret access to their library, she felt the lack of books almost as much as the loss of Sarah.

Her mind was full of her sister, how to get to America, how to protect her from Arvo. She had no money of her own and no means of escape. Stealing from the old man, running, wasn't an option. They were hundreds of versts from the sea and the Marinskys would run her down before she got far. Marinsky liked a clean house and Vincas liked fucking her, whether she protested or not. She couldn't easily sneak away in any case, with her birthmarked face, even if she did have the money. Marinsky, as a flour merchant, had contacts all the way to the coast.

The old man disturbed her almost as much as his son. He would stand behind her as she scrubbed the shop floor on her knees, silent but for the sound of chewing tobacco. When she righted herself, he would look away and spit. She tried to engage him, to seek his help in controlling the violence of Vincas, but he would quash any attempt at conversation. "You're his wife," he would say, his upper lip rising in a sneer. She began to think he liked to hear her cry.

As the winter gave way to spring, her belly grew bigger and even the old man commented. She felt the life growing within her with a mixture of excitement, bitterness, and disgust. Not for the new life but for its father. She longed for a girl, anything to save her from a little Vincas. He seemed not to notice her condition—whether he thought she was getting fat or didn't care, she didn't know.

Finally, feeling round and vulnerable six months after her marriage, she thought to spare herself a beating. She hoped too that Vincas would not want to take her as she grew big.

"I'm with child now, Vincas," she whispered when he grabbed her one night. He breathed vodka over her face, heavy, urgent.

"You think I care?"

"No, it will harm the child."

As soon as she said it, she wished it away. *No.* Not a word to use in that house, ever. The belt buckle cracked her jaw. "You say no to me, bitch? I say no." She curled away from him. The buckle caught the crown of her head. It clattered across the floor and for a hopeful moment, Bela thought he'd given up. He pulled her hair, exposing her neck, stretching her body. And then his fist crashed down on her midriff. Again and again until she could scream no more.

Later, after the pain and the tears and the confusion, came the blood. She felt the dead life in her fingers, a sickening crimson, a broken, miniature human. As the blood dried on her thighs, and the dark deep ache inside her dulled, a plan came to her.

Life with Vincas would forever be impossible. She knew what she had to do.

* * *

Wiggins had finally made it to Peter's place, supposedly a tea shop deep inside the 'Chapel. It was like no tearoom he'd ever seen. Not a woman in sight for one thing, he noted as he sat down opposite Peter. The table was scrubbed bare, without cutlery or plates. The walls were mostly bare, too, and the room had little natural light, other than a faint gloom coming from the alleyway. There were four or five other tables in the room, each with two men sitting at them. Saying nothing.

"Tea?" Peter said. "We have the finest samovar west of Riga."

Wiggins nodded, bemused.

"Don't look so shocked," Peter said. "This is Russian tea. No milk. Please, don't mind them." Peter wafted his arm around airily at the others, who had said nothing since Wiggins came in, neither to him nor to one another. "They are suspicious of you. But they are Russian. They are suspicious of everyone." He laughed. "Vodka?"

Wiggins examined his host in more detail. The gray streak in his hair gave Peter a certain elegance, an intellectual sophistication. His beard was trim and well kempt, quite unlike the other Russians he'd seen. The man's nails were clean and clipped. They shone. He looked like a rich man in a poor man's clothes. Or the devil. Wiggins turned his attention to the rest of the room. The clientele was similar to that of the drinking den—suspicious, restless, and hairy. A long trestle table ran down one wall. It was peppered with cups and dominated by a huge gleaming tea urn.

"Bonbon?" Peter placed a paper bag on the table and popped one into his mouth. "Very good."

He then made an extravagant show of serving vodka to go with their tea. In the dismal light Wiggins examined a string of flags and embroidered hangings strung up above the samovar. There were stars aplenty, but without getting up to see he couldn't be sure if any of the emblems matched the one in his pocket, the eight-pointed star.

"You have had haircut," Peter said. "Good. The fisherman must trim his line, if he is to get a bite."

The other customers had resumed their conversations. There were two chess games on the go. Despite this, Wiggins felt the gaze of one man in particular, leaning back in his seat, fat-cheeked with a shock of electrified hair climbing away from a high forehead. His eyes sat deep and his stare did not relent. He balled a teacup in his fist.

"You work today?" Peter said. "Tell me again, what you do?" He rolled a penny between his fingers, flipping it over his knuckles first one way, then the next.

Wiggins switched his gaze back to Peter. "I didn't tell you."

Peter's brow twitched but he said nothing.

Wiggins sipped his tea. "You was a croupier." he said.

Peter brought the coin to a stop between his second and third fingers. "Gambling is bourgeois," he said at last. "But you are right—when I was young." He looked at Wiggins. "I stood there in Riga and helped fat capitalists spend their money. They would think nothing of wasting a thousand rubles on a card, while outside people died in snow. For lack of a few kopeks. I wanted to be like them once, capitalists." He spat on the floor. "I can't think this now."

"Factory watchman, out Woolwich way," Wiggins said.

"You liked Comrade Kent's talk?"

"It rang some bells. But I don't do politics. All I know is the rich is still rich."

"But they don't have to be," Peter cried. "If a pack runs together, they can do more than an animal alone."

Wiggins raised his eyebrows. "And your plan is—?"

A chair scraped across the floor and the fat-cheeked man strode toward them. He shouted at Wiggins in harsh, guttural barks, finger jabbing. Peter leaned across to shield Wiggins, who couldn't decipher the language, but knew a killer when he saw one.

Wiggins stood up, arms outstretched. "Hey. Look. I don't want no trouble."

But Fat Cheeks went for him, pushing him to the floor. Before Wiggins could even grasp his cosh, the man had a snub knife at his throat. His face shoved right into Wiggins, their eyes locked, noses touching. He smelled of garlic and vodka. Saliva dripped from his rotten teeth.

"Who are you?" the man rasped.

Wiggins felt the point of the knife against his neck. "Wiggins. Woolwich watchman. Used to be a bailiff. Ex-gunner," he tried not to gabble.

"British Army?"

Something jangled against Wiggins's chest. He saw a flash of red on a string around the man's neck.

The door crashed open behind him.

A sudden stream of hysterical Russian broke in and the assailant relaxed his hand, allowing Wiggins to slither clear. Rough hands yanked him into a chair. His attacker stood, with Peter and a third man—a boy almost—crowding in on him. They spoke in quick, urgent tones, glancing every now and then at Wiggins. One word rose above the rest.

Arlekin.

Wiggins assessed his options. Heavily outnumbered, he had only one—stay still. Say nothing. Finally, the three men reached some kind of agreement. Peter stepped toward him.

"Forgive Yakov." Peter gestured to his attacker. "He trusts no one. Not even his own mother."

Yakov stood in the middle of the room, knife cast to the floor, panting heavily. Beside him, the younger man smiled.

"This is Yakov's small brother, Mikhail. He remembers you," Peter went on.

Wiggins nodded. "I let you go by London Bridge."

"When you were bailiff?" Peter asked.

Wiggins nodded. He remembered chasing the boy down Liverpool Street, to the river. The day when Kell first came calling; the eve of Bill's death, at the hands of a man like Yakov.

Yakov swiped his knife from the floor and strode toward the door.

Peter chuckled. "So, you are not lying—as Yakov thought. You do a good thing for Mikhail. Yakov owes you now. He trusts his brother. Only his brother."

Wiggins rubbed his neck. Then he held out his hand to Mikhail. "Thank you, fella," he said. "That's a debt repaid."

Mikhail showed no understanding but offered a hand, then skittered off after his brother.

Wiggins touched the wound on his neck and examined his bloody fingers. His heart still thumped, despite his calm exterior—not only from the exertion of the fight, but at the thought of what was around Yakov's neck: the flash of red, a small, eight-pointed star.

Peter sighed. "Yakov is quick to judge. His real name is not Yakov—he calls himself Yakov Peters, I call myself Peter the Painter. We all have different names, many names. What's a name? It is a way for government to control you, the Church. Names, always names. If you have none, how do they know who you are? You are a ghost. But sit, I want to tell you something. More vodka!"

The two men sat down again. Wiggins took deep breaths. He was *in*—he knew, now, that the eight-pointed star could be significant, that Peter and Yakov might know about Tottenham. He reminded himself to act the nascent revolutionary, a budding convert to the cause, eager for the battle.

Peter continued. "We go to Hyde Park soon. You come with us?"

"What for?"

"We march, for the workers, against Empire. Police, they don't like it too much. We need big brave men like you, powerful men. Good men, to show others how to act, to lead. Are you with me?"

Wiggins was with him. Of course he was, stuck with his only lead. Later, as they embraced on the street, Wiggins tugged at the thought that had been bothering him all evening.

"What's 'Arlekin'?" he said.

"Ha," said Peter and placed a strong hand on each of Wiggins's shoulders. "Not what, who."

11

"You're a romantic." Wiggins smiled.

"Nonsense," Kell bristled. "Now, tell me about Woolwich." The two of them sat side by side in the back of a hansom cab as it bounced and weaved over Westminster Bridge.

"I thought you'd prefer a motor to the hansom."

"Nothing like horsepower," Kell replied.

"The papers are offering a straight-up fortune for someone to fly the Channel."

"It will never happen. Why do you think the prize is so generous?"

They trotted on in silence for a moment. "Do you miss it?" Wiggins said. "London," he added, staring out into the Lambeth streets.

Kell felt the loss in Wiggins's voice, the pain of an old wound. For himself, he missed the horses, the great animals that pulled the city's wares across town, the magnificent dray horses, the dancing fillies of the cabs, the sleek and polished cavalry mounts on parade: the living, breathing beasts of London, its heart and bones. Soon they'd all be gone, even the emaciated nags tugging rag-and-bone men down the Old Kent Road. Disappeared, drowned out by motorcars and vans and omnibuses; by trains, over- and underground; by the tubular railway; by airships; and by telephone lines and telegrams and the Lord knew what else. Maybe Wiggins was right, he was a romantic.

"What has got into you?" he replied. "London is here." He swept his hand out of the cab. "This is for security. You remember I was almost killed in Hampshire? I still have a constable on my door. I still fear for my wife and family. We can't be too careful. What's happening at the Arsenal?"

Kell's authority was slipping, he knew.

Wiggins was a hard agent to control. And now he wouldn't even answer a straight question. At home, Kell's wife, Constance, laughed at him, or openly disagreed with him on many matters, in particular women's suffrage. She didn't even take the policeman on the door seriously. He suspected she thought it an affectation he'd dreamt up to impress her. His superiors at the War Office took little notice of him unless he could rustle up conclusive proof of German subterfuge. Only the buffoon Lieutenant Russell took any notice at all in the office. And did having power over a fool mean any kind of power at all?

"Here, you know much about these Rooski gangs. Anarchists and that?" Wiggins asked suddenly. He was obviously in contemplative mood.

"What has this got to do with Woolwich?" Kell cried. "I know nothing about them. Or rather, it's not our business. Melville in Special Branch spends his time chasing them. Apparently, half of them are simply hell-bent on creating chaos, some want revolution, while the rest are nothing more than common criminals. Although, between you and me, Special Branch often puts them up to it."

"The police?"

"Entrapment. Or else it could be some other foreign power— creating trouble for their own ends, probably."

"Other governments would pay for mayhem and murder?"

"This is not our concern," Kell snapped. Soapy's warning came back to him. "We must focus on Germany and her agents—leave the criminals to the police!" He took a breath as the cab skirted north of the Elephant, then began again. "I must insist you tell me of Woolwich—you have a name?"

Wiggins cracked his long thin fingers, lifted his brow, and nodded. "I reckon, but first things first—what about Tinsley, is he clear?"

Kell coughed. He'd followed Tinsley for a week and found nothing. Daily trips to Woolwich, afternoons and evenings spent hopping between steam rooms and gentlemen's clubs and Piccadilly eateries. The one place Tinsley rarely went was his home in

Kensington. He had many companions, men younger than himself, but Kell could never fathom their conversations or even work out who these other men were. Once, he suspected Tinsley was onto him when they bumped into each other in the revolving doorway of the Criterion Bar. Tinsley flashed a knowing smile and left.

At a loss to explain the man's behavior and exasperated, only the morning before meeting Wiggins, Kell had turned to Constance. "Do you know the Tinsleys, my dear? The Honorable Charles."

"Eunice attends a meeting every now and then," Constance replied, dabbing marmalade clear of her top lip. "Which doesn't surprise me."

"Why?"

"Well, you know, her husband. He's not very . . . attentive."

Kell cleaned the butter from his knife by inserting it into the side of a slice of toast. "Attentive how?" he asked.

Constance looked at him askance. "You know." She waited. "Oh, for God's sake—he's of the Grecian persuasion? A follower of Socrates? No, not philosophically, Vernon, really. I hope they don't have you decoding ciphers—it would take years. No, put as simply as I know how, Charles Tinsley prefers men to women in the, er, bedroom."

"Oh." Kell felt his skin prickle hot and his collar pinch. He thought of the Marshall Street Baths, Tinsley's steadying hand on his.

"Why are *you* so interested, anyway?" Constance asked, the corners of her mouth peaking.

"What? Yes, well. That's classified."

Constance's peals of laughter rattled the cups.

The cab turned back north over the river at Waterloo. Flowers of train smoke decorated the skyline to their left, out at Charing Cross. "He's in the clear, I'm sure," Kell responded gruffly.

"Thought so," Wiggins replied. "But you've got to check, given he's blackmailable."

"How so?"

"What with him being all Oscar and Wilde."

First Constance and now Wiggins. How did people *know* these things? Kell shifted uncomfortably on the seat and shook his head. "Look, we don't have much time. The Ministry's not made of money. You have a lead?"

"I know how the dirt gets out of Woolwich. But where it goes to, that's the key."

"A name?"

Wiggins ignored the interruption. "Hold up. We need to find the organ-grinder, not the monkey."

"The monkey would be a start."

"I can find the grinder too. What we need is fake documents. Something that looks like a secret, a trap."

"Is that all?" Kell asked. "How about a suite at the Savoy thrown in or an elephant howdah? Or the Koh-i-noor?"

Kell breathed in heavily as the cab swung through Covent Garden and back down to Whitehall. He wiped his brow with a handkerchief. "I will do as you ask," he said at last. "But only in return for a name—be it the monkey or the grinder, I don't care."

"But—"

"You have a week. But only if you give me a name."

Bela picked at the deep folds of her dress. "What do the three balls mean?" she said.

"Uncle, ain't it," Wiggins replied.

The room he'd taken was above a pawnbroker and the three golden globes of the sign dangled within view. "Pawn."

She pulled her hair free in a great tug and shook out her mane. "I know this. You think we don't know about pawnshop. I mean, why *three* balls?"

Wiggins looked at her as she undressed, captivated by her small, measured movements, her peachy skin and the amused smile as he struggled for an answer. "I don't know," he said at last.

"*Chudo*," she said. "It's miracle. You admit there's something you don't know."

"Steady on."

"I have decided. You know nothing. And you have too many clothes on."

The first time they'd made love she'd led the way, gentle, then hungry, grasping, offering herself to him completely and without restraint. Afterward, she had cried inconsolable tears. Wiggins had lain next to her, mute with incomprehension. They weren't tears of joy or physical pain, he knew, but what caused them he did not, nor how to stop them. All he could do was hold her hand while she wept.

She made no mention of the tears and they never reappeared. Instead, she would ask him questions about himself, about the "Anglish," about his factory job and about London. Then they would make love and she would continue to question him and stroke his hair, his smooth chin. It delighted him to talk about London, Sal and the gang, his one and only memory of his mother. He'd never talked as much in his life.

He even told her about his time with Leach and Son, the odious bailiffs. She wanted to know everything and he tried to be as truthful as possible. He remained quiet only about Kell and Holmes. To reveal one would somehow mean revealing the other and he didn't want to go down that road just yet. Though he wanted to unburden himself, his work for Kell *was* a burden that had to be carried. Something stopped him mentioning Bill by name too, a natural caution or the rawness of the wound he wasn't sure. It was as if Bill had yet to truly die, or rather, that fact was something Wiggins couldn't accept until he'd got to the bottom of his murder. It was a chapter yet to close. But the past, he reveled in.

That day, after she'd teased him about his failed knowledge of the three balls, after they'd made love again, lazily, slowly, as if Wiggins's battered watch had indeed stopped for good, she stroked her unmarked cheek against his chest and asked her questions. "Tell me about your work," she said.

So he told her again, the hellish Woolwich factory floor, Rayner's bitching, the lonely nighttime drudge.

"It makes guns?"

"Big ones. And shells."

"Why don't you ask me questions?"

Wiggins hesitated. He knew she'd been married, that she worked in the laundry, that she'd been badly beaten repeatedly in the past—but she hadn't told him any of these things herself. Deep scars on her back and arms told of the beatings, her shoes of the laundry, and the pale puckering on her ring finger bore witness to the past betrothal. But dare he ask anything more? Was Elsie the barmaid right: no woman wants you to know what she's thinking?

"I've asked you about your country, ain't I?" he said at last.

"And what do you know about it?"

"The Tsar's a total bollocks."

She laughed and swung her legs out of the bed. "Tell me more about Russia," he said, stroking her naked back.

"Latvia. It's cold. I come here for the weather. You Anglish, you always complain about the weather—but go there and maybe you don't complain."

"It can't be all bad, it's home at least."

Bela glanced back at him. "Home. This is a nice word, for you. Not for me." She fell silent for a moment and then exhaled. "I must go."

Wiggins examined her as she dressed. She'd refused to tell him where she lived, out of embarrassment or independence he didn't know. It meant he had no control, she could walk out of the door at any moment and never come back. He didn't want to give her any reason to leave but his curiosity burned still.

He gulped down his concern and risked a question. "Do you know what an eight-pointed red star means? That drinker, the day we met, they had it on the wall. I'm curious like."

She had her back to him. "Help me. Tie."

He strung together the back of her dress. "Maybe it is like your balls?"

"What?" Wiggins said. "What's wrong with my balls?"

She turned, a smile spread across her two-tone face. "The three balls. Maybe it's a pawn sign. I don't know what the star means. I am sorry. There is nothing wrong with you," she added as she smoothed her hand against his chest.

"By the way, have you . . ." He faltered.

Someone had been in the room while he was out. Small signs: the candle up-ended, the dust rings around the bed legs, a finger smudge on the sill. No one knew he lived there, other than Bela. He hadn't even told Kell his address. The same sense of unease that had prickled him when they'd walked from Jubilee Street came over him again.

"Are you all right?" she said.

"You can come here whenever you like. Even when I'm not here. This place is yours."

"Why would I come, if you are not here?"

They looked at each other in silence. Elsie's warning came back to him again, clouding his thoughts. Did he really want to know what Bela was thinking? Did he want to risk asking? No, he didn't want to ask her anything more, not about Russia, her past, or her friends. He simply wanted to stare at her forever, and the deep dark world outside could whistle.

What price Kell, the country, the Empire, when he had this, *her*?

He pulled her into a kiss. "Tomorrow night?"

Bela licked her lips. "You never take me out."

"I thought you liked it here?"

She smiled. "What do Anglish man and woman do? Where do they go?"

"I could take you to the flicks? We could go down Victoria Park, or see Lord Elgin's marbles in Great Russell Street. Anything you fancy."

Bela angled her birthmark away from him as she gathered up her canvas bag. "Something special. British, how you say, the Empire?"

Wiggins cast around the room for inspiration, charmed by her insistence. "Here you are, how about the Imperial Exhibition?" He held up a newspaper. "Down Wood Lane, near the Bush. It's got the Flip-Flap, a Wibbly-Wobbly, and everything."

"Vibbly-Vobbly?"

"Wibbly-Wobbly—it's a ride. You love a good ride, you. It'll be jam. We'll go on your half-day."

He watched from the window as she crossed the street and walked up to Essex Road. Then he proceeded to get dressed. It was only when he reached for his strides that he noticed she'd folded up his discarded clothes. A simple gesture, the sight of his trousers and shirt in a small neat pile, touched him to the quick.

* * *

Kerensky was the word on everyone's lips. Whispered, mouthed. Rumors from St. Petersburg rippled through Dvinsk. *Lenin. The Bundists. Menshevik, Bolshevik.* Every morning, the Marinsky shop hummed with the latest sensation, often unuttered. But Bela could tell in the glances, the murmurs, the fearful eyes. Something was going to happen. Russia was on the verge of an explosion. Of course, Vincas was too drunk to notice. Whenever politics came up, he'd shout down whoever spoke. Like all the truly ignorant, he did not even know the emptiness of his own brain. Old man Marinsky never mentioned politics either, but he at least had a cannier mind than his son. He affected not to be concerned about the ructions in the country, but Bela knew he was seriously worried when he brought home a box of gold coins from the bank.

What she didn't know was where he hid the gold. But it was the break she needed, all the same, for it must be in the house some-where. The shop had been awash with rumors for days, and there was even talk of a mutiny in the town barracks. The time had come.

Mrs. Kalina came in every morning, grumbling about one government injustice or another. Her piggy eyes flitted between the customers. "They are losing control," she scowled to no one in particular. She said things like this often, dangerous things.

Not dangerous for her, though. Mrs. Kalina, as Bela and most of the customers well knew, was an Okhrana informant. She would trawl Dvinsk, hoping to catch someone out in a stray word or thought, desperate to earn some extra kopeks from her masters. No one rose to the bait. "Maybe the Tsar is too old, or too weak," she said. Flour dust swirled in the silence.

Three days later, Bela was ready. A young woman she knew, buying for her family, approached the till. Bela ducked her head and spoke in a careful undertone, clear and just loud enough for Mrs. Kalina, farther down the line, to hear. "Vincas has such *views*—I don't know where he gets them from. I fear if there's a mutiny, he'll join the revolutionaries and leave me all alone."

Her young friend opened her eyes wide, surprised at such a public admission, afraid. Bela turned away blithe.

That night the Okhrana officers came, stinking of stale sweat and cheap tobacco. They pushed through the shop, upturning a sack of flour for effect. Bela, old man Marinsky, and Vincas were in the back room at dinner when three officers barreled through the door, their tunics dashed with white.

Marinsky tensed, his hands flat on the table. But his eyes flicked repeatedly at the fireplace.

"Vincas Marinsky?" the leader asked. He took off his cap and smoothed down the small island of black hair he had left.

"That's me," Vincas muttered. He tried to sound casual, bullish, but Bela sensed his fear.

"We have reason to believe you are harboring anti-tsarist views."

"I am loyal," he replied. "What do I care for revolution?"

"That is what we are here to find out." The officer jerked his head and his two underlings barged up the stairs.

"My son is a hard worker," Marinsky offered. Bela said nothing.

The officer held his cap in his hands but did not sit. He examined each of them in turn, unabashed, confident in his untouchability. Bela kept her head down but felt the officer's gaze. Above them, the heavy boots of the Okhrana clumped and rattled as they ripped the rooms apart.

"You will find nothing," Vincas said at last.

Bela glanced up to see him looking straight at her.

Before the officer could answer a great cry came from above, then the boots cascaded down the stairs. "Sir." The young deputy strode in. He waved the pamphlet like a handkerchief on a railway station platform. "We found this." In his other hand he held Vincas's rough jacket.

The officer grasped young Plov's stolen pamphlet.

"Is this yours?" He glared at Vincas. "You need to come with us."

"I know nothing about this," Vincas cried. "It is her, that bitch. She cleans the clothes."

Bela gasped, confused. "What does it say? I cannot read."

The two junior men took Vincas by the shoulders. They dragged him to the door, fear and confusion writ across his face. For he knew she could not read, yet how else could the pamphlet have got there?

The officer put on his cap and turned to Marinsky. "This is a serious matter. *Common Cause* is a banned publication. It is highly seditious. Anyone in possession of such material needs to be interrogated. Do not leave Dvinsk."

Marinsky called after him. "Leave Dvinsk? Where would I go?"

Long after she'd gone to bed, Bela heard Marinsky mutter and stomp. For all his meanness and sneering, he seemed genuinely distraught. Finally, in the hour just before dawn, she got up to join him in the downstairs room.

"I'll make tea," she said.

"I don't understand. What they say about Vincas, it cannot be true."

"Go to him. Everybody in the neighborhood knows you, Dvinsk knows you. You can save Vincas."

"Save him? Why, bitch? I know you hate him."

"He is my husband." Bela busied herself at the stove. "I don't want to be the wife of a traitor. It will stain us all. No one will shop here today."

Marinsky grunted but didn't disagree. They waited while Bela made the tea. Gray light stripped the edges of the outside door. Marinsky clapped his hands together and flung it open onto the misty morning. "What should I do?" he said at last.

"Go to the prison. Speak to people. You are an important man," Bela soothed, careful. "Isn't it the traders' meeting tonight?"

Marinsky scoffed. "What good will that pack of popinjays be?"

"It is influence," Bela said. "Sway. None of those men want to lose their sons to the Okhrana. It is all you have."

The old man blew on his tea a moment. "You sound like a Bolshevik." He spoke with no malice, however, and soon got up from the table. "Get me my overcoat." He gestured upstairs with a dismissive wave of his hand. "I need to help my son."

Bela remembered Marinsky's actions of the night before. Throughout the Okhrana's interrogation, he couldn't keep his eyes off the kitchen hearth. Once Marinsky left to go after his son, Bela knelt down to check. As she suspected, new brick dust sprinkled the floor on the right-hand side. She teased free one, two, three of the small bricks. Behind them, Marinsky's gold coins. He had taken some with him earlier, hence the new dust. After counting the money, enough to get her to the coast and onto a boat, she put it back and replaced each brick with care.

Marinsky returned that night, empty-handed. He muttered and cursed as he ate.

"What news?" Bela asked at last.

"This soup is disgusting." Marinsky pushed away his bowl. "No wonder my son beats you." He licked his lips. "I am going to bed."

Hours later, when Bela had checked and double-checked the old man's snores, she padded down the stairs to the kitchen. She'd wrapped a headscarf tightly around her face and mouth and wore her best and warmest clothes. The Plovs' driver had agreed to take her as far as Dunava, for a fee, and she would take a boat upriver to Riga. She felt her way through the kitchen, a space so familiar she needed no light. Once she was by the hearth, however, she had to see to pick the bricks away. She knelt down and scratched at the floor with a match.

The bright bloom flickered and suddenly went out, extinguished by a draft. Someone had opened the front door.

12

Sherlock Holmes had a sliver of ice in his heart. He called it reason, but a good detective's blood ran colder than that of any killer. It took days like today to remember this.

A fine rain misted Wiggins's view of the Woolwich factory as the gates swung open and the tide of workers swept through. Wiggins saw Royston Basil right away. His tinted circular spectacles, stiff homburg, and canary umbrella stood out in the sea of gray and brown.

But he wasn't there to follow Basil.

The preening underclerk's flashy clothes certainly came at a heavy price, well beyond the man's salary. But Wiggins had followed him home the week before, to the Deptford cottage Basil shared with his blind mother. Wiggins went back the next day, took tea with the kindly Mrs. Basil, and listened while she boasted about her son's important work for the government. "He's got a job at Woolwich," she said. "Working for my brother at the Arsenal."

Wiggins congratulated her on the good fortune. As she talked, he examined the blind Mrs. Basil's parlor. It didn't take long to dismiss Royston Basil as a suspect. A mean and despicable man, yes; a traitor, no. Wiggins noted the missing knickknacks, the empty dust-lined oblongs on the wall, the depleted silver canteen, and—most damning of all—the collection of unredeemed pawnbroker tickets on the top shelf of the dresser. Royston Basil had been pawning his mother's possessions to fund his taste in expensive clothes. It took Wiggins a couple more days to confirm this hypothesis, but it proved to be the case. Basil was a fashion-struck dissembler, a craven coward, and an exploiter of the most reprehensible kind. But he was no traitor.

That day, as the factory workers swarmed the streets, Wiggins waited for a different man. He had planted a set of documents in the design room, carefully left to look careless. Kell had instructed a draftsman to draw up plans for a flying bomb—the impossible dream of military expansionists everywhere—and Wiggins waited for the mole to take the bait. It was too tasty a morsel to ignore.

Sure enough, a couple of minutes after the factory horn, he saw the shape of his man cutting through the throng, his club foot swinging around him like a scythe. Milton the runner headed straight toward the railway station.

A runner? A nobody?

That's what Kell had said—surely he can't be the mole? It didn't surprise Wiggins. The runners could go anywhere in the factory, see anything, and not be noticed—they were *meant* to be everywhere. And they were paid a pittance. Any of them could have been spies—but it was Milton, poor foolish Milton. The way he kept his family was impossible on his pay packet. The dead father, ruined by the British Army, supplied additional motive—not that it was needed in Wiggins's eyes. It was no sin to need money. And Milton's nature was so open, easy, and biddable—a perfect mark for someone of an altogether more devious mind to take advantage.

Wiggins followed Milton onto the London-bound platform at Woolwich Station. The boy jiggled and jumped as he waited for the train. Wiggins hung back at the far end of the platform and boarded a different carriage. He changed hats, from a sailor's cap to a large worsted flat cap, an old trick. A man looking for a tail always looks at hats.

At each station, Wiggins got out and walked up the platform to the next carriage. Milton did not get off the train. Wiggins suspected that the young runner would stay on until the end of the line, and sure enough, Milton got out with everyone else at London Bridge. Wiggins followed him onto the concourse and watched as Milton used the public telephones. As he came out, he glanced at the huge station clock and then hurried toward Borough.

The rain fell heavier now and Milton ducked into the Bunch of Grapes in the shadow of Guy's Hospital. Wiggins waited in a doorway opposite. He could see nothing through the cloudy pub windows, but as the night closed, they shone ever brighter. A street-walker sashayed past. "Want company?"

"Not tonight."

Half an hour later, he became unsure. The Grapes didn't have a back exit, but Milton could be doing the deal inside—yet Wiggins knew the barmaid (he knew many), and it would be a risk to go in now. He stepped forward, hesitated. At that moment, the doors swung open and Milton appeared; he swung right, past the hospital, his gammy leg scraping on the ground.

Switching hats once more, Wiggins kept going. Milton looped under the railway arches, crossing Bermondsey Street, then Tooley, toward the dark warren of streets south of Tower Bridge. Knife territory, Wiggins thought as he felt the cosh in his pocket.

Finally, when it was full dark and the alleyways barely lit, Milton stopped by a small, deserted dock. Wiggins hid in the alcove of a warehouse. A single lamp swung from a wharf house doorway and Wiggins could see the outline of the dock, almost an inlet off the Thames. Milton clasped his hands together and jiggled from foot to foot. His head swiveled this way and that, and though Wiggins was too far away to see his expression, he could feel the boy's fear. Raindrops jumped off the flagstones. No good man would be out on such a vile night.

Wiggins heard a motorcar approach.

The headlights from the car almost swung a yellow wash over him as he ducked behind a discarded tea chest. The car, a Daimler, pulled up ten yards or so away. A man got out and strode toward Milton. The car juddered and strained against the handbrake, the engine still running. Wiggins watched as the man, six foot three at least, stepped into the light. He wore a cap and a tight-fitting sailor's jacket. His trousers barely reached his ankles; he looked like a child who had outgrown his wardrobe. Except there was nothing childish about the way he loomed over Milton.

Milton pulled out a stacked envelope, the fake documents provided by Kell. The man snatched them from Milton, weighed them in his hands. At a distance, Wiggins couldn't make out the conversation, but Milton nodded repeatedly, too eager.

The man reached into his own pocket. In the same movement, he put his arm around Milton's shoulder in an awkward embrace. Wiggins flinched—were they hugging? A blade flashed in the gaslight as the tall man pulled it free from Milton's midriff and plunged it in once more, again and again. He held Milton. Wiggins stood, stunned, gaping in horror as the runner shuddered his last.

The tall man dragged Milton's body to the dockside. With one smooth, effortless movement, he tossed him into the darkness beneath. Then he splashed his way back to the car, paused, and scanned the street. After a moment, he got into the motor, released the handbrake, and sped off into the night.

Seven miles north by northwest, across the dark metropolis, Kell looked out of a rain-streaked window and listened to the trees straining against the storm. His wife had not returned. She'd refused to listen when he forbade her attendance at the latest meeting of the Hampstead suffragists.

"I will not be detained in my own home," she'd said tartly. "This is London, for heaven's sake, I'll be fine."

He loved her for it, despite his worries. Wiggins would be out tonight too; his one agent in the field. He hoped the fake plans had found their mark.

The bushes in front of his house shook. Kell squinted and rushed to the front door. "Did you see anything, Constable?" he said. "Out there, in the laburnum."

"Nothing, sir. Wind." The young constable ruffled his rain cape. "No one would choose to be out on a night like this. If they had a choice."

"Are you sure? I could have sworn . . . Oh well, keep a weather eye out."

"A weather eye indeed."

Wiggins clung on. His muscles shook with effort, his palms burned. His head barely cleared the road.

He was holding on to the undercarriage of the car.

Milton's killer inches above him, Wiggins had jammed his feet above the rear axle and wrapped his upper arm around one of the pipes. But he couldn't last much longer. The hot pipes singed his jacket and he could feel his hair catching on the road surface. His grip slipped with each jerk of the suspension. Pain blossomed from his right shoulder. But if he let go now, he had nothing; Milton would have died for nothing.

They swung onto Westminster Bridge and his foot came clear, scraped the ground. Cold air numbed his fingers and he stifled a choke. He shot his eyes left and right, looking for markings.

Wiggins recognized the wide expanse of Piccadilly Circus, busy even this late. Light spilled off the road. The Daimler pivoted right, then left down a side street and finally came to a stop. He waited, dared not breathe. His stomach, arms, legs straining for stillness, for silence.

The engine died. After an age, the car door squeaked open. Wiggins saw the giant's feet striding across the road to his right. He lowered himself to the ground. From underneath the car, Wiggins could see the man on the far pavement. He looked about quickly, then let himself into an unlit shop and disappeared from view. Wiggins let out a great sigh. He breathed in the smell of car oil, hot metal, and horseshit. The road was smeared with sodden dung and Wiggins retched as he pulled himself clear. Shit caked his back and legs, but he didn't care—his arms and hands tingled with relief.

He stumbled to his feet, life slowly returning to his frozen limbs. Savile Row ran off to the right. Wiggins would be pinched for loitering if the coppers spotted him, especially in his condition. He crossed the road and peered into the shop window. There were a few flash antiques, but nothing to show where Milton's killer had gone. The shop itself only had one story, so there was no upstairs either.

Wiggins calmed himself and slunk into a doorway. They knew. Why else would they kill Milton? Poor, foolish Milton died a dog's death.

No.

Wiggins pulled himself up. He wouldn't let Milton die in vain, traitor or not; the boy only did it for the money. Two young 'uns to keep off the streets, all he wanted was a decent living. It was no worse than theft and theft wasn't really a crime if you needed the dosh, not in Wiggins's eyes. Only the rich thought otherwise. And now Milton was dead.

He rattled the shop door but it wouldn't budge. Glancing around for the beat copper, he took a deep breath, braced his foot on the jamb, and reached for the roof. The guttering held his weight as he levered his legs upward and landed belly down on top of the shop.

Ahead of him, stretching into the darkness, a long, tall brick building, golden oblongs stamped here and there along its length: the well-lit windows of expensive apartments. They weren't saving money on the gas. Probably electrified, given the constant glow. He crouched down on the shop's flat roof and counted.

One of the apartment lights went out. Just then, someone clattered through the shop beneath him. Wiggins dropped silently to his belly and peeked out over the edge. The giant had returned. Now sheathed in a billowing rain cape, he crashed through the door. Wiggins had no trouble recognizing him—he hadn't seen a man that big since ever.

The man sauntered back toward the Daimler. Not a slope in his gait, no sign of nerves jangling—he'd just killed a man, as cool as you like. He cranked the car into action and then swung it around in an arc away from the shop and down a side road toward Piccadilly.

Wiggins dropped down to the road and ran after him. In the distance, he could see the car turn right onto Piccadilly. He got there just in time to see the Daimler pull out. It veered in front of him, cutting up a cab. The horse rose on its hind legs and the cabbie cursed above the noise. Wiggins saw the tall man at the wheel of the car and caught a glimpse of the passenger he had just picked up—a flash of a dinner jacket, a top hat, and a black mustache. Then the car roared off into the night.

He turned back to where they'd come from and looked up at the most famous bachelor pad in London. The Albany.

"I'm still waiting."

"What do you mean?"

"You've yet to prove a thing."

Vernon Kell regarded his wife across their Hampstead drawing room. He tried to hide his relief at seeing her home safe. She shook free her umbrella and continued. "About women's suffrage—I've been waiting weeks now for your argument, for this great, watertight case. The evidence that women will ruin civilization if they get anywhere near a ballot box, let alone Parliament. I'm *agog*."

"My mind is on more important matters."

"But given that your mind is so much finer and more elevated than a woman's, surely you can think of more than one thing at a time?" Constance's eyes sparkled.

He smiled faintly, enjoying her company. Perhaps the constable was right: no one would choose to be out on such an evening. "Would you like a nightcap? Something to calm you down?"

Before she could respond, they were interrupted by a frantic banging on the front door. "I'll go," Kell said.

"You bastard!" Wiggins shouted in his face.

"I'm sorry, sir," the constable said. "This man says he knows you."

"Thank you, Constable. He does. Come in quickly." He pushed the door to. "Good God, man, look at the state of you."

Wiggins marched down the hall into the drawing room, glancing quickly at Constance, who gasped. Kell followed him in.

"You didn't need to kill him."

"What on earth are you talking about?"

Constance stepped forward. "Can I get you a towel, some hot water? Gosh, is that . . . ?"

Wiggins looked down at his dung-smeared strides and blistered hands. "I'm sorry, ma'am."

"Constance, I think some hot water might be a good idea—but best not ask Cook. Can we manage ourselves?"

"Of course."

When she was gone, Kell turned back to Wiggins. He was angry at the intrusion. But Wiggins didn't look as though he'd react well to a lesson on protocol.

"What is it?"

Wiggins took a breath. He stood in the middle of the room, dripping onto the carpet. "Milton's dead. The poor blighter's dead. You didn't have to—"

Kell raised his hand to interrupt. "I didn't have him killed."

Wiggins shook his head, stared into Kell's eyes for a moment, weighing up. "Then who did?"

"Why would I?"

"I give you a name and five days later he's dead. Murdered." He shook his head again, but slower this time, gentler. He'd seen enough men die to know that once the anger was gone, only the sadness remained. "You got a horn?" He looked up. "Get his body collected before the tide comes in."

Kell wrote down the directions and phoned through the details to the police. By the time he came back into the room, Constance had Wiggins sitting down, towels wrapped around him, his jacket hung on a chair and his hands resting in a bowl. Steam engulfed them.

"They'll find him," Kell said, his mouth set grim.

"Vernon?" Constance looked up sharply at her husband.

"What? Oh, yes. Introductions. Wiggins, my wife, Mrs. Kell. Constance dear, this is, er, Mr. Wiggins, an associate of mine."

"How do." Wiggins nodded his head as she sponged his hands.

"Mr. Wiggins must stay, Vernon. It's positively vile outside, and he seems to have had rather a shock."

Kell poured three stiff whiskies and waited until his wife finished cleaning Wiggins's hands. His trousers and shirt were surely beyond repair, Kell thought as he handed his agent the drink.

Constance shook her head. "I won't, thank you, dear." She gathered up the soiled towels. "I'll leave you. But Mr. Wiggins, please, there is a room free upstairs. Vernon will show you the way when you're ready. It was interesting to meet you. Good night."

"Much obliged, ma'am. Good night. Here, I'll have that if it's going." Wiggins gestured to Constance's undrunk whisky as they heard her feet on the stairs. "So if you didn't have him killed, who did?"

"Tell me what happened."

Wiggins did so, with the help of another whisky, while Kell smoked three cigarettes. "Did you get the registration number of the motor?" he asked.

"Course."

"And the killer drove to the Albany, you say?"

"Though he came and went through a back way—there's a shop, must have a secret door—the commissionaire would never have seen him. Then he left and picked up someone from the front. Someone who had rooms."

"A set."

"What?"

"Rooms in the Albany are called a set."

"What I want to know is who knew. Who did you tell about Milton?"

"What do you mean?"

"He was tumbled. Someone spilled. Who knew?"

"I can't discuss that. The distribution group is classified."

Wiggins crashed his glass down. "A man's dead. And you've got a bleeding leak."

"You work for me, remember? It's easy enough to change that." Kell took a deep breath. He disliked decisions made in anger. "Surely the man in the Albany must be behind it. That makes the most sense."

Kell lit another cigarette and watched Wiggins pour more whisky.

"What we must do is find out who this man is. The 'grinder,' as you put it. It is unfortunate that your man lost his life. But our task remains the same. I take into consideration the possibility that someone at the Ministry may have inadvertently divulged something untoward. Leave it to me to look into that. We will meet again once I've ascertained who owns the motorcar. Did you manage to find out the number of the set—the rooms—in the Albany?"

"I can tell which flat from the outside."

Kell raised his eyebrow.

"From the lights. One went off just after the big man came out, then he collected the gent."

"Very good. In the meantime, I suggest you stay at Woolwich in a part-time capacity. To make sure we have our man."

"We have our man. He's dead."

"Even so." They sat in silence for a time until Wiggins nodded. Kell stood up. "As my wife suggested . . ." He gestured half-heartedly toward the door.

"No, you're all right, sir. I'll take the Scotch though."

Kell saw Wiggins to the door, then went up to his room. He got into bed as quietly as possible but there was no need. Constance was wide awake. "Is he staying?" she hissed.

"No. He wanted to go home."

"Did he? He was very unlike your other clerks."

Kell sighed. "He's not a clerk."

"There was something, oh, I don't know, magnificent about him. Heaven knows what the ladies will say."

Kell raised himself up on his elbow and turned to his wife. "You will tell no one about this, ever."

13

"When you first arrive anywhere, Wiggins, set the scene in your mind—the entrances and exits, the loafer in a doorway, the innocent-looking hurdy-gurdy man: the whole milieu. Then, when it changes, you'll know."

So said Holmes.

Wiggins squinted down Oxford Street, checked the corners at Berners and Wardour. Milton loomed large in his mind—poor, club-footed Milton. And the sisters too, Mavis and the little one—what of them? Kell had urged him not to blame himself; Milton had died through his own treachery. And yet . . . A pair of sailors sauntered past, bright neck tattoos on show. Wiggins leaned down and handed his evening newspaper to a ragged child. "Back of the Metropole Hotel, they'll give you ha'penny for it."

The child took the paper. "Ponce," he said, and ran off.

Wiggins smiled as the boy stopped at a safe distance and folded the paper carefully under his arm.

"Always with the newspapers. Why?" Peter said from the sweet-shop doorway.

"Information."

"Huh! Does fish seek information from fisherman? Foxes from hounds?"

They resumed their walk down the clogged street as Peter went on. "Look at all these fools, buying, buying, buying—a fever. Happy life cannot be bought off shelf, wrapped in paper bag."

"What are we doing here then?" Wiggins pointed to the sweet bags Peter had just bought.

Peter laughed. "I am human, it is true. I love sweets." He thrust an open bag at Wiggins.

"H, H!" Wiggins whipped round at the voice. "Over here."

"Emily?" Bill's widow, Emily Tyler, was suddenly before them. She stood arm in arm with a tall, barrel-chested older man.

"I can't believe it, here on Oxford Street." She smiled.

Wiggins grinned tightly at Emily and avoided Peter's eye.

"I thought you might have come. After. I wanted you to," Emily went on.

Wiggins glanced at her companion.

"We're going to John Lewis," she said. "Why didn't you visit?"

"I couldn't," he said at last.

"Sorry, this is Robert. Robert, H."

Wiggins looked Robert up and down and nodded slowly.

Robert frowned. "Have we met?"

Emily placed a hand on his arm. "Won't you come to see me, H? Here's my new address."

Wiggins looked down at the card in astonishment. "Are you marrying again, already?" He stopped himself saying anything more. Peter sucked so hard on his sweet that Wiggins could hear. Robert was a copper—and like Wiggins, Peter knew police when he saw it.

"Sorry, Em, I got to go. Be happy."

He turned, pulling Peter by the arm.

"H?" she called after him.

Wiggins and Peter carried on toward the park. He barged his way through the crowds—the women in their dresses and straw hats, the men with hands tucked into waistcoats, elbows jutted. Seeing Emily, her face full and well fed, her clothes neatly pressed, and a new man on her arm, enraged him. So soon. Bill not in the ground six months. Would no one honor his name?

Peter plucked at his arm. "Down here." He pointed to a side street just before the park. "Good friends?" he asked.

Wiggins took a breath. Peter's hand was on his shoulder now. Not altogether friendly. It didn't do to have pals in the police, not where Peter came from.

"She was an old friend." Wiggins forced a grin. "I had her a few times. She was tasty once. Him, I don't know. Her bloke, I guess. A rozzer."

"Yes, I think so." Peter nodded. "This is kind of policeman I don't like. Alive." They walked on for a few moments. "But I understand. We cannot control old loves. It is not always nice to meet girls we used to know. Would you like an Unclaimed Baby?" He held up a baby-shaped sweet. "I like to bite head off first," he said, then did so.

"Don't go too deep."

"Why?"

"If you are in middle, you can do nothing," Peter said as they crossed Park Lane. They were on their way to a demonstration.

A great mob horseshoed Speakers' Corner. Key chains jangled, heavyset men sighed and mopped their brows. Wiggins strained to hear. Trade-union rights, better pay, holidays, the usual. The speaker was from the Socialist Party, but over the last few weeks he'd heard a Labor Party speaker, a Communist, trade unionists, and various self-proclaimed revolutionary anarchists. They all banged on about the same things, with varying degrees of anger. Not that he disagreed with what they said, it was just cloud-cuckoo in his experience. What employer's going to give the workers two weeks off a year? There's plenty of people out of work who want in, Wiggins knew, and so the bosses always get to choose.

"They are scared of police," Peter said. "But there is no need to be afraid, they don't have guns. So we come here, we help, we show people how to fight."

Wiggins eyed the ranks of bobbies lining the park.

"The police hate us. They are paid by the government, they hate anything that threatens change," Peter went on. They jostled through the demonstrators, keeping Park Lane to their right as they moved forward.

"Where are the others?" Wiggins looked around.

"Ha! Don't worry."

A new speaker ascended the small stage. He made some crack about Eton boys running the government like a school canteen. Laughter broke out, verging on hysteria, like a booze-soaked music hall halfway through the last house. Wiggins glanced again at the police cordon. "Did your lot shoot that copper up Tottenham way?"

Peter shrugged.

"Arlekin probably, I don't know. There are many plans. We need money to do our work. Arlekin directs us."

The crowd surged forward. Wiggins held his breath. "What's he like?" he tried, thinking of the boot marks in the cottage.

Peter grinned. "You will see, my friend, soon. You are like hungry bear."

Wiggins pushed up on his tiptoes and glanced back. Flags and banners fluttered like sails, red and yellow, bearing pictures of hammers and miners and mills and a star or cross, even a steam train.

"Where's our banner?"

Peter smiled but said nothing.

"What do the red stars mean?" Wiggins probed, emboldened by the crowd.

Peter nodded. "The star can be symbol. A movement, a brotherhood. But don't ask Yakov. Too many questions, he'll stab you in your liver."

"He owes me, cos of Mikhail."

"Sure, but you never heard of an unpaid debt?" Peter shook his head. "You, a bailiff."

But I believe in paying my debts, Wiggins did not say. He thought of Bill lying dead on the hard frozen earth of Tottenham. Arlekin must be the mastermind behind the Tottenham job. Peter, he knew, dabbled in more than demonstrations—you don't carry a Mauser for nothing. But Peter took his orders from Arlekin. Even when Yakov, Peter, and the others spoke in Russian, Wiggins could hear the respect in their voices, the reverence for this man Arlekin. He was the man Wiggins had to find. And kill.

He'd killed men before, on the battlefield, in fear and anger and confusion. And then there was the other thing. It was a different matter with time on his hands and nerves and calculation. But death had stalked him all his life. And if he couldn't kill for Bill, what could he do?

"Look at them. British," Peter sneered. "How well behaved you are. Your government bleeds you dry for order and empire, and no one creates trouble, no one fights, in name also of order. Workers die in factories, poisoned or maimed, servants wait on masters for little more than a meal. My friend Nikolai, he is mad now because of where he worked. And yet, everyone accepts."

Wiggins said nothing as the Russian went on. "Powerful men will always hold on to power and call it by any name they can—order, history, country—anything but chaos, they say. But it is power they want. All their silly schools and their silly games."

"Don't knock cricket," Wiggins said.

"I do not know this game, so maybe I am wrong, but for rest I speak truly. You British can fight but only for order. You don't fight real enemies—you fight poor in India, in Africa, everywhere. You need to fight at home. Look." He swept his hand toward the growing numbers of policemen. "Back home, we don't fight because they shoot us, but your police have no guns. That is why we are here. This is what Arlekin wants. Me, Yakov, this is what we do."

"So more of us should be like Yakov?"

Peter snorted. "Bloody British. Never serious. You people rule world." He shook his head.

"Where is Yakov anyway?"

"He is near," Peter said. "Stay close." The crowd moved again and the atmosphere shifted. The police linked arms. A shout rang out, then another, and soon the mob swayed.

"Now!" Peter broke clear and ran toward the police. He flung a stone at the line. Then Yakov appeared from the throng and threw a brick. More Russians emerged to fling missiles at the police. Yakov showed himself again, carrying a flaming bottle. He tossed it into the uniformed line. As the cops split apart, the bottle smashed in a stunning fireball. Wiggins saw shock, fear, then rage in the faces of the policemen.

They held for a moment, and then in a single charge they broke toward the rabble, truncheons drawn. Wiggins drove his fist into the face of the first copper he encountered, who was bearing down on Peter. A battle of fists and boots, of stray rocks and flagpoles, ensued. The peal of panicked police whistles broke the air. Wiggins felt his blood pump fast and, despite fighting the police, his heart surged in excitement and a strange kind of release. He took a strike to his arm and a kick to the shins but he felt ten years younger. All around him ragged, malnourished demonstrators fought with all they had. One swung a discarded police helmet around his head, a makeshift mace.

Wiggins saw Yakov gesture at Peter.

"Come." Peter grabbed Wiggins by the arm. "We must go. Horses will be here soon. Our work is done."

Five of them—Wiggins, Yakov, Peter, and two others—ran across Park Lane and through Mayfair toward Curzon Street. Peter laughed as they slowed down, out of view. "*Ura!*" he shouted, and then turned to Wiggins. "Success."

"What was in that bottle?"

"Vodka."

"Smart."

"Yakov's," Peter said as they hurried toward Shepherd Market. "When you have chaos in your heart, you can create chaos around you."

A shrill whistle cut through the air. Up ahead, a phalanx of policemen appeared. They spread out across the street as they grew closer, reinforcements destined for Hyde Park.

Wiggins gestured to an alley on the right. "Cut down there, quick. It'll take you to Green Park."

Yakov and his friends jumped to it, but Peter hesitated as the police approached. "I'll be all right," Wiggins shouted. "I'm ex-army. Run."

Peter grinned. "Sambrook Street, when you're out. Arlekin will thank you. We have plans."

"Go." Wiggins charged at the police, roaring.

As he plunged into the coppers, throwing punches with abandon, he knew he was one step closer to the man behind Bill's death.

"Anything new?"

"A minor riot in Hyde Park yesterday afternoon." Russell jumped up from his desk. "But that's only a rumor."

"Not that—I meant, any calls?" Kell snapped.

"Nothing, sir. Are we expecting news? Will we redeploy?"

Kell glared at the fool before him but did not reply. He slammed the door and dropped into his chair. The vehicle-registration people had failed to get back to him. It was all very well legislating a system of registration—the fuss it had kicked up at the time, he remembered, the attack on freedom—but if no one could find the files, then what was the point? Freedom reigned through incompetence. The story of the British Empire, he thought as he regarded a new pile of memoranda.

"*When will we hear news of German activity?*" "*Where is the proof?*" "*Cabinet loath to commit money.*" "*Anxious to see progress.*" The phrases repeated until Kell spotted a new one. "*Many other officers willing to undertake such work, if it is deemed necessary.*" If it wasn't bad enough to be run off the road and have his house under police guard, they were now threatening him with the sack. And all because he couldn't find an enemy to justify increasing the resources—resources needed to find and root out that very enemy in the first place. He threw the papers down in exasperation.

"I'm going out," he growled as he left the office.

"Where, sir? Perhaps I can help," Russell called out, but Kell had already gone.

"I'm interested in taking a set for the summer."

"Indeed, sir. Always nice to meet a new gentleman. Unmarried, I take it?"

Kell nodded.

"It is one of our more, er, popular rules, you understand?" the commissionaire lisped. "Have you visited the Albany before, sir?"

"How many sets do you have empty?"

"Just the three at present, two on the ground and one on the second floor."

"Show me the second, if you could."

"As you wish, sir." The commissionaire disappeared into a back office and returned with a huge garland of black keys. He gestured for Kell to follow him up the stairs. Kell covered his nose as they did so, for the commissionaire let out small gusts of wind from his gigantic backside with each step.

"What of the neighbors on this corridor—who lives here?" Kell pointed. He guessed, from Wiggins's description of the window, that the set they were looking for was two down from the door the commissionaire now opened.

"Ah, well, sir, I can't give you names, I'm afraid—we pride our-selves here at the Albany on our discretion. The gentlemen like to feel they can retain their privacy. This is not a club after all, sir; this is an apartment block."

"Quite," Kell muttered as they stepped into an empty sitting room. "I meant purely the kind of people, you understand? What one might expect from those on either side?" He wandered over to the large sash windows and peered down into the courtyard.

"A careful man, I see that, sir, and wise. This set is distinguished by nobility on one side, and the City on the other." The commission-aire gestured with his head each way.

"And beyond that?"

"Over there is a musical gentleman, puts on concerts and the like—very high class, so I'm led to believe."

"Oh no," Kell groaned theatrically. "I can't abide noise. Especially *music*."

"Don't worry yourself on that account, sir, for he does not play. He is the organizer, the promoter of concerts, not a musician. And he is often away on the Continent and such. He is in Brussels as we speak, I believe, and not due back until Monday."

Kell looked out of the window once more. "I suppose when one lives in London, one must put up with all sorts. What should I do if I want to take them?"

"You must write to the committee, sir, with references and the like, care of here."

"I will think on it. I once knew a chap who ran an orchestra and said he lived here, I wonder is it him? Very big man, enormous hands."

"Not him, sir, no indeed. The monsieur is a fine, delicate fellow."

Kell raced back to his office. Ignoring Russell, he squeezed the door shut, wound the telephone, and shouted into the horn: "Get me the classified desk at the *Evening Star*." He rat-tatted his hand on the desk—they had him! The music promoter must be the gentleman Wiggins saw in the car with Milton's killer; he matched the description. And he wasn't home until Monday, time enough to gather evidence, to break—

The door burst open and Ewart strode in.

"What's the meaning of this?" He waved a piece of paper in Kell's direction. "A message from Scotland Yard."

Kell stood up. "Sir?"

"You're bringing shame on the department, Captain Kell." Ewart didn't hide his irritation. "First some cock and bull story about a road accident in Hampshire, then a new body in the Thames, and now this?"

"What, sir? The body I've explained. If anything, it shows the efficacy of our work, not—"

"You are skating on ice, thin, thin ice. The Commissioner is hounding me for more information on the body—he thinks it's some lower-class robbery, so the devil knows why you're interested—and now there's trouble at Curzon Street Police Station that is apparently connected with you."

"Curzon Street?"

"Yes, sir." Russell appeared at Ewart's elbow. "A call from the Deputy Commissioner came through. I did try to tell you, but you said you were busy."

"Luckily Russell had the presence of mind to put it through to me. Where's my German intelligence, Kell? I want hard facts, not flimflam—did you follow up on the note about the cyclist?"

"An academic, sir, cursing in German to avoid offense—not, I think, a spy."

"I'm not sure how much I care for what you think, Captain. Russell, how about you?"

"Well, er, perhaps on this occasion Captain Kell has a point, sir."

Ewart tossed the note on the desk. "Very well. But you're hanging by a thread, Captain. This can't go on forever. The Ministry is full of able men."

When he was gone, Kell glared at Russell. "Thank you for your unqualified support, Lieutenant."

"What's happening at Curzon Street, sir, is it an operation?"

Kell swiped the telephone message from the desk. "How the hell should I know?"

"You came in the back?"

"Why did I have to?"

"I don't want to blow my cover."

"You called me, remember." Kell looked for a place to sit but there was none. Wiggins sat hunched on the police-cell bunk, gently touching a blossoming black eye. "What happened?"

"Best not say." Wiggins coughed. "I need you to get me out."

"Is that the only reason?"

To Kell's surprise, Wiggins laughed. "There speaks a man who's never been in stir. We're doing all right."

"You think? I have two agents dead, a policeman on my doorstep, and my only agent in the field's in a police cell. I'm about to lose my job, at best, and at worst some unknown foe will attack me and my wife."

"Steady on, sir." Wiggins stood up and raised a hand, though he didn't touch his boss. "What about the Albany? The registration number?"

Kell let out his cheeks, avoided eye contact, and gathered himself. "That's why I am here."

Wiggins smiled. "I thought you were here to get me out."

"I haven't decided about that yet. Something about your manner seems to suggest you rather belong here. Anyway, the point is we have to break into the Albany."

"What?"

"Tonight."

"You traced the car?"

"No. Look, the vehicle-registration service is new . . ."

"That's jam, that is."

"Never mind. My point is we know the set—you're sure of which window went dark?" Kell outlined his conversation with the commissionaire at the Albany. "Simple. We break in as soon as possible, find out what we need."

Wiggins sighed. "What about the cops?"

"But there's no evidence. I can't get a warrant, and we don't want to expose you. You're a secret agent, remember? If we put you into the open, that's it, forever."

Wiggins sat down again. Kell eyed him carefully. Despite his black eye, this budding agent had a fresher look about him, even after a night in the cell. His hair was shorter, smarter—still too long on top, but the black mop had gone. And his clean shave revealed a surprisingly youthful countenance.

"Why are you so pleased with yourself?" Kell asked.

Wiggins shook his head in mute reply. "Can't do tonight."

"Can't? You work for me."

"Saturday."

Kell opened his mouth to object, to upbraid his slipshod employee. But what was the point? He needed a happy agent.

"Very well. Tomorrow it is. Come to Hampstead for ten o'clock."

"Best not." Wiggins grinned. "Go to your gaff, I mean."

Kell nodded, despite himself. "I'll send you rendezvous details, the usual way."

"You's the boss. Sir."

They regarded each other for a moment, assessing the truth of this statement. Kell let it go, and pointed to Wiggins's shiner.

"The desk sergeant told me you attacked four of them without provocation."

"There was six," Wiggins said matter-of-fact. "And they was all armed with bloody great truncheons."

Kell pulled from his pocket a small square of felt and began polishing his spectacles. "The police say you were part of a violent mob in Hyde Park."

"It was a demonstration—ain't you read the papers?"

"It certainly won't be in the papers. You don't think the government allows them to print such things?" He put his glasses back on. "I should ask you what the hell you were doing, fighting with the police."

"You should . . ."

Kell hesitated, shrugged, then rapped on the cell door. "Now, I have permission to walk you out the back door, where I suggest we go our separate ways."

"Nah, you go out the back—I'll take the front. If anyone's watching, they'll think the cops let me go fair and square."

"Who would be watching *you*?" Kell asked.

"Can't be too careful." Wiggins winked with his good eye.

Kell shrugged, gave a curt nod to the constable holding open the cell door, and ushered Wiggins into the corridor. "Please, do not make any insolent remarks to the desk sergeant on your way out. My relationship with the police commissioner is not what it could be."

"Right you are, skip." Wiggins tipped his forelock.

Kell waited in the corridor as Wiggins tapped up the stairs to the exit. A moment later he heard the sergeant bellow, "You cheeky swine, I'll have your guts." Kell sighed as he made his way up.

"What did he say?" he asked the red-faced policeman.

"He didn't *say* anything, sir, he mooned me. Next time he's in here, he's not coming out in anything other than the wagon. Blasted cheek."

14

"Come up in five minutes. Or I'll kill you here and now. I don't care," Vincas whispered in her ear. His breath stank of cheap spirits. Bela nodded and turned away. She'd been lying down in steerage, feigning sleep among the other lower-class passengers, hiding. But he had found her. "Go through that door, there's a quiet space on deck. I bribed the steward." He made to stand up but then leaned close. "I know you hate me. But you fuck great. Why else do you think I brought you along?" He pushed himself vertical and stumbled away.

Bela let out a breath. She kept her eyes down. The huge cabin contained a hundred or so new immigrants, wrapped up against the cold, huddled for warmth. No one around her said anything. They all knew men like Vincas. Dim lanterns swung from the ceiling, shadows danced. She stood up, unsteady against the rolling of the ship, and teetered toward the door. An older woman, lined face squeezed tight by a headscarf, watched her as she left.

Vincas had escaped the Okhrana. Or rather, due to Marinsky's contacts and money, he'd been temporarily released—long enough to skip the country. "We must go," he hissed as he came through the door. "What are you doing in here?"

Bela had leapt back to the table when she heard the noise. She sat down just in time, her efforts to take Marinsky's gold almost discovered. "I couldn't sleep," she muttered. "We are worried."

Old Marinsky cried out upstairs and they heard him come down.

"It doesn't matter." Vincas placed a lantern on the table. "Father," he said. "We must go—they've let me out, but I'm sure they'll be back." He scrambled in one of the cupboards and pulled free a bottle. "God I'm thirsty."

"Vincas. It worked for the moment," Marinsky said. "But I stay. The business, the money."

"They will come for me. I'll follow Arvo."

Bela sat still, her mind abuzz. The chance of escape blown in an instant—there was no way she could flee now, steal Marinsky's money, or get to the coast. Yet, suddenly, this other chance to reach her goal—if Vincas were going to Arvo, to America, that meant he would be going to Sarah, too.

Marinsky knelt down in the hearth. "Take this, you'll need it for the passage." He pulled free the bricks and turned toward his son with a handful of gold coins and a roll of banknotes. Vincas stepped over to his father, hand outstretched. Then he swigged again from the vodka bottle. "How long do you have?" Marinsky went on. "And how are you going to get to the coast at this time of night?"

"I don't know," Vincas snapped.

"I do," Bela said at last.

Together, husband and wife traveled up to Dunava with the Plovs' driver, then caught the boat upriver as Bela had planned for herself. It took them a day and a half to get to Riga. They barely said a word to each other all the way. He didn't question her and she daren't break the silence, in case he asked her why she already had an escape plan. They were bound together—at least, that's what Vincas seemed to want.

At the port he bustled off to buy the tickets. They boarded a shabby, overstuffed, ocean-going steamer. Bela kept quiet and avoided the gaze of the other women, squeezed into steerage with their menfolk. It was only once they were well under steam that Bela realized the boat was not America-bound. She overheard two women discussing their relatives in the East End of London.

"Does this not go to New York?" she whispered when Vincas went for a piss.

"You joking? This tip will never make it that far. It's for London."

Bela hissed at Vincas when he returned: "We're on the wrong ship. Are we changing in London?"

"I can't be bothered with America. Arvo's a cocksucker. Anyway, I have friends in London. What? You want us to go to New York? Maybe we should." He looked into her hopeful eyes and laughed. "Then I could fuck your little sister too."

Bela's anger hadn't subsided in the three days since he had crushed her hopes. He'd got hold of some booze from one of the crew and had been drunk for the last twenty-four hours. She picked her way through the slumbering throng to meet Vincas on deck. Either to get fucked or beaten, she could never quite tell—nor could she really decide which was worse. She pushed open the door to the deck and saw her husband lolling against the rail.

"Wife," he shouted. "Ready to fuck?"

* * *

"Christ," Wiggins gasped. "That hurt."

"Don't be baby," Bela said. She examined his black eye with her hands. The blue-black had begun to give way to a greeny-purple in the twenty-four hours since the riot. She held her mouth firm. "Who did this?"

They sat on a public bench in Aldgate Station. Well-dressed gents strutted past and pigeons hopped between the scissoring legs, looking to score a feed. Wiggins enjoyed her fingertips on his face. He closed his eyes. His mother once caressed him in such a way before they were taken to the bone shop. An army nurse in Bloemfontein had cradled his head after his eardrum shattered on the veldt.

"It's nothing," he said.

She held his chin between thumb and forefinger. "Nothing? Only now you have nothing to say?"

"An argument with a copper is all. Don't worry, they let me go when they found out I used to be in the gunners—I got lucky."

Good liars almost always told the truth. You could get people to swallow anything if you seasoned it with facts. He needed to sell the same porky to Peter. It didn't come easy, lying to Bela, but he had no choice.

Instinctively he took her hand in his. "It really don't hurt," he said truthfully. "Not now. Let's get out of here."

They sat pressed up against each other on the Underground train. He kept her hand in his. Wiggins noticed odd looks and whispers from their fellow passengers. At first he thought it was his black eye, but they were talking about Bela's birthmark. Bela held her head high and seemed oblivious to the remarks but Wiggins was not. He grew angrier as the journey went on. As they approached Wood Lane Station, he heard a stifled giggle from across the aisle. He glared at the two women with such ferocity they clammed up. At the station, Wiggins led Bela to the platform. The two women exited the train behind them.

Wiggins paused, then turned back. "Yes, your fella *is* courting another woman, which don't surprise me. As for you, you'll never get a teaching job again unless you learn to count properly. Enjoy the Exhibition."

He took Bela's hand and walked her up the platform, leaving a stunned silence in their wake.

"How do you know these things?" Bela whispered.

"Lucky guess," Wiggins replied. "But if you was engaged to a bloke, why would you be going to the Imperial Exhibition with someone else on your half-day? She nearly ripped off that ring, worrying it."

"What about the teacher—with no job?"

"It's a school day, Bel—if she had a job she'd be doing it, and not carrying around a book of simple numbers and a flyer from the Wilkins Paget Bureau."

Wood Lane teemed with pleasure-seekers, young couples arm in arm, pensioners, and threes and fours of men and women heading to the Exhibition. And tourists too, clutching their Thomas Cook guidebooks. Wiggins stopped at a poster. It advertised a forthcoming fireworks display to celebrate the thirtieth anniversary of the defeat of the Zulus. Wiggins nodded at the image. "They had spears and we had Lee-Enfields." A dark blue woolen hat appeared in his peripheral vision. Odd for a hot day. Had he seen the same hat at Aldgate?

She put her hand on his arm and he shook his head. "Sorry." He smiled. "Miles away."

They entered the Exhibition. Pavilions of white alabaster with curlicue peaks and peeling plaster rose up against the blue sky. A great steel V-shaped contraption loomed over the pleasure gardens, its two prongs oscillating down to the ground and back up again, a viewing platform at each end. Who could be following *him*? Or were they following Bela?

"There's the Flip-Flap," Wiggins pointed, consulting the program, a guide to the Great White City. "This Exhibition is in 'honor of the Triple Entente.' Russia, Britain, and France are all pals now, so that's all right then."

"What about Latvia?"

"Sorry, love, there ain't no Latvian exhibit."

Bela took his hand again. "Well, Britain and Latvia can still be friends, no?"

They walked past exhibits from Austria, China, Denmark, Italy, Holland, and even Persia. "All these countries. Have you been to them?" Bela asked.

"Gibraltar, I've been to. That's just a bloody great rock. And South Africa in the war, but that's nothing like these gaffs. Mind you, I reckon none of these places are like this. Look at that model Chinaman—he don't look like no human being I've ever seen, not even down Limehouse."

"Do you never want to go somewhere else?"

"Holidays?"

"No, to live."

"Leave London? You must be up the pole."

Bela pulled him close as they strolled. Every now and then Wiggins caught her looking at him thoughtfully. They came upon the Russian exhibit, where Bela started giggling and couldn't stop. Four waxwork figures were arranged around a fire, while in the background stood hay bales, sickles, and a painted wooden cow.

"What is it?" Wiggins asked, before breaking into laughter himself.

"This is not Russia," she said. "It is, how you say, a joke."

Wiggins looked back at the diorama as Bela giggled. He thought of Peter and Yakov and the straggly beards of the drinking den. That was the Russia he knew. He was due back at Sambrook Street that week for more tea and vodka.

"Here, do you want an ice?"

"No," Bela said firmly. "I want to go on Vibbly-Vobbly."

Wiggins hadn't asked Bela much about her past. She shied away from questions, and he didn't have the knack of easy talk. He hadn't even asked her age. Mid to late twenties, he thought. But when they got on the ride, he saw what she must have looked like as a girl. Her face bunched up, she screamed, laughed, and bubbled as she clasped him. The contraption spun them around and up and down like a ship off the Cape.

Joy spread across Bela's face, but Wiggins reached out for her hand. "You scared?" she cried, laughing all the harder.

"No, no, it's just . . ." The ride lurched again, dropping Wiggins's stomach into his innards. His knuckles shone white as he gripped the handrail.

When it was over, Wiggins stumbled out onto the walkway, queasy and relieved. "Big strong man," Bela said as she followed after him. "Time for ice cream?"

"You have one," Wiggins said. "Let's get away from that thing. Even looking at it gives me a turn."

Bela laughed. "Men always say they are stronger, bigger, better. Look at you. Big muscles, weak stomach. Only women have the stomach for this life, I think."

"What do you mean?"

"If men had same life as women, I think the world would be different. Men can do as they like, women have to take *responsibility*. Is this the word?"

"I've been taking care of myself since I was seven," Wiggins said.

Bela squeezed his arm. A brazier burned chestnuts nearby, the smoke whirling close. Pleasure-seekers milled and chatted around them. She leaned toward him. "I am sorry. All I mean is—"

"Oi!" Wiggins shouted.

The blue woolen hat flashed off to his left and this time he pushed through the crowd, but the blue hat sprinted clear. Wiggins couldn't see his face, but he kept his eye on the bobbing hat.

"Stop thief!" he cried.

Onlookers fluttered aside. Wiggins gave chase. He sped past the fountain by the gates and into the street outside. Wiggins shouted out again but it was no use. He lost him in the confusion of the ticket queue. A huge after-work crowd pressed out into the street. At least suspicion had firmed into fact. He *was* being followed.

He went back for Bela, heart racing. She was nowhere to be found. He pushed past lolling ladies and guffawing swells, the chatter and laughter pressing in. A throng surrounded the French exhibit and marveled at the Dahomey warriors as they glistened dark against the waning early evening light. Wiggins cursed again.

"Hey." Bela pulled him around. "You forget me?"

"No, no, sorry. I . . . where did you go? I was looking for you."

"Where did *you* go? You run."

Wiggins shook his head. "I thought I recognized someone, but I was wrong. Sorry."

Bela searched his face but didn't speak for a moment, holding her hand on his chest. Wiggins tried to smile. He couldn't be angry for long, not with her so close, her lemons and laundry-soap smell all mixed up. "We go," she said softly. "I want tea."

"You're turning English."

"And then you have work, yes? We go back east—I don't like West London."

"Nor me, love. Wall-to-wall tossers from Sloane Square to Ealing Common. But I ain't working, not when I've got you to myself."

"You must." Bela looked at him sharply. "You have good job, don't miss it for me."

Wiggins's heart swelled at the concern on her face. "I'd miss anything for you. But I'm not on shift tonight. I won't be missing anything."

She nodded. "We go to Is-ling-town?"

"Too right."

They snuggled close on the train back, cocooned against the afternoon crush. Wiggins breathed her in. Outside the Angel, he bought a copy of the *Evening Star* and scanned the classifieds as they walked home.

He tossed the paper away when they reached his door.

"Tory rag," he muttered.

But he'd got what he needed.

Kell had advertised.

Kell hurried toward Berkeley Square. He'd paid the cab at Marble Arch, still thick with traffic even at this late hour, but the side streets were graveyard quiet. Kell felt his collar, itching in the heat. His shirt clung to his back and the air smelled of horse dung—the Mayfair mamas still insisted on horse carriages and it made the place stink. He'd told Wiggins to meet at ten fifteen on the dot. If Wiggins failed to show, Kell was to take a turn around the square and arrive again fifteen minutes later, and so on.

He glanced up Hill Street as he walked around the square, saw no one besides an old beggar and a bedraggled costermonger on his way home. He turned his eyes up at the gently rustling plane trees. For a moment, he thought himself back in Norfolk, a rural, unhurried quiet, a simpler life—no spies, no Empire to save, no unsolved murders. Should he go back, for his children, for Constance, back to that—

"Oi! Get orff me, you fat bastard. Ow!"

Twenty yards behind, under a street lamp, the old beggar had hold of a boy. "I'll call the rozzers," the boy screamed.

"I say, you there!" Kell ran toward them. "Unhand that boy now, do you hear? I'll take my stick to you." Kell held up his weapon.

"That you won't, sir." The beggar straightened from a stoop and revealed his face.

"Wiggins!" Kell cried.

Wiggins held the boy up tightly by the neck.

"Meet your latest tail."

"I ain't no tail," the boy cried. "Honest, mister. This ponce just nabbed me. OW!"

"Are you sure?" Kell ignored the boy.

"Eggs is eggs."

"What's your name?"

Tight red curls visible beneath his cap, the boy twisted and struggled against Wiggins's grip.

"Jax," he said. "Police!" he screamed. "Let me go."

Wiggins put the boy down, but only to tie his hands behind his back. "Shut your cakehole or I'll stuff it. We don't have time for this, sir."

"The police."

"West End Central?"

"We can hardly take him to Curzon Street, can we?"

Wiggins grunted and cuffed the boy once more. Kell went on: "My credit is pretty low, but I'm sure they'll look after him for a couple of hours."

"What's the charge, eh? I know my rights. What's the charge?"

Kell looked closely at the boy. The lamp hissed. He must be very young, Kell thought. No facial hair, and big brown freckles splashed across his cheeks. The enemy stooped low.

"We are not arresting you. We are going to put you in a police cell at West End Central, Savile Row. For your own safety, I might add. You will say nothing until we return. We will not harm you."

"Unless . . ." Wiggins said.

"Quite."

"So young."

"There's plenty younger," Wiggins said.

Something about the boy didn't sit right. He was Kell's tail, no question, but also uncannily familiar. Had they met before? Wiggins wondered. He shook the thought from his mind as he and Kell hustled down Savile Row. "You ready to break the law, sir?"

"Don't say that."

"It's you that's got us housebreaking by night, sir."

"Shush, here we are."

They arrived at the antiques shop. Kell kept watch as Wiggins clambered onto the roof and then dropped into the narrow courtyard of the Albany's main building. Despite the electric light, it was shadowy enough that he could get to work. He looked up and could just make out a small ledge in the brickwork that ran along the building, two feet or so below the windows.

Off to his left, a door swung open and he heard the start of an argument.

"I say, old man, you can't be serious."

Wiggins slunk behind a line of potted bay trees. Two gentlemen strolled toward him. A rakish fellow tapped his stick on the flagstone while a larger lummox ambled by his side, protesting.

"Why not?" the friend said. "We've pulled it off before, Bunny, we can do it again."

"But dash it all, what if we get caught—Mackenzie suspects, I'm sure of it."

"You leave Mackenzie to me," the man chuckled. "Have you lost your nerve?"

Their voices receded as they crossed the courtyard and left through the Albany's exit onto Vigo Street. Two toffs out on the town, Wiggins thought idly, except the way they carried themselves wasn't happy-go-lucky. He dismissed the thought. Two fewer tenants to worry about was all.

Wiggins looked up again, picking out a climb. He reached up into a small recess that extended up one side of the building's face and began to lever himself skywards. Propped into the right angle, he jammed his feet sideways and used his hands to scramble up the brickwork. He hoped Kell wouldn't give the game away trying to divert the doorman.

He prayed too that it wouldn't rain.

His hands slipped and gripped again. The soles of his boots stuck firm, though, and finally he reached the small ledge that ran the length of the building, eight inches wide at most. He straightened, his back to the wall, and took a breath, then edged himself along. Five unlit windows lay between him and the apartment. His toes hung over the edge, his heels bumped against the brickwork. He stepped past the first window ledge without problem, then the second and the third.

Where had he met Jax before?

As he approached the next window, the sash rattled but he kept his balance, paused, then resumed his steady shuffle.

An electric light went on. Wiggins startled, caught in the glare. His foot slipped, and then he was gone.

"I thought you'd come again, sir. You've got the look."

"The look?"

"Of a tenant, sir," the doorman said. "One of my gentlemen. Do you mind letting yourself in? I'm rushed busy here, sir."

Kell grasped at the key ring. "Of course." He left the doorman to his dinner.

As he walked down the wide corridor, Kell kept an eye on the door to their target's apartment. Was Wiggins already inside? He could hear nothing. Should he try the lock? No, best leave it to Wiggins. He entered the empty set he was meant to be viewing and switched on the electric light.

"Good God!" he cried, as a figure dropped from view past the window.

He pulled up the sash and thrust out his hand.

"Here. Quick."

Wiggins, dangling from the window ledge, clung on with his spare hand. Kell yanked him into the room.

"Christ," Wiggins gasped. "I near crapped my strides."

Kell coughed. "Thankfully not. You must hurry," he went on, unconcerned. "It's one window over. And let me in—the two of us together can search more quickly."

Wiggins clambered back out of the window and a minute later he opened the set door to Kell. Kell looked on, fascinated as Wiggins stared very intently at the objects in the room at lightning pace, muttering under his breath as he did so. He let out a high whistle and handed Kell a small, lozenge-shaped metal implement.

"Watch it," he cautioned.

Kell pressed a latch on the side and a sharp, thin blade sprung out.

"Knuckle knife," Wiggins said. "Nasty."

Kell then found a revolver, a collar studded on the inside with glass shards, and some particularly long needles. He didn't want to speculate about their use.

"Anything else?" he asked. He didn't mention the collection of pornographic photographs, though Wiggins raised his eyebrows when he saw them.

"Frenchman, or Belgian maybe. Thirties. This ain't his only residence. Waxes his mustache. Expensive tastes. Musician, or at least a follower. Cocaine man. Ladies' man."

"Anything incriminating other than these . . ." he searched for the word ". . . implements?"

Wiggins shrugged. "Try the mantelpiece."

Kell pulled out a shaft of papers from behind the clock. They were on the trail of a blasted Frenchman; the man didn't even have the decency to be German. What were the French doing sending men into Woolwich?

"Ah ha!" Kell cried, holding up a letter. "Our man is named LeQuin. Monsieur René LeQuin. Where have I heard that before?"

"We should skip," Wiggins said.

He reached a hand behind an unhung painting on the floor for one last look. "Here. He's got invitations here from all sorts."

Kell scanned them. "This is every embassy in town: France, Turkey, the Dutch."

"He's a boy, ain't he." Wiggins whistled softly.

"I must hand these back to the porter," Kell said, rattling the keys at the door. "I'll meet you back at Savile Row in twenty minutes."

* * *

"He's an agent then, agreed?" Kell said as they strode back to West End Central.

"Spies. Mr. Holmes used to have a list. Buying and selling secrets."

"But there was nothing there, no documents, no money even."

"Like I said, he's got another gaff, ain't he."

Kell clicked his tongue. "Maybe this boy can tell us more. You are sure he was following me?"

"Eggs."

They entered the police station and Kell nodded at the desk sergeant. "We are here to talk to our guest."

"Yes, sir." The sergeant automatically dipped his head and led them to the cells. "I must say, sir, that we are not used to this kind of behavior. We must arrest him soon, you know."

"I take full responsibility."

"All the same, sir, this is highly irregular."

"Say that again," Wiggins said.

The sergeant looked at Kell, then back at Wiggins. "It's highly unusual, holding without charge. Irregular."

"That's it." Wiggins clicked his fingers.

"What?" Kell said, as the cell door swung open.

"Oi, Copper," the boy shouted, shrill. "These ain't nothing but a couple of Oscars. It's illegal so it is. Let me go. There ain't no charge."

The cell door shut and Kell turned to the boy. "Listen here. What were you doing following me? And who do you work for?"

"It'll cost ya." The boy slumped against the wall, glowering.

Wiggins kept quiet, but examined the boy anew, the red curls, the upturned nose. It *had* to be.

"It will cost *you*, boy, if you do not give adequate responses to my questions. I will have you arrested, properly, and you will be sent to prison. I have that power. Now, if you please." Kell tapped his foot, obviously unused to disobedient youths.

Jax crossed his arms. But Wiggins could see the fear in his eyes. "No sauce," he said. "If you're straight, we're straight. French fella was it, told you to follow the gentleman—big mustache?"

"Nah." Jax looked at Wiggins. "No beard neither. Big bloke he is. Down the Cheese we call him the Big Apple cos of his Adam's." Jax pointed below his chin. "Anyways. I'm a runner, ain't I, for the papers and that. We all's hang outside the Cheese waiting for work."

"The Cheese?" Kell asked.

"The Cheshire Cheese, sir, a pub in Fleet Street."

"Who's this?" Jax gestured at Kell. "Tourist? Are. You. Not. From. Round. Here?"

"He's a very important gentleman, who has your life in his hands. So shut it. What's the Big Apple's name? Where's he from?"

Jax sniffed. "Dutch or German, something like that. Talks like he's about to spit in your face. Said his name was Rijkard."

"He pays you to follow me."

"You's sharper than a box of knives, ain't you? Is he your boss? Good luck with that. Yeah, I's to follow you in the day, home-office-home and anywheres in between. A general a day he gives me. That's all I know. Turned up at the pub a couple of weeks back. Hires me on the spot. He pays on time, so why wouldn't I? I ain't done nothing wrong. It's a free country."

"How'd you parlay vous?" Wiggins asked, glancing at Kell.

"A box at Charing Cross post office. I got my letters, see. It's open all night—in case you didn't know that, guv." Jax bowed deeply toward Kell.

"I knew that," Kell snapped. "Right. Enough of this nonsense. You'll be spending the rest of the night here, young man, and I imagine a lot longer than that. We can find a suitable institution for you, I'm sure."

"You can't do that; I ain't done nothing."

"Hold on, sir."

"He's been consorting with the enemy."

Wiggins pulled his boss out into the corridor. "Give me the night with him, sir. I can turn him. What if he worked for us, while still working for them? We could lure this Rijkard into a trap. If Jax fails to report, they'll know something's wrong."

"Hang it all, Wiggins, I can't just let him go."

Wiggins held his finger up, *wait there*, then dipped his head back into the cell. "Jax, your ma still living?"

"She's taken," Jax spat back.

Wiggins grinned.

He ducked back out. "I'll take him, sir. I'll turn him too. Gi' us a couple of shillings and he'll be ours, guaranteed."

Wiggins pushed Jax down the street. "First stop the GPO—you're going to post an all-clear to Rijkard."

"Or what?"

"You know what." Wiggins whistled as they skirted Trafalgar Square. Pigeons flew across the flagstoned expanse and shit on Nelson, while a policeman shouted vainly at the early-morning taxis.

Wiggins stood over Jax in the post office as he etched out his note. None of the clerks in the great echoing hall of the GPO saw anything odd in these two shambling specimens. The post office clanked and sang, gearing up for another big morning.

"Let's see your ma."

"Wot for? I don't know where she is, anyway."

"Take me to your mother," Wiggins repeated, his arm on Jax's shoulder. "Otherwise it's chokey."

The boy shrugged. "What do I care?"

They made their way across the river on the footbridge at Charing Cross. Morning shadows appeared, the sun tipped the top of St. Paul's in the distance, and Wiggins felt the tiredness suddenly prickle his eyes. He wasn't fifteen anymore. Once past Waterloo, they took a right into the shadowed backstreets south of the station.

"In there." Jax gestured half-heartedly at a green hut that stood at the crossroads.

Motor taxis and horse-drawn cabs crowded around the hut; the drivers called and joked. A furious cloud rose from a snub chimney.

"She's a cabbie?" Wiggins asked, surprised.

"Nah, she's the char."

Just then, a woman came out of the back door of the hut and threw a bucket of slops into the gutter. She looked up.

"Jax, my girl, where the hell have you been?"

"Girl?" Wiggins said, astonished.

"And what the . . . ?" The woman peered across at them.

Pink-cheeked, curly red hair, harassed, she was the living spit of her daughter (give or take a couple of stone). She held the large empty bucket in two hands, her face stern.

"Wiggins," she cried. "As I live and breathe."

"Hello, Sal."

15

Wiggins picked his way through the ill-lit side streets of Whitecha-pel. Ripper territory in the old days. One case Mr. Holmes never managed to crack, or at least never admitted to cracking.

"You must accept it, Wiggins," said the Grand Old Man (that's what the Irregulars called the great detective, though not to his face, mind). "Sometimes there simply isn't enough data."

"But Mr. Holmes, the Ripper's—"

"The Ripper's mad," Holmes snapped.

Touched a nerve. Wiggins didn't tell the others. It didn't do to question God.

Wiggins had finally made it back to Sambrook Street. He craned his neck but could see nothing through the tea shop windows. Less than a month earlier, he and Yakov had fought on the floor but now it had been cleaned out. An upturned table, a solitary chair, not even a chessboard. He felt a chill on his neck.

All his work with Peter, the riot in Hyde Park, even the batty-fanging he took from the peelers, all for nothing. It was the only address he had. Wind whistled in the high gables above.

A hand grasped his shoulder. Wiggins swiveled, arms raised, ready for the fight.

"No, no! Please. Viggins?" A small man stepped into the light, his head bent toward the ground, hands out wide.

Wiggins nodded. "Who are you?" The man tugged at his huge beard and beckoned into the darkness.

Through the cave-dark alleys, the man never slowed, only turn-ing to signal him on, half in apology, half in exhortation. Wiggins kept his eyes on the back of the bearded man's head as it ducked and weaved. Anxiety ebbed and flowed within him, at its height when they picked their way over shit-stench drains and fly hives, only to fall away when they crossed Whitechapel or Mile End or some other road he recognized.

Eventually, in the darkest, foulest alleyway yet, the man stopped at a small wooden door and rapped three times, waited, and rapped again. The door sprung open. A second man gestured them inward and they stepped through an anteroom lit by a single candle.

"Viggins," his guide said as he pushed open another door and thrust Wiggins through.

It was Yakov. Instinctively, Wiggins's hand went to the cosh in his pocket. Yakov had a blade. Were they going to fight it out, now and for all? Was this a trap? He cursed, jutted out his chin.

"Wiggins," Peter cried.

He sat at a table in the corner, half obscured by the open door.

"I knew you'd come." He got up and thrust out his hand. "I have vodka. For champion of Hyde Park, ha ha. That is a good wound, your eye, a brave wound."

Wiggins glanced back quickly at Yakov, at Peter, and smiled. He relaxed his hands. Peter poured two glasses as Yakov sloped across the room.

"Yakov, he said you would not come, but you have a strong heart. If the lion fights once, he fights again, no? That is why I sent Malev to wait. Help yourself to lemon sherberts." He popped one of the little yellow sweets into his mouth. "This is wonderful. How did you escape police?"

Peter smiled at Wiggins but his eyes stayed hard and steady. Yakov sat hunched at the only other table and picked at his finger-nails with a short knife. The lamps hissed. Wiggins gulped down his vodka. "They let me go," he said.

Peter showed no surprise. "Why?"

Wiggins took his time. Yakov stared openly at him; his knife clattered onto the table. "I'm British Army. The desk sergeant was a veteran. Half the force are too. Spun him some war stories, Ladysmith,

Bloemfontein. They held me for the night and let me go. I walked straight out the front door, didn't I."

Peter glanced quickly at Yakov. Then he slapped his hand on the table. "Ha ha ha! Yakov, you see, I told you." He followed this with a burst of Russian and more laughter. "Yakov, he is so suspicious. He went back. He waited by the police station and he sees you come out the front door, easy."

This Wiggins knew. He'd come out of Curzon Street nick the morning Kell had him released. Yakov made the single biggest mistake when tailing someone—he moved too quickly. If he'd stayed still, Wiggins might never have seen him, even though he was looking out for someone. But Yakov had ducked away around a corner and it was the flash of sudden movement that caught Wiggins's attention.

Running a tail was the most important job the Irregulars ever did. Wiggins and Sal trained the new recruits on the streets of Soho and Fitzrovia before letting them loose on Victoria Station, the big one.

"You'll never catch me," Wiggins would taunt the new kids, goading them on.

"Balls," Sal countered.

She coached the little ones. "Mind his shoes, trouser knees, and his hat. Always keep eyes on the hat and the way he walks. He can change the hat, so keep looking, but he can't change his gait for long."

With the knowledge of how to tail someone comes the knowledge of how to avoid it too. When Wiggins came out of Curzon Street nick and saw Yakov in the shadows, he turned down Piccadilly then cut across to Jermyn Street. He doubled back into a gentlemen's outfitters. The shop straddled the whole block and had an exit on both Jermyn and Piccadilly. Wiggins shifted through business, sailing, and motoring wear, then stepped back onto Piccadilly just in time to mount one of the turning buses going west. He knew Yakov would have to pause in the shop—unsure whether Wiggins would have gone upstairs or not—and as the bus pulled away he saw Yakov finally emerge, head twisting from side to side, defeated. Street craft, the boys called it.

Peter crowed from across the table, pointing at Yakov. "This bad Russian man thinks you not come back. He thinks you yellow Englishman. But I think you are a soldier and you are with us."

Yakov shrugged.

"Admit it, you are wrong," Peter went on as he poured more drinks. He gestured Yakov over. The glowering wretch shuffled forward and drained the liquor in one gulp. He nodded at Wiggins.

"You got a nod. For Yakov that is a big hug." Peter shook his head, amused. "He doesn't treat his women this well."

Yakov muttered in Russian and he and Peter exchanged a few more words. Wiggins heard mention once more of Arlekin.

Peter then fixed him with his interrogative stare.

"Did you see newspapers, about Hyde Park—our riot?"

"Nothing."

"Exactly. Your press is like puppy dog to government. They print nothing. They don't even need to make laws, they wink and chuckle and people know nothing. So, Arlekin thinks we need to act bigger, so that no one can ignore. And you can help."

"Can I meet him?"

Peter shifted his focus. "You work at shell factory, yes? We need materials. You can get them for us. It is a plan."

Wiggins tried to recall when he had told Peter about Woolwich—he wasn't sure. That was the problem with getting drunk. Peter looked at him expectantly, but the thought still nagged. Did he mention it, the last time at Sambrook Street?

"A bomb," Peter went on. "This they cannot ignore. Arlekin is counting on you. *I* am counting on you."

Wiggins had known from the first time he met Peter that he was a man who carried a Mauser pistol. Yakov had pulled a knife on him. Fisticuffs was one thing, a bit of rough and tumble with the coppers. That was almost affectionate. A bomb was different. He stared at Peter and thought of Kell—maybe he should bring him in, get these bastards rounded up. But he couldn't tell Kell, Holmes had said, and Kell himself had told him to steer clear. And even if he did go to the police, he wouldn't get justice. Not the kind of justice he craved.

Peter glanced at Yakov and back to Wiggins, urging. "We need your commitment. Show it to me, to our cause."

Wiggins thought of Bill, dead in the ground because of people like this. That was a cause to believe in.

"I like to know who I'm working for. I'd need to meet Arlekin," he said at last.

"Of course, this will happen. Get the materials and you can meet Arlekin. Let us drink to it."

"It ain't that easy, getting in and out of Woolwich with a bag. And it's the death penalty if I get caught."

"You will think of something," Peter intoned. "I saw you at Hyde Park. You are smart, you are quick, you are brave."

Wiggins chewed at his mouth. "Have you got a gun?"

"I don't," Peter replied.

"What are we meant to be blowing up?" Wiggins pushed his cup forward.

"*Da!*" Peter clicked his fine fingers. "I knew it. But I do not know all plan. Only Arlekin knows everything. Now, *Na Zdorovie.*"

Wiggins waited outside Bela's laundry, hoping she was about to finish the late shift. He'd made his excuses to Peter and gone to meet her, his mind awash with vodka and indecision. Could he filch the stuff from Woolwich? Six months previously, he'd been half-heartedly chasing debtors across town, and now he was up to his neck in an East End criminal gang while being paid the King's shilling to tail a spy ring. He rubbed his hands together, breathed in the carbolic-rich steam of the laundry and thought of Milton's gigantic killer, Rijkard; of the young girl Jax; and finally of Sal, his oldest friend.

"What a turn-up," Sal had said that morning. "You're wearing the age, I'll say that, bar the shiner. Still got a lovely barnet, trimmed and all. Very ooh la la. Who's the lucky lass?"

Wiggins helped Sal and Jax prepare breakfast for the cabbies. They served tea and rashers with doorsteps. Afterward, Wiggins pulled Sally aside and gestured silently at Jax. "She's in with a bad crowd, Sal."

"I knew she was running down Fleet Street. But she's nearly fifteen, it ain't my place no more. She's got to make her own way."

"She can work for me."

"You?" Sal cackled. "Make an honest woman of her, will you?"

"It's kosher."

Sally blew on her tea. "Fifteen years and suddenly you turn up in my shop, Jax on your arm, without a by-your-leave. Where did you go?"

Wiggins hesitated, looked toward the young girl. "Army."

"I know that, you dafty, but why didn't you come back, after?"

"It wasn't that I didn't . . ." He looked at his hands. Soot-black dirt filled his fingernails, grime from the Albany's brickwork. "Mary-the-bones, remember?"

"You never could say it right."

"You don't look any different," he said. "Neither does Jax. She's your spit. That's how I knew."

Sally raised her eyebrows, then drained her tea in two great gulps. She pulled a sleeve across her mouth and grinned.

Wiggins gestured at Jax. "Any more?"

"Nah, one's enough."

"Father?"

"Why, you interested in applying for the role? I'm kidding. He's long gone. Swine. Now, I've got to get on." She stood up. "I can't stop Jax working for you—it's legal you say? Not that it ever stopped her. But make sure no harm comes to her, Wiggins. She's my babe. And that salt cellar's not worth ha'penny, so leave it where it is."

"I'm a changed man." Wiggins held up his hands, grinning.

He looked over at young Jax, red curls hanging loose. So like that little girl he used to know who broke him out of St. Cyprian's, who lived with him in the back ways of Paddington all those years ago.

"Jax," he called over and pointed to the bench next to him. "You and me's got to parlay. Matters of import."

"You!" Bela pointed from the laundry doorway. "You never leave me alone."

"I was lonely," he said, pulling her into a kiss. "I could walk you home."

"You don't know where I live."

"True. If you won't tell me, it means you have to come home with me. Right now."

Back in his Islington room, Wiggins gave her a bottle of perfume. A simple gesture, but he'd never got the hang of giving so much as taking. When you had nothing, it was the only way. But now, with her, he wanted to do things differently. He'd even paid for the bottle.

She smiled, dabbed it on her wrist and sniffed—then flicked some in his face. He grabbed her around the midriff and they ended up on the bed, the room pungent with rosewater and almonds, the vodka on his breath, the carbolic on her hands, and the smell of freshly spent sweat. Later, as she lay sleeping, Wiggins traced the outline of her birthmark. Could they make a life together, away from laundries and factories and the East End; away from her unspoken past, her secret present; away from gangs and bomb plots and violent friends; could they speak only of now and what was to come, and not of the shadowed past? And could he tell her what he now did for money? Was it possible, he wondered, to live one life at home and another out on the streets, keeping secrets, risking lives, taking orders from on high?

16

Wiggins gunned the Enfield as they swung down Hampstead High Street, swerving in between the buses. "Are you political, Mr. Wiggins?"

"Pardon, ma'am?" he shouted over his shoulder. He jiggled at the wheel impatiently. The car bounced and jerked down the hill toward Camden Town as Wiggins tugged at the control sticks.

"You sure you've driven before?" Kell asked from the back seat. "There's no hurry."

"Oh, don't be so rude, Vernon. Mr. Wiggins and I are having a conversation. I asked him about politics." Constance waited for Wiggins to respond.

Wiggins swerved out of the way of a drunk. "Watch it, sozzle," he shouted. "Politics? It don't make a difference. The world's still the way it is, whatever the politicians say."

"But surely you can't really believe that?"

"I think he may have a point," Kell said, thinking of his work in Whitehall. Most of the politicians weren't even interested in government at all. Parliament was just another one of their gentlemen's clubs. These dilettantes were nevertheless preferable to those politicos who actually wanted to do some work. They were the ones who really caused the problems.

"No, I can't credit it," Constance went on. "There may be some very bad politicians, incompetent, lazy, self-serving. It doesn't help that they all come from the same schools. But politics itself, that changes things."

"You Liberal or Tory, ma'am?"

"Ha!" Constance cried. "Neither of them, nor this new Labor Party either. Though I *am* very political. I belong to the NUWSS."

"Please, dear, I'm sure Wiggins has no interest in such things."

Wiggins maneuvered the car between the trams of Charing Cross Road. Hawkers called out the names of the music-hall shows and, off to their right, the ladies of the night paraded.

"Nah, go on. What does that stand for?" he called through the glass.

Constance lifted her chin in Kell's direction. "National Union of Women's Suffrage Societies. I'm a suffragist."

The car swung into open road as they approached Trafalgar Square and Wiggins tested the acceleration. "I had you down for a suffragette, if you don't mind me saying, ma'am. What with all those meetings you go to, and the placard-making."

"How did you know that?"

"It's a trick of his," Kell muttered.

"Well, the WSPU are a little more active. But we are all campaigning for the same thing, for the right to vote, whatever you call us. What do you say to that?"

"I suppose I'm for it," Wiggins said after a moment. "In my experience women know as much about what's going on as men do."

"You see," Constance said to Kell. "A man of enlightenment."

"Not that it matters," Wiggins continued. "If voting changed anything, they'd abolish it."

Kell laughed. Constance ignored him. "No, Mr. Wiggins, you are wrong, quite wrong. Have a little faith," she said as they reached their destination.

Carlton Terrace rose resplendent above the Mall, and the German Embassy stood out, its windows ablaze in the warm summer evening "We're here," Kell called.

"Seconds out," Wiggins grunted in reply.

The vehicle-registration office had finally got back to Kell and confirmed that the green Daimler driven by Rijkard on the night of Milton's murder was indeed registered to a René LeQuin, resident of the Albany. Kell had dug a little deeper and found out, from a friend at *The Times*, that LeQuin staged intimate private concerts. It was clear that Milton's killer worked for LeQuin, but they didn't have enough evidence to arrest the Frenchman.

Instead, in the few weeks since they'd broken into the Albany, Kell had obtained an invitation to a party where LeQuin was organizing the music. Wiggins, as the Kells' driver, was to dig around for information among the staff.

Torches fluttered either side of the embassy's big double doors and guests bunched at the entrance, the men in top hat and tails or uniform, the women in corseted dresses and expensive jewelry.

"Take it round the back," Kell said loftily as he helped Constance to the pavement. Wiggins grunted. "Wait." Kell stepped forward and whispered through the window. "Anything new at Woolwich?"

"Nah, clean as. I told you it would be. Milton was the mole."

"You've been there long enough now since his death, I think. We'll need you full-time on LeQuin and Rijkard."

Wiggins paused. "I've got to give notice."

Kell pulled on his gloves. "Well, as quick as you can."

"Why did you bring your wife? Tonight I mean."

Kell mustered as much disdain as he could, raising his chin, and giving Wiggins a damn-your-eyes glare.

"Oh, I get it." Wiggins grinned. "She's the one with the invitation. Nice." He released the brake and rolled away.

"I do like him," Constance murmured as they waited to be announced.

Kell had eschewed uniform for tails. Constance refused to be seen in public with a soldier. He knew she was proud of him, she used to say so, but ever since she'd started marching to the suffragist drum, the epaulets had been banned. Another war would change that, he mused. There'd be no embarrassment about soldiery then, and all this "Votes for Women" nonsense would be scotched as soon as the war bells rang.

They were greeted by a lavish spread. Mountains of exotic fruits, pineapples and bananas; platters of meats and cheeses and great hunks of black bread; pastries and salads and shucked oysters on beds of crushed ice; lashings of champagne and hock, all toted around by grim-faced waiters.

An electric chandelier cast light on the main hall.

"Show of strength," Kell said under his breath to Constance. "They are parading their power. It's one great Teutonic pantomime, paid for by the Kaiser."

"Oh, grow up, Vernon, it's a party. I think I'm going to have one of those gorgeous-looking ginger biscuits."

Kell swiped another glass as the tray passed and surveyed their fellow guests. For all the anti-German feeling abroad in the British press, the place crawled with recognizable faces from society. They didn't seem to care who hosted the party, as long as the wine was good, the food fair, and the ancestry of the other guests impeccable.

"Captain Kell?" a German voice sounded behind him. "Please let me introduce myself. I am Count Effenberg. Welcome to this humble corner of Germany."

Effenberg smiled. He stood half a head taller than Kell, with straw hair and a chin that could split ice. One hundred percent Prussian from his sapphire eyes to his heels that clicked right on cue.

"A pleasure, Count. But please, Mr. Kell will suffice—I am ex-army."

"Oh?"

"The civil service is much removed from the military one." Kell forced a smile.

Effenberg nodded. "It is true. I am the cultural attaché here, a very different role from the army."

"But you still wear the uniform." Kell gestured with his glass. "Ceremonial too, I see."

"It is a very important party for the embassy."

"Careful with the deviled eggs," Kell said. "They'll make a mess of those whites."

They stood in silence for a moment. "Did you see the terrible disturbances in the park the other day, Captain Kell? Most troubling."

"No, I don't think I did."

"Terrible. A mass riot. I find it very worrying when disciplined countries like ours cannot control our subjects. Don't mistake me. This is a challenge for us all. But when it happens on the streets of London . . ."

"I thought you said it was the park."

"Correct." Effenberg clicked his heels again. "Still, one wonders about the strength of such a country." He smiled. "It might be thought of as weakness. Maybe the Tsar will cancel his official visit, in view of such a volatile situation."

Effenberg broke off and inclined his head.

"Who is this charming lady?" he said.

Kell turned. "Count Effenberg, my wife, Mrs. Kell. My dear, this is Count Effenberg, an attaché, I believe. Was it culture or military? I've forgotten."

"*Kultur*. Only culture. *Enchanté*, madame." Effenberg took Constance's hand, bowed, and clicked his heels.

"That's quite a uniform," Constance said.

"*Danke*," Effenberg replied. "Mrs. Kell, may I show you around the embassy? It is extremely well appointed. Captain, do you mind?"

"Not at all," he said as Constance raised her eyebrows and took Effenberg's arm. "Creep," he muttered to himself.

He took a turn around the party, keeping an eye out for anyone matching Wiggins's description of LeQuin. Despite his inquiries at *The Times* and elsewhere, he still didn't have a photograph of the man.

Earlier that week, Kell had been wheeled out again by his boss Ewart to talk to the Committee for Imperial Defense. Ewart beat a loud drum about the LeQuin business, and had even got Haldane, the War Secretary, to attend.

"Gentlemen," Ewart had boomed, "we have conclusive proof of espionage—"

Kell tried to interrupt. "Er—"

"Of German intervention, spying, on a huge level."

"I wouldn't quite say—"

"The proof," Ewart went on, regardless, "that will convince you all of the need to properly fund the department. Captain Kell, over to you."

Kell stood up with all the enthusiasm of a condemned man climbing the scaffold. "Yes, well. We think that a spy infiltrated Woolwich and sold the results to Germany. A Frenchman, we suspect, named LeQuin."

"French? I thought you said Germany."

"Doesn't sound like proof to me."

"By God, if we had to set up a Secret Service Bureau to investigate every suspicious Frenchman, we wouldn't have a penny left for the King."

The room erupted in laughter. Even the grim-faced Haldane's upper lip twitched. He collected himself. "Major General, there is nothing conclusive here. It's all a little thin."

"Thin," Churchill boomed. "We're about to go to war, and you say it's thin."

Haldane stared at him, all levity gone. "We are not about to go to war, Winston, however much you may wish to."

"The streets are crawling with enemy agents," Churchill went on.

"There is no proof."

"We must be ready."

"No proof. I see the Captain's reports. Ewart petitions me weekly. But it's the stuff of fiction. We rule the waves—as president of the Board of Trade you must know this—and there is no appetite for war across the Channel. This obsession with Germany, with war, is folly."

Kell watched as the committee members nodded their agreement. Even Soapy.

"Now," Haldane went on. "I take it all necessary preparations are in place for the Tsar's state visit?"

Ewart left without saying a word. Humiliated. The meeting closed soon after. When Kell got back to his office, there was a telephone call holding for him. It was Churchill.

"We must act. If we don't, we're doomed to be behind the game when war breaks out. It could cost us everything. Do your utmost to sink this man LeQuin."

"What do you suggest? There is not enough evidence."

"Open his damned letters," he lisped. "That'll get you proof."

"Is that strictly fair, sir? Is it even legal?"

"Nonsense. Why do you think Charles the Second set up the post office in the first place? We must use every weapon at our disposal so that we—the government—can do everything necessary to protect the commonweal, to unearth the traitorous, to vanquish our enemies."

"Yes, sir."

"If I were Germany, I'd be listening to this call—if that can be done. Can it be done? Find out. Presumably we can insert agents at the exchange."

Kell coughed. "There is a certain threshold of legal proof. Might I ask, does your request come under the auspices of the Board of Trade?" Kell knew it didn't.

"I won't be president of the Board of Trade forever, Captain. Mark my words."

Kell took another glass of champagne and scanned the party for LeQuin. It was true, Churchill would soon move into another government post and would at some point likely become his boss, if Kell lasted that long. He sighed. What annoyed him most about the committee and Churchill and the whole of Whitehall, all those pompous men, was that they didn't care about Leyton and Sixsmith: who killed them and why. The bigwigs cared only about appearances and hierarchies and departmental segmentation; about votes and prestige and honor. They cared not one whit for two good men dead and a spy ring unchallenged. It was down to him and Wiggins to bring LeQuin and the murderous Rijkard to justice.

He gripped his glass and edged into the next room, a huge affair decked with flowers and looked down upon by a portrait of the

King's nephew, the Kaiser. At the far end, a small string orchestra tuned up. Fussing around them, prominently mustached as Wiggins had described, was LeQuin. Kell started. The steam baths on Marshall Street, the man who had shown an unnatural interest in him. He knew he had recognized the name. René LeQuin. Kell had been too busy keeping an eye on Charles Tinsley to bother, but now it made sense.

LeQuin must have been onto him all along.

Kell lingered by the doorway, nursing his glass. He tried to apply Wiggins's methods. LeQuin wore a Savile Row suit—a clear indicator of money and good taste. He was of average height, despite a raised heel in his shoe—thus self-conscious about his lack of inches. Build, slight to medium, although Kell noted with satisfaction that he appeared rather heavy around the lower chest, suggesting gluttony and lack of exercise. And the musicians feared him. He could see the violinist quake as LeQuin put a hand on his shoulder and the cellist visibly blanch when spoken to.

Otherwise, Kell could glean very little. The mustache was too long to be fashionable, and too oiled to be anything other than deeply vulgar. He looked in his thirties, though it was hard to tell because his hair was raven-black—it must have been dyed. Kell sniffed.

He felt a tap on his shoulder. "Hello again." Charles Tinsley stood before him, holding two glasses of champagne. "Enjoying the view?"

"Erm, I'm sorry, you have the advantage of me," Kell fumbled for an excuse.

"Charles Tinsley." He gestured at LeQuin. "I do love watching men at work. It's so stimulating, so vital. Am I right in thinking we met at Marshall Street?"

"Really, I can't recall ever being there. Vernon Kell." Kell thrust out his hand, only to find Tinsley placing one of the two glasses into it.

"Yes, I think we move in similar circles."

"I don't think—"

"Are you a member of the Drones? No, that can't be right. Wellington's steam and rub?" Kell shook his head. "The Savile?" Tinsley raised an eyebrow and smiled at him.

"Yes—oh, here's my wife."

Constance landed on Kell's arm. "Charles Tinsley, may I introduce my wife. Constance, Charles Tinsley."

"Charmed." Tinsley brushed dry lips across her hand.

"Pleased to meet you, Mr. Tinsley. I know your wife, Eunice. Is she here tonight?"

"Indisposed, I'm afraid. I shall pass on your best." He finished off his drink. "Now, will you excuse me, I'm parched."

"Dreadful man," Kell muttered. "He shouldn't be anywhere near Woolwich."

Constance readjusted her butterfly brooch. "He is rather well connected." Kell grunted, but she ignored him. "Anyway, Rudi was a most charming host, thank you for asking."

"Rudi?"

"The Count Effenberg. He's from Hanover."

"He looks like a stuffed bear in that ridiculous uniform. Click." Kell clicked his heels together. "*Danke.*"

Constance laughed. "You're jealous. He looked splendid."

"Ha. You won't allow me to wear my uniform."

"That's because it's *green*. Now, can that really be the Kaiser? What a truly monstrous portrait. Don't tell me you're going to stand here and listen to the music all night."

The orchestra had struck up and Kell fixed his eyes on LeQuin, who'd drifted away from the musicians.

"This is incidental music, Vernon, we're not meant to be an audience. Why don't you get us another drink?"

Kell craned his neck, ignoring his wife.

"Oh wait, is that him?" she hissed in his ear. Kell nodded slightly. "So this *is* work."

"Indeed."

Constance turned away. "He's a handsome man, in that very French way. An Alphonse perhaps."

"That's not a particularly helpful observation," Kell said as he glanced at her. "How can you see?"

She nodded into the large mirror above one of the buffets. "You're so obvious," she whispered. "My, he does have a cruel mouth, though, doesn't he? Is he a sadist, do you think?"

Kell kept his eye on LeQuin as he merged into the partygoers. He edged toward the double-fronted glass doors that opened onto the garden. Kell strained for a better look. "Sir, sir, I say, Captain Kell."

He swiveled round. "Oh God, it's you."

Lieutenant Russell, uniformed, gangly, and keen, stumbled up to them. "Jolly good party, wouldn't you say, sir? I fancied I saw you earlier but I wanted to make sure."

"Of course you did." Kell looked over his shoulder but, as he suspected, LeQuin had disappeared. "Lieutenant Russell, my wife. Constance, Lieutenant Russell—a member of my staff."

Constance twinkled at the young officer. "You must be the *invaluable* Lieutenant Russell. Vernon talks of you often." She held out her hand and he shook it vigorously.

"Gosh," Russell stuttered, staring at her.

"Would you be terribly gallant, Lieutenant, and find me a fan. It's so awfully hot and I forgot my own. I believe they may have some spare in the cloakroom."

Russell bounded off.

"Is he gone?" Constance asked.

"Yes, I lost him over by those French windows."

"Who is he?"

"I believe he may have been responsible for the death of at least one man, possibly more. I need to find him, but he knows who I am already, I fear."

"Be careful."

"You too—Russell might trample on you by mistake."

Kell went out into the garden and quickly realized that LeQuin could be anywhere—he might even have left—and the embassy was too big to cover on his own. And even if he did find him, he couldn't approach him. LeQuin knew him by sight. It was down to Wiggins.

* * *

Motorcars lined the mews at the back of the embassy gardens. Wiggins followed the directions of one of the flunkies and jerked the car into a space. A gaggle of drivers stood and smoked at the servants' entrance.

"Steady there, mate, it's not no nag," a driver called out and they laughed. "Looks like it's alive."

A few horses and traps nestled between the gleaming motorcars. By the back entrance—a small door to the embassy garden—the staff had set up a trestle table with refreshments.

The older driver was holding forth. "They're Krauts, mate, what do you expect? Believe you me, there'll be war within the year."

"But they left out a crate of beer—can't be all bad."

The first driver spat out a mouthful. "They call this shit *lager.* Give me a pint of ale any day. Rank so it is, never catch on."

"I don't mind it." The younger driver pulled on his fag. "And hospitable, like. Lady Argyll don't give the staff nothing at her dos."

"It's to stop you stealing."

Wiggins grabbed a bottle for himself and joined the circle. "So you think war?"

"Who you with?" a younger driver asked.

"Kell. I'm a ringer."

"Course. These Krauts are warmongering swine, so they are." He spat again and glanced at one of the embassy staff, who heaved another crate of beer onto the table. "Swine," he repeated loudly.

Wiggins stepped toward the man with the beer crate. "*Guten Tag,*" he said. "*Danke.*"

The young man nodded. "*Bitte.*"

"Have you got an opener? Sorry, my German don't go much above pleasantries." He gestured opening the bottle with his hand.

"Yes. Here."

"Anyone famous in tonight?" Wiggins went on. "Anyone special?"

"The guests are you speaking of? I don't know who they are. I work in the kitchens," the boy replied. "I know only the German ones. My English is very bad."

"It's top-drawer, mate. Pisses on my Deutcher. Here, take a swig of this—you look all heated up."

"I cannot." The boy glanced back down the garden and then to the beer bottle.

"Go on, no one's looking."

The boy grasped the bottle and took a huge gulp. "*Danke*."

"*Bitte*." Wiggins grinned. "Who are the Germans there, then—any bigwigs?"

The boy flushed a little with the booze, and leaned in to Wiggins. "There is a new man here from Germany, very special."

"Hans!" A stream of harsh German followed, too quickly for Wiggins to understand anything but the tone.

The boy leapt to attention and hastily forced the bottle back into Wiggins's hand. He hurried away toward the embassy. A tall major-domo type came striding into view through the garden and cuffed the boy around the head as he walked past. The majordomo came out into the mews.

"Lady Argyll's driver?" he called. "Lady Argyll? She wishes to leave."

One of the men flung his half-smoked cigarette to the ground. "That's me, lads. The old bird's probably had a turn." He fixed his cap on. "Either that or she needs a shit." He left, pursued by laughter.

Wiggins went back to the car and made sure he had a good view. A single electric light illuminated the small doorway into the garden. Most of the drinking drivers gradually moved away from the trestle table and settled in their cars or fussed over their horses.

He kept an ear out for announcements, but it wasn't until much later that people started to leave in numbers. The mews became busy as first one butler and then another came to the door and called out names. Traps bounced past and drivers barked farewells, crunching gears or cursing lazy nags.

"LeQuin. Monsieur René LeQuin."

Wiggins tensed.

At the far end of the mews, the green Daimler gently pulled out. Wiggins ducked his head down. The car slipped past and as it did so, Wiggins caught sight of the driver. He wouldn't have mistaken that Adam's apple anywhere, it almost cast its own shadow: Rijkard, Milton's killer.

Wiggins turned back to the embassy doorway, expecting his own call at any minute—Kell wouldn't stay much longer once LeQuin had left, he guessed. He watched as a young woman stepped from behind the German butler. She nudged the man sideways to get past. As she did so, her upturned face caught in the light for an instant.

Bela.

17

She stepped out into an ocean-cool night. The wind tugged at her hair. She squinted against the darkness until she finally picked out Vincas, lolling by a lifeboat.

"Over here," he hissed. "We have ten minutes. Hurry, each minute cost me a fucking ruble. And don't cry this time." He fumbled at his trousers as she came close. "Lie down."

"Take your belt off," she said as she settled. "It digs."

He grinned as the belt slithered through the loops. The odor of cheap rum and rotten teeth washed over her as he knelt. They were by the railing that edged the deck, hidden from view by the bulk of the lifeboat. The wind whistled and screeched, the ship groaned. Bela shifted her hips to the side.

"Want it, do you?" Vincas gasped.

She bucked against him, to the side once more, and moaned. "It has been weeks," she mewled into his ear, her hips swaying from side to side under him.

He grunted harder, faster. The ship tipped and rolled, but he kept on, rum dribbling down on her as she shifted. His pace increased, she felt his stomach muscles stiffen and in that moment of release, she used all her strength to pitch him sideways. Surprised, disoriented, drunk, he tumbled over the edge toward the black sea.

At the last, his hand clung to the upright railing. His back bounced against the hull. "Bela, help me," he screamed.

She leaned over the side, steadying herself against the rail. With her free hand, she pulled the long belt toward her.

"I have the money," Vincas cried. "Pull me up, please."

The ship pitched forward. Vincas's body swung against the hull again. One hand gripped the railing. His arm shuddered with the strain. Bela threw the belt buckle toward him.

"Here," she whispered. "Your belt." In one swift move, she looped it around his neck and buckled it to the metal upright.

"Hey . . ." His shout faded to a gurgle as the leather caught his windpipe. She pried his hand free from the railing. His feet kicked at the hull, his hands scrambled at the belt biting into his neck. "The money," he gurgled again. "You'll die without money."

She unbuckled the belt.

Vincas disappeared into the void. His body slithered against the hull as it went, gone in an instant.

Bela held the buckle in her hand, felt its sharp points, its heft. Then she tossed it into the rumbling sea below and turned back to steerage, a widow.

*　*　*

The party was a total bust. Kell spent his time bored rigid by a succession of guests complaining about the mooted imposition of an income tax. As if he had any power to alter the budget, or to rearrange the visit of the Tsar. He hadn't seen Constance since Lieutenant Russell went for her fan, and LeQuin had disappeared. In the end, he lounged by the front door and drank champagne. He even treated himself to a German sausage.

Constance batted him on the arm with her fan. He started and dropped the last of his bratwurst. "Some lookout you are," she said.

"Where have you been? I've been looking everywhere," Kell said.

"Do you know, I think women would make much better secret agents than men."

"Shush!" He glanced around.

"No one knows what secret agents are, darling."

"Haven't you read the papers? The *Daily Mail* speaks of nothing else."

"As if anyone here reads the *Daily Mail*." Constance smiled. "This is a very upper-class soirée."

"And what about Conrad, *The Secret Agent*? Eh?"

"That's a book, my dear. This class of people doesn't read books at all. I think I just saw Monsieur LeQuin skulk off. Does that mean we can leave?"

Kell asked a servant to call for his car. As they waited, Constance threaded her arm through his.

"I know you think women are the equal of men in every regard, but why did you say they'd make *better* agents?" he asked.

"We are much better at looking. We're brought up to observe. You men can run around with your swords and your guns and your goodness knows what else, but we *see* everything, and we're not threatening. Women, I find, also make much better confidants than men."

Kell was unnerved by this but listened as Constance went on. "I know you find this a little distasteful, Vernon, but women also have what I believe they call Sex Appeal."

"Sex Appeal?"

"Yes. A woman can often find it very easy to get a man to do something, given the right circumstances. Take your Monsieur LeQuin."

Kell goggled at his wife. "What have you done?"

"You didn't think I stayed with that tiresome lieutenant all night, did you? Monsieur LeQuin was most charming. He became particularly attentive when I let slip—ever so accidentally—that I was married to a man in the War Office. I, of course, was most interested in his musical career and his artistic sensibilities. 'Tell me . . .'" her voice lifted to a girlish lilt "'. . . where did you get your great gift for music, monsieur? I so admire it.'" She laughed.

Kell couldn't believe his ears. "That could have been incredibly dangerous—what were you thinking?"

"What was he going to do, brain me with one of the prize pineapples? No, it was perfectly safe. You needed to know more about this man, it would have been pointless for you to talk to him yourself—you would have found out nothing. The empty-headed wife, however . . ."

"Constance, I really don't know what to say."

Half of him raged with anger at the danger of it, the impromptu folly; the other half blazed with admiration for the woman beside him.

"Well, I am your wife, I should be able to help every now and then. And in any case, why should you have all the fun?"

"So what happened?"

"We're to meet again next week, at the National Gallery. He's desperate to show me the Delacroix, apparently. I think he's also interested in seducing me. Don't worry, Vernon, I would never go for a man with a waxed mustache. In any case, I'm sure he's not interested in my body. I'm under no illusions about my own attractiveness."

"But my dear—"

"Bless you. No, he may be as sex-obsessed as the next Frenchman, but I get the distinct impression that he fancies you too."

"Good God."

"No, dear, not like that. He likes the idea of you and your position. He wants to seduce me to get information. I don't know how he got the idea that I might be prepared to do that." She laughed again. "Silly old me."

Kell shook his head. "Where the deuce is Wiggins?"

Wiggins sat in the car, his knuckles shining white against the wheel. He'd ducked as Bela walked past, her boots clip-clopping along the cobbled streets. In her wake trailed the faint smell of carbolic and too many questions for comfort.

"Kell," the butler sang out. "Kell! This is a call for Kell."

Wiggins brought the motor round to the front.

"Where the hell have you been?" Kell snapped.

He put the car in gear and headed north. They'd gone straight over Marble Arch and up Edgware Road when a bus pulled out in front of them. Wiggins swerved and narrowly avoided smashing into a shop window. He pulled on the handbrake.

"Wiggins, are you quite all right?"

"Sorry, sir."

"You've been all over the place. Why are we up in Marylebone?"

Wiggins shook his head clear. "Miles away," he muttered.

"Stay here for a moment. Let's catch our breath."

Kell looked at the back of Wiggins's head, concerned. Wiggins twisted in his seat to face them. "Sorry, ma'am, about the fright."

"Any news on LeQuin? What did the servants say?" Kell pressed.

Wiggins gestured to Constance. "Oh, don't mind her," Kell said airily. "She knows more about him than any of us."

"Rijkard definitely works for him. Driver. Bodyguard. In the Daimler." He took a deep breath. "What did you make of LeQuin?"

Kell outlined the observations he'd made, down to the letter.

"Right. That matches. But you've missed out anything of any use."

"What do you mean?"

"You saw but you didn't observe. It's the details what counts, the details. You've given me almost nothing. Or at least, your deductions are all skew-whiff."

"What about the shoes, and that he's putting on weight—"

Wiggins sighed. "No one puts weight on like that. The thickening around his ribs but no gut? That's not fat, sir, that's paper. Documents most like. He must be the type who carries his most important stuff on him, if we're right about him."

"And the lifted heel?" Constance asked.

"Probably false. Seen that dodge in the nick—hollow out the heel and you can put all sorts in there. Money, keepsakes—or, in his case, I'll take a shot at keys. His business is secrets, right, so he needs the means to lock 'em up."

Constance clapped. "Wonderful."

"It's just a trick," Kell said. "I could be right."

Wiggins and Constance shared a look.

Kell continued. "I'll wager you don't know where LeQuin will be next Monday?"

"That I do not know."

Kell enjoyed explaining the gallery date, although by the end of his explanation, he realized that the three of them were now locked into a plan to trap LeQuin. He'd gone to a party and ended up launching a covert, unofficial spying operation with his wife.

Wiggins drove them home. Constance fluttered up the steps, hallooing to the police constable, but Wiggins called Kell back. "That LeQuin, is he a stirrer? Might someone sling him a few quid to make trouble?"

"I don't see why not. From what we know of him, he buys secrets but also employs murderers. He killed Milton, probably Leyton and Sixsmith too—it seems he'll stop at no degradation to make money. But we must concentrate on his connections with Germany, how the information got to Krupp's. That's our only concern, that's what I need."

Wiggins nodded absently. "And what's his full name again?"

"LeQuin. René LeQuin."

Wiggins caught a late bus from Hampstead down to the Euston Road. The air around the station was still thick with smoke and soot. Fine grains pricked his eyes as he cut south of St. Pancras and dived into the Wounded Hart. He'd hardly drunk since meeting Bela. She was the first girl ever to get him off the sauce, but right now he needed a drink. He wanted to push through the elephant and the Hart stayed open until the last drunk croaked.

It was gone one by the time Wiggins neared his room off Essex Road. He struggled to force the key home, cursed, tried again, and dropped it. Only then did he notice the "tell" on the floor. Every time he went out, he wedged a sliver of wood between the door and the jamb. The sliver had fallen.

As he squatted down, his own door swung open. "What the—" A boot caught him under the chin.

Wiggins fell back to the pavement. A blade flashed. The assailant pressed in. The knife point at his throat. He flung off the man with one great heave.

They regained their feet. The man thrust at him, knife first. Wiggins sidestepped and the knife caught in his heavy jacket. He grasped the man's hand.

"Who are you?" he shouted.

The blade sprang free, clattering against the flagstones, Wiggins's jacket torn. The man looked up. Then he ran.

Wiggins pulled at his ripped coat and ran after him. He recognized the blue woolen hat from the day at the Exhibition. The man's face played in his mind too.

He followed, straining his eyes each time the man darted through the bright islands into the unlit spaces between the gas lamps. Then the hat disappeared. He must have dropped down onto the towpath of the canal. Wiggins ran down the steps to the canal and stopped to catch his breath. Up to his left lights twinkled from the warehouses at City Road Basin. The water lapped gently. Someone was opening the lock.

Wiggins heard the cries of the boatmen. He could just make out their narrowboat entering the lock. Wiggins took in the length of the canal past the wharfs. Off to his right, the canal vanished into a pathless tunnel. Wiggins turned to his left toward the lock and inched along the path, wary of the undergrowth and the water. He came level with the end of the lock, the boatmen ahead oblivious.

A rustling to his left, a blur, and his jaw sang with pain. The man's fist caught it flush, but as he fell Wiggins grabbed hold of his attacker's lapels.

He bucked and fought, but the blue-hatted man smothered him. He had weight on Wiggins. And he had him by the throat.

Wiggins's head hung over the side of the emptying lock. His eyes bulged. Rushing water sounded in his ears. The sluice roared.

He gurgled, struggled. His vision blurred. A last breath died in his throat.

With one final effort of will, he relaxed. Unbalanced, the attacker jolted forward and Wiggins used the momentum to tip them both over the edge into the lock.

In this topsy-turvy moment, as their heads plunged side by side into the void, Wiggins caught sight of the scar on his chin. The last time he'd seen him, the man was about to behead him with a scimitar outside the drinking den. Bela had saved him then.

The attacker's head crunched on the brick sill before plunging into the deep. Sucked under by the current, Wiggins struggled for purchase on the slime-slicked sides. He realized in horror that he'd been sucked under the boat. Foul water filled his nose, his eyes, his mouth. He didn't give a second thought to his attacker as he scrambled against the hull, his limbs heavy, weak. The boat creaked.

Wiggins couldn't swim.

To die in the shit and the stench and the litter-filled waters of an industrial canal, to drown, with all those unanswered questions . . . Pressure built in his head. Scrambling. Why was Bela at the embassy? Bela, Christ, he didn't want to die. Bill, Kell, Holmes, they'd think he fell in drunk. Not Bill, Bill's dead and so would he be unless—

Suddenly, the boat shifted free of the lock. Wiggins rose to the surface, gasping for air. He shouted. Nothing came out.

The backwash engulfed him once more.

18

Bela breathed in the smell of books. She loved it. Not just the dry paper aroma, but the silence too—so different from the constant cries and traffic of Stepney, or the steamy belches and incessant chatter of the laundry.

Newspapers rustled on the reading tables. An elderly man glanced at her as she passed. Bela headed straight for the Fiction section, nestled in the far corner of Whitechapel Free Library. Free. Books teetered high above her. She could read any of them she liked. No one commented, no one complained. Once a week, on her day off, she would spend the time reading, improving her English, learning about the world. Today, she wandered down the Romance aisle. Her boots tapped out a slow rhythm on the polished floorboards.

Unseen, one aisle across, another pair of shoes beat out a similar tempo. Bela stopped. So did they. She started again, hurried. The steps followed, at a quicker pace. She turned at the end of the aisle and passed through into History at the back, glanced around. Saw no one. Heard them. The library shelves pressed in, no place of comfort now. She pushed through the fire exit and ran.

Vincas was eight months dead. Lost to the North Sea. Bela was teaching herself not to fear. She'd even stopped looking over her shoulder.

When she first went back to the steerage deck after his death, she had expected to be hauled away at any moment, a hue and cry to break out above deck. But there was nothing. A couple of the men asked around. No women did. Bela kept her eyes down, but she felt the gaze of the other women, an old one in particular. One man kicked up a bit of a fuss—"Hey, your husband, where is he? He owes me fifty kopeks." Bela shook her head, shrugged.

"No one cares," the old woman whispered to her the next day. "That man was a monster. Where are you going?" She sucked at toothless gums.

"We—I—have passage to London. I don't know anything else. I have no money."

"Help me with my bags, girl. I can't promise anything. I am Marta."

They disembarked in London, surrounded by all kinds of vessels from tiny fly-pricks to great clippers and steamers. Bela was used to feeling small, but never had the world around her felt so big. People buzzed about the huge ships like flies around a horse in summer. She and Marta edged warily into the East End, north of the river. Bela carried Marta's bundles as well as her own small one. On the steerage deck, their fellow passengers chatted mostly of the money they would make, how London could offer a better life for them and their children, as yet unborn. Bela did not join in such talk. Now in London, as she and Marta walked through the shit-streaked streets, with dirty children barefoot and ragged women spilling out of small doorways, Bela's heart surged. Marta spieled on, disgusted at the poverty, but Bela simply stared, awestruck. The streets went on and on, with no end in sight. London was immense. And in an immensity, you could get lost, start anew, become something else, anything else.

The two women passed a bar with frosted windows. A gaggle of drinkers lounged out front, loud and looming. Marta shrank behind Bela. A man stepped forward and called out in a language Bela didn't understand. He gestured with his hand and his friends laughed. Marta and Bela carried on. But then Bela stopped, turned, and took two steps toward the man. He grinned, spoke again. She simply stared at him, unafraid, steady. The man, red-faced with drink, faltered under her glare, silenced. Bela turned in her own time and took Marta by the arm as they continued. In this city, she could be whoever she wanted to be. Not Vincas's wife, not her father's daughter, not a victim, not a mute, not one of the suppressed. That time, her old life, was over. No one would know who she used to be, what she wanted or where she came from—and they need never know. She'd killed a man, justly, and she would fear men no more.

Marta's family lived in a tiny room north of Cable Street, and her son was aghast when his mother turned up with an extra body to house. But Bela soon proved herself valuable. She got a job at the laundry and helped fund a move into bigger rooms. New York was still an ocean away. It might take Bela years to raise the money to get there, even if she could find out where Sarah lived. Marta introduced her to the Union, a society of mutual aid in the East End, and Bela started to investigate people-finding agencies in America.

"We must help each other," Marta said.

Bela went further. She found the Anarchist Club on Jubilee Street and would attend meetings whenever she could. Pamphlets like the one she found at the Plovs' were allowed in London and there seemed to be nothing like the Okhrana. Her greatest discovery, though, was the free libraries—islands of books in the urban grime.

And yet—what a fool she'd been. You never truly left a man like Vincas. Evil never dies. She hustled down the alley behind the library, sick with fear. Was it Arvo? Had Vincas's brother come back to avenge his death? Or was it the law?

She burst out onto the street and straight into the chest of a heavily built, well-dressed man.

"Don't be scared," he said, in perfect Russian. He clamped his hands around her wrists. "Vincas can't hurt you now."

* * *

The loud horn sounded the end of the shift. Wiggins approached the gates at Woolwich with a hurried step, his last weekend on the job. Rayner would have another go at him for tardiness. But then that would be refreshingly normal compared to the last few days.

A hand on his arm.

"Keep walking," Peter said.

"What are you doing here?" Wiggins hissed, startled.

He'd only just recovered from his near death in the canal. With his very last ounce of energy, Wiggins had caught a trailing slip rope. The boatmen came to his aid and, amid much excitement, pronounced him a lucky swine. They gave him shots of gin and slaps on the back. He didn't tell them about the other man, the man whose head wound must have sent him to the bottom. The Russian with the blue hat and scarred chin, who'd followed him in White City, been in his room, tried to kill him, and who had now met his end in the oil-slicked soup of Regent's Canal.

Peter stood too close to be friendly, breathing in his ear. "I worry. When you throw a stick, you expect your dog to bring it back."

"I ain't no dog."

"A saying." Peter's eyes sidled to and fro as people passed. "Of course you're not dog. But you are only one man. I think it's not so easy to steal from this factory. You need help."

"I don't need no help," Wiggins snapped.

Was he really about to steal highly combustible material from a government armaments factory, where capture meant the death penalty? So far he'd become involved in Kell's hare-brained plan to honeytrap a murdering spymaster; his girlfriend had some connection with the German Embassy she'd somehow forgotten to mention; and now he was being physically manhandled by a gun-toting Russian who expected his help in making a bloody great bomb.

He could have been standing in a railway carriage, like any normal person, on his way home from work, looking out over the chimney stacks of South London, bracing himself against the jolting of the points.

Instead, he was in the grip of Peter the Painter. It was a long way from Baker Street.

"We're on for tonight." Wiggins softened his tone. "What's the rush?"

Peter studied him intently and shifted his body slightly. Wiggins noted the heavy hang of his right pocket—the gun.

"Good," Peter said at last. "I will wait. Tomorrow I will collect it. Here, this is for you." He handed Wiggins a carpet holdall. "I am a generous man, no?" He slipped into the crowd of workers leaving the factory.

The fact Peter had turned up made it unlikely that he was behind the blue-hatted assailant at the canal. A small comfort, but Wiggins nevertheless took heart from it as he waited for Rayner's torrent of abuse. He approached the guardhouse.

Rayner appeared in the doorway.

"You're facking late." He spat a ripe phlegm ball on the ground between them. "If I'd shown that kind of ill discipline in my unit, half the men would have been killed."

"What, of food poisoning?"

Rayner's eyes bulged. "That's it! You're fired, get out of it."

"That ain't your decision." Wiggins paused. "Cooky."

"How dare you?" Wiggins really did think the old man might drop dead there and then of apoplexy "I . . . I . . ."

"Listen, you old fucker. You can't fire me and you know it. What you can do is go to the boss first thing and make your strenuous recommendations as to my future employ, which I know you've done already, by the way. Well, don't trouble yourself. This is my last day. But someone's got to mind the shop this evening, and that'll be me. Now, I'm not doing this out of any respect for you—but for the job. I'm a patriot, so I'll watch out as good as always and tomorrow you can bring in whoever you like. Now piss off home."

Rayner stepped back, shocked. He nodded dumbly and collected his hat and coat from the guardhouse pegs. As he headed toward the gate, he turned slightly, his head bowed. "I was the best cook in the line, so I was."

Wiggins had a momentary pang of pity for the old fool. Still, it gave him the perfect excuse to leave work with the bag—and the old watchman would tell all and sundry he'd given him the boot.

Once the factory floor had emptied, Wiggins reconnoitered. Two other watchmen took random turns themselves, stationed at different workshops. Every half hour or so, he'd hear the heavy tread of

Tomkins in particular, an enormous man with a cauliflower ear. He would snap Wiggins in two given half a chance. Finally, unable to settle, Wiggins could wait for his opportunity no longer. He kept his step steady and slow and filched what Peter wanted. Then he padded back through the deserted factory, the hulking machines eerie in the silence. It took all his willpower to resist the urge to whistle. He got back to the guardhouse and stowed the deadly ingredients in the carpet bag.

Moments later, Tomkins thrust his head around the door. "Got a brew?"

Wiggins nodded. Tomkins sat down and proceeded to relate a tale of marital woe. Wiggins continued to nod and tried not to look at the bag, nestled as it was beneath Tomkins's monstrous arse.

In Hampstead's NW across town from Woolwich's SE, Vernon Kell made love to his wife. Married couples throughout the city were no doubt doing the same, but for the Kells it had become routine in the execution and rare in its frequency. All that had changed after the German Embassy party. The pursuit of LeQuin brought them together—the excitement of the chase and the chance to talk about something other than the children or women's suffrage or the invitation list for the latest dinner party. Seeing the spark in her eye and her quicksilver mind kindled something within him, and he could see in her eyes that he was no longer the staid civil servant she'd become used to. What surprised Kell most of all was his own ardor. The danger of Constance's impending meeting with LeQuin troubled him, but it excited him too.

Afterward, Kell stared at the ceiling and wondered whether letting women into the workplace was really such a bad idea after all.

"What the fack's this?"

Wiggins woke with a start. He'd fallen asleep in the chair outside the guardhouse. Rayner rooted around, pulling at the holdall. "You ain't allowed nothing here."

"Hey, leave it," Wiggins growled as he stood up. "That's my change of clothes. I'm done here for good, if you've forgotten."

The sun had yet to rise and the night chill clung to Wiggins. Rayner, his mean and morose self once more, bent over the carpet bag.

"Tell you what, old man. You let me get on my way nice and friendly, and we'll leave it at that. Play up and I'll let everyone know yous was a cook in the army and not some hooting tooting warrior likes you claim. Your choice."

Rayner glared at him. "You wouldn't." He hesitated, then threw his withered hands in the air. "Oh, what do I care anyway? Fack off out of it and take your poncey gear with you."

Wiggins walked slowly toward the station without averting his gaze. It only took a few minutes for Peter to fall in step beside him. "You have it?" he said.

"Everything."

"*Otlichno!*" Peter exclaimed. He bent down to take the bag from Wiggins. "Thank you."

Wiggins pulled away and switched the holdall to his other hand. "No you don't."

Peter looked askance but said nothing. They walked on in silence until they reached the station. "Where next?" Wiggins said.

"What are you doing?" Peter opened his arms. "We are friends, comrades. Don't you trust me?"

Wiggins scoped the platform, busy with a Sunday morning crowd. If the coppers picked them up now, it would be hard for Kell to save him—not with what he had in the bag. But he had no other cards left to play. If he pulled out, the road to Arlekin would be closed forever. He could see it in Peter's expression.

Wiggins whispered, "I want in, proper like. I want to meet Arlekin. That was the deal."

The train clattered into the station, all noise and steam and pistons. "We go to London," he said. "I knew I liked you." Peter put his arm around Wiggins's shoulder. He squeezed hard, let go, and thrust his hand into his pocket. "Here, I have humbugs."

Wiggins kept a tight hold of the bag.

A great scrum funneled through the ticket gate at Charing Cross. As the two approached, Peter cursed.

"What's wrong?"

"I have no ticket," Peter replied. "In the middle of the day, there is nobody. But now."

Wiggins glanced around, noted a bored policeman on the far side of the gate. "Follow my lead. Just walk through a second after me, you'll be fine."

"But how? If we are found with the bag . . ."

"Stay behind me."

Wiggins stepped in front of Peter and confidently strode up to the gate and tried to pass through without showing his ticket. "Oi, you—stop!" the inspector barked at him. Wiggins turned back, patted his pockets, and eventually produced his ticket while at the same time Peter walked straight past along with others, the inspector distracted.

"Brilliant," Peter said when they met again on the concourse. "So simple."

"They love to find a cheat," Wiggins muttered.

The Irregulars never paid a fare. Wiggins never allowed it. "We're street kids," he'd say. "The trains are ours. And we can keep the Grand Old Man's expenses."

Sal got caught once on the Metropolitan at Portland Street. The guard stood her by the gate and sent his mate for a copper.

"Here, Tommy," Wiggins whispered. "Look sharp before the mutton-shunters get here."

"Sharp?" Tommy, a boy of thirteen with sandy hair and a button nose, was Wiggins's left-hand man. Not that he knew his left from his right.

Wiggins ushered him back into the ticket concourse, in full sight of Sal and the guard.

"Sorry, Tom," Wiggins said.

"What for?"

Wiggins punched him in the face.

The fight escalated quickly. Tommy went wild, swinging his arms left and right, kicking and scratching. Wiggins held him off as best he could before they were pulled apart by a great crowd. Sally escaped in the chaos, while Wiggins and Tommy ran off into the park.

"Why'd you do that?" Tommy sniveled.

"It was the duck and dive, Tommy. A dodge. Look, there she is." He pointed as Sal emerged from the bushes. He knew she'd be here, just as she knew he would. Regent's Park was their manor. The rhododendrons offered some of the best cover in central London.

"You took your time." She brushed a pink petal from her chest. Wiggins felt his face go hot all of a sudden, as if he'd met Sal for the first time. "Cat got your tongue?" she said.

"We ran the dodge." Tommy ducked his head. "So you could get clear."

Sal eyed Wiggins. "You look all poked up."

Wiggins coughed. "Why'd they nab you?"

She shook her head slightly as the three turned north to Camden. "I'm too big, is all."

"You're fine," Wiggins protested.

"I'm old. Too old to be hopping rattlers. Look at me." Wiggins didn't. He couldn't guarantee he wouldn't go red again. "Here, Tommy," Sal went on. "Nail us some nuts from the zoo. Bet you can't."

"Can so," Tommy cried, and ran off ahead. Always ready for a rob.

Sal and Wiggins strode on in silence for a minute. "It's no good, Wiggins. We's proper now, we's all grown up."

"I'm fourteen."

"'Zactly."

"You want to give up on the Grand Old Man?"

"Can't duck and dive forever."

* * *

Still ducking and diving, Wiggins thought as he and Peter threaded their way across the concourse outside Charing Cross. As they moved to the Strand, Otto the German beggar beckoned to Wiggins.

Wiggins shook his head and Otto called out instead: "Change. Any change for a poor Luxembourger? Good gents, any change?"

After they passed, Wiggins turned back and flicked a coin at him—mouthing "Luxembourg?" Otto shrugged.

"Disgusting," Peter said as they walked on. "This is richest city in world, heart of huge empire, bleeding colonies dry. Yet on streets, poor man must beg to eat. Where does money go? I tell you, Wiggins, into pockets of royals and capitalists. Who can support this system?"

The question hung in the air between them as they skirted Covent Garden—the dying cries of the costermongers jangling down the side streets as they took fruit to the city. "*Straws, straws, two punnets a* penny . . . *Yorkshire rhubarb, get it fresh.*" They cut up Henrietta Street, where barrow boys and flower girls spilled out of the morning pubs and traded filthy banter.

At the top of Shaftesbury Avenue, Peter gestured to a doorway. "It is here," he said. A corner shop selling umbrellas bustled with custom just to the left. "We are above. Top room."

Wiggins followed him up the thin stairs, around the landing, and up again twice more to the attic room. A single door squatted at the top of the staircase and Peter flung it open theatrically.

"*Bozhe!*"

Yakov stood before them, knife in hand, like an irate butcher. He unleashed an angry torrent of Russian and pointed furiously at Wiggins.

While the two Russians shouted at each other, Wiggins took in the scene. A greasy sash window looked out over the tops of the nearby buildings. Two cane chairs and a tea chest made up the furnishings along with Yakov's table. On it lay a collection of implements, bolts, and bits and pieces, like a disassembled engine or clock. Eventually Yakov calmed down. Peter cracked his neck, grinned, and sat. "Yakov was surprised to see you."

Wiggins handed over the bag. Yakov dived in and pulled out the jar of phosphorus. He grunted at Wiggins.

"He says thank you."

Wiggins sat on the tea chest. "How long will that take him?"

Peter and Yakov shared a look, before Peter answered. "Six days. Maybe five."

"What about the rozzers?"

Peter pulled up the spare chair. "Police know nothing. Klaus is back in Jubilee Street, trying to trick stupid people into throwing bricks at windows—then they can arrest them. This is how your police work here—fools. They think they are cats and we are mice. But if we keep secret, they will never know. Are you scared, Englishman?" He grinned and popped another humbug into his mouth.

"What's the target?" Wiggins said. "And no, I ain't afraid."

"We don't know. Only Arlekin knows."

"When do I meet him?"

"Questions, always questions, Wiggins. Arlekin will meet you in time."

Wiggins glanced again at the table.

"I want to take the bomb."

"Why?" Peter asked, astonished.

"Look at the pair of you, Ivan the Terrible and Genghis bloody Khan. You're not worried about the coppers, but I ain't never seen two more suspicious-looking villains."

Peter glanced back at Yakov, unsure. "It is up to Arlekin."

Wiggins stood up. "Let Arlekin tell me the target, tell me the time, and I'll set the bloody thing off myself."

19

"You have a point." Mr. Holmes fiddled with his cigarette. "Obsolescence comes to us all."

"Obsolescence?"

The Grand Old Man strode to the window and looked out on Baker Street. "The new century is not far away, Wiggins, and I fear there is no call for men like me. This will be the century of the machine."

He was in one of his moods. Wiggins stood in the doorway and waited. He'd only come in to report back on a serial adulterer out in Putney, small fry. He happened to mention his age—he couldn't get Sal's words out of his mind—and how his work might be changing, and Mr. Holmes had been prosing on, becoming blacker and blacker. He was often like this without the Doctor. "What will you do?" Holmes asked suddenly.

"I, er . . ."

"Come on, out with it. You can't live on the streets forever, a man of your talents. And my practice cannot support you for much longer—look at you, you're almost as tall as I am. You are distinctive, the criminal fraternity will cotton on soon. No, it's all up, Wiggins."

The front door opened. Wiggins heard clattering in the hallway. "Ah," Holmes went on. "The good Doctor, here to surprise me."

"Good day, Holmes," the Doctor hallooed from the landing. "Wiggins, my how you've grown." The Doctor clapped his hands and walked to the fireplace.

"As ever, Watson, you've found exactly the right words to describe our predicament. Wiggins is old."

"What was that? Oh, I see. Yes, bit of a problem out there on the streets. Hardly blend in. Tall as a telegraph pole."

"But what should he do now?"

Watson looked on Wiggins with friendly eyes. Neither he nor Holmes showed any interest in Wiggins's own opinion on his future prospects. "Army? I can put in a word with the Berkshires."

"Yes, of course," Holmes cried.

"Army," said Wiggins at last.

His eyes popped open. "Wiggins!" Bela stood by the bed, her hand on the curtain. "You are moving everywhere. I wake you. You have bad dreams?" she said.

He put a hand to his sweat-damp chest and squinted, adjusting his eyes. Bela loomed above him, dark against the late-afternoon sunlight. "Hot, is all. You startled me." Her scent infused the room, waking his senses.

Bad dreams. Like blowing up yourself and half of Soho with a jerry-rigged bomb. Like watching on as your best mate bleeds out in the dust of Tottenham Lea. Or listening to your mother as she slices a shiv down her wrists and stifles her own cries. He'd lived enough bad dreams to last the long sleep.

"Do you want me to go?"

"No, course not." He forced a smile, shook his fears away. Dust motes danced around her as she hesitated. "Come here." He swiveled his legs over the side of the bed and pulled her into a kiss. She tasted of plums.

"I have food," she said after a moment. "You don't eat." She spread out a cloth on the bed.

"Anything to drink?"

Bela frowned. "Lemonade."

Wiggins bit into a pickled egg and grimaced. He examined Bela's precise movements as she arranged each item of her picnic, then he gazed at her face—the same face he'd seen earlier that week as he waited outside the German Embassy. She passed him a bottle of lemonade and they ate in silence. Wiggins couldn't take his eyes off her. He imagined this was what home felt like, at last. But did happy homes have secrets?

"Where have you been? I've missed you."

"I work. What is wrong?"

He picked at his food. "Nothing," he said. "Do you remember who tried to kill me? The night you saved me, down Cable Street."

She blinked. "I don't know. Bad people."

"I could've sworn you said a name, is all. You said he'd come back to get me."

Bela looked at him carefully, then turned her shoulders away.

"Nikolai," she said at last. "Everyone know him, every Russian. He is mad. From the paint factory, he goes mad. And now we are careful. If you see him, cross the road, that is what we do. Poor, sad Nikolai." She looked down at her lap.

"Did he have a scar across here?"

"You've seen him?" Bela asked quickly. "Where?"

"Nah," Wiggins lied. "I just remember, is all. I didn't mean to upset you." They ate in silence until Wiggins tried again, the questions mounting in his mind. One question, above all the rest, could he ask it? What was she doing at the embassy? "I've been going to Jubilee Street, sometimes like," he said at last. "There's a lot of sense in all that politics." Bela put her hand out and took his, but said nothing. "I don't know what I'm trying to say. Thank you, I suppose. I don't hold with all those rioters, I'm not up for killing or nothing, but maybe things can change. What we need to do is stick together, ain't it, support one another. You showed me that, so thank you. I'm with you, girl, I really am."

She offered the ghost of a nod.

"I cannot stay," she said. "Work."

"Be late." He pulled her toward him again and this time they fell into the picnic things, tenderly, passionately, and, Wiggins felt as they lay together afterward, all the more united. He watched as she fussed with her skirts.

"I go now." She stood by the door, ready. Her head to one side, she wore an expression he couldn't read. Care, worry, resolution—he didn't know.

"Here, let me give you some lolly for that grub. It must have cost a bomb." He searched the floor for his trousers. "I'm flush."

"No," she said. She opened the door to leave. "It is gift."

He got up and stood before her in his underwear. "You know, sometimes we do things for money that we don't want to do. It's nothing to be ashamed of. All of us have been there, love." *What were you doing at the embassy?* The question pressed in on him. Was she selling herself? No shame in whoring. Could he say that? The barmaid's words again—no woman wants you to know what she's thinking. Was Bela any different? And what would he do if she told him, anyway? She could walk out the door and never come back, and that would be the end of it.

"You need money?" She searched his face with anxious eyes.

"Nah, that's not what I meant." He put his hand on her heart. "Life's tough, I know. And we got to do what we can, and sometimes we got to keep them things secret. For ourselves. And that's all right, we can keep it locked in here. I don't need to know, you don't need to know. I got money now, enough for both of us. For the future, like."

She took Wiggins's hand from her breast and held it in hers. "You are a good man, Wiggins, a kind man. You could drink less." They smiled. "But you are these things. It is not so usual a woman can find this." She paused and looked away. Wiggins sensed something else, the unsaid, rising to the surface, struggling to get out. Bela opened her mouth, leaned her head to the side, and shook the thought away. She squeezed her eyes shut for a moment, then looked at him once more. "Stay a good man. For me." She rose onto the tips of her square-toed boots, kissed him on the lips, and was gone.

A good man—he wasn't so sure. He went to the window, but she didn't turn around. Her dainty, doll-like figure quickly disappeared on the Essex Road. He didn't know whether to feel unsettled or reassured by what had happened. Bela's tone was wistful, almost melancholy, yet her affection for him seemed to match his own. What could make a man happier than the woman he loved telling him he was a good, kind man? There would always be secrets, they had both lived too hard for it to be any other way; he didn't need to know what she was doing before him, about the scars on her back, the absent (or dead) husband, the nighttime visit to the German Embassy. All he needed to know was that she loved him. As to the rest, he didn't care as long as she was his.

She'd also provided him with the name of his blue-hatted assailant: Nikolai. The body had been dredged up two days earlier from the City Road Basin. Jealousy, madness—whatever the motive, Wiggins had nothing to fear from a dead man. One worry scotched.

He dressed, finished off a sausage roll, and went outside, headed up to the Angel, then doubled back down Upper Street. Reassured he was alone, he bought an evening paper and glanced at the personals column: "*Fishing trip as planned. Tomorrow 2:15 p.m. Come to the hotel, Winnie.*"

The next morning Wiggins found himself outside the Blackheath Orphanage for Girls. High gables jutted into the sky, warding off the angels. The railings stood like jailers, spears at the ready. He couldn't bring himself to enter the gates, even after all these years. Nothing like an institution to make you feel seven again. The black metalwork, the small windows designed not to let children see out. Sal had escaped with his help twenty-six years earlier, and they were still locking up girls. He waited in the street until a small child padded down the steps with a brush.

"Oi," Wiggins called to her. "Want to earn a penny?"

The girl, a waif with an angry rash on her forehead, hesitated, then scurried toward him.

"Two sisters, name of Milton. Get one of 'em out here."

She bit her lip, then thrust a hand through the railings. Wiggins plopped the penny in it. "You get another one from the Milton girl, once she's come out—so don't nick it."

He stepped back into the shadows and watched as the little girl finished brushing the yard and then disappeared inside. Sometime later, Mavis Milton wandered out from around the back of the building, armed with a bucket and mop. She searched through the railings, but when she didn't see Wiggins she drove the mop into the bucket.

Wiggins paused. The eldest of Milton's two sisters had the same innocence about her, the wide-set eyes and fair hair. She looked about thirteen. He closed his eyes for a moment and then snapped to.

"Over here," he beckoned.

"What do you want, mister? I had to get punished to be here." She brandished the mop. "Do I know you?" she said, edging toward him.

"Here's a sovereign." Wiggins passed the money through the railings and into her belt-scarred hands. "Give this penny to the girl who told you. And look after your sister."

Her eyes burned in astonishment. "Did you come to the house once, soused?" She stuffed the money away in her dress. "I don't want to do nothing, I don't owe you."

"I was a friend of your brother's," he said. "I'll try to come again."

The doors behind her rattled and she jumped back to the stoop and gripped the mop. "Mavis Milton, get in here at once. You are to clean the steps after scullery duty."

Wiggins retreated into the road and observed the matron with an even stare. "Morning, ma'am," Wiggins tipped his cap.

"Get inside this instant." Mavis hustled under the woman's arm and the door shut firmly behind them.

He stood for a moment longer, regarding the child prison in front of him. Was Peter right—was this really a system worth defending? A way of life that made it all right to lock up children until they were old enough to beg. The newspapers were full of the Empire's wealth—the richest the world had ever seen. Yet on the streets of its greatest city, the poor died for being poor.

Wiggins's thoughts turned to the Russians holed up off Shaftesbury Avenue and their bomb. Yakov was a liar, and Wiggins didn't trust Peter either. But even though Wiggins knew they might be lying about how long the bomb would take to make, he guessed that he had at least three days, until Thursday, before it would be ready. If Arlekin let him carry the bomb, then he'd have the means to stop it and he'd have the means to kill him and avenge poor Bill.

As Wiggins had these thoughts his eyes fell once more on the sign on the orphanage gate. Under the name of the institution, it bore the following legend: Principal MR R. LARKIN, Esq.

Kell flicked shut his watch and placed it back in his waistcoat pocket. "It is one fourteen. He should be here any minute."

Constance pirouetted a parasol on the floor beside her. They sat in the bustling lobby of the Northumberland Hotel. The room was very ornate with high ceilings, marble floors, and a fleet of burgundy-clad porters, their brass buttons glinting in the light. Constance eyed the guests carefully, guessing at who was a genuine adulterer (the hotel was notorious) and who was simply arranging a divorce. She turned to her husband after a moment. "I understand you arranged the hotel, but how does he know what time? I mean, he doesn't have a telephone or an address, so how do you communicate?"

Kell showed her the previous day's paper and pointed to the personal ads. "There," he said. Despite his anxiety at the thought of Constance meeting with René LeQuin, he enjoyed working with her. She was unnervingly good at subterfuge.

"But it says two fifteen here. Do we really have to wait an hour?"

"No. Wiggins's idea. When we set a time to meet, the actual time is one hour earlier. In case the messages are intercepted—standard protocol."

Constance raised an eyebrow. "And who is Winnie?"

"Oh, that was me. We used to call Churchill that at Sandhurst. Infuriated him."

Constance glanced over Kell's shoulder at the door. "Here he is, on time. Handsome devil, isn't he?"

Kell twisted to see Wiggins striding toward them in a state of great agitation. His hair fell hugger-mugger over his brow and his collar flapped open. He'd been sweating. Constance whispered into Kell's ear, "Handsome, but not my type."

Wiggins sat opposite them both, hands on knees. His left leg twitched. "Let's kill him," he said. "Hear me out. This LeQuin's a menace, agreed? Let's bin him. I can do it, that's an end to it. It's finished. Over."

Kell lifted his hand. "Waiter, can we have a pot of tea for three, please. Is everything all right?"

"Course."

"I admire your zeal and, er, commitment. But obviously we cannot kill LeQuin. We are the British government, not a gang of Italian desperadoes. Assassination is not how we do things. In any case, he's a conduit. Bumping him off on a dark night in Waterloo won't help us in the long run."

Wiggins slumped back in his seat. The tea came and it wasn't until Constance handed him a cup that he spoke again. "I could do it off the books?"

Kell examined his biscuit. "Is this what they call a bourbon?" he said.

"Did he kill the boy from Woolwich?" said Constance and Wiggins nodded. "How sad."

Kell checked over his shoulder, suddenly anxious. "Is this really the best place to be having this kind of conversation?"

"Best spot to hide is always in plain sight—no one gives a monkey's."

Kell had to admit it, no one cared about three people having tea in the lobby of a grand hotel. It was what London did best, ignoring other people's business.

"You all right with this, ma'am? Meeting LeQuin?" Wiggins said. "I could always dip him instead, see where that gets us."

"Dip?"

"Ain't you read *Oliver Twist*? I used to be one of the best dips in London. Mr. Holmes didn't like it."

"Far too risky—you could blow the whole thing," Kell said.

"That won't happen. See that fella over there in the boater? Watch and learn." Wiggins stood up and approached the man as he neared the concierge desk.

"Good God, no." Kell leapt up and grabbed Wiggins before he got there, desperate to avoid any kind of scene. "Come back here."

"You're right," Wiggins said. "Pointless risk."

They sat back down and Constance looked between the two, amused. "You're like a double act in some kind of revue," she said. "Or a married couple."

"I don't know about that, but we shouldn't dawdle. Now, how long have we got before the meeting? Oh, where's my watch? I had it a second ago."

Wiggins put down his teacup and produced from his jacket Kell's shiny new pocket watch. "Need a watch, guv'nor? I could sell you this for a little bit of sugar."

Constance laughed, delighted. Kell snatched the watch back in annoyance. "Well, I, how did you, I mean . . ."

"Once a dip."

Kell harrumphed. "We should stick to the plan. This is an unnecessary complication, and could place Constance in even more danger."

Wiggins nodded, chastened. "Right you are, skipper. What's the plan?"

Kell glanced at Constance and leaned forward. "We're all agreed we need to find out LeQuin's other residence. His 'safe' house, as it were."

Wiggins sipped his tea and nodded.

"So, Constance is to secure an invitation using the lure of some important documents . . ."

"What's the bait?"

"Is that me?" Constance interjected. "Because I am here, you know."

"Sorry, my love. I'm talking about what you'll promise LeQuin." Constance raised an elastic eyebrow and Kell suddenly cracked. "You know, on second thoughts I don't think this is a good idea at all. It's far too dangerous."

Constance took his hand. "I'm going to the National Gallery, my dear, not deepest Soho. Let's see if he likes what we have to offer, and then we can decide how to proceed."

"What's the offer?"

Kell pushed his spectacles back up his nose. "Constance is going to tell him that her husband is setting up a Secret Service Bureau and that she's seen, and can perhaps procure, documents that detail various particulars."

"Christ, that's a bit close to the bone."

"But believable. There's nothing that sells a lie like the truth. LeQuin will fall for it, of that I'm sure."

Wiggins nodded.

"It's time," Constance said.

"Don't worry, my dear, we'll be watching. I shall be in the gallery and Wiggins will wait outside."

"No chance," Wiggins said. "He knows you're the husband."

"He didn't see us together."

"You didn't see him seeing you together. But he was at the party. He knows who you are, it's his job. I'll go."

Kell opened his mouth to object. But Wiggins was right. He hated to admit it, but Wiggins would probably make a better guardian to the bargain. "You can't walk around the National Gallery dressed like that," he said at last.

Wiggins looked down at himself, momentarily self-conscious.

"You'll have to change," Constance agreed. She seemed to find the whole spy game rather droll. "Vernon, Mr. Wiggins is a similar size to you—why don't you two toddle off to the gentlemen's cloak-room and exchange suits. But do hurry, we wouldn't want to be late for Monsieur LeQuin, would we?"

As Constance approached the gallery steps, Wiggins fussed and twitched inside the unfamiliar clothes. Kell's suit was far too stiff. His eyes never left Constance as he idled amongst the sightseers and birdseed sellers bunched around the base of Nelson's Column.

Out of the corner of his eye, he spotted LeQuin and then Rijkard, rising above the crowd; a moment later, Constance met them. LeQuin chuckled and kissed her hand. He dismissed Rijkard with a waft of his hand and ushered Constance into the gallery.

Wiggins hastened to the east entrance, bile rising in his throat. All the calmness instilled by the Kells back at the hotel had dissipated. René LeQuin. R. LeQuin. Arlekin. Why hadn't he seen it earlier? Wiggins cursed as he rushed to catch up. He'd been blind to the coincidence, precisely because it *was* a coincidence. If only he had a knife.

Constance was an expert flirt.

Wiggins found her and LeQuin by the Delacroix, as promised. She knew her mark perfectly, flattering with questions and observations, playing the unworldly wife. As they walked through the grand halls of the gallery, she touched LeQuin's arm fleetingly. Wiggins watched as the two of them sat down on a bench opposite a panoramic naval scene. He paced from one exit to the other, eyes on the back of LeQuin's neck. Sweat beaded on the fatty roll just visible above the brilliantly starched collar. It wouldn't take much to snap that neck. A length of red cord hung by an attendant. Long enough and strong enough. But then he'd hang too. If he killed LeQuin there and then, Kell couldn't save him from the drop, for all LeQuin's crimes.

A sharp noise behind him shook Wiggins out of his reverie.

"Oh, silly me. Thank you so much, René," Constance said as LeQuin handed her the parasol.

They were five or six paces past Wiggins, having left their seat, and he hadn't noticed. Constance continued in a loud, light voice: "No, I cannot dine with you at Goldini's, René, but it's very sweet of you. My husband is expecting me, so if you could help me find a cab . . ." Wiggins followed, chafing against the unfamiliar suit. He'd almost lost them, but for Constance's presence of mind.

Outside, Wiggins stayed close, following LeQuin's fat neck. LeQuin pushed and jostled Constance to the curb. Buses and motorcars rattled past. Constance said something else to LeQuin as she got into a cab. She waved like an excited schoolgirl as the taxi drove off. Wiggins pressed closer, the road near. One push, well timed, and it would be over for LeQuin. A police wagon powered up the inside of the street, bell clanging. Wiggins stepped forward, an inch away from LeQuin's back, and—

"This way, monsieur." Rijkard steered LeQuin by his arm. Wiggins dropped away and shrank into the throng.

Rijkard ushered LeQuin to the waiting Daimler. Wiggins breathed heavily. He watched as the car accelerated toward Pall Mall, swerving through the traffic. Suddenly, he was surrounded by a swathe of twittering tourists led by an excitable guide. "Make sure you stay in the group, everyone. If you don't stay with us, you won't be able to claim your free tea and cake in the cafeteria. Monday is normally Dundee."

There would be more chances. Wiggins took another turn around the gallery to calm himself, to gather his thoughts. He deposited Kell's perfectly tailored jacket in the cloakroom, pulled out his shirt and crumpled the sleeves, back to his normal look. Then he cut up St. Martin's Lane and through Seven Dials. A horse reared up on the pavement, fretting in the heat. The small streets around the Dials were dusty and airless, crying out for rain. The city stank of drains and rotting fruit. Ragged children sat outside the mean doorways of Monmouth Street, too tired to play, dirty faces upturned as he passed.

Wiggins waited opposite the umbrella shop with a clear view. A heat haze crinkled the air. The New Oxford Street tram rattled and sang over the junction. He took a deep breath, crossed the road, and went in.

Yakov leapt up from the table.

"Easy," Wiggins said.

He held his hands up and inched through the door. Yakov's dead-eyed stare followed his every move, but he sat down nonetheless. The room had gained an army bedroll, a glass bottle, and the detritus of lunch. In the corner, a piss bucket stank. Yakov, shirtless, sweaty, and heavily haired, looked at him with ill-disguised hostility. In front of him, the bomb had taken a more solid form. It still didn't look ready, though, Wiggins noted with relief.

"Where's Peter?"

Yakov shrugged. He picked up a screwdriver and tipped his eyes to the table. He no longer wore the eight-pointed star around his neck.

"When will it be ready?" Wiggins asked.

Yakov ignored him. Wiggins examined Yakov's pile of clothes on the windowsill, his meager belongings.

He tried again.

"You're Arlekin's tool," Wiggins taunted. "No master, no God, eh? Just following orders. No idea what for, or why." He cast a look out of the window and went on, unable to stop himself. "Is that any way to live? Hardly an anarchist ideal, just taking the shilling all the same, with a different name on the coin. That's what you are, mate, a total fucking tool."

Yakov clenched his fist around a hammer until the knuckles shone. His brow wrinkled, his shoulders shook, but he didn't stir. Instead, he dropped his eyes to the table and continued working.

As he did so, he spoke in a deep, low tone. Each word heavily accented. "I don't like you. I don't trust you. I don't care what you say. You save my brother, so I don't kill you. Yet. Peter will come, maybe. I am not his keeper. I am happy for things to be as they will be. You call me a tool. I say—yes! I am a tool of revolution. We all serve something bigger than ourselves. So, you stay or go, foolish English. It is all one thing to me."

Wiggins laughed mirthlessly. "Fair enough."

Yakov got up and walked over to the bedroll, where he reached down for a bottle. He drank slowly.

"So where's the wife and kids?" Wiggins said.

Yakov dashed the bottle against the wall and sprang on Wiggins. His hands clawed at his throat and the two men crashed to the floor. Yakov held him by the neck. "How you know my family? You follow me?"

Wiggins relaxed for a moment and then pushed back hard. Yakov rolled away. They both staggered to their feet, breathing heavily. Wiggins's eyes darted to the table. Yakov's knife was just out of reach. Wiggins rolled on the balls of his feet. Yakov jumped for the knife.

The door swung open. "Hey!"

Peter stood in the doorway. "*Bomba*. The bomb," he repeated in English in a hushed tone.

Yakov screamed at him but didn't take the knife. Wiggins dusted down his shirt, slowed his breathing.

The three of them stood, sweating, eyes flickering from one another to the table to the bomb. At last, Yakov raised and dropped his hands and sat down carefully at the table, keeping his eyes fixed on Wiggins.

"Wiggins. When I see you, I feel like huntsman whose favorite dog is with puppies." Peter smiled. "New soldiers. Yakov feels different, but you know already. You surprise us," he went on. "This is like Easter one week early. We did not expect you until later. It can be dangerous to surprise Yakov—when he has a gun he shoots first." Peter scrambled around in his pocket for a sweet. He didn't offer them. Instead he walked toward Wiggins and placed a hand on his shoulder. Wiggins felt the squeeze. "Problems?" Peter asked.

The fingers pressed a little deeper. "I'm keen, is all."

"Good." Peter let go.

He slid the tea chest into the center of the room and sat arms akimbo, straightening his back. "Arlekin says Friday, when bomb is ready. Come at noon."

Wiggins hesitated. If Peter was waiting for Arlekin to say the word, then all Wiggins needed to do was to take out Arlekin. Or René LeQuin, as he now knew. R. LeQuin. He almost blurted it out in Peter's face—what are you doing working for the French? Why? It made no sense. Peter looked at him quizzically, and Wiggins realized he needed to stay in character, keep up the charade. "I'll meet Arlekin?" he said at last.

"Yes. Noon, Friday. We will hear great plan. But now I must go. You too, I think. Don't worry, Yakov doesn't leave."

As they reached the door, Yakov muttered at Peter in Russian. "Wait, please tell Yakov how you know about his family. For me," Peter urged.

Wiggins glanced back into the room. "His shoes, his shirt, and the lining of his hat there on the sill. *Do svidaniya*," he called cheerily as he left.

He'd be damned before he gave Yakov any kind of satisfaction. Hopefully the bastard would spend the next two hours examining his clothes for any signs. Wiggins had felt a baby's rattle in Yakov's pocket when they fought months earlier. The fact that Yakov's hat and shirt had been oft repaired spoke of someone else at home—the rattle owner's mother. He mentioned Yakov's shoes just to fuck with him.

Peter hurried off, muttering something about a woman. But as Wiggins left him, past the Old Crown, he knew Peter was watching. Making sure he left. It wasn't until he zigzagged through Covent Garden that he was confident Peter had gone. He went back to the gallery, picked up Kell's jacket, and set off on foot to Essex Road, via the Strand.

At Holborn Viaduct Wiggins felt secure enough to buy an evening newspaper. Dark blooms of locomotive smoke streamed down from the railway lines above. The press had taken to calling this time of day the "rush" hour, now that so many folk lived out of town. Wiggins would never live out of town. Camden was too far north for him.

A young newsboy shouted above the din. "Tsar sets off for London, Tsar to London."

Wiggins tipped the boy and discreetly scanned the paper as he walked. Kell had already placed a new message. Constance had succeeded. As the Grand Old Man used to say, the game's afoot.

20

The front door creaked. A foot tested the stair. Wiggins scrambled out of bed as quietly as he could. He grasped the cosh in a sweat-slicked palm and waited behind the door.

Ten minutes earlier he'd been dreaming of Bela and now he stood naked, waiting for God knew what. The floorboards on the landing bent loudly and the door cracked open. A dark figure crept toward the bed.

Wiggins leapt on the assailant, clamping him in a headlock.

The figure screamed in high-pitched, pure street. "Fack off."

"Sal!" Wiggins stood back, startled.

He struck a match. Sal's face loomed up, red raw. "It's Jax. She's gone."

"Hold up. She'll be right as, trust me. We's due to parlay tomorra," he said as he lit a candle.

Sal grasped her hands. "Nah, nah. She was taken to Lots Road in a cab. She got a message to me through the cabbie. She's in trouble. You said you'd protect her and now she's gone." The words tumbled out of her.

Wiggins stared, open-mouthed. Jax was blown. Rijkard must be onto them. And Rijkard was a killer. "I'll sort it."

Sal pushed a shirt into his chest. "Get dressed. Herbert's got the cab waiting."

Wiggins looked down at himself, still naked.

Two minutes later, they were in the back of Herbert's motor cab, juddering through town. Mist hung heavy and the first signs of day-light bruised the sky. "What do you know?" Wiggins asked, tying his bootlaces.

"Just the message—all the cabbies know me cos of the hut."

"How did you find me?"

"I used to be an Irregular too, remember? She's my only babe." Sally clung to him. "The cops don't care about a kid like Jax. But I knows it's all wrong. She would never have sent for me unless . . ."

Wiggins patted her hand and she fell silent. The cab wheeled left toward the river. The streets were empty. When he was an Irregular, this had been his favorite time of day. The street kids owned the hour, a break between the fear and uncertainty of the night and the bustle and stress of the day.

"I'm enlisting," Wiggins mumbled into the dark space.

"Listing more like," Sal hissed. "Are you elephants?"

Wiggins tripped over and cursed.

"You'll wake the others," she whispered.

The Irregulars lived in an abandoned railway arch out past Paddington. It was dark, it was damp, but it was safe. Eight or so of the street urchins bunked up together on bedrolls fanned around a smoldering brazier, presided over by Sal. That night, as the little ones slumbered, Sal sparked up a lantern and padded over to the entrance where Wiggins sprawled. "Here, take a sip. What you been drinking for?"

Wiggins burped. He wasn't used to the liquor. "I've taken the shilling."

Sal gasped. "But I thought—"

"You were right, Sal," Wiggins groaned.

"Shush," Sal said again, arching away from his gin-reek breath. "Come here." She led Wiggins outside, down the side alley, away from the little ones. Sal was a great Irregular, one of the best, but as she and Wiggins had grown, she'd found herself keeping house more and more, trying to make the arch some kind of home. "You'll wake the lot of them," she said.

Wiggins lolled against the wall of the ill-lit alley. Away to their right, a few late-night revelers wandered past down toward Westbourne Grove. "You's rancid with the ale. What's this bull about the army? You're only fifteen."

"You told me. I needed to sort something. Mr. Holmes and the Doctor. The Berkshires . . ." He tailed off.

Sal held him up by the shoulders. "I didn't mean join up. I thought, I meant . . ."

"Whoa ho! Lovers' Lane, is it?" A coarse West Country voice echoed from the street. "Take a look at this, lads, here's a right set-to."

Sal glanced up. A bandy-legged man walked up the alley toward her, his cloth cap askew. "How much, doxy? I've got half a crown," he cackled.

If she hadn't been so distracted, she'd have sent him on his way with something sharp and sassy. But Sal had Wiggins in her arms. "Oh, piss off, farm boy," she muttered.

"What you say, whore?" The man leapt forward with surprising speed and yanked Sal's arm.

"Sling it," Wiggins slurred. The man drove a fist into his chin. Wiggins slumped to the floor, unconscious.

"Fuck off," Sal cried. Boxed in, she scratched at his face. The man sidestepped, then backhanded her to the ground.

"I is a farm*hand*, not a boy. And fucking is something we farm-*hands* know all about." He kicked her in the stomach, held his foot on her torso, and pulled out a short stub knife. "Don't buck too frisky."

Sal screamed, but the man dropped to his knees and clamped her mouth shut in an instant. His calloused paw covered her nose and mouth completely. Wiggins did not stir. The farmhand's eyes glistened, mean with drink. His knife clattered to the ground as he scrambled at his fly with his free hand.

She squirmed, kicked, and bucked, but the man bore his weight down upon her. "I likes 'em eager," he whispered as he mounted her. "Full of spirit." Her hands scrambled on the wet stones to the side, searching for purchase, anything, as her skirt rode up past her hips—

"Oi!" Wiggins shouted, rising to his knees. "What the . . ." The farmhand turned his head, faltered.

Sal plunged the discarded knife into his groin.

The man screamed once and writhed as Wiggins pulled his body clear. Blood pumped from his upper thigh, like a burst water pipe.

"I only meant to wing him," Sal said, helpless.

Wiggins, sober now, put his hand to the wound but it gushed through his fingers.

"What do we do?" Sal said. "No, no, no."

Wiggins looked down at his palms, back at the road, up at Sal. The farmhand closed his eyes, his body tensed, then went limp, and still the blood ran fast and thick.

"You hit something, a vein? He's dying."

Sal sat on the ground, her back to the alley wall, shaking. "I didn't mean to, he just . . ."

"Did he?"

She shook her head. "No . . ."

A horrible choking gurgle rose from the farmhand, a last rattling gasp. His chest gave a final heave, then flattened, still.

Wiggins looked down at his hands, his clothes, blood-drenched. "We've got to go, Sal. His mates will be back, or the mutton-shunters. We could hang for this."

"I didn't mean . . ."

But Wiggins was already moving. He gently took the knife out of her hand, slipped it into his own pocket. "Listen. No one's hanging you."

"But he's dead."

He knelt down beside her and ripped clear a blood-splattered portion of her skirt. "There's the evidence gone," he said as he put it in his other pocket. "Roust the others first thing. None of you can stay."

"The Irregulars?"

"It's over, Sal."

"You?"

"I'm your suspect, ain't I? A bloodied male, leaving the scene. The cops'll buy straight up. I'll dump the knife."

Sal looked up at him. His long dark hair hung over his face, but she reached up and touched a cheek. "Where?"

"I'm joining the army, remember."

He helped her up and they hustled to the end of the alley. They hesitated, eyeing their separate ways, Sal to go back to the Irregulars, to pack up the base, Wiggins to a new life. They held hands for a moment, then Sal turned her face up to his and kissed him fiercely on the lips.

"I'm glad you was my first," she said.

The cab hurtled westward along the Embankment toward the upturned table of Lots Road power station, visible now in the dawn gray. Sal hadn't spoken for the rest of the journey, but she'd held Wiggins's hand. Wiggins thought of the long years since that hurried goodbye, the long years with no one's hand to hold. He looked down at Sal's calloused fingers, burned red by work. Then he thought again of Bela's own hand in his, the rightness of such a feeling, complete at last.

Sal shivered. Her fears filled the small cab and Wiggins felt every sinew in her body tense.

"Here'll do," Wiggins called to the driver. "Down there."

Wiggins pointed as he and Sal got out. A mooring of boats threw jagged shadows. Beyond them loomed the power station, standing guard over Chelsea Reach. In its shadow, a crowd of small wharf houses tumbled into the river. "One of those." The perfect place for a man like Rijkard. Easy access to the river and to town, deserted half the time. The best waste-disposal service in London, flowing past your door.

Wiggins bit his lip. "Give me thirty, Sal, then go to the rozzers. If they sauce you, tell 'em to ring Vernon Kell in the War Office. Say my name."

"The War Office? What's going on?"

"Wait."

He jogged along a wooden gangway that ran in the lee of the power station, scanning the boathouses and wharfs. Dawn had cracked. Nothing stirred. Six or seven small warehouses stood empty and closed, facing each other in a dusty square abutting Chelsea Creek. The minor waterway fed into the Thames. Wiggins picked his way through half-painted boats on blocks. He heard the river lap gentle. Beyond it, the lights of the malthouses and mills at Battersea winked. Creosote tinged the air, and then off to his right, he caught the whiff of smoke, a fire.

A strangled cry broke. Wiggins spied a decrepit godown by the river. "Help!" a girl's voice shouted out again.

Wiggins surged through the open door. There, lit by a burning brazier, stood Jax—terror in her eyes. Beside her the giant Rijkard, a bright-tipped poker in his hand. Jax reached her hands toward him. "Wiggins," she cried.

Rijkard turned without surprise, grinning. Wiggins rushed forward but then faltered, confused. Something didn't look right. He felt a sudden movement behind him, a whoosh and a great crack. And then he fell, his head afire with pain.

"Again." Rijkard nodded. "*Snel.*"

He *is* Dutch, Wiggins thought as he slipped from consciousness, his nose full of cloves and burning coal.

* * *

"What does Wiggins say?"

"He's gone."

"Gone? How very inconvenient of him."

Kell poured himself more tea. "We may have to postpone."

"Never." Constance crashed her cup down among the breakfast plates. "We have René right where we want him, we'll never get another chance."

"I wish you'd stop calling him that," Kell sighed. But his wife was right.

Constance had played her part to perfection. A refusal to see LeQuin at the Albany—"Too many friends *there*, René, for a married woman"—and the feigned impropriety of an hotel: "Tawdry, René, tawdry."

LeQuin eventually suggested a meeting at the Natural History Museum—"I have a place nearby, *cherie*," he'd mumbled in her ear. A tryst.

"Do we need Wiggins?" Constance continued. "You have the might of the War Office behind you, dear, you can rustle up a squad to follow. Otherwise it will all have been for nothing. Where is he anyway?"

"I don't know," Kell answered grimly. "He didn't turn up at our last rendezvous yesterday."

"He's probably with his new woman."

"Woman?"

"You must have noticed? He's cut his hair, polishing his boots, *washing*. It's been a total transformation since I first met him."

Kell shook his head, amazed his wife could tell so much when he noticed so little.

"In any case," she went on. "I'm sure he'll turn up. And in the meantime, we can go on—we *must* go on."

Kell grunted. "I have to get to work. And you're right. We don't need Wiggins, he is but one man." He said this as much to reassure himself as Constance. It didn't make it any more believable.

Kell chose to walk to work that day but he regretted it as soon as he hit Camden. Roadworks, railway works, half-built blocks—the air swirled with dust and smoke. It was hot, and the smell of rotting fruit tinged the air all through Covent Garden. No wonder society chose to decamp to the countryside each summer, leaving the city to the masses. As he went into the office, Kell's abiding hope was that Lieutenant Russell might have gone off to a country estate somewhere for an extended rest.

His heart sank when he heard his deputy's braying laughter echoing along the corridor. A moment later, Russell opened the door and ushered in their boss, Ewart.

"Kell, what the hell are you doing here?" Ewart rasped.

"Well, this is my office."

"Russell, wasn't this . . . ? Oh, I see. Yes, right. Lieutenant, can you leave the room for a moment?" Ewart dusted his hands and eyed the far wall. He did not look at Kell.

Russell shrugged an apology in Kell's direction and stepped out. "What is it, sir, if I may be so bold?"

"Best be clear about it, Captain. Can't go on, you understand, of course? Last straw it was, the other day. We have younger men, more energy and so on. You understand?"

"No. I do not."

"Hang it all, Kell, you're a disaster. The unit is a catastrophe. We've been demanding evidence of German espionage for months and you've given us nothing."

"But—"

"I'm sorry. It's over. It pains me to say this, but you're stood down. Can't have you running things anymore, you've lost control. You know what broke the camel's back? I saw you come into the office the day before yesterday dressed like a tramp. Awful get-up, can't have my officers looking like they've slept in the gutter."

Wiggins's jacket after the gallery. "That was part of an operation, sir, it wasn't—"

"It's not fitting, not fitting at all. Russell! In here."

Kell opened and closed his mouth. He knew it was coming, but not now, not with Wiggins missing and Constance about to enter the field. "Sir, I'm in the middle of a very delicate scheme—a week, five days even . . ."

"What was that? Ah, Russell. There's nothing for it, Kell, I am afraid. Any operations, agents you have in the field, best hand them over to the lieutenant here—he'll be taking over."

"Him?"

Russell grinned. "No need to worry, sir. I've got everything in hand. What's this scheme you're working on? Is there an agent I don't know about?"

"There, you see, Kell—keen as mustard, fresh blood. That's what this service needs. And don't worry about pay and that sort of thing.

I'm sure we can find you something in the Quartermaster's division." Ewart swept out of the room. "Carry on, Russell."

Russell saluted and then turned to Kell.

"This plan," he demanded. "I need the details. What, where, and when. And who is the agent?"

Kell stared. Russell's whole demeanor had transformed. His shoulders squared, his eye steady, his chin had lost its wobble. "It's a strange thing, Lieutenant," Kell said as he gathered up his belongings. "How the mind works. One minute, you have it, the thought, right there in front of you. And in the next moment, it's gone. If I remember anything, a name, an operation, I will of course let you know. Until then, goodbye."

He strode out of the room, holding the one document that had Wiggins's name on—he had one ace left. But only if that card came to the top of the deck in time.

His head throbbed, full and heavy. His body wobbled. A dull sound echoed in his ears.

Wiggins opened his eyes. He'd obviously been moved to another location, away from the river, but he wasn't sure how long he'd been out. A thin light seeped into the room from a window that ran along the bottom of the wall. There was no furniture. He tried to move but his hands were tied tight behind his back. The pounding in his head made sense. He was hanging upside down, trussed by his ankles like a Smithfield's carcass.

He arched his head upward. His bound feet were attached to a hook in the middle of a ceiling. He looked beneath his head at the floor. The stone surface tapered slightly into a drain. Wiggins could see liver-colored stains. Butchers' stains.

A roar built again, shaking the walls before it waned. He tried to piece together what had happened. One moment, he'd seen Jax, Rijkard, and the hot poker, and then nothing. Except . . .

He thought back to the scene. Rijkard hadn't been surprised to see him. Nor had Jax. The Dutchman had grinned. No binding on Jax's hands. Had she been scared for herself, or for him?

A door crashed open behind him.

"Ah, Englishman. Good. You are waking, after a day. I thought maybe never," Rijkard joked.

"Where am I?" Wiggins croaked.

"I don't answer questions. I ask them. Now you will tell me what you know." He scraped a match on the wall and lit a cigarette. The small room filled with the smell of smoke and cloves.

"Indonesian," Wiggins grunted.

"Correct," Rijkard said and nodded at another man, who stood at the bottom of the stairs. "This English knows things." He pulled deep on the cigarette, studied its glowing tip, and grinned. "Things he will tell me."

Wiggins fiddled behind his back. Damp rope, bound tight. "I can tell you one thing," he said, breathing slow. "You're the ugliest fucker I've ever seen."

Rijkard shrugged, bent down, and pressed the tip of his smoke into Wiggins's forehead.

Wiggins screamed into his throat.

Rijkard grinned. "You will tell me more, I think."

He tossed the cigarette aside, hesitated, then slowly went through the ritual of lighting another.

"You work for Captain Kell, we know this. What does Kell know about us?" Rijkard dragged on his new cigarette.

Eyes wet, jaw clenched, Wiggins reviewed his options. Was there a shadow at the top of the stairs?

"Captain Kell . . . Kell knows. He's planning to . . ." He breathed more heavily, the pressure building in his skull, his forehead stung, his leg muscles cried out for relief. "He's planning to set up a unit at the War Office, to . . ." Rijkard squatted down, his face close to Wiggins, straining to hear. The now familiar rumble shook the walls. Wiggins sighed, exhaled. "He fancies a career in the circus, to be honest . . . Seen you clowns . . . reckons he can do better."

"*Ja, ja*, I see. Funny man. The English always funny men. But I don't have time." Rijkard stood up, gestured to his underling. "Get me the cleaver."

21

Kell strode twenty paces behind his wife. They walked down from the park and entered Cromwell Road. He noted the bobby at the corner, the police box up Exhibition Road. But they were on their own now. Up ahead, a wide, shallow staircase swept toward the great arch of the Natural History Museum entrance. Gargoyles perched on its ramparts, ready to swoop, stark against the velvet sky. Visitors flocked around the doors. White calico, boaters, bowlers, and summer feathers fluttered in the breeze. Constance had remained undeterred.

"We must continue, Vernon," she said. "No matter what that unutterable prig Ewart says. This is for England, is it not? For Leyton and Sixsmith."

"But without Wiggins, without police backup."

"We can manage. We must manage."

And so he tailed his wife alone as she went for her meeting with Monsieur René LeQuin on the steps of the museum. Wiggins was still missing. He'd now missed rendezvous three—Tuesday, Wednesday, and a last gasp attempt that morning, Thursday. Finally, Kell had broken protocol and sent full written instructions to the post office box where the money went—outlining where and when Constance was due to meet LeQuin. He'd even posted the details in the newspaper twice in a desperate attempt to find his agent.

The doors to the museum opened and Kell panicked, trying to keep sight of Constance. She'd placed a huge peacock feather in her hat and he caught it again, by the foot of the steps, fluttering in the wind. The crush closed around him. He jostled and pushed. LeQuin flashed into view, a top hat—the French, so vulgar—reflecting the sun.

LeQuin's hat bent toward the peacock feather. The Frenchman kissed Constance's hand. But then the crush closed on Kell once more. He looked for the feather. He needed to get closer. Out on the street, a fire engine rattled past, bells jangling. Kell swiveled his head toward the noise. Someone barreled into the back of him and he missed his footing. His hand crashed to the floor amidst the boots on the stairs. "Wait, excuse me, wait!" He leapt up immediately, pushing a schoolmistress out of his way. His head jerked left, right.

The peacock feather had gone.

A fly as big as your eye. One two, five six, a swarm. Get them off him. Get them off. He's dying, Bill. Don't mind the flies. Reload. Reload, the major cried.

We got no fucking Billy, sir.

Take cover, take cover, the major cried.

Stretcher, stretcher. Knightly dying in the dirt. Stretcher. Bill shouting.

The ambulance, Ladysmith's only one, ringing its bell. Ringing for the dead. Ringing in his ears.

"It's ringing. The telephone."

"Answer it then."

"I don't know how."

The Dutchman swore and grunted something in Dutch.

Wiggins opened his eyes. He'd been drifting in and out of consciousness for what seemed like days—the pain, the exhaustion, like Ladysmith all over again. And now, once more, he saw his own blood. Slow, fat droplets dripped on the floor beneath him. The monstrous Dutchman, Rijkard, cleaned the cleaver against his massive thigh and waited for the telephone to stop.

"It's the boss," Rijkard's thug called down.

Northern accent. English. Traitor. Wiggins caught sight of a mouthful of blackened teeth. But there was another voice there too, a woman's.

"*Fok.*" Rijkard disappeared up the stairs in two great strides, leaving his accomplice with the black teeth to stand guard. Wiggins craned his head. A pair of familiar boots just visible in the doorway, the owner of the voice, the girl who didn't know how to answer the telephone.

Wiggins kept his eye on those two small feet. Rijkard's grunts echoed downward. Then he shouted for his man. "Miller!" The guard spat and lumbered up the stairs into the hallway, past the small boots of the waiting girl, just visible in Wiggins's eyeline.

"Jax," Wiggins hissed.

Her feet flinched. She crouched down and he saw her face for a second, unsure, fearful. He urged her with his eyes.

She tiptoed down the stairs. "Pretend to give me some of that water," Wiggins gasped, nodding toward a bucket.

Jax approached warily, glancing above her. The sounds of the conversation between Rijkard and Miller filtered down to them, but Wiggins couldn't make out the details.

Instead, he whispered, "I don't blame you. But you've got to get me out of here."

She pushed a cup of water to his mouth but still couldn't speak.

"Ask Sally, ask your mum. How she knows me."

"I can't," Jax whispered at last. "There's two of 'em." She searched his face, pushed the cup at him again. "I didn't think they'd hurt you," she said, placing a hand on his forehead. "I'm sorry."

"Gi' us your sharp."

"I ain't got no sharp."

Wiggins widened his eyes. The men upstairs talked on. "Put it in my hand. Quick."

He felt the sharp sliver of metal in his palm. Jax leapt away from him just as Rijkard reappeared. "Get out of here," he muttered.

"I just gave him a drink, mister."

"Why water a dead plant?" Rijkard backhanded Jax as she went past. "You are lucky, Englishman, *ja*. I will come to kill you in a few hours. Think about that—you can die quick. If you speak. Or it can be painful."

The cleaver clattered across the room, into a corner. "I will put it there, to help you think. Miller," he shouted up the stairs. "Watch our friend. I go." Rijkard reached down toward Wiggins and rammed a petrol-stained rag in his mouth.

"What about the girl?" the heavy Miller asked at the top of the stairs.

"I do not care," Rijkard said. "But if you do her, make sure—" The door swung shut and Wiggins heard no more, other than the key turning in the lock.

Left dangling on Rijkard's slaughtering hook, Wiggins worked the shiv. He knew Jax would carry a sharp, they all did. The shard of metal bent and twisted in his grip as he sawed at his bonds. He held it between finger and thumb and it worked well enough, but he needed to be quick. Miller was about to move in on Jax, and—thanks to him—she was now unarmed.

The rope was Brummagem tat, cheap cord rather than proper sailor's rope. It frayed twine by twine. Wiggins struggled for breath against the gag, a petrol tang in his nose. Up above, a chair scraped back. A muffled cry. The rope was almost free. Suddenly, a great crash of crockery, a high-pitched scream, muffled.

Wiggins ripped the rag from his mouth, gasping for air.

"Help," he shouted, hoarse. "Help!" The best hope for him and Jax was to spook Miller.

Wiggins placed his wrists behind his back, sharp in the palm of his hand, and screamed again.

The basement door swung open.

"Shut the fook up, or I'll stick you." Miller crabbed down the stairs. He pulled at his balls, a gorilla in underwear. "How you get that out?" Miller grunted as he saw the gag, assuming it had been spat free. He crouched down to pick it up, then stepped over to Wiggins. "Here you go, matey."

Wiggins swung his hands around, grasped Miller's legs and clamped his teeth on the man's cock. He bit hard. Miller screamed and Wiggins stuck the sharp in his exposed side. He crashed over.

"Jax," Wiggins shouted. He pulled himself up to the hook, his body bent double, but the effort defeated him and he flopped down. Miller groaned on the floor. "Jax! Hurry," he shouted.

She rushed down the stairs, her shirt loose, hair wild, and launched a boot into Miller's face.

"Leave off," Wiggins gasped. "Untie me, 'fore I snap."

The young girl stopped and gulped. Miller was silent, still. "He . . ." She couldn't finish the sentence.

"We'll sort him later. Get this bleeding knot."

She reached up and untied the binding on his feet. Wiggins subsided to the floor, gasping in relief. The two of them hauled Miller up onto the same hook, and covered his head with a burlap sack. Wiggins glanced at Jax—Miller would live. Jax looked pale and agitated. "You all right, girl?" Wiggins asked. "He didn't . . ."

"No."

Wiggins pulled the sack tight around Miller's torso and hastened to the door. "What day is it?" he asked.

They'd reached the hallway. Wiggins took a swift look around the house and gathered all he needed to know. A drawing room, an office, bedrooms upstairs. He knew exactly where he was.

Jax looked dejected. Shirt ripped, her red curls askew, her bottom lip jutting. Wiggins wiped the blood from his face with a wet cloth then dabbed at the cigarette burn on his forehead. He put a hand to Jax's shoulder. "I don't blame ya. My fault for keeping you involved. They's bad medicine. Now, what day is it?" he asked again.

"Thursday."

"Christ." He glanced at his watch. "Is there anyone else likely to come back?"

"Nah, just them two far as I know. I ain't never been here before." Jax pulled her hat on, tucking her hair away.

"Sling it, back to Sal's. You got any blunt?"

"I don't need money for the bus, I can bunk it."

"For me."

"Why?"

"I need to buy a paper."

Wiggins hobbled from Gloucester Road to South Kensington. Life slowly returned to his wracked limbs and he picked up speed. He sent a fleet of pigeons into the air at the corner of Stanhope Road and, now at a run, swerved through the traffic, over the Cromwell Road toward the museum. His limbs burned with exertion. As he flitted across the grassy verges that fringed the museum, he scanned the visitors. He checked his battered watch, dried his sweating palms in his hair, and looked at Kell's advertisement in the paper once more. No sign of Kell, Constance, or even LeQuin. Too late.

Then he saw him.

When Wiggins first met Vernon Kell, the man had been the perfect picture of a staff captain—trim, dapper, sharp. Now, his hair blown awry, a shirt tail loose, a crushed hat in his hand, eyes wild as he searched the oblivious masses, he looked broken. Wiggins barged through to his boss and gripped him by the elbow. "Sir?"

Kell started and took a moment to focus. "She's gone."

"With LeQuin?"

"A peacock feather. I was meant to track the feather but it's disappeared. She's disappeared . . ."

Wiggins regarded him. "Think, sir, you must have an idea where he's taken her."

Kell's expression lifted. "Not the Albany, and not a hotel. Constance forbade it. But other than that, I have no notion."

Wiggins led Kell away from the museum and into the street. "I can guess where they've gone," he said.

Kell gasped. "Are you sure?"

"It ain't far—but we'll need backup."

Kell's whole body straightened and he jammed on his hat. "I've been fired out."

Wiggins gaped. "What?"

"I've lost my job."

"Still need backup."

They walked purposefully, retracing Wiggins's route. "There is one person I can call," Kell said, eyeing the police box on the corner. "But it's a long shot."

As they jogged side by side through the streets of Kensington, Kell's heart thumped. Wiggins gasped out his story between breaths. "The big fella, Rijkard, took me to some gaff on Cranleigh Gardens."

"Here?"

"Yep. Basement's a bloody mess."

"And Jax?"

"No sign. We need to hurry, sir."

They picked up their pace. Kell noted the open wound on Wiggins's forehead, the bright burn too. "Fiends," he muttered. There was no need to say more.

What of Constance? He had visions of a solitary breakfast, an empty bed. How could he ever explain it to her mother, to the children? How would he forgive himself?

A police inspector waited at the corner of Collingham Road, together with four large constables. "Good old Winnie," Kell said.

"Captain Kell?" the inspector asked. His dark red mustache twitched.

"Inspector . . ."

"Carlton, sir. We came as soon as we could."

"Do you have a battering ram?"

"We've got Constable Trubshaw, sir." The inspector indicated a uniformed mountain of a man.

The wide West London street, dappled and rich, was the kind Wiggins used to be turfed out of in his youth. Too dirty, too poor for this part of town. For all he worked on the right side of the law, Wiggins was dirt to the peelers. At least, he used to be. Today, he urged the constables on. "Number seventeen," he cried. "Don't bother knocking." Kell drew his pistol as the cops thundered into the door.

Boom. Boom. Boom. The door splintered and finally broke. "Police! Police! The game's up," Trubshaw bellowed.

Wiggins and Kell rushed into the hall after the policemen. Rijkard appeared from the side door, his Adam's apple bobbing. He felled the first copper with a huge fist and roared as two more closed. Wiggins burst past him and through a door off the hallway.

The room, which he'd only glanced in earlier, stretched the length of the house, with bookcases lining the far wall and two matching fireplaces. Constance lay by the front window, her hat askew. Before Wiggins could go to her a pain seared his arm. LeQuin, armed with a poker, charged down a small staircase at the rear of the room. "Constance!" Kell ran to his wife.

Wiggins, arm stinging, chased after LeQuin. He jumped down the stairs and caught sight of him clambering out of a sash window at the back of a small parlor. LeQuin then dropped from view. Wiggins cried out in surprise. He thrust his head out the open window.

Below him, LeQuin rose from all fours. The Underground's tracks ran directly under the windows of the terrace, in a deep, open trench that arced beneath the ground at either end. A set of signals glowed red. LeQuin had jumped onto the roof of a stationary train held at the light. He glanced up at Wiggins, as if to utter some triumphant parting shot.

Fear flashed across the Frenchman's face as the train lurched into life. LeQuin stumbled backward, arms windmilling, just as a roar rumbled from the tunnel. A second later, LeQuin fell from the roof of one train under the onrushing wheels of the other. Wiggins watched in horrified fascination as LeQuin's legs were thrown clear—severed by the wheels—while his torso disappeared under the engine.

"Christ." Inspector Carlton appeared at his shoulder.

The train directly below them eased off in the other direction, leaving LeQuin's remains spread across the tracks. "We'll have to get down there. I'll telephone the station," Carlton said. "That bodyguard's a beast. It took four men to subdue him. We've got him in the back of a wagon."

"There's a man in the basement," Wiggins said. "He won't put up much of a fight. Mrs. Kell?" Wiggins remembered, and hurried back to the drawing room.

Kell held Constance in his arms. It was the look of tenderness in her eyes, the shape of Kell's body, the affection, love, between them . . . Wiggins hesitated, brought up short by the sight.

"Ah, Mr. Wiggins." Constance smiled at him. "Please come in. I am quite well, there is no call to be alarmed. A little buffeted."

"LeQuin?" Kell asked.

Wiggins drew his hand across his neck twice in a quick but decisive gesture.

Kell stood up and looked at Carlton. "And what of the other man?"

"We have him, sir. He's out cold and currently being sat on by three of my constables. A formidable opponent."

"Show me."

Kell and Wiggins followed Carlton outside. The constables were in various states of disrepair: all helmetless, two had bleeding noses and a third sagged as he stood guard at the front door. Carlton swung open the van doors.

"Move aside, lads, give us a butcher's," he said. The three policemen crouched aside, revealing the body of Rijkard. He stretched over six three and wore a collarless shirt and a heavy coat, despite the heat.

"That's Rijkard all right," Wiggins said. "He killed Milton. I'll swear to it."

"Look at those hands." The inspector whistled. "What a boxer he'd have made."

Kell pushed back his spectacles. "Did you find anything in his pockets?"

A constable stepped forward. "Not much, sir. Matches, fags. A nice watch, though." Kell picked up the gold timepiece and was about to hand it over to Wiggins for some of his analytical tricks when he saw the inscription on the back. His face clouded over and his head dropped.

"What does it say?" Wiggins asked. Kell handed it to him.

Wiggins read it out dully: "'L. F. Leyton, presented to him on the occasion of his wedding, all my love, your new wife, 6th June 1908.' This is . . . ?" He turned to Kell.

Kell nodded and muttered quietly to himself. Then he took a deep breath and handed the watch to Carlton. "That may very well be evidence of another murder, Inspector. Guard it well. This man must never see the light of day again."

"It would be my pleasure, Captain Kell. There's another of the brutes out cold in the basement. In the meantime, I'll leave a constable on the door—I shall have to return to deal with the, er, body. I've telephoned through and the line has been suspended."

"What line?" Kell asked.

"You'll see," Wiggins said as they returned to the house. Constance was adjusting her hat in the mirror. She handed Kell a broken peacock feather.

"Did you see where he kept his papers, ma'am?" Wiggins asked.

"Not clearly. He was quite charming to begin with. His man, you know, the Dutchman with the Adam's apple, picked us up and drove here. But he'd hardly left us alone for a moment before he quite broke in upon us. He went downstairs then came up shortly after, shouting and screaming. They started to pack up and Monsieur LeQuin disappeared into the back half of the room. I tried to leave but Monsieur LeQuin got rather angry. Thank heavens you arrived when you did. I think he'd forgotten I was there for a moment. But he must have known I was against him. I'm terribly sorry, dear." She looked at Kell. "I gave myself away."

"It is not your fault, my love. I should never have allowed it. Luckily Wiggins got us here just in time."

Wiggins examined the rear of the room, searching for the safe. "Where is it?" Kell asked. Wiggins shook his head and walked the length of the room again, scanning the walls and both fireplaces.

"Ah ha!" he cried at last. He yanked at the bell pull and then reached up the chimney. Gradually, a small strongbox lowered into view on a pulley. It nestled in the empty hearth.

"How on earth?"

"*Two* bell pulls in the room?" Wiggins said. "And this grate ain't seen fire in years."

Kell used LeQuin's telephone to call a car for Constance. Wiggins listened as they fretted and cooed over each other in the hallway, and it wasn't until she was gone that Kell returned to his side. "Now all we need is the key," he said.

"In the heel of LeQuin's shoe, I reckon."

"Well, where's his body then?"

"Not in the same place as his foot."

Gloucester Road's stationmaster met them on the tracks. "You must be quick, gentlemen. We've got to have this open by four, else the system will jam. There's a fireworks show on at Wood Lane later—it'll be bedlam, sir, utter, total bedlam. Not to mention the Tsar at the palace. Embankment will be overflowing."

Kell, Wiggins, and the inspector hurried along the track. "Was he a jumper? We get them more and more every year; tragic it is. Don't they know these machines are killers? I wish they'd do it on Sundays," the stationmaster added.

Kell had seen corpses before, but never one so reduced. The scene resembled the sweepings of a butcher's floor. Kell shuddered inwardly and wondered whether this was indeed what happened when man came up against machines.

He shed no tears for LeQuin, though, or for the murderous thugs in his employ. Kell had finally found Leyton's killer. Rijkard would not escape the noose—for Milton's murder, and for Leyton's too, possibly even Sixsmith's. Kell had been unable to protect his agents, but he would avenge them. If he ever got back into the War Office, that would be his watchword. He didn't care if the enemy were French, German, or Sudanese—if they threatened his own, they'd suffer.

Wiggins walked toward him between the rails, holding up a shoe in one hand and a key in the other. "Let's go."

By the time they'd opened the safe, they could hear once again the rumble of the trains easing back into operation. London stopped for no man. The strongbox contained a raft of manila envelopes full of documents, £150 in notes, and a snub-nosed revolver. In addition, Carlton found a document girdle on the tracks containing a few letters and a small pocketbook. Wiggins riffled through the documents but threw them down in disgust. "Is this French?"

"There's no need for panic," Kell said. "I speak the language."

Wiggins cursed and shot through the door out into the hallway. As Kell sifted through the papers, he could hear Wiggins crashing about upstairs. His agent then made a great show of pushing back into the room. "Nothing," he shouted, then disappeared again. He came back a few moments later. "There's nothing here."

"Are you all right?" Kell asked. Wiggins's feet jiggled in agitation and he couldn't keep his hands still.

"Anything on the East End? Tottenham, Whitechapel?"

"Tottenham? Why on earth? No, I don't think so. It will take time to go through it all thoroughly—as you say, they are in a number of different languages. But I speak several."

Wiggins paced to the window and looked out into the street. "It can't be . . ." he tailed off.

Unnerved by Wiggins's demeanor, Kell nevertheless felt a kind of grim elation. The documents were a trove indeed. In particular, a letter with a German diplomatic letterhead informing whoever it may concern that the bearer should be afforded every assistance. Taken together with the Krupp's connection and the death of Milton, the document in itself could be proof enough to get Ewart what he wanted—to start a whole new department.

To get his job back.

It didn't help that LeQuin also appeared to have a similar letter from the British government's own Foreign Office, as well as from representatives of the governments of France, Turkey, and Austro-Hungary.

"How about Russian?" Wiggins said.

"Funnily enough, that appears to be the only one missing."

"What? I meant, do you speak Russian?"

Kell looked up at him. "A little. It's an interesting language, forever in flux. Russians often take words from somewhere else and adopt them, speaking in their own accent. Did you know their word for train station is *Voksal*, all because of some government visit or other a few years ago—they wanted to see the new inventions and a bigwig showed them Vauxhall train station. And they thought it referred to all stations, so they took the word as was. A straight transliteration.

"Funny you should ask that," Kell went on. "On today of all days."

"What's today?"

"The Tsar's visit. Give it another hour and he'll be rolling down the Mall to the palace. Are you sure you're quite all right, Wiggins?"

As Kell had told this story, he'd noticed a strange transformation come over Wiggins. His face tensed, his foot tapped, and he began gnawing at his fingernails.

Wiggins leapt at the door. "We must stop him."

"I beg your pardon."

"Stop the Tsar's procession. I can't explain. Someone's going to try to blow the bloody thing up. Trust me."

"But—"

Wiggins had already gone. Kell sighed. Curse the fellow. Stopping a state visit in its tracks was near impossible. Still, he had his evidence, and he had the direct line of the one person in Whitehall who might believe him. He picked up LeQuin's telephone and made the call.

"What is it now, Kell? Get to it."

"I have reason to believe the Tsar's procession may be the target of a bomb, sir."

"Good God, sir. What do you expect me to do about it?"

Kell coughed. "You know my current situation."

"This is highly irregular, Captain. It will not make me popular with the authorities. If I am to succeed—I must add this—my chances are slim. Will it be worth my while?"

"Sir, thanks to your intervention with the police I now have cast-iron proof of German espionage on a large scale, I have one enemy agent dead and a murderer under lock and key. I will be reinstated, we will get more funding, and you will get the credit. But, of course, only if the Tsar lives."

"I will try, Captain."

I bet you will, Kell thought, as he put the telephone back on its hook. Winston Churchill was the most pompous, glory-hunting man he'd ever met. If he could claim the credit for saving a royal's life, the King's cousin no less, then he'd surely move heaven and earth to do so.

Kell went back to the documents spilling out of LeQuin's safe. There must be all the evidence he needed here, if he only looked hard enough. It took him another ten minutes, as he gathered and sifted the papers, to realize that his agitated agent had taken the £150 in notes. Wiggins the dip indeed.

22

"Who's there?"

"Vot's wrong with your leg?"

Wiggins looked down at his knee. It jiggled uncontrollably. "Not now, Otto," he said out of the corner of his mouth. "Tell me."

The beggar looked up at him from his spot on the pavement. He shrugged. "Spare change for an old Luxembourger. Spare change," he shouted and then muttered under his breath. "Vere have you been?"

"I got held up." Wiggins glanced up and down New Oxford Street and caught his breath after the headlong rush from Kensington. "Are you gonna tell me who's in there or what?"

"Spare change!" Otto called again. The old beggar coughed, then spoke through his hand. "The good-looking von, Peter, he is upstairs. I don't see the other von leave. And no man with the big mustaches. Spare some coins, any coins! Peter, he come about von hour ago."

"I owe you."

"My takings are three shillings down from the Strand."

Wiggins scanned the frontage. The umbrella shop door rang, its wares lined up in the window like rifles. Upstairs, unseen, Yakov and Peter plotted their mayhem, at the behest of Arlekin, in that piss-stink hellhole of an attic room. Arlekin. Not René LeQuin. Wiggins shook his head at the stupid error, playing silly games with words. Of course LeQuin wouldn't be mixed up with the likes of Peter, with the Tottenham job. Wiggins cursed. For one moment, as he and Kell closed in on LeQuin, he'd thought he had the man responsible for Bill's death.

But now Bill's death would go unavenged, the shadow Arlekin would be lost to him forever, unless . . .

He bolted across the road. "Vere are you going, Viggins?" Otto called.

Wiggins barged through the door and vaulted the stairs two at a time. His heart hammered hard, and not just from the stairs. Peter and Yakov didn't trust him, but they still didn't *know* he was on the other side. If he could string them along for a while more, he might get a chance to confront Arlekin *and* foil the bombing. Ever since Bill's murder, he'd been looking for this man, Arlekin, the man behind his best friend's death. Arlekin was waiting for him, justice was waiting for him. It all came down to this moment. He had to keep his cool.

He swung open the door to the attic room without knocking.

"*Dyavola!*" Yakov exclaimed.

"You!" Peter said.

The two men stood opposite him in the small room. They were fully dressed, and even had their hats on, ready to leave. The bomb was nowhere to be seen and the bed had been rolled up in the corner. Peter's hand strayed to his coat pocket, but Wiggins took a breath and kept his voice calm.

"I was passing by," he said. "We still on for tomorrow? Noon?"

Peter hesitated, glanced at Yakov. His eyes involuntarily flicked to a hatbox under the table. "Yes, yes, of course. It's good to see you." He smiled wolfishly. "A surprise. Nice surprise. Here, have one of these." He held out a brightly colored pellet. "Wine gums. Delicious. Capitalism's only gift to world."

Wiggins shook his head.

"You are sure? It gives a little to your teeth, like good meat, but then it breaks in two, easy." Peter bit into the small sweet and held up the other half between finger and thumb. "See. A clean break. No juice."

Yakov stared intently at Wiggins then sloped back to the table. "You are mess," Peter went on. "What have you been doing?"

Wiggins shrugged. "I'm fine."

Peter barked out a sharp laugh. "So English," he said.

"You going out?"

Peter put his arm around Wiggins's shoulder and drew him toward the window. The arm weighed heavy.

"London," he said, pointing with his free hand. "We make our mark here. It is center of world, even for us Russians. This is where revolution starts. Over there, only two streets away, Karl Marx wrote *Das Kapital*. And Lenin lived near here. Even our very own Tsar is parading in streets today! This city is heart. This is where it starts."

As Peter talked, Wiggins sensed Yakov shifting around the room. He followed his movements in the reflection in the windowpane. The Russian knelt down and gently pulled the hatbox from under the table.

Peter went on. "I came here to make something for myself and to make something for my people. This is not always a nice thing to look at. Sacrifices have to be made. World is hard. If I told you stories of my childhood, you would not believe; you would not believe I could be standing here, hundreds of versts from my country. I survived." Peter paused. "But I refuse to be defeated. Revolution takes different forms. We learn this. We all have our own wars to fight."

His hand squeezed Wiggins's neck, the thumb dug deep. "This is not your war. Not your way."

A hand on each shoulder, he forced Wiggins round so that they were now face to face. "I like you, truly. You are my favorite Englishman, I think—a man who can drink vodka and fight police. This is a good man to know, my kind of man. But Arlekin says we cannot trust you with this job, it is not your way."

"But—" Before Wiggins got any further, Peter drove a fist into his solar plexus. Wiggins doubled over in pain.

"I am sorry," Peter said.

Wiggins squinted up at the handsome Russian, his mouth twisted in regret. Yakov then burst past Peter, his fist balled around a snub-nosed knife. He drew his hand back but Peter shouted out and yanked him away. "*Niet!*"

"Sorry for Yakov. He is very angry you stole compound spring from his bomb parts. Lucky we have spare. You have very good fingers." Peter shrugged. "All of us poor, we learn to take things. Yakov would kill you. I like you. What can I say, I am human. *Do svidaniya.*"

Peter dragged Yakov away.

At the door, he turned back. "One day, we drink again. Until then, my English friend." He swiveled on his heel and pushed Yakov in front of him.

Wiggins clambered to his feet.

"Wait!" he shouted down the narrow stairs, stumbling after them. "Bombing the Tsar won't change anything."

Peter turned at the landing, puzzled. He looked up at Wiggins and shrugged his shoulders in resignation. "She was right," he mumbled. Then he pulled the Mauser from his pocket, straightened his arm, and fired.

Wiggins flew backward. A jolt of pain exploded in his shoulder. A blinding light flashed in his eyes like a reel of cinematographic film unspooling. And then it went to black.

Kell sat on the floor of LeQuin's drawing room, documents strewn around him. They included a number of compromising letters and other scandalous material about various royals—not only British, but those scattered across Europe. They would need to be handled carefully, as would the few technical papers—the importance of which he didn't yet know. The constable previously posted on the door now fussed about the room, helping Kell sort through the documents. There were also Leave of Passage letters from the diplomatic departments of Europe and even the State Department of the United States. Bloody Yanks, pretending they believed in isolationism while paying spies.

It would take weeks to go through all the information, to untangle what exactly LeQuin was doing and for whom. Kell decided to keep it all to himself for the moment, until he could analyze it properly. All except the German one. That letter, combined with the case against LeQuin and the arrest of Rijkard, would be enough to get him his job back.

One item puzzled him particularly. LeQuin's pocketbook contained figures and letters but in no discernible pattern. The constable coughed. "You want to keep these, sir?" he said, holding up a sheaf of receipts.

"Of course," Kell snapped, his concentration on the numbers. "One plus eight?" he muttered to himself.

"Is that numbers, is it?" the constable asked. Kell looked up. The policeman had a long, thin face, split by a crooked nose. "There are numbers," Kell replied. "But I have no idea what they mean."

"Do you mind if I . . . ?" The policeman put his hand out, like a shy child.

Kell handed him the book, surprised. "What's your name?"

"Stoner, sir," he said. He scanned the numbers and letters quickly. "It appears to be a code."

"Yes, thank you for that. It's good to see the Metropolitan Police is training its officers properly."

"Sorry, sir. I meant, maybe it's a transposition code." The constable started reading out letters: "P, E, R." He looked down at Kell. "Best take a note, sir."

Kell grasped a pencil and began writing, repeating the letters and numbers as the policeman spoke.

"That's page one, sir. It don't seem to mean much, but I'm sure that's it."

Kell searched the letters. "Of course," he cried. "It's in French! *Allemagne*—four hundred pounds. *Autriche, Turquie*, et cetera."

"Sounds like a ledger, sir."

"By God, it is, it is. How do you know so much about this, Constable . . . ?"

The young policeman blushed.

"Stoner, sir. My old man's on the tic-tac. He's a bookie, sir, to be honest, and not entirely legal like, so please don't tell. But me and my brothers, we're all dab with the numbers."

Kell held the book in his hand. "This is marvelous."

It was the final piece, proof positive that LeQuin had been working up until that very day for Germany. LeQuin used Milton to get the information out of Woolwich, the intelligence that ended up in Krupp's; he'd had Leyton killed to protect the secret; and Milton had met his death when he was blown. Lord knew what Sixsmith had done to deserve his demise, but it would be in the ledger.

"Read out the rest, Stoner."

Kell took down the names and figures with mounting glee. "Say that last one again," he called out, scandalized.

A grin spread across his face. "Stoner, find me a cab. We will finish this later. I must get to Whitehall at once."

It all made sense. What a fool he'd been.

"Is he dead?"

"Oh Gawd, he's dead."

"He's not dead, you daft ha'p'orth."

It was this broad Lancashire accent that caused Wiggins to pop open his eyes. The view was fringed not by angels but by whores. A big woman, the madam, scattered the young girls and bent to his side. "There you go, love. You best get off if you can. I can't have my customers disturbed. They won't pay." She leaned down and gently cradled his head. "Can you walk?"

Wiggins felt his shoulder. His hand came away hot and wet. "This suit is ruined," he laughed nervously. "And it's not even mine."

"Viggins, Viggins. Are you all right?" Otto clambered up the stairs, breathing heavily. "I see the two men, they leave and nothing. Oh my Got, vot is this? You need the hospital."

"No." He winced, suddenly aware of the pain. But it had the effect of clearing his mind. "There's no time. Gi' us a hand."

Otto and the madam helped him to his feet and the old tramp put his head under Wiggins's good arm. Wiggins grunted to him. "Gower Street. Twenty-four A."

Wiggins felt better on the street. His mind, awash with adrenaline and pain, was sparking back to life, making connections like the telegraph wires strung across the city, the train tracks. The sewers.

Arlekin.

They arrived at number twenty-four and Wiggins rang the bell with his good arm. Otto stepped away. "I should go," he said, wary of officialdom in all its forms.

"Thanks, Otto."

The door swung open. "How many times must I say the surgery's hours are—Great Scott, Wiggins, is that you?"

"It is, Doctor. I wonder if . . ."

"Of course, here, take my arm . . . Martha! Martha. Bring the brandy into my room." In seconds, Dr. Watson had Wiggins lying on a raised bed. He pulled back the jacket and ripped Wiggins's shirt clear. "Bring the ethanol," he shouted. "Now, Wiggins, I'll deal with this first on the promise that you'll tell me the truth of the matter afterward."

"Of course, Doctor, I ain't never lied to you."

As the good Doctor went about his work, Wiggins examined him. His mustache was grayer, a little longer perhaps, the wrinkles deeper, the skin of his neck dappled by brown spots, his hair scrappier than before, not quite groomed. But his eyes still burned kind.

Dr. Watson went on. "This is going to hurt, but I can pull the bullet out with these. It may not feel like it, but for some reason the wound is shallow. Take another brandy. Here goes." He yanked the bullet free. A jolt of pain shot down Wiggins's arm, up into his neck, and across his chest. He passed out again.

When he came to, his shoulder was bandaged and he reeked of ethanol and brandy. He saw Watson hold up something to the light by the window. "Remarkable," the Doctor said as he twisted the bullet between finger and thumb.

Wiggins took another pull at the brandy bottle. The pain dulled slightly. "Weren't you wounded by a bullet, Doctor? Was it your leg or your shoulder? I can never remember."

The Doctor appeared not to hear, for he turned to Wiggins earnestly. "This could have killed you. Something must have significantly slowed the velocity of the bullet—or was it at long-range?"

"Look in the breast pocket." Wiggins pointed with his good arm. "There!"

Watson lifted up his old battered Hunter watch and gazed in admiration. "You stole this from me years ago," he murmured.

"I didn't mean . . ."

"It was a gift of sorts, Wiggins, we let you take it." He turned over the watch and they saw the hard bullet mark scraped along the front cover. "You know, I do believe this saved your life," the Doctor said finally. "This is one for the annals."

Wiggins got up and stood next to the Doctor by the front window. As he did so, he heard a heartily sung anthem coming from the street outside.

"*The people's flag is* deepest . . ."

"The Tsar!" Wiggins cried as he hustled to the front door.

A gang of trade-union demonstrators were trying to cheer themselves with a rendition of "The Red Flag" as they walked northward. Their banner trailed sadly behind them. "What happened?" Wiggins called after them.

"A dead bust." A young man in a baggy cap turned toward him.

"Huh?"

"Six hours it took us to get here, supporting our comrades in Russia. Six hours and then he cancels, don't he?"

Another man lifted his banner tamely. "That's the imperialist for you. Unreliable."

"Grand Imperial, my arse."

"A wasted day out," the men carried on, grumbling as they went. "Should have gone to Wood Lane."

Wiggins looked after them. Kell must have got the message through. And yet. Grand Imperial.

"What's the time, Doctor?" He turned back into the hallway.

"Just gone five."

"Have you got a telephone? It's urgent."

Watson fixed him with a stare. "Is this legitimate, Wiggins? You turn up here with a bullet in you, what am I meant to think?"

"I work for the government, Doctor, honest. Ask Mr. Holmes."

"Holmes!" Watson exclaimed. "Of course. The telephone is in my office. But you really need to rest."

Wiggins strode to the door, strengthened by the brandy in his belly and the bandage supporting his shoulder. The Tsar had never been the target at all. Too hard, too obvious—but the bomb was going to go off all the same. He needed to stop it and he knew exactly where it was going. But first he had to make a call to give himself a chance. He held the receiver in his teeth as he wound up the instrument with his good hand.

"Get me Whitehall 412."

Wiggins, made lopsided by his injured shoulder, barreled out into the street and hailed a hansom cab.

"Wood Lane. A fiver down if you do it under forty."

The cabbie sneered. "You ain't got no fiver. And I don't want no bleeding in the cab." He raised the reins to gee off but as he did so, Wiggins ripped a note from his pocket and brandished it theatrically.

"I don't have time," Wiggins said, the note flapping in the wind.

"Sorry, sir. My eyes aren't what they used to be, sir. Wood Lane you say? Jump in."

The horse near bolted before Wiggins even took his seat. They flew down into Shaftesbury Avenue, the cab bouncing and flitting. But the roads gradually filled, and by the time they'd reached Piccadilly they were at a complete standstill. Wiggins squeezed his leg with his good arm, fighting the pain in his shoulder.

"Fack sake," the cabbie cursed. "First the Tsar's parade and now this? Facking Underground up the spout. Never trust 'em."

He gestured at the crowds streaming from Dover Street Station. They'd come to a halt by the flashy new Ritz luxury hotel and Wiggins stood up in the cab, scanning the road ahead. A wall of idling motorcars, lorries, carts, four-wheelers, taxis, and hundreds of bobbing hats—bowlers, boaters, derbies, homburgs, liveried caps, bonnets, feathered elegances, and even an ivory topper. A sea uncrossable.

"How much for the horse?" Wiggins said.

The driver's small eyes widened in astonishment. "Wot?"

"Fifty quid for the horse and tack. That's double his worth."

"You want it now? I mean, wot for?" The old cabbie chewed a moment and spat free a tobacco cud. "You know, on reflection, I don't know if I could bear to part wiv him, sir. He's been my constant companion since my missus passed, bless her soul, and without Monty here—a stunning nag if I say so myself—I don't know if I'd have pulled through. It would be too much of a wrench to lose him too."

"Sixty."

"Done."

The driver hastily unbuckled the horse and helped Wiggins mount. Pain shot down his arm as he gripped the improvised reins. He hadn't been on a horse for more than ten years, but he'd grown up on the streets of London, a city—then—that ran on horsepower. He'd ridden on cabbies' nags, on the drays, on the wizened old coal horses, and the old stagers plodding the Regent's Canal; he'd passed the time with the stable hands behind the grand hotels, picked up all the dodges. Even as the horse neighed and jittered, he dug his knees in sharp, thrust out his toes, and turned onto the pavement.

"Oi, watch it!"

"This is a public footway, you thug."

Pedestrians rippled aside as Wiggins and his horse clip-clopped under the colonnade of the hotel. A second later a policeman whistled. "Orff that horse, now!"

Wiggins kicked his heels, Green Park in sight. He veered through the gates and into the park. The horse stretched out, reveling in its freedom. Wiggins clung on, teeth clenched against the pain of his wound, his sights set west.

"You can't go in there, sir."

"Really?" Kell said as he strode confidently through the Cabinet Office entrance. "Refer any complaints to the Undersecretary. Failing that, talk to Mr. Churchill," he continued, the agitated clerk fluttering in his wake. If Soapy had any guts left, he'd stand up for him.

"But they're discussing the cancellation of the Tsar's parade."

"I know," Kell called over his shoulder. "That's my fault, so I'm sure they'll want to talk to me."

Kell had gone to the War Office only to find the whole team across at the Cabinet rooms.

He reached the grand entrance of Cabinet Briefing Room A. Behind him, the clerk called shrilly for the police. Kell threw open the doors and held his head high. The room had so long been the scene of his fruitless attempts to make a case for an espionage agency, Kell now allowed himself a grim smile.

"What the devil?" Soapy looked up at the interruption. "Oh, Captain Kell. To what do we owe the pleasure?"

Soapy actually looked amused, unlike the dour-faced elders packed around the table. Even the army's true overlord, the Secretary of State for War, Haldane, was there.

"How dare you, sir," Haldane glowered from beneath bushy eyebrows.

"Kell," Ewart bellowed. "Leave at once. I've just been informing them about your reassignment. As I was saying, sir, Lieutenant Russell here is the man in charge now."

"Ah yes, Russell." Kell dwelled on the name for a moment. "We'll get to you by and by. First, I must inform the committee of my findings."

"I say, Kell, dear chap, aren't you behind this parade fiasco?" Soapy drawled. "You may as well tell us what the devil's going on. The police are livid, and I hear Tsar Nicholas is distinctly put out at having the whole thing canceled."

Churchill coughed theatrically.

"I can answer that, if I may be so bold. There was an imminent threat to the very body and being of His Imperial Majesty—as detected by Captain Kell—and it was my duty, to the crown, to the country indeed, to protect His Majesty from any violent action, be it—"

"Yes, thank you, Winston," Haldane said. "Captain Kell. Ewart here tells us you are no longer working for the counterintelligence bureau. So, explain yourself quickly, man, before I have you arrested."

Kell nodded. "I have here written proof of a spy ring, financed by the German Government, which stole secrets from Woolwich

Arsenal and has been responsible for the death of at least two of my agents. Two men are under arrest for murder; a third man—the spymaster, a Monsieur René LeQuin—died trying to escape. See for yourselves—the problem is real, it is big, and it will only grow." A shocked silence fell on the room. Only Churchill seemed unsurprised. He sidled over to Kell and began looking at the documents.

Finally, Ewart spoke. "But, I, er, Kell. Um, Russell, what say you?"

The lieutenant blanched. His lower lip sagged. "I . . ."

Kell grimaced. "I suggest, Major General, that you put this man Russell under arrest. If you look at page five of this ledger, you'll see Russell—I imagine we can drop the 'lieutenant' now, eh?—was also in the employ of LeQuin. His information led directly to the death of at least one man and possibly more."

"That's utter rot, sir. How could I—I would never."

"Save your protestations for the police," Churchill growled, pointing the policemen—who'd arrived at the behest of the clerks—toward Russell. "That's your man, Constables. Arrest him at once."

The police hauled the lieutenant away. He haw-hawed his innocence, but the men at the table sat stoney-faced. Ewart opened and closed his mouth, silently aghast.

Churchill had taken charge of the meeting. "This doesn't augur well for your organization, does it, Ewart? You sack the one man who has succeeded and hire an agent of the enemy. Well, sir, well?" He pulled a cigar from his waistcoat and examined it carefully. "Haldane? There can be only one course of action, surely."

Ewart stood up, still unable to speak. He nodded to Haldane, picked up his hat, and left the room.

"How did you get all this, Kell?" Haldane asked, fingering the documents with awe.

"I had one agent left, sir. The best."

23

Wiggins galloped across Shepherd's Bush Green, where the road traffic gave way to a carnival of pedestrians heading for the Imperial Exhibition and the fireworks display. It was due to start in thirty minutes, and the crowd was thick and loud. He tried to pick out Yakov or Peter in the crush. The bareback horse with the winged rider attracted the odd curious glance, but Wiggins hardly noticed, his search desperate. Yakov and Peter would stick out among these middle-class pleasure-seekers, Wiggins knew.

He also knew they wouldn't be there.

Twenty minutes later he saw the figure he dreaded most. Dreaded and expected. Approaching Wood Lane from a side street, he saw the hatbox first, round, striped like a cut cake, held out in front with two hands. She looked like a respectable lady's maid, out running errands on a busy day. A policeman wouldn't give her a second glance, except perhaps to note the unusual birthmark spread across half of her face.

* * *

He looked good on a horse. Strange, to see him in this city, a beautiful man cutting through the crowd like a hussar, his head hatless, one shoulder hunched.

Watch them. Join them. Tell me what they say. You needn't betray anyone. His Russian was perfect. But he was not Russian. That first day in the library, he'd sounded so reasonable, so easy, so rich. In the beginning, he (she did not find out his name until later) asked only for tidbits, gossip, general chatter. They met in public libraries, exchanging hurried conversation between the shelves. He paid her little, but it helped. She contributed more to Marta and her family, made their lives better. And if she were going to get to New York, to Sarah, she needed to start somewhere.

Back in Dvinsk, the idea of being an informer would never have occurred to her. But she was not in Dvinsk anymore. She did it for the money at first, of course, but she never thought she was doing anything wrong, not really. They were stupid little boys playing stupid little games—one side wore suits, the other stubble. One side did it for their "King and country" the other for "the workers." Or so they told themselves.

No one did it for the women.

Van Bork treated her with respect. He would ask her where she wanted to meet. He would pull out a chair for her. He was always polite. This was new. At his suggestion, she inveigled herself into the political meetings around Whitechapel. She was so successful, melted into the scene so seamlessly, that Van Bork began asking more.

Names, places, numbers.

And then one day he said, "Lead them. Everybody wants to be led. Especially the anarchists. I will pay you more. You needn't betray anyone."

A different, younger Bela would have laughed behind her hand and turned her face away. But she didn't have to be that Bela anymore. She didn't have to be anyone's Bela but her own.

She began to visit him periodically at the German Embassy, always at night and always through the servants' entrance. Ask for Van Bork, he told her, though she didn't know if that was his real name. He wanted her to cause trouble, to provoke action. He wanted fights, demonstrations, unrest.

"Why?" she asked, the first time he met her at the embassy.

"For money, of course."

"No, why do *you* want this?"

He unfolded his insect-long limbs and stood up. "That is a bigger question. You've heard of the Triple Entente? It doesn't matter if you haven't. What I want, what Germany wants, is chaos and disharmony between Great Britain and Russia. We want disaster on the streets of London, and we want Russia to get the blame. You can help us. But you needn't betray anyone." He'd been walking up and down as he talked, but at this last line he turned and smiled. "There," he added. "I have given you a gift—I have told you why I want what I want. It makes me weaker to do so."

"You think I can do this? I am only a woman, they will not listen to me."

Van Bork slowly rubbed his hands together. He examined the palms before he answered. "They will listen to you. I see it in your eyes. You are a leader. I know you."

"What if I refuse?"

"Must we go through this? Really? You have been working for the imperialists, you have been *spying* for the imperialists. Your new friends . . ." he tailed off, the implication clear. "Let's not be childish."

Trapped again. But she was never going to refuse, even though she asked. It was the only way she was ever going to earn real money on her own. And maybe Van Bork was right. She *could* lead.

Peter was the key. She'd seen him out and about a number of times, at the drinking dens north of the 'Chapel, at the clubs. People spoke in hushed tones when he passed. There's the Painter, they'd say, as if he'd decorated the Sistine Chapel. When Bela looked at him, she thought of a different art. His thick hair, his languid smile, the symmetrical features—he could have been on the stage. She watched as he strutted about with his gang of toughs. But Bela saw the sadness around his mouth when he smiled, recognized the dissatisfaction in the machismo performance.

"Petty crime is very glamorous," she said to him as he exited the Anarchist Club one night.

"What?" He turned.

"It must make you feel good. To contribute to the cause."

"I am against the law, as all anarchists should be."

Bela shrugged. "Of course, it is as I say. It makes you feel good."

He waved a hand at her in dismissal and strode off into the night. She knew he would return. The way to charm a peacock is to give him what he knows he does not have—the one, most beautiful feather in the plume. In Peter's case: a sense of mission.

"Why should I listen to you? Who are you anyway?" he said, the next time they met.

And that's how she reeled him in, under Van Bork's instruction. She suggested targets for robbery first, but targets that struck at the state and not simply for the crime itself. These targets changed to include demonstrations, focused acts of violence and mayhem. Peter christened her Arlekin, Harlequin in English, the multi-colored fool—her two-tone face like the clown's mask. He came to follow her, like a child behind a piper.

He used her too, of course. Each of his various schemes he dignified to his followers with the same old "It's from Arlekin," although half the time she only found out later. But Peter began to trust her. She was so much better at planning than he was. The Tottenham job would never have been so botched had it been up to her—what kind of idiot holds up a payroll outside a police station?

The bomb was her last job. Van Bork put down enough cash to take her to New York and a new life, away from anarchists and Peter and Yakov and men playing their silly little games. All she'd needed was access to the materials to make an effective bomb—and then Wiggins fell into her lap. A new convert, a worker at Woolwich, eager and ready. At least, that's what he'd said to Peter—ready to go into battle for the cause. Yet that wasn't the man she knew, her Wiggins. But then, did she know him at all?

Wiggins. A good man. She used to wonder whether they existed, where. And there he was, a magnificent drunken white knight, fighting for her on the street, buying her perfume, holding her hand. Gentle and true. Why did he have to be so true? Didn't he know the poor can't afford love?

And now here he was, her good and beautiful man—on a horse, like a real knight. Not what she needed at all.

Wiggins slipped from the horse, steadied himself against its flank, and headed toward her. She stopped when she saw him but didn't try to run, didn't show much surprise beyond a delicately arched eyebrow. He moved quickly, despite the pain in his shoulder. She had a faraway smile on her lips, sad, knowing, maybe even amused, but as he neared, Wiggins saw her expression drop.

She gestured with her eyes. "You're hurt?" Wiggins realized she wasn't smiling at all. Her eyes were bloodshot, her face pale.

"Not here," he said.

With his good arm, he gripped Bela but not too tight to rattle the box. "This way." He guided her from the crowd. Wiggins pulled her down first one street, then the next and a third, his teeth clenched, his brow sweat-streaked, and his shoulder throbbing. Neither of them spoke. He could barely keep his eyes from the hatbox, Yakov's bomb. Phosphorus he had stolen inside, the nuts and bolts and springs and murderous cunning of Yakov.

"Is it live?" He had to check.

"I knew you'd steal something," she whispered. "Yakov got another spring."

"Is it live?"

"Yes."

Their shoes beat on the flagstones as they headed north, down terraced streets. Windows glowed golden as the evening closed in. Wiggins dug his fingers into Bela's arm. His eyes flicked again at the box, heart pumping. The pain stung his shoulder, chiming with every heartbeat. Bela's breathing grew quicker beside him, wheezy, short. Her hands shook with tension. The box. The bomb. Wiggins pushed on.

A rocket screeched above their heads and multicolored flowers lit the sky.

"Christ," Wiggins ducked. "That's the display."

"We don't have time," Bela gasped, eyes on the box in front of her. "We must leave this."

Wiggins glared at her but carried on. "It'll kill people here."

He half dragged her over a barge-choked canal and then a set of train tracks, until they reached a wide main road. A horse reared up and a motorcar swerved. Someone shouted, but Wiggins kept on.

Up ahead, an ornate gate with a huge stone architrave. They hurried under the arch and into a grand cemetery. The night closed, blacker there amid the gravestones, the mausoleums, and the high, hanging trees. It was deserted as they went deeper in, away from the roads and the surrounding houses.

"Give it here," Wiggins muttered at last. He took the box in his hands, his left arm shaking with the pain, and trod carefully into the stairwell of a large crypt.

Bela waited for him, though he could barely make out her form in the gloom. She waved an arm above her head in one slow movement and he headed toward her. "Here is safe," she said.

They sat side by side on a public bench and eyed the far-off crypt. Wiggins glanced up and down the path.

He hadn't trusted himself to talk—his anger too difficult to control. Not anger at her so much as at himself, for missing the signs. Now, as they waited for the bomb to explode—the device he'd helped create—Wiggins thought of the shadowy Arlekin, responsible for Bill Tyler's death, who now sat beside him with her hands in her lap.

"You're hurt," she said. "What happened?"

"Arlekin. That means harlequin in Russian, right? Your face—they call you Arlekin."

She said nothing.

"You've been running me all along. As soon as you found out where I worked, you knew you could use me. 'Don't leave your job, Wiggins. It's a good job. An important job,' you said. Woolwich factory, military hardware. You and Peter playing me like a fucking piano. Christ, what a mug I've been." He shook his head. "This is your big job, ain't it, the big score. You couldn't trust the others to do this one. No one would suspect a woman, would they, not a peach like you. Wouldn't hurt a fly." He barked out a laugh and then fell quiet. "You know, I loved going to the Exhibition with you—normal, like. We went on the ride. I thought you was interested in me, in days like that. But you was just casing the bloody joint, fucking recce. That's why I'm here, that's why I knew. I clicked at last." He exhaled long and slow. "Did you ever feel anything for me?"

Bela sighed. "You know this."

"Do I?"

He felt her hand gently rest on his bad shoulder and despite himself, her touch calmed him. He breathed in her scent.

"What happened?" she said again.

"Peter," he replied. "I'm all right. At least, my shoulder is."

"I told him not to hurt you," she whispered. "Why did you come?"

"You can't kill innocent people, it ain't right, Bel."

"It's not about killing. I am to destroy the Vibbly-Vobbly, that is all . . ." Her voice trailed off.

Wiggins spat. "Have you ever seen a phosphorus bomb? Seen a body ripped apart? It's not the bang you remember, it's the waiting after the bang and before the screaming. Funny, it seems like hours when it happens, that silence between the cause and the effect. That's what stays with you." As his muscles relaxed, he suddenly felt very tired.

The bomb waited in the far-off darkness, unexploded.

"I only went along with the bloody plot so as I could kill you," he said at last. "Kill Arlekin. I should do it too—you sent my best mate to the grave. Bill was the best man I ever knew and you and your fucking games—you!—sending those stupid bastards out robbing, you killed him."

"I had nothing to do with your friend's death. This is true."

"Ain't this your bloody gang?" He pulled from his pocket the red enamel eight-pointed star and thrust it awkwardly into her hand. "You ran the Tottenham job, sent those fuckers up there with a shooter and collected the cash. Christ, what a mug," he repeated.

"This is not my gang. The star means without state. I have no gang." She placed the small star back in Wiggins's lap. "Peter and Yakov are common criminals. Peter has a good face, he is handsome, yes, but they are no good. They shoot for fun, for anything. I never sent them to Tottenham. It is foolish thing, this robbery. It means nothing." She took a breath. "This is the sign of an old gang—they change the name all the time, to give reason for their stupidity. You must talk to Peter about your friend. He was at Tottenham."

"You say it Tot-num, two syllables," he muttered. "You swear you had nothing to do with it?"

"Nothing." She stroked his back.

"Then what are you doing trying to blow up half of Hammersmith? I knew you was into the politics, but Bel, *this*? Running with the likes of Peter, bombing folk? What good would it do?" He grunted in pain. "But it ain't even political for you, is it? That ain't the half of it."

Wiggins shook his head sadly as he thought through each of the steps leading to this point. Bela as Arlekin, the Exhibition as the bomb target, Bela pulling all the strings. He thought he knew why, though not quite the reason behind that why.

"They don't know about the Germans, do they?" he said.

Bela's hand stiffened and withdrew. "I don't understand."

"I saw you, Bel, at the embassy."

The night exploded. A great flash of light and a shuddering, hollow boom, rubble, then smoke and green-white light in a great bloom. Wiggins saw Bela's face, lit up, startled.

She turned to him. "We must go. The police will come." She stood up.

He grabbed her wrist tightly. "I'm not going anywhere. Tell me who you speak to at the embassy? Have they been paying for all this?"

She swept her eyes around as the light from the bomb died. In the distance, they could hear faint cries, the peeping of a whistle.

"His name is Van Bork. He pays me to set up these things—the demonstration, a fight, a bomb. That's all I know. He found me, a long time ago. And he pays me."

"But why?"

"We must go, the police."

"Tell me." Wiggins squeezed her wrist hard and wouldn't let go. "Is there a child?" he said in a softer tone. "Is that why?"

Bela said something he didn't understand and then switched to English in a violent burst, harsher and quicker than he'd ever heard—barked and hard-edged.

"No, there is no child. Is this only reason for woman to act? Is woman's life about child and nothing else? Woman cannot have the same life as man? All men I have met think this. My father, my husband, the Plovs. Peter, Yakov, and now you. Women are not allowed their own thoughts and feelings. You would never ask this question of a man. For man it is all right to be greedy, evil, it is his decision. But woman, it must be child. This is what all men think and you think it too. I tell you. I did it for the money, Wiggins, for new life. My life. For this bomb, Van Bork will pay me a hundred pounds. I go to America. Do you know what a woman's life is in Russia? Misery and work. And here? For me, not better. With this money, I go. I find my sister. A new life." She drew breath, and brought her other hand around to Wiggins's wrist. At the cemetery entrance, a lantern jogged and winked in the darkness. Shouts and voices punched the air. Phosphorus smoke bit their eyes. "You can come with me, to America. Please . . . ?"

He held on to her wrist. "You once told me I was a good man. What would a good man do?"

She stopped struggling against his grip. The far-off shouts were getting closer. "You don't need to be so good. Not this time. Come with me."

He released her. "I can't do it, Bel," he said. "But if you go, go fast, get out of London. You've got the most beautiful face I've ever seen, but it ain't hard to recognize. They'll be after you. In no time," he added, placing fifty pounds in her palm. "Don't go back to the embassy. Don't go back to Peter neither—they'll know you was a German snout. Working for the imperialists. I can't have you going back there."

"Come, please," she pleaded.

"Did you ever love me? No, don't answer that—it's pathetic. How can you fall in love with a mug?" He breathed out. "Do you swear you had nothing to do with the Tottenham job? You weren't in the cottage?"

"It is not me. It's Peter."

"That's a fifty." He stabbed a finger at her. "Not a bloody love letter, so don't ditch it. That'll get you anywhere in the world."

"Who are you?" she said. And then a thought struck her. "What did you do to Nikolai?"

"Nikolai?" Wiggins said, thrown. "He worked for *you*?"

She cursed. "No. He follow me, he liked me. Once there was something but he is mad. Now he has gone."

"Yes, Bel. He's gone."

Outraged cries. The bomb was drawing a crowd. Bela collected her skirts, ready to run, raised onto the tips of her small, square-toed boots. The lanterns glowed close. She hesitated a moment.

"Who are you, my handsome man?" she asked again, her voice soft.

"Wiggins," he said as his chin dropped to his chest. "That's who I am."

24

Vernon Kell whistled as he high-stepped toward Victoria Station. He looked up at the faddish new Westminster Cathedral and decided that, on reflection, he approved. The red and white stripes added vim to the area, even if the overall impression was rather cake-like. Why not celebrate every now and then? Less than a month after the death of LeQuin, and Kell had the top job, a whole new-fangled bureau, Ewart was on his way out (they'd have him doing something at the palace), and the threats from abroad were being taken seriously at last. The Woolwich case had been wrapped up to everyone's satisfaction. René LeQuin's demise had shattered his spy network—without the head, the rest fell. Rijkard would hang. The other thug, Miller, would do fifteen years for conspiracy. Woolwich was leak-free. The only problem that remained was the connection to Germany, or the lack of it. They were no nearer to discovering the identity of the embassy man who ran LeQuin, though they now had the means to set about finding out.

"No cab?" Wiggins appeared behind him, as if out of nowhere.

"I thought I told you to wait outside the station?"

Wiggins sighed. "I saw you coming. The blind man selling matches saw you coming."

"Let's go." Kell clicked his heels. "I need to introduce you to someone. How's the shoulder?"

"Mending," Wiggins said in a manner that struck Kell as unut-terably sad. A contrast to his own fine mood.

"Excellent. Our work is about to grow considerably. With no small thanks to you," he added. "I can keep you on the same pay scale, and maybe there'll be additional expenses. We will be

recruiting, training, and I'll need your help. There's a spy school
to think about, new agents, protocols. You know the sort of thing;
you're good at it."

"Is that what the big boss said? 'Give that Wiggins a slap on the
back.'"

"Well, obviously, we try not to reveal the name of our operatives.
Your anonymity is to protect you."

"While the credit goes elsewhere?"

"Let's not argue now, Wiggins, this is a new beginning. There are
great challenges ahead."

"How's Mrs. Kell?"

"Wonderful," Kell said, then corrected himself. "Mrs. Kell is very
well, thank you. She's happy our work together bore such bounteous
fruit."

"Any leads on Van Bork?"

"Strangely, he's not on the embassy lists. That's priority number
one."

They turned down one side street and then the next. High red
apartment buildings shaded them on either side. "How about the
leak?"

"Bad business." Kell cleared his throat. "My deputy, Lieutenant
Russell. Gambling debts, I believe. Would never have credited it, to
look at him. LeQuin had him in a vise, I think. Blackmail."

"How long did he get?"

"Good God, he hasn't gone to prison. He's been posted to the
Quartermaster General's office."

Wiggins exhaled in theatrical frustration. "Look," Kell went on.
"Russell's uncle is an earl . . ."

"And?"

"That's the world, Wiggins. But don't worry, he won't be allowed
anywhere near our work again."

They walked on in silence. Kell thought of Milton, dead in the
river for a crime hardly worse than Russell's. A thought he knew
must be in Wiggins's mind too. The agent's feet scuffed angrily on
the newly cut pavement flags.

"If it's any consolation," Kell said, "the crypt you so spectacularly destroyed in Kensal Green belonged to the family of one of Russell's relations."

"They're all fucking related though, ain't they?" Wiggins said, though he did manage a small grin.

"Nobody's perfect. By the way, we never discussed LeQuin's money. A hundred and fifty pounds was it?"

"Expenses," Wiggins said.

They walked on for a moment until Wiggins filled the expectant silence. "Most of it went on stopping that bloody bomb. The rest went to the Miltons. He'd never have died if it weren't for us."

Kell looked at Wiggins. His hair had grown long again, like some jungle native. Stubble had reclaimed his chin, his collar flapped open. A man of the streets, tough, razor-eyed, and battle-weary. But Kell would trust him with anything, except money and a woman. Too damned handsome to leave alone with the ladies. They continued around a corner back onto the main road.

"I don't suppose anyone will come forward to claim it," Kell said at last. "The office is here on Victoria Street, but it's safer to take a circuitous route, don't you think?"

"What's the story?"

"Ah, yes. Mansfield Cumming. He won't like you at all, at least not on first impressions. But be yourself, Wiggins."

"Why should I care?"

"Double pay, of course, double the excitement. Cumming is to take on the foreign half of the Bureau. And the committee was so impressed with your work they want to use you as much as possible. Haldane was particularly interested in the terrorist connection, as it happens. So your—how should I say—freelance work has also been much valued. We've decided to call you Agent W, by the way. Ah ha, here we are."

Kell tapped up the short steps to an imposing block of residential apartments and pushed open the door.

"Coming?"

* * *

Wiggins hesitated. He looked up at Kell, the elegant, wealthy, well-dressed owl, waiting in the doorway—a representative of power and privilege, but a source of money too, and excitement. They'd wrapped up the Woolwich job nice enough between them, a good team—Constance, Kell, and him. Wiggins had managed to keep Jax out of the tidying up, for Sal's sake, though he had a feeling he'd see them both again. Something about Jax still tugged at his mind, an unscratchable itch.

And Peter was still out there, scheming, killing, creating havoc in the name of all sorts of bollocks—him and the evil bastard Yakov. And what of Van Bork, whoever he was? Directly or indirectly, Van Bork had Milton's blood on his hands. Bill was dead, Emily was married, and Bela was gone. What remained?

"Who the devil's this?"

Kell coughed. "The, er, gentleman I mentioned?"

"Gentleman!" Mansfield Cumming exploded. "I see no gentleman." The old man marched out from behind his desk, his right leg swinging in an exaggerated limp. "And how many times have I told you to use my code name?"

Wiggins stood in the doorway of the office. He watched as the sharp-chinned Cumming strutted back and forth, upbraiding Kell. "I'm looking for agents, men of steel, intelligence, and class. Not this . . ." Cumming waved a hand, searching for the words to describe Wiggins ". . . Whitechapel scruff! What can *he* possibly offer the Service?"

Cumming turned back to his desk, his square frame closing like a door. Wiggins stepped forward.

"You're right, guv'nor," he said, deliberately playing up his accent. "I'm gutter class. I don't know what you gents are cooking up, but it's beyond me."

The old man looked at Kell—*I told you so*—and began writing at his desk but Wiggins continued, the twinkle in his eye evident only to Kell.

"What I would tell you, if I was asked like, is that the crank shaft on the Rolls-Royce Phantom IV is a real pig, especially when you're running a heavy oil like you do." Cumming stopped writing. "As to you, guv'nor, all I can tell you—only if you asked, of course—is that you sailed in Malaya and spent time in Singapore, though I reckon you was born in India? Either way, you're short-sighted, twice married, you take snuff but your wife don't approve, and you're partial to the odd biscuit. Oh, and you suffer from gout in your right toe that you try to pass off as a war wound. Other than that, I can't tell you a thing."

Cumming leapt to his feet, his face red. "What did you tell him, Kell?"

"Nothing."

"Then how . . . ?"

Wiggins paused. "I was taught by the best."

Kell forced him to explain. The oil stains on the inside of Cumming's wrist, his snuff box (inexpertly hidden), the ship's-biscuit crumbs on the ink blotter. The old man's weathered skin and leathery tan spoke of much time in the East, and he wore his shirt cuffs in Malay fashion. The gout passed off as a war wound was something of a long shot in terms of a deduction, but Cumming looked like the kind of man who lived a life of gout but didn't want to admit it.

Cumming sat back at his desk as Kell recounted once more their recent adventures: the unmasking of the leak at Woolwich, the discovery of LeQuin, and the capture of his murderous henchman.

"Well, well," Cumming said finally. "So this is Agent W, eh?"

"It is. The Admiralty insist after W's rather exceptional work—and his skills—that he be made available to both parts of the Bureau. On missions, of course, but he may also have a role in any future spy school. Training, recruitment, et cetera."

"That's certainly a clever trick you've got there in judging people. But my leg, truly, was injured in Borneo. I certainly don't have gout."

"Of course," Kell murmured. "The method is not infallible. Merely a guide."

Wiggins cleared his throat. "So you want me to work for both of you?"

Kell sniffed and addressed Cumming. "Of course, as the senior, official Service, I shall have first call on Agent W—but there may be times when you might need his, er, skills."

"Yes, I can quite imagine we would. We can hardly call him Agent W as well, though, that would never do. Can't be confusing the two divisions of the Bureau. Home and foreign, keep everything separate." Cumming looked over at his young clerk.

"What do you say, Michaels, you're a Cambridge man, a new code name, do you think?"

"Rather. I say we could always call him Agent double O—instead of the double U, if you see what I mean?"

"Yes, I like that, very clever."

"And then if we have any more special agents, we can give them an extra number, like double O–one, double O–two, double—"

"I can count, thank you, Michaels." Cumming turned to Kell. "Right. It's settled. Your Agent W is my double O."

Kell looked across at Wiggins.

"You can call me what you like, as long as I get paid," Wiggins replied.

At that, Cumming rose again from his seat and thrust out his hand, the first real gesture of acknowledgment he'd managed since Wiggins entered the room.

"Agent double O," he said. "Welcome to the foreign arm of the Secret Service Bureau. You can call me C."

HISTORICAL NOTES

Some of the events and many of the characters depicted in the novel have a basis in historical fact. In particular, events at Tottenham, the establishment of the Secret Service, and the lives of Peter the Painter and Yakov Peters.

The Tottenham Outrage
Constable William Tyler lost his life at the hands of Jacob Lepidus and Paul Hefeld after a payroll robbery in Tottenham on January 23, 1909. The crime and subsequent pursuit became known as the "Tottenham Outrage," a cause célèbre of Edwardian London. The events surrounding this day were much as they are described in the novel.

The Secret Service Bureau
After a series of meetings of the Committee for Imperial Defense, a Secret Service Bureau was formally established in August 1909. It was subsequently split into a home service, headed by Captain Vernon Kell, and a foreign service under Sir Mansfield Cumming. These services later became known as MI5 and MI6.

Peter the Painter and Yakov Peters
Peter the Painter probably existed. Certainly, someone of that name was operating in London at the time. Yakov Peters definitely existed, and you'll find out more about what happens to both of them in a subsequent novel.

The Baker Street Irregulars
In his own accounts of Sherlock Holmes's work, Dr. Watson briefly acknowledges the role of the Irregulars on three occasions. Young Wiggins is cited as the leader of the gang working on two cases—*A*

Study in Scarlet and *The Sign of the Four*—while in a third case, Wiggins is mistakenly identified as "Simpson." Dr. Watson's accounts are notoriously hazy on dates and names, however, and most historical sources are convinced that the Irregulars, and Wiggins in particular, played a far more substantial role in Holmes's work than Watson credits. This would be in keeping with the mores of the time, where it was rare for lower-class people—and street "Arabs" or urchins in particular—to be given prominence. It may also be that after the cases referenced above, Holmes himself wanted Wiggins's name taken out of any accounts so as to maintain the effectiveness of the child agents.

ACKNOWLEDGMENTS

Thanks to my agent, Jemima Hunt, and my editor, Nick Sayers, for making the book better and for believing in it. I'd also like to thank Cicely Aspinall and everyone at Hodder, as well as Caroline Johnson for an exemplary copyediting. Any faults or errors in the text are mine alone.

In the same spirit I would like to thank Nathaniel Marunas, Amelia Ayrelan Iuvino, and all at Quercus USA for their support and painstaking work on the book.

Thanks also to the staff of the British Library, where much of this book was researched. I drew on too many historical sources to name them all here, but I must mention the following: *The Defense of the Realm* by Christopher Andrews, *The Security Service 1908–1945* by John Curry, *Outrage! An Edwardian Tragedy* by Janet Dorothy Harris, *MI6: The History of the Secret Intelligence Service 1909–1949* by Keith Jeffery, *The Quest for C* by Alan Judd, and *Six: The Real James Bonds 1909–1939* by Michael Smith.

I would also like to thank my sister Buki Armstrong, Julia Caithness, Giles Foden, Stephen Guise, Adrienne Maguire, Dan Teper, the redneck DW Wilson, and especially my brother, Tom, for introducing me to Sherlock Holmes and for his continued vigilance over the text.

I must pay homage to Sir Arthur Conan Doyle, whose skill and imagination sparked the whole enterprise in the first place.

Most important, I'd like to thank my family—R and E, who hopefully will enjoy the book one day, and especially my partner, Annalise Davis, who is supportive, inspirational, insightful, and always funny.

ABOUT THE TYPE

Typeset in Minion Pro Regular, 11.5/15 pt.

Minion Pro was designed for Adobe Systems by Robert Slimbach in 1990. Inspired by typefaces of the Renaissance, it is both easily readable and extremely functional without compromising its inherent beauty.

Typeset by Scribe Inc., Philadelphia, Pennsylvania.